SHIELDED HEART

THE INFINITE CITY #2

TIFFANY ROBERTS

SHIELDED HEART

He's an alien crime boss who always gets what he wants—and what he wants is the shy, timid human female who happens to be his fated mate.

Arthos, the Infinite City, is a place of alien wonders and indescribable beauty—and, most importantly for Samantha, it's also halfway across the universe from her abusive ex-fiancé. She came to the city desperate for a fresh start, but she finds herself downtrodden on a world of aloof alien beings with little hope of finding her place—and a good chance of being kidnapped or killed before she can even settle in.

At least until she is saved by an irresistible alien with piercing eyes and a seductive smile.

Alkorin is the living embodiment of temptation, and he makes no effort to disguise his desire for her. But when his past threatens to drag her into a dangerous underworld, she discovers he isn't who he claims to be. After enduring so much suffering, can she bear to take a leap of faith with this mysterious alien? Can she trust him with not only her life, but her heart?

Dedicated to Sam Griffin, whose talents helped bring Arcanthus to life—including his naughty bits. May your imagination continue to be an inspiring source of devious, alien delights.

ARCANTHUS
SHIELDED HEART

ONE

Arthos, the Infinite City
    Terran Year 2105

THE PRESS OF A BUTTON—IN this case, a button which displayed the amount of credits loaded onto the chip in Arcanthus's hand—was all it took to change the bokkan informant's standoffish demeanor.

The bokkan's stony features softened as he led Arcanthus and Drakkal to somewhere more *private*—a dark, deserted alleyway. Arc exchanged a glance with Drakkal; that glance was enough to tell Arc that he and his azhera companion were on the same page.

The change of location suited their purpose well.

Arcanthus's thick tail swung from side to side. He willed it to slow; as eager as he was to conclude this business and head home, he couldn't rush this. He knew this was the informant they'd been searching for, but he needed to hear confirmation from the bokkan's lips.

After they were well beyond the main street's neon lights, the bokkan stopped and turned to face Arcanthus and Drakkal. "So, uh..." His eyes dipped to Arc's hand, which was closed around the credit chip.

Arcanthus raised his left hand and splayed his metal fingers, revealing the chip on his palm. "This? Oh, you have to earn *this*, my friend."

"Just...just a little, then, as a token of your good faith?"

A grin spread across Arcanthus's lips, and he chuckled. "We've not pulled any weapons on you. That's token enough, I'd say. Though we could do things that way, if you'd prefer..."

Shifting his eyes to Drakkal—whose burly frame nearly filled the narrow alley—the bokkan shook his head.

Arcanthus closed his fingers over the credit chip and lowered his hands, clasping the right over the left. "I've only four questions. Answer to my satisfaction, and you will receive all due payment."

The bokkan's dull purple tongue slipped out and ran over his craggy lips. "That's not how this sort of thing usually works. You pay me for—"

Drakkal cleared his throat, dragging out the sound into a low growl as he bared his fangs. The azhera's fur—taupe with patches of copper and umber—bristled. The bokkan snapped his mouth shut.

"Did you give information to a female with blue and black hair and a male with facial scars?" Arcanthus asked.

Eyes rounding, the bokkan nodded. "You're not the first to ask after them either. Some people dressed all in black had questions too, but none of them actually spoke. They used holo-text to communicate. Seemed unnatural."

"A perfect segue into my next question. What did you tell the black-clad individuals who asked after the couple? I suggest, for your sake, that you omit nothing."

The bokkan flicked his gaze toward the alley entrance. "Look, there's people involved in this who I'd rather not cross, and I don't—"

Drakkal moved closer to the informant.

"Okay, okay!" the bokkan cried, pressing his back against the dirty wall. "I told them that yes, those two had come to me. I, uh...told them that the female did most of the talking, and she was asking after a forger. Said they'd heard of one with a reliable reputation. And I, um... I really shouldn't be telling you any of this, okay?"

Arcanthus lowered his chin, tightening his hold on his own hand. The gentle hum of his cybernetic limbs exerting pressure coursed up his arms and into his shoulders. "Such a shame. I *really* wanted you to earn your payment today."

The bokkan cast another frightened glance at Drakkal and held up his hands. "All right, all right. I gave both groups instructions on how to find this forger, okay? I told the ones that didn't talk that I'd sent the couple over there. That's all I said."

Arc's tail picked up speed, but he kept his hands down and clasped together. "What do you know about this forger?"

"You didn't hear any of this from me, okay? He's a real secretive one. I've heard he doesn't give his name out to many people, likes it to be hard to find him. He's got a reputation for being trustworthy—he doesn't double-cross his clients, even when the bounty on them is bigger than his asking price for his work. Supposedly doesn't even share the names of people he does work for. Goes by Alkorin."

Arcanthus took a single step closer to the informant.

The bokkan glanced up, meeting Arcanthus's third eye, and slid half a meter away along the wall.

"And he expects the informants who send people in his direction to be discreet," Arcanthus said. "Expects them to guard his potential clients. That's why he ensures said informants are well compensated. That's why *you* have been well compensated—a thousand credits per month, plus kickbacks for referrals that result in new business."

The bokkan shrank back, as though attempting to force his body through the wall. "H-how could you know—"

"Remember, I'm asking the questions, and we've arrived at the last one. I trust the answer should come to you easily enough. You seem to have no problem passing this information to everyone who comes asking." Anticipatory electric currents coursed through Arcanthus's cybernetic limbs. "What is my name?"

The bokkan's eyes widened, and, somehow, his rocky skin paled. "A-Alkorin the Forger?"

Arcanthus nodded. "Good. It's too bad you seemed to lack any amount of intelligence when you sold out my clients. I do not appreciate my business being compromised. I would tell you to remember that, but..."

He shifted his thumb and flicked the credit chip high into the air. The bokkan looked up to follow the chip's arc. In the same moment, Arcanthus opened the concealed compartment in his left forearm. The compartment launched the hilt of a hardlight blade into his waiting hand as he extended his arm. He activated the weapon before he'd fully closed his fingers around the grip. The blade—like a sword forged of translucent yellow crystal—formed instantly and pierced the bokkan's neck.

Releasing a choked grunt, the bokkan informant lowered his eyes to look at the blade before meeting Arc's gaze again.

Arcanthus lifted his right hand and caught the credit chip as it came back down. "Sorry. People like you simply don't align with the ethics of my business."

He deactivated the hardlight blade.

Blood oozed from the hair-thin wound on the bokkan's

throat. Arcanthus turned away, slipping the hilt back into its hiding place. He'd taken a few steps toward the end of the alley before the bokkan collapsed; the *thump* of the body hitting the ground did not give him pause.

"You really just mention ethics while you had a blade in someone's throat?" Drakkal asked from behind Arcanthus.

"What of it?"

"You're irritable lately."

Arcanthus stopped a few paces from the alley's mouth. "I am *not* irritable."

Drakkal chuckled dryly but said nothing; it seemed to Arcanthus a sly means of having the final say without speaking.

Arc spun to face Drakkal. The frustration and stress of the last couple weeks bubbled to the surface, but as he looked into Drakkal's green eyes—which glowed with reflected light from beyond the alley—those emotions subsided. None of this was the azhera's fault.

"Shut up," Arcanthus muttered as he turned and walked into the street, continuing toward the hovercar waiting a few blocks away.

"Problem's solved," Drakkal said, falling into place beside Arcanthus. "Leak is plugged. No need to stress."

Arcanthus waved a hand dismissively. "There should never have been a problem in the first place. I'm sure the damage to my reputation has already been done."

"You know the terran and her mate didn't tell anyone what happened."

"That's not the point, Drak."

"It is. And I won't let you do this, Arc."

"And what, exactly, do you think it is I'm doing?" Arcanthus kicked a chunk of rusted scrap metal across the ground; his cybernetic limb registered the impact and relayed that information to his brain, but it was nothing like feeling it for himself.

"Brood."

"I am assuredly *not* brooding, Drakkal."

"You're whinier than a thirsty cub begging for its mother's teat."

Arching a brow, Arcanthus turned his head toward his companion. "Is that really what you're going with?"

Drakkal shrugged his broad shoulders. "Being honest."

"No, you're not. You accuse me first of brooding, and then of whining. Which is it, exactly?"

"Both. You've been...off since dealing with that terran."

Arcanthus sighed. "Would it hurt to lie once in a while, if only to raise my spirits?"

"Yeah. It'd hurt *you.*"

"Couldn't possibly be more painful than the bruises you constantly leave on my ego."

"More likely to bruise myself on your ego than the other way around, Arc."

Arcanthus opened his mouth to reply but realized quickly that he had no retort; there was no arguing against what Drakkal had said.

They continued onward in silence, and the Undercity streets grew crowded and noisy as they left the alleys and side streets behind. Arcanthus was more eager to get back home with each step. Business that forced him out of his sanctuary was rare, and it always irked him. There was too much that could go wrong out here, too many variables beyond his control. If he had to be away, he found it far more pleasant to be doing what he wanted rather than cleaning up messes or putting out fires.

When they arrived at the hovercar, Drakkal climbed into the driver's seat and Arcanthus into the passenger's. The control boards bathed the pair in a soft, bluish glow as Drakkal engaged the engines and began their ascent to the express tunnels.

"We're alone now," Drakkal said. "Talk."

"I've nothing to say," Arcanthus replied.

"*Arc*. Out with it."

Arcanthus released a heavy breath. "I want a terran."

Drakkal glanced sharply at Arc, narrowing his eyes. "What the hell do you mean you want a terran?"

"I used the simplest language I could."

"No, just the vaguest."

"I want a terran. A *female* terran." Raising a hand, Arcanthus swept back his long, black hair, tucking the loose strands behind his horns. "I fail to see what's so difficult to understand."

"You just going to call a purveyor and buy one? *Kraasz ka'val*, Arcanthus, you should know better after what we've been through."

Arcanthus glared at Drakkal. "I didn't say that, damn it. Terrans have been migrating to Arthos for two years. I'll locate one who's already here." When the azhera just stared at him, Arc added, "I'm *not* abducting anyone, Drak."

"I know you. You bend the rules when you want something."

Hovercars and express tunnel walls flitted by in a blur outside the cab.

"You wanted me to talk about it," Arcanthus said.

"Yeah. So I could tell you not to be stupid."

"Says the one who swallows a kilogram of his own fur over the course of every year."

"I told you," Drakkal growled, "there's scientific research that proves azhera tongues are some of the cleanest in the known universe."

Arcanthus smirked. "Have you looked around the universe,

my friend? The standard isn't set particularly high. But if you *must* know, that female terran intrigued me. Hell, if she hadn't been mated to the zenturi, I'd have had her bent over my desk by the end of that first meeting. I saw it in her eyes."

Drakkal snorted and shook his head. "You say that about every female. Have you forgotten how much trouble you've caused because you can't keep your pants on?"

"I don't wear pants. Only a very long loin cloth."

"*Vrek'osh*, you know what I mean!"

"Now who's irritable?"

"Arcanthus, I will—"

"I promise you, Drakkal, this is different."

"How?"

"Because it is, all right? What harm is there in finding a curious terran, bringing her to my workshop, and potentially learning a few new ways to give and receive pleasure?"

Drakkal shook his head, lips curling to display his fangs. "You met *one* terran, and you've been obsessed with them ever since."

Arcanthus pressed a hand over his chest. "You wound me, old friend. I'm merely intrigued. Nothing more."

"Obsessed," Drakkal repeated, glancing out the side window. "You need new hobbies."

"What difference does the way I spend my free time make?"

"With as much as you pushed that zenturi, I have a right to be concerned. You were outgunned on that one."

"I could have dispatched him if I'd wanted to."

Drakkal laughed; the sound, deep and rich, seemed to rise from his belly. "No, you couldn't have. You're a top-grade fighter, Arc—the best I've ever seen—but he was a *killer*."

"Is there a difference, azhera?"

"When you were messing with his mate, yes. He would've taken you out."

"Do you recall our earlier discussion about telling little lies to help me feel better?"

"I do. Especially the part where I implied it wouldn't happen."

Arcanthus threw up his hands. "Fine! You win, Drakkal."

"Good. You're finally—"

"I'll make sure *my* terran isn't spoken for."

The string of curses that tumbled out of Drakkal's mouth—all in the obscure dialect of his clan, which translator implants seemed unable to decipher—made Arcanthus laugh whole-heartedly. His laughter only provoked fresh oaths from the azhera.

When they arrived home, Drakkal left Arcanthus to his own devices, muttering to himself about how he should've gone back to his homeworld years ago to become a fisher, a shop-keeper, or a trash collector—anything other than Arc's business partner.

Arcanthus's humor lingered until he was alone in his work-shop. He entered through one of the rear passages; the huge blast door at the room's front was used only as an entrance for clients, one of several visual representations of how seriously he took security. He wanted his guests to know they were safe under his roof—and that any attempts to harm him would be swiftly and wholly thwarted.

He sat down behind the wide desk at the edge of the raised platform, leaned back in his chair, tail swishing slowly through the cut-out at the base of the seat, and swept his gaze over the large chamber.

Low couches ran on either side of the carpeted walkway, and exotic sea creatures drifted in large tanks built into the walls. An autocannon hung from the ceiling in each of the four corners. Crimson and violet lights set the tone of the room, their relatively soft glows creating deep shadows in many places.

Arcanthus frowned; the lights didn't suit his current mood. With a flick of his wrist, he brought up a dozen screens—two physical, the rest holographic projections—on the desk. He navigated the menus and commands with little conscious thought.

A moment later, the lights changed to blue; they were light-colored, with a touch of green, inside the tanks, and darkened near to black on the patches of wall in between.

Arcanthus shook his head. "A bit much, don't you think?"

But he didn't change the lights again; he shifted his attention to the screens and hacked into the Consortium's identification database. He'd told himself it was a business matter when he started checking it daily a little over a week ago—he needed to keep informed regarding registration and immigration trends to be as effective as possible in his work. But he'd stopped several days ago, after realizing how much time he'd spent browsing the files of terran immigrants.

He'd been unable to justify his diligent perusal of those files.

"Drakkal is wrong," he muttered as he entered his search criteria. "I'm not obsessed."

A list of the Infinite City's most recent immigrants—all having been processed in the last three days—populated one of the screens. Seventy-eight thousand, nine hundred and forty-two names.

Without thinking, Arcanthus sorted the list to display the terrans on top.

"Whoops."

He extended a finger to undo the change, but his hand froze before touching the control. There were only eleven new terrans; what was the harm in looking a little closer? Maintaining his relaxed position, Arcanthus perused the files. Five were related to one another—a terran diplomat, her husband, and their three children. He flicked them aside, dropping their files to the bottom of the list. The next two appeared to be former soldiers, possibly here to seek work with one of the many private security firms based out of Arthos. His own soldiering days had been brief and so long ago they felt like they'd occurred in another life; he had no desire to brush up against that world again. He dismissed both files.

Arcanthus continued his perusal, moving swiftly through three more files—a male and two females, none of whom sparked any interest in him. What had it been about the terran who'd come to him that set her apart from the rest? What about her had intrigued him?

He reached the last terran file. The name, translated phonetically into Universal Speech, was *Samantha Dawn Wilder*. He opened the file.

A tingle sparked across his *qal* marks when the terran's life-sized head appeared as a hologram over the desk. His eyes widened.

The slightly bewildered, overwhelmed expression on her face was oddly endearing. Dark, naturally arched eyebrows rested over large brown eyes with thick lashes. Long brown hair framed her delicate face, contrasting her pale skin and pink lips.

She was beautiful.

For an instant, a strange, disorienting feeling overcame him, like he *knew* her despite the impossibility of it. The only terran he'd ever met—Abella—hadn't produced nearly this strong a reaction in him.

Arcanthus raised his hand to touch Samantha's cheek; his fingertips moved unhindered through the insubstantial hologram. He lowered his fist to the desk's surface, his pang of disappointment swallowed by growing excitement. He hurriedly read the information in her file—no registered family in Arthos, no listed employment, and a residence in one of the city's many Consortium-sponsored immigrant housing complexes.

He returned his gaze to her eyes and smiled.

"*Samantha*," he said. "I think you're the one."

TWO

Today was the day, Samantha decided, that she would venture out into this new, amazing world in search of work. The day she would start her new life. *Nothing* would stand in her way.

Well, nothing except her apartment door.

And her jerk of a neighbor.

And her own damn anxiety and fear.

Samantha clenched her fists at her sides and stared at the first of her obstacles. The metal door stared back at Sam, mocking, taunting, and tormenting her. It spoke in her mind in a cruel, familiar voice.

You're worthless. Weak. That's all you'll ever be. I protect you. You need me.

She pressed her lips together and shook her head.

No, I don't.

Samantha drew in a deep breath and slowly released it. "You can do this, Sam. Just one slap of the button and you're done. Door open. Easy."

The door glared at her.

She glared back.

I can do this.

Squaring her shoulders, she strode forward and swung her hand up.

Her hand stopped mere centimeters away from the button, trembling as dread chilled her from the inside.

What if Rakkob was waiting for her in the hall?

Samantha carefully pressed her ear to the door, closed her eyes, and held her breath. She heard nothing from the hallway, but that didn't mean he wasn't home, didn't mean he wasn't out there. The beating of her own heart steadily loudened to fill the relative silence.

She'd only encountered her borian neighbor—a large, powerfully built male with long, elf-like ears—once face-to-face. It had been two days ago, when she'd first moved into her unit. The same day she'd arrived on Arthos.

Since then, Rakkob had come to her door several times. He'd attempted to coax her out, calling her *little terran* and trying to sound sweet, but he'd resort to pounding on the door and demanding she come out when she didn't respond to his coaxing.

During those times, Samantha had cowered in her bathroom, wondering why she'd come to the Infinite City. This was supposed to be a new start, a *safe* start, and she'd yet to feel safe here. She felt foolish to have left everything she'd known to come to this wholly alien place.

But this was the farthest she could get from Earth, and it wasn't like she'd had the luxury of time to plan. She'd only had time to act.

Beneath her fear ran the knowledge that she couldn't hide in her apartment forever. The residence had been provided by the Consortium—the group of alien species who ruled Arthos—as part of their immigration policy, and the United Terran Federation's Emigration Assistance Initiative had arranged for a monthly credit allowance to pay for her necessities. But both were temporary. The support was guaranteed for only one year.

The only thing Samantha currently had to her name was the bag of personal belongings she brought from Earth. The UTF's Emigration Assistance Initiative had allowed for more, but she hadn't owned anything else. She was completely dependent on governmental support for now; they would ensure she could buy food and clothing for herself, and she was a registered citizen, meaning she could find work, but all of that was only attainable *outside the damned door*!

Before she could think on it any longer, she hit the button and ducked aside, flattening herself against the wall.

The door slid open.

After a few seconds of silence, she peered around the door-frame. The door across the hall—Rakkob's door—was closed. She leaned out and looked up and down the corridor.

Empty.

Releasing a relieved breath, Samantha slipped out of her room, waved her wrist in front of the scanner on the wall—which was programmed to respond only to *her* Consortium-implanted identification chip—and hurried down the hallway once her door was closed.

Her anxiety grew when she entered the elevator, which was not empty. She eased to the back, nestling herself in the corner with shoulders hunched and head bowed as aliens entered and exited on almost every one of the twenty floors on the way to ground level. Some were silent, others chatty and boisterous, and several stared at Sam curiously when they noticed her.

She wiped her sweat-dampened palms on her pants. She'd never been surrounded by such a diverse crowd. Several alien species had become commonplace on Earth—primarily volturians, azhera, vorgals, and borians—but there were more peoples on Arthos than she could count. They were all so different from each other, so different from her, that she couldn't help but feel as though *she* were the strange one.

Once the elevator finally reached the ground floor, Sam quietly followed the large group into the lobby and proceeded out onto the Undercity streets. It was by far the most unusual place she'd ever been—not that she'd traveled very far from her hometown before this—and she wasn't sure if she'd ever get used to it. Everything was enclosed here. There was no sky, no clouds, no moon or stars, only an uneven ceiling riddled with catwalks and supports high overhead. Day and night didn't exist here; the Undercity ran nonstop, never slowing, never quieting.

The city above the surface was just as busy, but at least there was a sky and natural light up there. The Undercity was lit primarily by neon lights and pulsing holograms. She'd never thought she would miss the sun—her pale complexion was a clear indicator of her lack of a relationship with it—but she had a feeling she would grow desperate for its warmth after long enough down here.

Samantha did her best to study her surroundings, noting anything particularly unusual she could rely on as a landmark. Though her breathing had eased since leaving the tight confines of the apartment complex, her anxiety had not. It would be so easy to get lost in the crowd, so easy to vanish; there were many beings near her size or smaller, and many, many more who were big enough to make her feel like a child.

She eventually worked her way through the flow of bodies to reach the outskirts of the crowd. The streets were lined with food stands, merchant booths, and storefronts. Standing on her toes, she strained to see over the heads and shoulders of the nearby aliens and get a better idea of her surroundings. It all seemed so big, so impossible; a dark shroud of doubt settled over her mind.

No, I can do this. I just...just need to go talk to people.

Sam approached a booth with shelves of footwear on display, seeking out the owner, who she assumed was the dacrethian kneeling before a volturian male, holding a pair of shoes in each of his four hands.

Samantha cleared her throat. "Um, hello?"

The dacrethian and the volturian continued their conversation without acknowledging her. They probably hadn't even heard her meek voice considering all the noise from the bustling street.

Sam brought her hands up to her middle and nervously clasped her fingers together.

"Hello?" she said a little louder.

Their conversation ceased. The volturian lifted his faintly glowing blue eyes to meet Samantha's; there was only coldness in his gaze.

The dacrethian twisted his torso to look at her and said in Universal Speech, "Yes?"

Samantha swallowed and forced a smile. "Hi. I was... wondering if you were hiring?"

The dacrethian's gaze dipped to trail over her body before returning to her eyes. "No."

He turned back toward the volturian.

"Nothing?" Sam asked. "I don't mind doing tedious jobs. I—"

"Are you here to buy?" the dacrethian asked.

Sam frowned and shifted her weight from one foot to the other. "No. I'm look—"

"Then leave."

Ouch. Guess I'm dismissed.

The volturian, now smirking, stared at her a moment longer

before looking down at the shoes the dacrethian presented to him.

With a sigh, Samantha left the booth and returned to the crowd.

She visited a long string of shops and booths. Despite the diversity of their wares and operators, most of the people she spoke with reacted similarly—they gave her a once-over, found her somehow lacking, and sent her away.

Her discouragement was so deep that she was caught completely off-guard when someone said in a deep voice, "I can put you to work, terran."

Samantha's heart skipped a beat, and she turned to find a bulky, shirtless vorgal with black, *moving* tattoos depicting various beasts looking at her.

A swell of hopefulness spread through Sam's chest. "Really?"

He smiled, drawing her attention to the short tusks jutting up from his lower jaw, and nodded.

Sam's stomach sank when she looked past the vorgal; the door behind him was unmarked and dingy, with faded graffiti on its face, surrounded by similarly grungy walls. She lifted her gaze to see a holographic image projected over the doorway—a naked, dancing volturian female. As the dancer went through her motions, her body morphed, cycling through various species, all nude, all undulating to the dull beat thumping from behind the door.

"Oh." Samantha returned her attention to the vorgal and offered him an uneasy smile, retreating with her hands up and palms facing him. "No. No, that's okay. Thank you though. That's uh...not really the kind of work I'm looking for."

"A terran would make good credits. More if she takes cock." The leering vorgal stepped toward her, reaching out with one hand. "Why don't we see what you—"

She leapt away as though his hand was aflame. "No!"

Her back slammed into something hard. It took her an instant to realize it was a person—a purple-skinned tralix who was three times as wide as her and at least a meter taller.

Before Sam could utter an apology, the tralix spun toward her.

"Watch it!" he snarled, swinging an arm as thick as a tree trunk.

The action reminded Samantha of how someone would move when swatting at an annoying insect. Unfortunately, *she* was the insect in this case. His arm struck her with enough power knock her off her feet. She hit several other people on her way down, getting spun around and disoriented in the process.

She cried out in pain as her hands and knees struck the concrete. Tears stung her eyes and blurred her vision. Shakily, she lifted her hand and turned it. Her palm was scraped, with droplets of blood oozing from the torn flesh.

A heavy foot came down on her leg. Samantha cried out again, struggling to stand. Before she could get her footing, someone bumped into her, sending her sprawling back to the ground. Reflexively, she drew her limbs inward in a desperate attempt to protect herself. The crowd rushed around her in an endless stream, none of them caring about Sam or her predicament as they bumped, kicked, and stepped on her.

Trampled to death on an alien planet. Not how I thought I'd go.

A hand closed around her wrist in a powerful but not painful grip. Before she understood what was happening, the hand yanked her up. Her legs wobbled, unwilling to accept her weight, and she felt herself falling again.

She was stopped when a solid arm snaked around her waist, pulling her close to the alien to whom it belonged.

"This is why I avoid going out," said a deep, smooth voice very near her ear. "So few decent people in this city."

Samantha threw her arms around the male, clutching tight in fear she'd get swallowed up by the crowd once more. He was slightly stooped, leaving her looking over his shoulder and unable to get a glimpse of his face. But she certainly felt his body; he was dressed in a black, silken garment that lay in a thin layer over the hard sculpted muscle of his torso.

And his scent? It reminded her of sandalwood, woodsy and sweet, at once comfortingly familiar and enticingly exotic. Unable to help herself, she tightened her arms around him and inhaled, drawing in his smell to fight back the pervading stench of too many bodies crammed into too small a space.

Her mysterious savior lifted Sam off her feet and carried her toward the edge of the crowd, shoving people aside with his free arm as he moved. He showed them as little regard as they'd shown her. As mean as it was, she took satisfaction in it. Finally, they emerged from the flow of alien bodies, and he stopped in the entryway of a wide alley.

"Are you all right, little terran?"

"...little terran?" Samantha blinked away the moisture in her eyes. A strange haze had settled over her mind. Was she all right? Only a moment ago, she'd been sure she was about to die, but then she'd been picked up by strong arms and enveloped in the most delicious scent. "I...think so. Thank you. For saving me."

"No need for thanks." He eased Sam onto her feet. "I'm just glad you're safe."

Samantha took a step back to look up at her savior. Her breath hitched, and her eyes flared. Her gaze met not two eyes, but *three*, all a luminous yellow with slitted pupils. They were utterly alien and utterly captivating—especially the one in the center of his forehead, which was turned vertically.

Dark, slashing eyebrows rested above his other two eyes, leading to a straight, sharp nose, and full, sculpted lips. His dark gray skin was contrasted by glowing yellow tattoos on his face and neck—angular, flowing lines on the left side of his face, including a crescent around his left eye. There were smaller marks on his lower lip and chin. His ears were long and pointed with identical piercings—a loop and three studs—in each one.

Her gaze flicked up to the pair of dark, curved horns at his temples, which swept back from his face. His long black hair hung around his muscular shoulders, some of it arranged in thin braids, with a shorter portion swept to one side of his face. Her eyes dipped lower. His silken robe was reminiscent of a kimono. The garment was partially open, revealing the sculpted muscles of his chest, where there were more glowing tattoos.

As Sam stared at him, her heart quickened, and her pain vanished.

Call me a sinner, because he looks like a demon, and I am tempted.

A flicker of movement called her attention lower still to find a long, thick tail swaying lazily behind him.

"I certainly hope you like what you see," he said, drawing her eyes back to his face. One corner of his mouth was upturned in a lopsided grin that offered a glimpse of white fangs.

Annnnd I'm just standing here like a creep checking him out. Way to go, Sam.

Heat flooded her cheeks, and she took another step backward. "I'm so sorry!"

He arched a brow. "Why would you be sorry? I can't blame you for looking. In fact, your staring has given me ample time to stare back at you." Moving slowly, he tipped his chin down and took her wrists in his hands, turning her arms so her scraped palms faced upward. "You should get these cleaned up."

Sam glanced down. He was wearing gauntlets of some sort, made of charcoal-colored metal with segmented fingers. The undersides of his fingers were padded by a softer material, all of it strangely warm.

She trembled in his grasp; she told herself it was just the aftereffects of adrenaline overload after nearly being trampled to death—not because he was so close, not because of the way he was touching her, not because of the way he was staring at her.

Her awareness of her injuries returned in the wake of his words. In addition to the burning, stinging scrapes on her hands and knees, she was sure she'd have bruises in several places.

"I'll...I'll get them taken care of. Thank you again for what you did." She tugged on her arms.

He frowned, and his center eye remained on her face while he looked down at her palms. Though he seemed to make no effort to mask his reluctance, he released her. "You're new to Arthos, aren't you?"

Nodding, Samantha dropped her hands to her sides and loosely curled her fingers. "I've only been here for two days and..." She glanced toward the ceaseless flow of people on the street. "I'm a bit out of my element."

"Sometimes I think these crowds are connected by some animalistic hive mind." He turned his head to follow her gaze. "That they sense when someone doesn't belong and subconsciously seek to devour them."

"That's, um..."

"Not very comforting, I know." He looked back to her and smiled, the expression as warm as it was hungry, as charming as it was devilish. "What is your name, little terran?"

Little terran. It was the same thing Rakkob called her, and yet it didn't make her feel uncomfortable coming from this male.

"Samantha. Some people call me Sam. And yours?"

His lips parted, and he hesitated before replying, "Alkorin. It is a pleasure to make your acquaintance"

It was a pleasure just to *look* at him.

His grin widened; for a horrified moment, Sam wondered if he knew exactly what she'd been thinking, or if she'd said it out loud without realizing.

"I can bring you somewhere to clean up if you'd like, *Samantha*," he said, caressing her name with his sultry voice. "I know this city can be daunting to navigate." He eased a little closer, and his tantalizing scent filled her nose again. "It would please me to assist you."

Tingling warmth spread through her. She squeezed her fists despite the pain it caused in her battered palms. Why was she reacting this way? Why did it feel like her panties were wet just because of the way he said her name? Alkorin was gorgeous; his three eyes, horns, and tail only heightened her desire to touch him, to run her hands over his skin and feel its velvety smoothness over the hard ridges of his muscles.

And his lips... Would they be soft or firm against her own?

What is wrong *with me?*

Samantha's powerful attraction to him scared the hell out of her. He was an alien. She didn't know him, and even if she did, she'd already proven herself a poor judge of character. She couldn't let herself fall into another trap because of a charming smile. Not when she'd come here seeking inedpendence.

Not when she'd come here seeking safety.

"No. I...I should go," she said. "It's getting late, and I need to find my way back home."

"I could walk with you, if you'd like. Just to make sure—"

"No!" She winced at the sharpness in her tone, and softened her voice when she said, "No. It's okay. I'll find my way back. You've...already troubled yourself enough. Thank you."

"You've not troubled me, Samantha." He offered her a slight bow, the sleeves of his robe swaying as he put his arms to the sides. "Have a good evening. And try not to fall again."

Sam smiled as she backed away. "I'll try not to."

She forced herself to turn around before she was tempted to linger and hurried back into the street. She kept to the outskirts of the crowd, walking close to the buildings and booths.

Don't. Don't look back.

Unable to help herself, she glanced over her shoulder.

Alkorin was gone.

Disappointment struck her harder than she'd expected it to.

Well, what did you expect? That he'd stare longingly after you?

Samantha looked down at herself, and her cheeks blazed with shame. She was a mess; her clothes were filthy, her hands torn and bloody, and her hair disheveled. She couldn't imagine what her face looked like. Alkorin had probably been laughing at her behind his smile, laughing that someone like her had the nerve to ogle someone like him as though she stood any chance of having him.

You're worthless.

Sam's throat tightened, but she refused to let those terrible memories rise to the surface. That life—and James along with it —was behind her.

She crossed her arms over her chest and kept her head bowed as she continued back toward her housing unit. It was hard not to feel like a failure, but she took pride in her effort— even if she'd nearly died because of it. That she'd ventured outside her apartment door was a feat on its own.

I won't be trapped again.

Eventually, the crowds of the busy main streets were behind her, and she found herself walking down relatively quieter side streets, many of which were lined with large residential complexes like the one she lived in. There were still people around—other pedestrians and alien beings standing or sitting around the apartment building entrances, often talking in languages that sounded strange but were totally understandable due to her translator implant.

She was a couple minutes away from her apartment complex when a voice from behind chilled her blood.

"What's a pretty little thing like you doing out here alone?"

THREE

Samantha glanced behind her to see four aliens approaching. She only knew the species of one of them—a reptilian ilthurii. They were all dressed in dark clothing with glowing, electric blue accents; and the two aliens who had hair sported the same color within it.

Sam faced forward and quickened her pace. Clamping her jaw shut, she struggled to remain calm, but she was terrified.

Almost there. Almost home.

But it wasn't really home, was it? She'd lost her real home, her only home, to time and space. Why had she thought Arthos would be safer than Earth? She'd only been here *two days* and had already been threatened, knocked down, nearly trampled, and now...

Her chest constricted as her fear solidified, making it difficult to breathe.

Now...

A hand clasped her upper arm and brought her to a halt.

Samantha spun and swung her fist. She hit the alien in the face, and something crunched against her knuckles.

The alien cursed as his head snapped back, dark green blood running from his nostrils to stain his bared teeth—jagged, pointed teeth that could put a shark's to shame. He had no lips to conceal them. Raising a hand to his face, he wiped the blood away from his leathery skin.

Samantha stared in horror as he narrowed his beady eyes on her. She backpedaled quickly, turned, and ran right into a living wall—the ilthurii.

He wrapped his arms around her, lifted her off her feet, and chuckled. "Looks like this pretty little thing is mine. You're too weak for her, Jurgol."

"I demand the first taste, Te'shek!" Jurgol snarled, grasping a fistful of her shirt.

"Let me go!" She fought Te'shek's hold, her breaths so quick and strained that black spots danced in her vision.

No! Not this, not here! Please!

"I'm really not in the mood to kill anyone tonight, so please let go of the female and leave," said a familiar voice.

Samantha looked toward its source to see Alkorin standing at the entrance of a dark alley. She stilled. Had he followed her? Why? And why would he place himself in danger for her? What could he hope to do against four people?

She thrust her questions aside; they didn't matter. She didn't give a damn about his reasons—she was immensely grateful that he'd followed her home.

One of the other aliens snickered.

Jurgol spat blood on the ground and tightened his grip on her shirt. "You'll have to find your own pretty. This one is ours."

Alkorin stepped out of the alley and walked toward the aliens at a casual pace, empty hands in full display. "While I'd hate to disappoint you, I have to make it clear that the female is under my protection. Let go and walk on."

Te'shek snorted. "You are terrible at your job, sedhi." He moved his scaly face closer to Sam's, and she cringed when he extended his long, thin tongue to lick her cheek. "Next time you ought to tell your *ji'tas* to watch themselves in our territory."

Alkorin stopped a few meters away from the group, his stance startlingly nonchalant. He sighed. "Last chance, my friends."

"Fuck off, sedhi," one of the aliens said. "This *ji'tas* is in our territory now."

Raising his arms, Alkorin rolled back the sleeves of his robe, revealing the sleek, charcoal-colored metal, which was run through with yellow highlights matching his tattoos. The armor on his right forearm was bulkier, as though it were reinforced.

"Should've taken a moment to stretch," Alkorin muttered as he splayed his fingers and curled them into fists. "I'm not quite as spry as I used to be."

"Deal with him already," Te'shek snapped.

"Don't tell me what to fucking do," Jurgol growled as he and the other two aliens stepped toward Alkorin.

The fear coiling through Samantha's insides knotted, making her stomach churn. These aliens were all big and rough-looking—not that Alkorin was small, but he seemed so *refined* compared to them, like a pampered movie star facing down three street-hardened thugs.

One of the thugs lunged, and everything seemed to blast into light speed.

Sam barely saw Alkorin move as he slammed his fist into the side of the attacking alien's face with a meaty *thwap*. The alien was knocked aside with the impact, spinning as he fell. Something clattered to the ground at Sam's feet; she glanced down to see a pair of bloody, cracked teeth on the concrete.

Jurgol took a swing. Alkorin blocked the blow with his forearm. Sam heard bone crack before the alien yowled in pain. Alkorin twisted his hips and kneed the alien in the gut, the sides of his robe fluttering apart to reveal what appeared to be a thigh-high armored boot on his leg.

Eyes bulging, Jurgol doubled over and crumpled to the ground.

Te'shek threw Sam aside. She gasped as her hip took the brunt of her heavy landing. Gritting her teeth, she pushed herself up on her elbows and watched the reptilian alien charge toward Alkorin.

The ilthurii and the other alien still on his feet drew weapons from their coats. At the touch of a button, pulsing energy blades formed from the hilts in their hands. Alkorin backed away, dodging their swings as both aliens attacked simultaneously.

"I said I *didn't* want to kill anyone." Alkorin raised his right arm as one of the blades sped toward him in a downward arc. The bulky armor piece on his forearm lit up, and a round, segmented shield formed in the air above it, comprised of a translucent yellow material; it took Sam a moment to realize the seemingly crystalline substance was hardlight.

The energy sword struck the shield with a flash. Alkorin deflected it to his right, twisted his arm to grab the alien's extended wrist, and hammered his left fist into the alien's elbow. The joint snapped inward, bending the alien's arm in the wrong direction.

The alien dropped his weapon and stumbled aside. Screaming in pain, he grasped his broken arm and fell to the ground.

Te'shek pressed his attack, swinging wildly. Alkorin danced backward, swaying to avoid the sword, and swept his tail forward between his legs. It wrapped around the ilthurii's ankle and pulled.

As his leg was lifted high by Alkorin's tail, the ilthurii threw out his arms and fought for balance, but his struggle was in vain; he crashed onto his back. Before he could recover, Alkorin swung his right arm. The shield darted forward and struck Te'shek in the face, knocking his head back against the concrete.

The ilthurii went limp.

Releasing Te'shek's leg, Alkorin straightened. The shield dissipated, and he rolled his sleeves down. His third eye fell upon Sam before he turned toward her fully. She stared in stunned silence as he hurried over to her.

He crouched in front of her and offered a hand. "Are you all right, Samantha?"

She glanced at the aliens; two were unmoving, while the other two were on the ground, writhing and groaning in pain. Hesitantly, she placed her hand in Alkorin's and looked up at him. "You...followed me?"

As he rose, he drew her upright in a smooth, effortless motion. "I did."

Sam searched his face, meeting his third eye briefly. "Why?"

Alkorin held her gaze—and her hand. "I saw them tailing you. This city isn't the safest place for your kind, little terran. You're considered an exotic race, so I assumed their interest in you was neither passing nor innocent."

Something in his gaze suggested that *his* interest in her wasn't passing or innocent, either, and part of her thrilled in that.

Despite that thrill, her shoulders slumped in defeat. "If it's so unsafe, then why...why would the UTF *pay* to send me here?"

He shrugged. "Who can guess at the motives of governmental organizations?" His gaze dipped, roving over her from head to toe. "Now answer honestly—are you hurt?"

Sam tugged her hand free from his. "Just a few more scrapes and bruises. Nothing serious...thanks to you. Again."

He lifted his now empty hand and swept back a few strands of his straight, black hair, tucking them behind his pointed ear. "As understandably reluctant as you must be to trust anyone in Arthos right now, I insist on walking you home. Your day has been difficult, I imagine, and I'd like to spare you further terrible experiences. This city isn't all bad, but it seems you've stumbled into a lot of it, anyway."

Samantha looked at the ground; her hair fell into her face, shielding the tears welling in her eyes. She tugged her sleeves down to cover her wounded palms and curled her fingers into the fabric.

This city isn't all bad.

Alkorin was the first good she'd experienced in the Infinite City, and it wasn't quite enough to change how weak, defeated, and miserable she felt. Her entire body felt like one big bruise; that was a sadly familiar sensation, one she'd hoped to never feel again. She wished she could just disappear, wished she could leave all this suffering behind.

Even if she couldn't bring herself to believe there was more good to be found out there, Alkorin was right about one thing— she didn't trust anyone here. She had a neighbor who wanted to do questionable things to her, she had been snubbed, looked down upon, and nearly killed. And then there was whatever these thugs had wanted to do. Sam didn't want to even spend the mental energy to speculate.

Alkorin was it; a single shining beacon of kindness in the vast darkness.

He'd saved her twice in a single evening—twice in an *hour*. Either time, he could've easily walked away, could've decided she wasn't worth the effort and just walked on. But, despite the risk to himself, he'd chosen to help her.

Even if he hadn't saved her twice, she would've found herself wanting to trust him—he had that smooth, friendly demeanor, and a casually arrogant air that was surprisingly disarming. She felt safe standing here with him. And, if he hadn't been there for her today...

It was confirmation of her weakness, of just how ill-prepared she was for life in Arthos. She'd come here with nothing and no one; how could she have thought she'd survive on her own? How could she have thought she'd be safe? She couldn't even leave her apartment without psyching herself up. And apparently being a terran made her some kind of exotic attraction.

Samantha sniffled loudly. Tears streaked down her cheeks and fell to the concrete beneath her feet.

Through the curtain of her hair, she saw Alkorin lift his hands to waist level and hesitate, fingers partly bent. She couldn't blame him—she was a mess, and she'd have been hesitant in his position, too. This was the moment when he'd lower his hands, back away, and leave her alone and crying in the middle of an alien street. That's how most people back on Earth had acted—like they couldn't see her bruises, her black eyes, her split lips. They either ignored her because they didn't want to get involved, or they just turned up their noses and walked on like *she* had been the bad one. Like she'd asked for what she had received.

She drew in a shuddering breath when he wrapped his arms around her and pulled her close, cradling the back of her head with one of his hands. Her cheek settled against his warm chest, and her tears flowed over his muscled torso and onto his silken robe. Alkorin didn't seem to care.

"You're all right, Samantha," he said, his voice soft. "I have you."

Samantha squeezed her eyes shut, slipped her arms around his waist, and slid her hands up his back, clutching him as though he were her lifeline. Fresh, hot tears spilled down her face.

When was the last time someone had held her and told her everything would be okay? Her father had died five years ago, but he'd always had a hard time showing physical affection. Her elderly grandmother—who'd passed away two years before Samantha's father—had been the only one to regularly hug her.

She breathed in, and Alkorin's heady scent filled her nose. She pretended that was all she could smell, that his warmth was all she could feel, that his gentle voice was all she could hear.

Sam remained against Alkorin, holding him close—being *held* close—until her crying eased. Embarrassment and exhaustion quickly swept in.

What am I doing?

She abruptly stepped back, horrified to see what her tears had wrought. Alkorin's robe was soaked and wrinkled, and his dark gray skin shone with moisture from her tears. She hurriedly wiped her face with her palms and winced when the salt burned her scrapes.

"I'm sorry," she said. "I shouldn't have—"

"You don't need to apologize, Samantha," he said, raising a hand to brush stray strands of hair out of her face. He glanced at the alien thugs; the conscious pair were struggling to their feet. Alkorin moved to stand beside Sam and placed a hand on her lower back. "Come. We should be on our way before they feel well enough to call their friends. I would feel bad if I had to rough up an entire street gang tonight. I can only imagine what it'd do to their reputation."

Samantha let out a soft, airy laugh then nodded and began walking at his gentle guidance. Sniffling again, she peeked up at him; his center eye was staring down at her. She quickly averted her gaze.

It was so...*weird.*

He chuckled and shifted his hand to her hip, drawing her against him.

She should've resisted, should've pushed away and put distance between them, but at that moment, she didn't want to move away. After all he'd done for her, after the way he'd fought, she felt like the safest place in the universe was here at his side.

"One of them called you *sedhi.* Is...that what you are?" she asked.

"Yes. That is what my people are called."

Taking a deep breath, she blurted, "What's it like seeing out of three eyes?"

His laugh was full and genuine. "You're the second terran to ask me that, and I've only met two of you."

Her cheeks heated even as his laughter coaxed a little smile onto her lips. "I'm sorry. That was rude, wasn't it?"

"It doesn't bother me. I'm just as curious about what it's like for you to see out of two eyes. Do you have a blind spot between them?"

"No, there's no blind spot."

"Hmm. I wonder, then, what's the point of my third eye?" He turned it toward her again and smirked. "Apart from being hypnotic and intriguing, anyway."

Her blush deepened.

Intriguing is putting it mildly.

"Alkorin, are you a professional fighter or something?"

"No, I'm not. I *was,* some years ago, but I've left that behind me. I'm in...document verification these days. It's a relatively safer line of work."

Samantha shifted her eyes to his legs, which were encased in those tall, armored boots. "But not so safe that you don't have to wear armor?"

He glanced down, and his hold on her tightened for an instant. "I'm afraid that's not armor, Samantha."

She looked up to find his eyes on her. "It's not?"

"These"—he lifted his free hand and turned it slowly—"are the result of an unfortunate accident."

"Oh. *Oh!*" *Way to go, Sam.* "They're...prosthetics?"

"They are. But the accident was a long time ago, and they've served me well enough."

His tone, paired with the vagueness of his answer, suggested he didn't want to speak on it any further. Samantha understood his reluctance; she could only imagine how traumatic it must've been to have lost all his limbs in an accident. Besides, she was a stranger. He had no obligation to share anything with her, especially something that must've been so devastating.

He lapsed into silence for a time before asking, "What were you doing out in the city today?"

Sam frowned; his question reminded her how much of a failure she was. "I was looking for work."

"Looking for a particular type of work or just work in general?"

"Something, anything—wait, no, not *anything*. *Almost* anything." She was not going to sell her body. She had nothing against sex workers, but that profession was just not for her. "I don't mind labor. I just... The Consortium gives new immigrants housing for a year, and my homeworld is paying me a monthly wage for the same amount of time. I just wanted to...to get ahead for a change, I guess. I figured if I worked during this first year, I could save the extra because my necessities would be covered, and that would leave me in a better position to move somewhere nicer, someplace safer."

Samantha pressed her lips together. She'd been rambling like a fool. Fortunately, when she looked ahead, her apartment complex was in sight, offering her a means of escape before she embarrassed herself more than she already had.

She slipped out of his hold and stepped away. "Um, this is me. My building, I mean."

Alkorin looked at the building and furrowed his brow before returning his glowing yellow gaze to her. "I would be more than happy to pay for a hotel room in a nicer sector of the city, Samantha. It would be safer for you, and likely more comfortable."

His offer floored her. Her lips parted, the word *yes* perched on the tip of her tongue, but she snapped her mouth shut and shook her head.

Alkorin was a complete stranger! Why was she contemplating saying yes for even a moment?

And one night wouldn't make a difference, anyway. She'd still have to come back here tomorrow. "I can't ask that of you or accept it. But thank you—for the offer, and for all your help today."

He frowned, but he didn't argue. Stepping closer, he reached out and gently took hold of her left wrist, laying his warm metal fingers along its underside and guiding her arm up. His touch sent soft electric currents through her; she gasped at the pleasantness of the sensation.

His thumb curled around her wrist, brushing lightly over her skin, until it touched the activation button on her holocom. When the holographic projection screen appeared, Alkorin dipped his chin. "Unlock it."

Samantha raised her free hand, and though she hesitated, she did as he'd commanded.

The fingers of his left hand flicked through the menus rapidly, almost too fast for her to see what he was doing, as he went into her contacts and added new information. There were only a few entries there, none of which were personal.

Except for the new one listed as *Alk*.

He dismissed the screen and took her hand between both of his. "If you need anything, Samantha, do not hesitate to contact me." His fingertips trailed lightly over the underside of her wrist; it seemed innocent on the surface, but it sent a thrill straight to her core. "*Anything.*"

Samantha shifted on her feet, squeezing her thighs together as an entirely new sensation flooded her.

"Why?" she asked breathlessly. "Why are you doing this for me?"

"Because I know what it's like to go through difficult times," he said, his gaze slowly running up her arm until his eyes met hers. The yellow markings on his face pulsed brightly and his voice grew huskier when he continued. "But don't mistake me for a hero; I've not acted selflessly tonight." He raised his other hand and ran the back of his fingers down her cheek. "You're beautiful, Samantha, and I find myself eager to be in your company."

FOUR

Arcanthus watched Samantha walk away, unable to remove his eyes from her until she disappeared inside the housing complex. Part of him longed to continue following her even knowing he'd already pushed too far. His little terran was a delicate flower in an unforgiving city—at least outwardly. Somewhere inside her was a tristeel core that would bend but not break. She was awash in discouragement and despair, alone and lost, but she wasn't yet defeated.

Her vulnerability, though distressing, could be made to work to Arc's advantage. As much as he hated that fact, he knew it would not stop him. The time he'd spent with her this evening had only confirmed what he'd known the moment he'd first seen her face—Samantha Dawn Wilder was *his*.

He adjusted his robe as he turned away from the building, clenching his jaw against the ache in his groin. His cock had throbbed almost nonstop since he'd seen her emerge from her apartment earlier today; at one point as he'd followed her through the Undercity streets, he'd been forced to duck into an alleyway and tighten his under wrapping over his pelvis to ensure his shaft didn't extrude. The delay had become doubly frustrating when he'd stepped out of the alley and was unable, for several harrowing seconds, to locate her in the crowd. To his relief, she'd walked out of a nearby shop shortly after, and he'd resumed shadowing her.

His heart had pounded at the thought of losing track of her, and panic had briefly set in, heating his skin. That panic—as silly as it seemed—had been nothing compared to what struck him when the tralix knocked her down. His flare of rage at seeing her harmed had only been overpowered by his fear for her safety. Arcanthus had never forced his way through a crowd so quickly.

As Arc walked away from her building, he glanced down at his metal hands. They relayed information on pressure, texture, temperature, and moisture to his brain with immense accuracy, but despite their sophistication, they would *never* replace the sensation of touching anything with his own flesh-and-blood fingertips. He'd yearned to touch her with his own hands as he'd helped her out of the crowd, but even the contact between her skin and his cybernetic limbs had amplified the electric hum she produced in his *qal*.

Though he'd not even seen her body—her oversized clothing obfuscated her shape—everything about her called to him. It had taken one glimpse into her dark, expressive eyes for him to know what she was to him.

After a few minutes, he arrived at his hovercar. It unlocked at his touch. He climbed inside, closing the door behind him.

"Damn it," he muttered, releasing a shaky breath. "She's my *mate*."

Saying it out loud only gave the word new weight; it hung around him, thickening the air, and settled heavily upon his chest.

Mate.

There was no other explanation for the way she made his *qal* react, no other explanation for why he'd just spent half his day following a stranger through an entire Undercity sector as she, with steadily increasing desperation, searched for employment.

Obsessed, Drakkal grumbled in the back of Arcanthus's mind.

"Yes, because she's my *mate*, you ornery fur ball. That's how it works."

He powered on the hovercar's engines but didn't take hold of the controls.

His interest in terrans had begun recently, when he'd met one for the first time—Abella. He'd made no effort to disguise his want of her; some of his forwardness had been to provoke her mate, a foul-tempered zenturi, but the terran female's looks had been tempting. Even more appealing had been something less tangible; something about her personality, her spirit, had drawn him in, something he couldn't describe apart from it being *terran*. He'd thought about Abella often and had even come to envy her mate for having her.

And yet Abella hadn't triggered a fraction of the response in Arcanthus that Samantha did. *No* female had.

"Don't be stupid, Arc," he said in an exaggeratedly guttural voice as he accessed the plexus through the hovercar's onboard computer system.

After double checking that his safeguards were in place to make his source untraceable, he called one of his guards—a cren named Kiloq.

"Yeah, boss?" asked Kiloq when the audio connected.

Arcanthus flipped through several files on the hovercar's holographic display. "Sending you some information. I need you to come to this address and keep an eye on this female. Discreetly- she can't know you're around."

"Sounds good. Is she trouble?"

"No, she's *in* trouble. She caught the attention of some thugs from the Blue Threshers. Do what you must to ensure they don't touch her again." Sweeping his fingers closed, Arc compiled the files and sent them to Kiloq.

"Got them, boss."

"Bring your brother with you. I want you to keep track of her whereabouts at all times, and make sure she's safe while she's out." Arcanthus turned his head, glancing in the direction of Samantha's building, which was out of sight a few streets away. There was little to distinguish it from the surrounding complexes—they were all big, bland, dirty buildings with hundreds of windows that looked out on the windows of neighboring units. This place was meant as a start, but these sectors were often rife with criminals targeting the unfortunate and desperate. "Should anything happen, make her safe and report directly to me."

"We'll keep her safe, boss."

"I know. That's why I'm putting you on this. Check in later."

"Right. We'll be on our way in five."

Arc cut off the call. As he grasped the controls, he paused; part of him wanted to stay and watch out for trouble until the two cren arrived, just to be sure.

Part of him wanted to go into that building, walk up to Samantha's door, kick it down, and sweep her into his arms. That would be the quickest way to have her, after all. The most direct route to getting what he wanted. He'd sacrificed so much over the years just to survive; wasn't he entitled to taking the easy way every now and again? With so much having been taken from him, wasn't it all right to take a little for himself?

"Stupid," he muttered. He piloted the hovercar up and began his journey home.

He'd always enjoyed the game, had always enjoyed maneuvering boldly and brashly, throwing his opponents off guard with his audacity. He was a champion, not a conqueror; he would win his mate, not steal her. She'd already shown some interest in him. Even though she'd openly fought that interest, it was a start. It was enough for him to work with.

Drakkal was waiting with his thick arms crossed over his chest and his brown, taupe, and copper fur bristling when Arcanthus drove the hovercar into the garage. Despite the dark tinting of the hovercar's windows and windshield, the azhera seemed to meet Arcanthus's gaze instantly with a heavy, angry glare.

"So it begins," Arcanthus said. He opened the door and exited the vehicle.

He approached Drakkal at a leisurely pace, tilting one corner of his mouth up in a smirk. "It looks like something has your fur rumpled. Did Razi annihilate you in Conquerors again?"

"Six hours and twenty-two minutes," the azhera growled.

Arcanthus stopped in front of Drakkal. "Well, you kept at the game for a long time. I admire your persistence, but sometimes you just have to know when to surrender."

"This isn't a game, Arcanthus. How am I supposed to keep you safe when you disappear for six and a half hours without a word? When you turn off all communication? Are you—"

"Stupid? Yes, I suppose I'm *quite* stupid sometimes." Arc waved a hand and walked past the azhera into the hallway. "I'm fine, Drakkal. It's been ten years, and as far as they're concerned, I'm dead. My real name isn't out there anywhere. There's nothing wrong with me going out for some air every now and then."

Drakkal's footsteps sounded behind Arc as the azhera followed him down the hallway. "If you believed that, you wouldn't live inside a small fortress and constantly cycle through twenty different aliases."

Frowning, Arcanthus stopped and turned to face Drakkal. "That's just...habit by now. They aren't looking for me because I no longer exist. Simple."

Drakkal sighed, though it came out as something closer to a snort. "All for a terran?"

Arc narrowed his center eye. "The terran has nothing to do with this. I was feeling trapped. Does it truly come as a surprise that sometimes I just need to get outside these walls?"

"I know you sent Kiloq and Koroq to watch out for her."

Arcanthus's brows fell. "Then I suppose I will have to have a conversation with them regarding discretion, won't I?"

"You wanted me to head up your security. That's what I'm doing. If you want me to be effective, you keep me in the know."

"I can take care of myself."

Drakkal's expression spoke clearly—*really?*

"*Sometimes* I can take care of myself, then. Does that make you happy? Does it satisfy your craving to be needed?"

"I don't want to walk into a scene like I did back on Caldorius, Arc."

A pang struck Arcanthus's chest; he wasn't sure if it was guilt, sorrow, pain, or something else. "Well, the good news is that there's not too much left to be chopped off, if you think about it."

Shaking his head, Drakkal dropped his arms to his sides. "Just be careful. You're too soft for this city."

"Surely you jest. I've often some trouble telling, as you seem unable to modulate the volume and tone of your voice."

"You're offended. Just proves my point."

Arcanthus lifted both his arms, curled one hand into a fist, and knocked on his opposite forearm, producing a dull, metallic clang. "If you'd like to discuss *soft*, we can compare. Your fur is looking particularly fluffy today, so I'd advise you avoid this conversation if you don't want to be embarrassed."

"Come here," Drakkal said, spreading his arms wide. "I'll hug your pain and bitterness away."

"You are *not* my mother, azhera."

Drakkal's mouth curled into a smirk. "Stop acting like a child and you won't trigger my maternal instincts."

There was too much going on in Arc's head, too many emotions beyond his understanding roiling in his chest, for him to be standing here, quipping with Drakkal, but he couldn't help laughing. "You're lucky I like you so much, Drakkal. Any sensible employer would've fired you ages ago."

"You can't fire me, Arcanthus."

"And it irks me to no end that you're aware of it."

Smirk fading, Drakkal lowered his arms. "Keep me in the know, all right? That's all I'm asking. It's not safe for you to go wandering the streets like that."

"All right, Mother. I will endeavor to make better decisions in the future."

"One day you'll give me a serious answer, and I'll drop dead in shock."

Arcanthus and Drakkal walked deeper into the compound —Arc's holdings spanned several blocks and buildings, all inter-connected by various tunnels and passages—and eventually parted ways.

As he entered the workshop, Arcanthus removed his robe and tossed it aside. He glanced down at his body before he sat; the scars around the edges of his surgically implanted cyber-netic sleeves were as prominent as ever, the result of the hasty patch job that had saved his life ten years ago. Even with all that time to adjust, it still felt strange when he stopped and *looked,* when he let himself think about how his body just...*ended* at those points. That what existed past those scars, though connected to him in every way that mattered, wasn't *really* him at all.

Those thoughts led to thoughts of the Inner Reach Syndicate as he sat at his desk. The Syndicate had begun as a conglomeration of criminal organizations on distant Caldorius, but had extended its fingers across the universe, even into Arthos. Every decision Arc had made in the last ten years had taken the Syndicate into consideration; every move had been calculated to keep him out of their notice, even as his reputation in the Infinite City's criminal underbelly had spread and grown. All his security measures existed to keep them away.

Why hadn't he thought about them a single time when he'd decided to seek out Samantha and follow her? Why hadn't he realized the risk and abandoned the foolish whim before he'd pursued it? He'd even given her a means of contacting him directly—only Drakkal and a few of his most trusted guards, people he'd worked with for *years*, had his commlink ID.

"She *must* be my mate," he said as he prepared his screens. "Either that, or I've been too long without a female's touch."

He had work to complete. He was the foremost creator of false identification chips in Arthos, and both his reputation and his business relied upon him fulfilling his obligations. But he instead found himself scouring the plexus for information on terrans—their culture, their biology, their everything.

At some point, he brought up the copy of Samantha's file he'd taken from the Consortium's database. He read through the information several more times, though it provided him little insight into her. She was from place called *Seattle, Washington* on the planet *Earth*, the terran homeworld. No criminal history, no background in government or military—not much documented history at all. His shy little terran was something of an enigma.

His flicker of disappointment was fleeting. It would be exceedingly more satisfying to learn about her directly, to coax out every bit of who she was from between her pink lips.

He'd wanted so badly to kiss her for the brief time he'd had her in his arms. The feel of her against him, of her heat radiating into his chest, had been exquisite, and the soft, inadvertent brushes of her lips against his skin had nearly been his undoing. And yet his main drive had been to comfort her, to lift her spirits, to take away her pain. That he didn't think he'd succeeded in that goal was maddening.

Arcanthus's attention returned to the hologram of her face. Her expression, captured forever in the Consortium database, seemed only more apt now—she was out of her element, desperate to find her place but unsure of how to go about it. How simple would it have been to offer her a position in his own organization? He could've maintained a semblance of legitimacy and legality at least for a little while as he eased her into the true nature of his business, and he would have known she was safe and provided for in the meantime.

His third eye dipped to the options beneath her holographic face, lingering on the one that would pull up the full body scans that were standard for every citizen of the Infinite City. They hid *nothing*.

He lifted his hand and extended his index finger but stopped himself before moving it forward. Just the thought of seeing what was hidden beneath her baggy, shapeless clothing was enough to send a rush of heat to his groin. Yet what would it accomplish? What would a peek do other than silently break the bit of trust he'd built with her?

Why look now when he would eventually see her flesh directly with his own eyes? That was the real prize, that was the real thrill. Holograms could not compare.

That inevitable moment when she finally gave herself over

to him, when she finally revealed her body to him of her own accord, *that* moment would be special beyond words. It was a moment worth waiting for.

The anticipation alone would add such a thrill to the ultimate reveal that it would be foolish not to wait.

He dropped a hand to his crotch and pressed it over his slit. Despite the restraint of his under wrapping, his cock struggled to emerge, creating a pulsing ache in his pelvis. He leaned forward in the chair to tighten the cloth again. The relief provided by the extra pressure was minimal.

Moving her file to one of the side screens, he took a few minutes to check through the security feeds from around the compound and its various entrances. There was a separate entry correlating to each of the eight forger aliases he used, identities separate from those he cycled through on his own ID chip. Everything seemed quiet; the streets of Nyssa Vye—the Undercity's largest black-market sector—were as busy as ever, but the traffic flowed past the discreet entrances without anything suspicious to catch his eye.

Satisfied, he moved Samantha's file back to his primary display, dismissing everything but her holographic image. Leaning back in his chair, he propped an elbow on the armrest and settled his chin on his hand. He stared into her dark eyes. Faint tingles flowed along his *qal*.

The longer he stared, the clearer it became that he would not be able to ignore his body's needs any longer. He lowered his hand again, loosening his under wrapping. His cock slid free.

He released a groan and curled his fingers around the base of his shaft. "You'll know soon enough, Samantha...you're mine."

FIVE

After patching up her cuts and scrapes with the first-aid kit in the bathroom, Samantha had gone to bed. Her sleep had been disjointed; she'd tossed and turned, unable to find a comfortable position thanks to the aches racking her battered body. As if her many bruises weren't enough, her mind raced with a thousand what-ifs.

What if she wasn't strong enough to make it here? What if she never found work? What if she ran into that gang again while she was alone?

But, more than anything, she couldn't stop thinking of a certain sedhi whose lightest touch had set her body ablaze.

She woke the next morning feeling more exhausted than she had when she'd lain down. Raising her arm, she traced her fingertips over her wrist, touching the same place Alkorin's fingers had so gently brushed. It didn't matter that his hands were cybernetic, it had been *his* touch.

And his eyes...

They'd captivated her, had looked through her, directly

into her heart, and it felt like he already knew her. His intensity frightened Sam as much as it tempted her.

He's dangerous.

Sam repeated those words in her head as she waded through the crowded Undercity streets in search of work. She almost hadn't gone out; the thought of leaving had made her nauseous, but the thought of giving up, of acting like a coward, was more sickening still.

In a city filled with billions of people, Sam was just a speck of dust. She was lost, with no direction, no guidance, no friends, no family. But that didn't mean there was no hope. There was a way forward, there was a future for her here somewhere. She just had to keep moving forward if she wanted to find it.

After three hours of wandering the streets, her feet were sore, and weariness weighed heavily upon her bruised body. Whether she wanted to or not, it seemed like she'd have little choice but to head home soon. That familiar discouragement began falling into place after another shopkeeper turned her away.

Until a female borian met Sam's gaze and approached her.

Samantha froze, swallowing hard. The muscular borian was at least a head taller than her. The woman's hair was weaved into countless thin braids that were pulled back and tied behind her head in a thick bundle, and her deeply tanned skin made her piercing blue eyes stand out. There was an intimidating intensity about the borian.

"I hear you're looking for work," the woman said in Universal Speech.

Samantha's heart leapt. "Yes!"

"Good." The borian grasped Sam's wrist and all but dragged her into a nearby booth; Sam had to jog to keep up with the woman's longer stride.

Once they were inside the booth, the borian released

Samantha and turned to face her. "Today only. That spawn of a skek left me to run the kitchen by myself." She pointed toward the back of the enclosed booth. "You wash and clean as I cook. Understood?"

Sam smiled and nodded. Even if it was only for a day, it was more than she'd expected. It was a start. "Got it."

The day flew by at a hectic pace. The borian, Sarai, took orders and cooked with speed and confidence, multitasking effortlessly. Sam scrubbed every pot, pan, skillet, plate, and utensil that was brought to her, kept all the counters clean, and mopped the floor several times to keep it free of grease and bits of food.

The work was demanding. Samantha's breaks were barely long enough to catch her breath, and by the time Sarai closed the booth, Sam was close to collapsing.

But it was fulfilling work.

She helped Sarai straighten up and prep for the next day. When they were done, the borian grinned and slapped Samantha on the back, nearly knocking her over.

"You did well, terran!" Sarai eyed Samantha critically. "Your size is deceiving. In truth, I did not expect you to keep up. You surprised me."

Samantha smiled. Were her cheeks not already flushed from exertion, she was certain they'd be red from the praise. "Thanks for giving me the chance, Sarai."

Sarai grunted and plucked something from her apron. "Here."

Sam extended her hand, and the borian dropped a credit chip onto her waiting palm. It didn't matter how much was on it. She closed her fingers around the chip and held it to her chest as an immense sense of accomplishment swept through her. "Thank you. Thank you so much."

Sarai arched a thick, black brow. "Never seen anyone so happy to wash dishes."

"I just... You have *no* idea how much it means to me. That you gave me a chance. It's...it's been hard."

The borian woman stared at Samantha silently for a moment before she patted Sam's back, softer than before. "It's rough down here, but you have strength, terran. Here." Sarai turned, picked up a food container, and held it out to Samantha. "You earned it."

Samantha accepted the box; it was warm, and wisps of steam drifted out through the tiny gaps beneath the lid. "Thank you, Sarai."

The borian grunted and turned away, but not before Sam caught a change of color on her cheeks. "Now go home. And watch your back."

Samantha left the food booth feeling better than she had since arriving in Arthos. It gave her hope that there were others out there like Sarai, others willing to give her a shot.

Alkorin came to mind on the heels of that thought.

But don't mistake me for a hero; I've not acted selflessly tonight.

He'd been kind, yet by his own admission, he'd not helped without expecting something in return. But what did she have to offer? What could he possibly want from her?

You're beautiful, Samantha, and I find myself eager to be in your company.

Biting the inside of her lower lip, Samantha clutched the food container closer to her chest. There was nothing special about her. How could someone like him find *her* beautiful? She was...

Worthless. Weak.

Sam quickly silenced that voice, locking it in the depths of her mind.

Thankfully, she made it back to her apartment complex without trouble. She'd kept to the outskirts of the crowds, avoided open alleyways, and checked her surroundings frequently; she wouldn't forget the lessons of the previous day.

She entered the building and took the elevator up to her floor, standing against the back wall and avoiding eye contact with the other passengers who came and went.

Once the elevator reached her destination, Samantha slipped out. She crept to the corner of the elevator space, which was offset from the main hallway, took in a deep breath, and leaned forward to peek into the corridor.

Rakkob stood outside his apartment, speaking to an unfamiliar azhera.

Samantha straightened.

Damnit!

Just need to move fast, ignore him, and get inside. I'm not going to let him ruin my day.

Wrapping her arms securely around the food box, Samantha slouched down, bowed her head, and turned the corner. She walked swiftly toward her apartment, keeping close to the wall.

"Little terran!" Rakkob boomed as she neared.

Of course it was too much to hope that he wouldn't notice me.

Grinning, he stepped away from the doorway of his apartment and approached her. He extended an arm and placed his hand against the wall in front of Sam as though to block her path. "Look here, Cida. Didn't I tell you a pretty terran lived here?"

The azhera turned and settled his orange eyes on Sam. He made a rumbling sound in his chest.

Samantha didn't slow; she ducked beneath Rakkob's arm and hurried to her door. Before she could raise her ID chip to the scanner, Rakkob caught her wrist in a vise-like grip. She released a startled breath and nearly dropped her food as he yanked her closer. A sweet, smoky scent wafted from him.

Rakkob leaned down until he was eye level with her. His grin was gone, having been replaced by a scowl. "It's rude to ignore someone talking to you. Didn't they teach you that where you come from?"

"Let me go," Samantha said quietly.

He tightened his grip on her wrist; much more pressure, and her bones would snap. "I don't think I will."

Cida leaned closer and sniffed, his cat-like nostrils flaring. "She smells good beneath the stench of food."

"Perhaps a taste, then?" Rakkob said, bringing her hand to his mouth.

Samantha smashed the box of food into his face. Rakkob released his hold on her and reeled back, throwing his hands up to grab the container. It was enough of an opening for Samantha to dash to the door, scan her ID chip, and get inside. She slapped the interior control and looked up to see Rakkob's furious expression—with bits of food clinging to his face—as he lunged at her.

The door slid shut just before he could cross the threshold.

He slammed into the other side, producing a heavy, metallic *clunk*, and Sam leapt away.

"You'll pay for that, terran *ji'tas!*" Rakkob yelled over Cida's laughter.

Samantha stood, trembling, as the cren pounded the door— it felt like hours passed, but it couldn't have been more than a minute before he gave up.

"What am I going to do now?" she asked herself quietly.

Rakkob was pissed, and he didn't strike her as the kind to keep his hands to himself even when he was calm.

If you need anything, Samantha, do not hesitate to contact me.

She looked down at her holocom.

Anything.

Had Alkorin meant it?

No, she couldn't bother him. He hadn't really meant for her to call him for anything, it was nothing more than politeness. Just an attempt to make her feel a little better before he moved on with his life.

You're beautiful, Samantha, and I find myself eager to be in your company.

Those words replayed over and over inside her head, with one sticking out more than the rest.

Beautiful.

But I'm not. I'm not...beautiful.

And yet the way he'd looked at her as he said it *almost* made her believe it was true.

After a final glance at the front door, she turned toward the rest of her apartment. It was a simple unit, with the living room, bedroom, and kitchen contained within one space. Only the bathroom was a separate room.

Sam was exhausted, but she was also starving. She walked to the kitchen and opened a cupboard, pulling out a wrapped food tray. Placing the tray on the counter, she stared down at it for a few seconds before releasing a sigh.

"So much for the food Sarai gave me," she muttered, but her lips tilted up into a smirk as she recalled the bits of vegetable clinging to Rakkob's eyebrows. "Serves him right."

She unwrapped the tray, slid it into the heating unit, and started the device. As she waited for the food, her eyes strayed again to her holocom. Turning her arm, she brushed a finger along the inside of her wrist. She could almost imagine the feel of Alkorin's touch.

The heating unit beeped, snapping her back to reality.

Stop it! Stop doing this to yourself.

She removed the food tray, sat down at the small table, and stared blankly at the floor as the food cooled. Once she was sure it wouldn't scald her mouth, she ate; she barely tasted anything.

Several times, she caught herself glancing at her holocom. It was as though the device called to her subconscious.

No, it wasn't the holocom. *He* called to her. The alien with hypnotic, glowing eyes—three eyes, how crazy was that?— horns, a tail, and one hell of a sexy body.

"And what would I say? Oh, hi, remember me? The pathetic human who cried all over your masculine chest?"

Samantha huffed and shoved the half-eaten tray away. Scooting her chair back, she stood and walked to the bathroom. She stripped along the way, tossing her filthy, grease-spattered clothing onto the floor.

She stopped in the bathroom doorway and looked back at her discarded clothes. Her fingers twitched with the urge to pick them up. The mess was so minor, so insignificant, but it would have been a massive issue while she was with James.

Locking her legs in place, she drew in a deep breath. She didn't have to pick them up now. This was *her* life. She was in control, not him. If she wanted to leave her dirty shirt on the floor for a day, a week, for the whole damned year, it was her choice.

Samantha faced forward, entered the bathroom, and took a hot shower, relishing the soothing feel of water cascading over her aching body. Her mind summoned images of Alkorin every time she saw the holocom on her wrist.

While she'd worked with Sarai, she'd been too distracted to think about him, but now, with nothing else to occupy her thoughts...he was *all* she could think about. Worse, her body reacted to those mental images; the memory of his touch, however innocent it may have been, created a new ache inside her.

After her shower, she hurriedly dried off, threw on an over-sized shirt, brushed her hair, and checked her palms. Looking at her hands now, no one ever could've guessed they'd been scraped to all hell the day before. As basic as this apartment was, the first-aid kit contained some pretty amazing supplies. Too bad there wasn't a full-body salve she could slather on to heal her numerous bruises.

Sam exited the bathroom, turned down the lights, and crawled into bed. Once she'd settled down, she stared up at the ceiling. Despite weariness creeping in from all sides, she lay awake and restless for some time. Eventually, she turned onto her side and stretched, extending one arm in front of her.

Her eyes fell on the holocom, and she frowned.

What if he really *had* been serious about her calling if she needed anything? Wouldn't it be stupid *not* to take him up on that offer? Rakkob wasn't going to leave her alone. If anything, he was more likely to seek her out and harass her. She'd gone well beyond ignoring him now.

She'd smashed greasy food into his face.

What would it hurt to call Alkorin? The worst he could do was say he didn't remember her.

Sam rolled onto her stomach. Her hair fell around her face as she activated her holocom, bringing up the control screen. She unlocked it and went into her contacts.

Her heart quickened.

"This is dumb. He was just being polite. He doesn't actually want to talk to me."

ARCANTHUS'S FINGERS flew through commands as he pieced together a profile for the identification chip he was working on. Despite the distractions that had risen over the last few days, he'd managed to bury himself in his work, his state of focus enhanced by the almost total silence of his workshop. Even the tanks on the walls were quieted thanks to the sound dampening fields he'd enabled.

So, when his holocom chimed with an incoming call, its sound was more like a grenade detonating beside his ear than a gentle alert. He jumped up with enough force to hurt his tail—which caught on the top of the cutout in his chair—and came down hard on the cushion.

He grimaced. "Fuck!"

Heart pounding and jaw clenched, he released a heavy breath through his nostrils. He was annoyed at both himself and his people. He'd told them no interruptions until he stated otherwise, save for those concerning Samantha. But Kiloq and Koroq had been sending him information via text, not through calls.

Without looking, he brushed a finger over the holocom's activation button to connect the call.

"What is it?" he demanded.

"I-I'm sorry. I shouldn't have called," said a soft, feminine voice before the call went dead.

Arcanthus froze. For a moment, it was difficult to breathe, and the thumping of his heart echoed in his ears. He turned his head to look down at his holocom. Its display was inactive.

Maybe I'm overworking. Pushed myself to the point of auditory hallucinations.

It couldn't have been Samantha calling him; she seemed much too timid for that. She'd been genuinely grateful for his help last night, but she'd also been frightened of his closeness, embarrassed by his offers of further assistance. His plan had been to allow her a couple days before arranging another *chance* meeting.

Frowning, he pulled up the communication log from his holocom on one of his desk screens. *Samantha Dawn Wilder* was listed as the most recent incoming call. He'd entered her information into his system when he'd first found her file, a pesky fact of which she never needed to learn.

He reached forward to initiate another call only to stop when he realized how he'd greeted her.

"Shit. That wasn't my finest moment, was it?"

Sighing, he raked his fingers through his hair, tugging the long strands back, and initiated the call.

Soft notes played as the system sought a connection, waiting for her to accept. He'd never been so impatient for that sound to end. Seconds passed, each feeling longer than the last, and he dipped his chin, cursing himself for a fool. She'd reached out to him—a wholly unexpected move—and he'd scared her away.

The soft notes ended, and Arcanthus thought the call had disconnected until he heard her voice.

"Hi."

Arcanthus straightened in his chair. "Samantha?"

She sounded surprised when she said, "You remembered me."

He grinned. If he'd not had work to do, he'd likely have spent every moment thinking about her today—he nearly had, even with that workload. "I don't see how it'd be possible to forget you, little terran."

"I...I don't know how to respond to that."

"You don't need to. I didn't think you would call. Is everything all right?"

"Is it a bad time? I don't want to disturb you. You sounded—"

"Irritated?" He chuckled.

"Yeah."

"I'm sorry about that. Like I said, I didn't expect you to call, so I assumed it was one of my employees contacting me even though I asked not to be disturbed. Had I been smart enough to look before I answered, I'd have spoken in a far more pleasant tone."

"You don't mind me calling you, then?"

"The only thing I would rather be doing right now is *seeing* you, Samantha." He leaned back in his chair and lifted one leg, settling his ankle over his opposite knee.

"You could," she said, and, after a gasp, hurried to add, "I mean that the holocoms have that option, not that that we needed to meet up, but... I mean, we *could* if you wanted and..." She groaned, and her next words were slightly muffled, as though she were covering her mouth. "Oh, I'm babbling."

Fully aware of his state of dress—he wore only a loincloth, which would be below the optical receptor—Arcanthus moved his hands behind his head, locked his fingers together, and curled his long tail forward, flicking the command to enable image sharing.

"You're...oh." A moment later, Samantha's image appeared in front of him. "Oh!"

She stared at him, wide-eyed, with her long brown hair hanging loose around her face. One of her shoulders was bare. She lay on her front atop a bed, the blanket rumpled around her, with the fabric clenched in one fist.

Arc's grin widened; not only was her exposed shoulder more than he'd seen of her body thus far—the most tantalizing bit of flesh he'd *ever* seen—but she was in bed, in the dark. A wave of desire coursed through his veins, making his cock stir. "Handsome? Ravishing? Enticing? Please, stop me, or I'll go on for a long while...and I'd much rather talk about *you*."

Her eyes dipped, and interest sparked within them.

"Gorgeous..." she breathed, then quickly covered her mouth. "I can't believe I just said that."

"I can. What's harder to believe is that you seem unaware of your own beauty."

She lowered her hand to the bedding. Her pink lips fell into a frown as she looked away. "You don't need to lie to me, Alkorin."

Dropping his raised foot to the floor, Arc leaned closer to the optical receptor and propped his elbows on the desk . "Look at me, Samantha."

She hesitated but did as he asked.

"I've told many lies in my time. I cannot deny that. Truth has not always been my friend. But when I say this to you, it is meant with more sincerity than I can rightly express: you are the most beautiful female I have ever seen."

Samantha ducked her head, and her hair shifted to partly shield her face from view. "I really don't know what to say around you."

He shrugged, forcing his arms to remain on the desk; his urge to reach toward her image was a foolish one, and it would only disappoint him when his fingers passed through the hologram. He wanted to show her just how beautiful she was. He wanted to touch her.

"You can say anything you want, Samantha."

"It felt easier before. When...when you couldn't see me. Or, at least, I thought it was easier. But..." Her gaze returned to him. "I like seeing you."

"If one of us is going to be self-conscious, shouldn't it be me? I'm underdressed for the conversation, it would seem."

"I'm...not wearing much else, either," she replied, cheeks turning red.

One corner of his mouth tilted farther upward. "I just learned something new about you, Samantha."

"What did you learn?"

"That you enjoy teasing me."

"That I—? I was just—" She covered her face and lowered it into the bedding. Her new position gave Arcanthus a fleeting glimpse of the curve of her lush bottom, clad in the white fabric of her underwear.

Arcanthus caught his lower lip between his teeth and only held in a groan by exerting all his willpower. The tip of his cock extruded farther out of his slit, straining painfully against his loincloth's under wrapping.

Whether it was intentional or not—and it really didn't seem to be—she *was* teasing him. And it was the most exquisite torture he'd ever experienced.

But it was too much. If this continued, he would either scare her away or become aroused to the point at which he'd be unable to control himself. He doubted she would appreciate him stroking his shaft in front of her.

Though, based on the heat that had been in her gaze when it trailed over his bare chest...perhaps she *would* appreciate it.

Finesse, Arcanthus. This requires finesse.

"You never answered me before, little terran," he said. "*Is everything all right?*"

Samantha raised her head and ran a hand through her hair, pulling the strands back and to the sides. She lowered her brows as a troubled gleam entered her eyes. Arcanthus was instantly on guard, curling his fingers into fists. He knew without her saying anything that she'd had another unpleasant encounter.

"I...don't really have the means, and I don't know my way around the city, but I was hoping that you, or maybe somebody you know, could, well, take me on a tour of the surface? I...

really don't want to travel alone. I know it's a lot for me to ask, and I completely understand if you say no because you're busy—"

"Tomorrow."

She drew her head back slightly, confusion wrinkling her brow. "What?"

"I will pick you up tomorrow, Samantha. Will the morning work? Whatever is morning to you, I mean."

"Wait. You *will*?"

He leaned his chin on one of his hands and grinned. "I'm a fool, but not so much of one as to pass up a chance to spend time with you."

She blushed again; this time, it was accompanied by the hint of a smile on her pink lips. "I'd...like to see you too. In person, I mean."

"Good. I'll send a message before I leave."

Her smile strengthened, shining in her eyes. It completely transformed her—for the duration of that smile, Arcanthus saw the vibrant, carefree female trapped in the prison of self-doubt and timidity she seemed to have constructed around herself. And she was breathtaking.

"Okay," she said. "Goodnight, Alkorin."

"Goodnight, Samantha. Dream of me. I'll be dreaming of you."

Her cheeks reddened further before she ended the connection.

Arcanthus sagged back in the chair, licked his lips, and finally released the groan that had been building in his chest. He dropped a hand to his pelvis and pressed down on his throbbing cock, which his loincloth could no longer hold back. His tail flicked back and forth over the floor.

"How am I going to show her around the surface with this jutting out the entire time?"

He grinned to himself; there were far worse problems to have.

Less than a minute later, the rear entry door—designed to blend seamlessly into the wall when shut—slid open, and Drakkal strode in.

"I said I wasn't to be disturbed," Arcanthus said.

"Since when do I take orders from you?" Drakkal stopped beside Arc's chair.

"I suppose I'm going to have to start restricting access to those doors in defense of my privacy."

"Whatever, sedhi. There's talk on the streets that someone's planning a big smuggling job. Might have a lot of business about to come our—"

Drakkal's words faltered when he glanced down at Arcanthus. "Why are you grinning like that?" His eyes dipped lower. "And why are you fondling yourself? You're supposed to be *working.*"

Arc didn't move his hand. "Would you like me to *work,* Drakkal?"

"Just because your arms are made of metal doesn't mean I can't tear them off."

Snickering, Arcanthus moved his arms to the armrests of the chair, his cock thankfully retreating into his slit. The interruption had been enough to kill the mood. "I was hard at work. It's only recently that I was diverted by a delectable distraction."

Drakkal sighed and rolled his eyes. "The terran?"

"You know me so well. I'll be taking her to the upper city tomorrow to show her the bountiful wonders."

Drakkal growled. "Arcanthus, did we or did we not just have a talk about this?"

"Relax, Drak. I'll be safe the entire time."

"Why, because you're going to be careful? I don't think you even know what that word means."

"Careful? Me?" Arcanthus scoffed. "I'll be safe because *you* are coming with me."

Drakkal's darkening expression only made Arcanthus's grin stretch wider.

"You will have the honor of being my driver tomorrow, azhera," Arc said.

Nostrils flaring and fur bristling, Drakkal asked through bared fangs, "Have I ever told you how much I hate you?"

"You have, but we both know it's not true." Arcanthus turned back to the screens on his desk. "Now get out. I have work to do, and you're distracting me."

SIX

Samantha was a nervous wreck as she waited outside her apartment building. She shifted her weight from one foot to the other, tucked her hair behind her ears only to shake it free a moment later, and fiddled with the cuffs of her sleeves. Her eyes scanned her surroundings in a ceaseless search for Alkorin. Was he coming in a hovercar, or was he walking? What if she somehow missed him? What if he missed her?

She'd received a message on her holocom twelve minutes ago—*Be there in fifteen, little terran*—and her stomach had been fluttering ever since.

No, not just since the message. I've felt like this since I talked to him last night.

She couldn't quite believe their conversation had been real, couldn't believe that she'd taken active part in it. He'd flirted with her, and Sam... She'd flirted right back. His holographic image had been delectable, to say the least. If he'd been with her in the flesh, she feared she wouldn't have been able to keep herself from reaching out to touch him.

Dream of me, he'd told her.

And oh, how she'd dreamed of him. His words had triggered something powerful in her subconscious. She'd dreamed of him sliding his metal hands up her legs and over her naked body, caressing and teasing her flesh, coaxing moans from her lips. She'd dreamed of his mouth brushing over hers. And in her dream, she'd welcomed him, opening her legs to take him into her body.

She'd woken with a start, her skin hot and sweaty, her sex pulsing and wet. A need unlike anything she'd ever felt throbbed at her core. The details of her dream had faded quickly, but she could still feel the aftereffects of his ethereal touch.

What am I doing? This is crazy.

She'd only just met Alkorin, barely knew anything about him, yet she was in danger of placing herself in the same position she'd sought to escape by leaving Earth.

No, he's different. He's not like James. He wouldn't...he wouldn't...

But he could. Anyone could. She would never have guessed what James was capable of—what he would *do*—in the beginning.

She already knew Alkorin was capable of violence. She'd seen him in action—he'd taken out four aliens within seconds of their attack, a couple of whom had heavier builds than him. And he'd been smiling and joking as things escalated, like he was completely unconcerned with the prospect of facing four hostile gang members at once.

As if it were a game to him.

They deserved it, though. He didn't fight without reason. He was protecting me.

Samantha turned her head to the left, scanning the street nearby.

Someone grabbed the front of her shirt and spun her to the

right. She gasped, lifting her gaze to her assailant as she grasped the hand clutching her shirt with both of hers.

The eyes she found herself staring into were unsurprisingly, terrifyingly familiar.

Rakkob leaned down until his nose nearly touched Sam's. "I could have shown you a good time, terran *ji'tas*, but you chose to dishonor me instead. So now I'll *take* my pleasure from this weak little body of yours."

You are mine. You exist only for my pleasure. Weak. Worthless. You're nothing.

Sam's blood turned to ice.

Rakkob tugged her toward the apartment building's entrance.

She scratched at his arm and dug her nails into his hand, leaning back to force her heels against the concrete. "No!"

Something—*someone*—darted past her; she caught only a flash of crimson cloth and long, dark locks before the newcomer grabbed a fistful of hair on the back of Rakkob's head.

Alkorin!

Rakkob spat some sort of curse before his hand fell away from Samantha's shirt. She stumbled back, raising her hands to her mouth. Rakkob seemed about to turn on Alkorin, but the sedhi was much faster. With one arm, Alkorin swung the borian around and slammed him face first into the wall.

Grunting, Rakkob lifted an arm to fight back, but Alkorin caught his wrist and forced it down.

"Fuck you," Rakkob snarled.

Alkorin pulled the borian's head back and hammered it into the wall again. Rakkob's knees buckled, but Alkorin held him upright by his hair.

"I don't understand what's wrong with the people in this sector," Alkorin said. He looked at Samantha over his shoulder. "Who is this?"

She lowered her hands and curled them beneath her chin, pressing them together. "My neighbor."

"Has he done this sort of thing before?"

Samantha nodded. "He's...why I called you last night."

"Oh. Here I was hoping you called me because you couldn't get me off your mind." He smiled a lopsided, roguish smile before he turned back to Rakkob and leaned his mouth close to the borian's ear. When he spoke again, his voice was unlike anything she'd heard from him thus far—it was a low, bestial growl. "If you touch her again, if you so much as *look* at her wrong, I will break every bone in your body one at a time. Do you understand?"

The borian nodded, scraping his cheek against the wall.

Alkorin squeezed the borian's wrist, and bone cracked. "I want you to *tell* me you understand."

Rakkob cried out in pain. "I do! I understand. Won't touch her. Won't look!"

"Good. Now go back to your room, and make sure I don't see you again." Alkorin pulled the borian away from the wall and shoved him toward the door.

Rakkob dove inside the moment it was open.

Alkorin straightened the silky fabric of his robe, tucked one of his long, thin braids behind his pointed ear, and turned to face Samantha again. His expression was serious as his eyes raked over her, the eye on his forehead moving independently of the other two. "Are you all right, Samantha?"

He stepped closer to her and settled a hand on her cheek, tilting her face up so she met his gaze. The pad of his thumb brushed her cheekbone. It sent a shiver through her that had nothing to do with fear.

Hesitantly, she grasped his wrist and held his hand there, pressing her cheek into his palm. Though it was a simple gesture, his touch calmed her, grounded her, melted the icy fear that had welled in her heart. She needed it, craved it.

"You're always saving me," she said.

His smile tilted, becoming a mischievous smirk. "Anything to make me look better in your eyes."

Samantha laughed. His humor in the face of what had just happened was a welcome change from the usual, just the distraction she needed at that moment. Her smile stretched wide, making her cheeks feel tight, and she tilted her face down as a fresh wave of heat flooded her cheeks. "I don't think you *can* look any better. It's already hard for me to believe you're real..."

Her lips parted, and her breath hitched when his tail sensually brushed along her calves. She longed to feel it against her bare skin.

Alkorin leaned closer. His cheek almost touched hers as he spoke in a low, sultry voice. "Oh, Samantha, you have no idea how difficult it is to resist, do you? No idea how much you tempt me..."

Samantha drew her head back and met his eyes; all three glowed bright, their slitted pupils expanded wide. She released a shaky breath.

Then don't, Alkorin. Don't resist.

She wanted to say those words aloud so badly, but they lodged in her throat and refused to budge. All she could do was stare, torn between her undeniable attraction to him and her fear of letting go. Her fear of trusting him.

She couldn't understand why—why her? She didn't know what the standards of beauty were for alien species, but she couldn't imagine many women not finding this sedhi sexy as sin. What could he possibly see in Samantha?

Alkorin looked past her for a moment, and a strange,

mirthful glint entered his eyes. "Are you ready to leave, little terran? My driver is somewhat impatient, and I'd hate to inconvenience him."

Sam turned her head to follow his gaze, breaking contact with his hand. A sleek, black hovercar idled on the street just outside her building, its windows tinted as dark as its external paint, which made it impossible to see into the cab.

"That's *your* car?" she asked. "And you have a driver?"

"Yes, and yes," he replied, lowering his hand to the base of her spine. He gently guided her toward the vehicle. "I hope you don't mind. I simply wanted the freedom to focus on giving you as wonderful an experience as possible."

"I guess document verification must pay well. What, um... what exactly does that entail, anyway? Do you work for a big company?"

When they reached the car, Alkorin stepped forward and opened the rear door for her, standing aside. "I work primarily with Consortium identification documents. It's lucrative enough to keep me comfortable."

"Would they happen to be hiring?" she asked as she entered the car. She slid along the seat to allow room for Alkorin.

"It's...contract work, mainly. Difficult to obtain without relevant experience," he replied as he climbed in behind her and closed the door.

She glanced toward the front of the car, and her eyes widened when they met the driver's, who had twisted to look back at her. He was a very large, gruff-looking azhera with intense green eyes. Like all his kind, his features were reminiscent of a big cat's—a lion, or maybe a leopard—blended with a lupine hint and something vaguely human. They looked like... well, like werecats. But it was this azhera's coloring that caught her attention; the tan and brown of his fur was similar in hue and pattern to that of her grandmother's old cat, Mister Wiggles.

A wave of homesickness rushed over her, dragging the sorrow of loss in its wake. Mister Wiggles and her grandmother were gone. Her father was gone. She'd never see the only people she truly loved again.

The azhera shifted his gaze to Alkorin. "You know people saw you, right?"

Alkorin stretched out his legs, leaned back in a leisurely slouch, and shrugged. His tail lay between him and Sam on the seat, hanging partially over the edge so its slowly moving tip ran up and down her shin.

"And?" Alkorin asked.

The driver released a low, frustrated growl. "We've talked about this before. Very recently."

Alkorin turned his head to face Samantha. "Don't mind him. He's just a bit of a worrier."

Samantha glanced between them. "You won't...get into trouble for what you did, will you? To Rakkob, I mean."

"Your neighbor? He would have some difficult questions to answer if he tried to go to the Eternal Guard, wouldn't he? There's nothing to worry about."

The driver released a heavy breath through his nostrils. "Arc—"

"Anyway," Alkorin interrupted, directing a pointed glare at the azhera, who snapped his mouth shut, "I should properly introduce the two of you. Samantha, this is Drakkal. He's worked for me for a long time. I haven't had the heart to let him go, even though he's often rude and steps out of line."

Samantha smiled at the azhera. "Hi."

Drakkal's eyes flicked to her. "Hello."

"Now that introductions are out of the way, shall we get to it?" Alkorin asked.

Drakkal muttered something that Samantha's translator couldn't decipher, turned his face forward, and directed the hovercar into a smooth ascent.

Alkorin settled a hand on Samantha's thigh.

She jumped at the unexpected touch, but he didn't pull away; he kept his hand in place with such nonchalance that it seemed to belong there. Her heart fluttered. The longer she stared at his hand, the more she yearned for it to move upward, to slide between her legs...

"Just relax and enjoy the ride, Samantha," he said. His voice was so smooth and sensual that she couldn't help but find extra meaning layered in his words, couldn't help but hear the promise of something more in his tone.

But she couldn't relax—not with his hand on her thigh, not with his tail stroking her leg, not after the dreams she had of him, and especially not while a fire burned low in her belly. That heat built to a throbbing ache in her core she couldn't ignore.

Turning her head slightly, she glanced at Alkorin, catching her lower lip between her teeth as she studied him.

He was reclining with such leisure that it seemed the most natural position in the world for him. The sides of his robe were spread outward slightly, exposing a wide expanse of his chest. She raked her gaze over his delectable gray skin and toned muscles, shifting it up to his yellow tattoos.

A glint of metal caught her attention; his right nipple was pierced. Were she someone else—someone bolder, someone more confident—she'd have crawled onto his lap and run her tongue over that piercing and every one of his glowing marks.

Just imagining that scenario intensified the ache between her legs. The sensation spread up to her breasts, and her nipples hardened. Breath quickening, she tore her eyes away from him.

Oh my God. I'm getting turned on right next to him, and all he did was set his hand on my leg!

As desperate as Samantha was for release from the ache, she didn't dare squeeze her thighs together; it would've been a dead giveaway of what she was feeling.

"Tell me about the city," Samantha blurted.

Alkorin chuckled, calling her attention back to him. He smiled down at her, his gaze burning with want, and she had the sense he knew what was really on her mind.

"Arthos is very big and very old," he said. "It's not without its blemishes, as you already know, but neither is it lacking in beauty. Still, I find myself as unable to put that beauty into words as I am to encapsulate yours in any language I know."

Drakkal snorted.

Samantha's cheeks flamed in embarrassment. She tried to ease away from Alkorin, but his hand tightened around her thigh—not enough to hurt, but enough to halt her retreat.

"It is something to behold, not to describe." He leaned toward her, his face stopping extremely close to hers. "Embrace yourself, Samantha. Embrace this world. There is happiness to be claimed here, with a little boldness."

Samantha turned her face toward him, but she didn't meet his eyes. Instead, her gaze fell upon his lips. His bottom lip was fuller than the top, and the glowing mark at its center only made it more tantalizing.

"I'm not...bold."

His lips stretched into a grin, revealing his fangs. They should have given her pause, should have frightened her, but they only aroused her further.

"You are." His hand slid a centimeter closer to her pelvis. "You just haven't realized it yet."

Her heart leapt, and she dropped her hand over his. A thrill pulsed through her, igniting a flood of liquid heat between her legs. Panic and desire warred in her mind, each threatening to conquer her, to reduce her to an unthinking creature driven only by instinct.

This...this wasn't normal. Couldn't be. She'd never felt anything close to this, her body had never reacted like this.

Samantha's arm trembled; she didn't know if she wanted to prevent his hand from moving higher or *force* it to. Her craving for his touch equaled her fear of it at that moment; she was afraid of what he made her feel.

What is he doing to me?

"Hmm..." Alkorin's grin softened into a smile. He brought his free hand to her face and brushed her hair back, tucking it gently behind her ear. His fingers lingered there, lightly stroking the rounded shell, his touch delicate despite the size and strength of his hand. After a few moments, he lowered that hand to grasp her chin and tipped her head back, making her lift her gaze to his.

"You will blossom soon enough, little flower," he said softly, "and then you will realize your own beauty. I look forward to witnessing it."

He stroked her lower lip with the pad of his thumb before he pulled away, returning to his prior position. His other hand remained upon her thigh.

Samantha stared at him as he looked out the window; she ran her gaze over his profile, from the piercings in his long, pointed ear up to his dark horns. She squeezed his hand a little more firmly. She wasn't sure how long she sat there ogling him, but it felt like it had been both much longer and not nearly long enough when the world outside finally caught her attention.

She leaned forward to look past Alkorin as the hovercar emerged from the tunnel it had been traveling through. The windows—which had been crystal clear from within despite the dark tint on the outside—dimmed slightly to soften the bright light from the sky.

She'd seen Arthos from above after completing the registration process, had stared out the window of the shuttle that had brought her to her new apartment complex with her jaw slack and her eyes wide, and the sight was no less astounding this time. The city was comprised of countless buildings of staggering height and variety. Metal and glass gleamed everywhere, an endless stream of vehicles filled the air, and people of every size and shape bustled beneath a colorful sky dominated by an immense quasar.

The Undercity was all deep shadows contrasted by flamboyant neon lights and pulsing holos; the city above was polished chrome and gold complemented by pure, natural light and the vibrant greens, purples, and reds of living plants—at least the parts of each area she'd seen for herself. Like Alkorin had said, it was impossible to put Arthos into words.

They called it the Infinite City, and Samantha understood why; it seemed to go on forever, stretching to the distant horizon and beyond, ever changing and yet all one.

Samantha was so absorbed by the sights that she didn't realize how close she'd come to Alkorin until he dipped his head, pressed his nose to her hair, and inhaled.

He groaned softly and lifted his hand from her thigh, moving it to her lower back. "It's becoming increasingly difficult for me to believe you're doing this by accident, Samantha."

Sam stilled. Had he really just *sniffed* her? "D-Doing what?"

"*Teasing* me."

Her eyes widened. "I'm not! I swear! I was just—"

Grasping Samantha by the hips, Alkorin turned her toward him and drew her onto his lap so she straddled his muscular thighs. She put her arms out, flattening her palms against the back of the seat to either side of his head to prevent herself from falling against his chest. Her hair tumbled down, brushing over the exposed skin of his chest, and Alkorin grinned up at her, his half-lidded eyes gleaming with desire.

"Whoops," he said. "I can be so clumsy sometimes."

"That was on purpose," Sam shot back.

His smile tilted to one side. "The burden of proof rests upon you, whereas *you* rest upon me."

Her face heated. Despite her position on top, he was entirely in control, and she felt more vulnerable than ever.

Without looking away from her, Alkorin said, "Drop us off at one of the entrances to the Ventrillian Mall, Drakkal."

"Don't you think that's a bit crowded, *boss*?" Drakkal asked.

"We'll be fine. I'll take every precaution to avoid standing out."

Samantha couldn't imagine Alkorin not standing out.

Alkorin slid his hands down to her thighs, and Sam's breath hitched as he tugged her closer. "My little terran has seen some of the worst this city has to offer, and she deserves to see some of the best."

Samantha heard a soft creaking sound from up front, as though Drakkal were tightening his grip on the controls, before the hovercar angled into a gradual descent.

She leaned forward slightly and whispered, "I don't think he likes your idea."

"He's just upset because I woke him up earlier than usual today," Alkorin squeezed Sam's thighs gently. "I'm far more worried about whether I'll be able to bring myself to exit the car once we've landed."

Samantha frowned. "Why? What's wrong?"

"I'm not sure I'll have the willpower to let you go." He lifted his pelvis slightly, rubbing it against her center.

Her breath hitched. She curled her fingers into the back cushion as realization struck her. Lowering her gaze, she took in her current position, and desire flared within her.

Never in Sam's life had things escalated so quickly between her and a man—she couldn't even imagine things moving this fast. She'd only met Alkorin the night before last! Why wasn't she panicking, why wasn't she freaking out and darting for the opposite door to escape?

Because for some inexplicable reason, despite how strong he's coming on...

I feel safe with Alkorin.

As much as she should've wanted him to release her, she... didn't.

Their bodies swayed gently as the hovercar slowed to a stop.

"Here," Drakkal growled.

Alkorin made no move; he just stared at Sam, his eyes and the markings on his skin brighter than ever. "I suppose we should step outside. Drakkal would only put a damper on the mood if we stayed in here."

I'm straddling him while his driver is right there.

Samantha's skin was so heated that she might've mistaken it for a sunburn had she not known better. She opened the door.

The pure light of the quasar—the sort of natural light Sam hadn't seen for days—flowed into the cab through the open door, making Alkorin's long, straight hair shimmer.

Alk's tongue emerged briefly from between his lips. "After you, then?"

Sam hesitated for an instant before she hurriedly, but carefully, climbed off his lap and stepped out of the hovercar.

"I'll let you know when we're ready for you to pick us up," Alkorin said to Drakkal as he exited the vehicle.

"Be careful, *boss*," the azhera replied.

"Don't worry, Drak. I'll be fine."

Drakkal uttered another guttural, untranslatable oath before Alkorin closed the door.

Standing up straight, Alkorin turned to face Samantha with a wide grin. "Well then, here we are. I don't know that anyone can see the entire city in one lifetime, but this seems a good place to start."

SEVEN

Sam quickly lost track of time as Alkorin escorted her through the Ventrillian Mall, a huge pedestrian area filled with all manner of shops, eateries, gardens, sculptures, and performers. The sights were alien, wondrous, and beautiful, and the open air and ample lighting gave the area a sense of oddly comforting immensity. They sampled strange foods from several places, most of which were delicious, and stopped to watch a troupe of alien acrobats perform an amazing show using palm-sized hoverpads to levitate high over the audience.

Soon after the acrobatic performance, they came across a group of aliens playing music atop a raised platform. Midway through the song, Alkorin took Samantha's hand and pulled her close, leading her into a dance that was both sensual and exciting. She fast overcame her initial self-consciousness, forgetting everything and everyone around them as her attention focused solely on the male who had his arms around her. She let go and simply *felt*.

The dance was thrilling; she had no doubt it was primarily because Alkorin was her partner.

The area had to be at least as crowded as the main streets down in the Undercity, but it didn't feel that way—especially with Alkorin beside her the entire time. She was surprised that, after the way he'd made her straddle him in the car, he didn't so much as take her hand outside their dance.

But, before long, *she* took *his* hand. He twined his fingers with hers as though it were the most natural thing in the world.

Throughout their time in the mall, many aliens cast curious glances at her; she wasn't sure she'd ever get used to it, but she understood. Humans were extremely few in Arthos. She was new to these people, offering them a rare glimpse of an unknown species.

At least once, one of the other pedestrians even took a picture of her. That's what Sam guessed, anyway, when a groalthuun—a thick-necked alien with a scaly, goat-like head—lifted his wrist and a brief holographic flash emanated from his holocom, which he'd directed toward her. She moved a little closer to Alkorin and continued walking, brushing aside her suspicions.

She didn't want anything to ruin their time here.

Throughout their sightseeing, they talked. Samantha's shyness faded with every moment in his company; his unique blend of arrogance, humor, boldness, and flattery put her at ease. Though he teased her every now and then, he was gentle, and he never made fun of her—though he poked fun at himself more than once.

They stopped at one of the mall's many fountains. It was a tiered, horseshoe-shaped pool, each tier hovering in the air about a meter over the one below. Water poured down from each level in shimmering streams. She wasn't sure what method they used to conceal how the fountain operated, but there were no visible connections between any of the tiers. Despite the seeming lack of any means to replenish the contents of the floating portions, each remained at a steady water level.

Alkorin turned away from the fountain and leaned back with his elbows on the railing separating onlookers from the monument. His tail swayed lazily behind him. He seemed completely oblivious to everything around them—all the awe-inspiring plants and displays, all the interesting people, all the tempting storefronts. All his focus was upon her.

"Well, Samantha, what do you think? Does Arthos have at least a few redeeming qualities?" he asked.

She offered him a soft smile before turning to face the fountain. Alkorin by himself was enough to redeem Arthos in her eyes.

"It does," she said. "Thank you for showing me all this, Alkorin."

The Undercity had its own sort of beauty, an *odd* beauty, but the city above the surface was in an entirely different league. Feeling the warm light of the quasar on her skin, seeing the sky, and breathing in the surprisingly fresh air reminded Sam of the best parts of Earth.

"My pleasure. I don't often have a chance to leave my workshop, so this is a welcome opportunity. And the view is a pleasant one."

Sam knew, even without looking at him, that his attention hadn't left her. It filled her with a giddy pleasure. "Have you always lived here?"

The tip of his tail settled over her foot, curling slightly around her ankle. "No. I've called a few worlds home before this one."

"What made you come here?"

"Necessity." He shifted closer and leaned back farther, entering her field of view again. "I'd...headed a business venture on another planet before I came here. I was overly ambitious, and my competition came together to destroy my livelihood."

She turned her face toward him. "The fighting?"

"Yes. I'd tried my hand in a more...let's say, managerial role. I didn't have anything left by the time they were done with me, so I came here." He raised one of his hands, palm up and fingers splayed, gesturing to the city around them. "Arthos is supposed to be a city of opportunity. At least that's how they sell it. What about you, little terran? Why did you leave your homeworld?"

"Necessity," she said.

"Were the males of your planet simply not attractive enough?"

"Compared to you?" she asked, grinning. It felt nice to be playful with him.

"I meant in general," he replied with a smirk. "Obviously, *all* males are lacking compared to me."

She couldn't stop her gaze from dipping to his chest. He hadn't bothered closing his robe since they'd left the hovercar, and it gaped open, leaving his chest—with its luminous tattoos and nipple piercing—on display.

As though of its own accord, her arm extended, and her fingers brushed over one of his yellow markings. The tattoo pulsed with light. "What do these mean? And why do they glow?"

Though the movement was subtle, she felt his muscles tense beneath her fingers, and he dipped his chin to glance down at her hand. "They are my *qal*. All my people are born with them. A result of our volturian ancestry. I'm afraid I can't tell you why they glow, however. They just...do."

Volturians had been one of the first alien species to befriend humans after making first contact about thirty years ago, and many had settled on Earth in the years since. Now that he'd mentioned it aloud, she recognized the similarities between Alkorin and the volturians she'd met back home.

He sported many of the same elfin characteristics—the pointed ears, the sharpened, refined features, the straight hair and natural markings—but it was his almost-monstrous traits that made him into something unique and utterly alluring. The horns, the tail, the black sclerae, the third eye. Those wicked, arousing fangs.

"You're related to the volturians?" she asked, if only to get her mind off how beautiful he was.

"Sedhi are what many refer to as a hybrid species. We're descended from volturians and tretins."

"Tretins?"

"Yes. Large, mean things with a proclivity for conquering and enslaving entire species. You could probably consider your-self fortunate if you go your entire life without ever meeting one."

Sam's eyes widened.

Alkorin chuckled and trailed the backs of his fingers down her cheek. "Nothing you need to worry about, little terran. I won't allow any such thing to happen to you. Now then, we must address the real issue here—once again, you've avoided answering my question to any reasonable degree." He placed a finger beneath her chin. "What necessitated your coming to Arthos?"

The lightness of the day suddenly dissipated, allowing dark, heavy shadows to sweep in. She wanted to look away from him, but she couldn't. How much could she tell him?

How much did she trust him?

She already knew she couldn't trust the part of her heart that wanted to tell him everything, that wanted her to throw caution to the wind and leap into his embrace. It had betrayed her before.

Would it betray her again?

ARCANTHUS SAW HER MOOD SHIFT—IT was an obvious change, and if she was capable of masking it, she made no effort. The light that had shone in her eyes snuffed out suddenly, and she seemed to sag as though under a great weight. The sight made his heart ache.

"I...needed a fresh start," she finally said in a small voice.

He didn't need to know much about terrans to tell that she didn't want to discuss it further, that she wasn't ready to talk about it. Everything he'd worked toward so far was threatened in that moment—and worse, he couldn't bear the thought of having been the catalyst of her sadness.

"So, it seems we have similar stories," he said, keeping his tone as light. "You said you were looking for work in the city. May I ask you a hypothetical question?"

Samantha nodded.

"If you could choose any sort of work to earn your living, what would it be? What is your ideal career?"

She was silent before she said, "Art."

A small smile tugged at the corners of his mouth, but he didn't give in to it yet. "Art. One might say you've made an art of being vague, little terran."

That light sparked in her eyes again, delicate and tiny but undeniable, as she laughed.

"Tell me more," he coaxed, brushing his finger across her jaw. His tail wound farther around her leg.

"I'm...not sure what to say. I had an old tablet as a kid that I carried with me into my adult years. My family... We didn't have a lot. The tablet was a gift from my dad, who worked extra hours for months to save up for it, and I *loved* it. I'd draw on it for hours and hours. It was the only thing I really enjoyed, the only thing... The only thing that I felt good at."

She raised her hands and glanced down at them as she fiddled with the cuffs of her sleeves. "But when you're poor, you're not offered a lot of choices. I got my first after-school job in a restaurant when I was fifteen so I could help my father, and when I wasn't working, I was helping care for my grandmother, who had taken a bad turn. I eventually had to quit my job to take care of her, but...she didn't make it. After that, my old boss let me work at the restaurant again. I didn't have the time, the energy, or the funds to pursue anything else. Once I graduated, I went to work fulltime, and picked up all the overtime I could. And then my father..."

Tears welled in her eyes, and Arcanthus's chest tightened. He cupped her face in his hands and guided her gaze back to his. "Tell me about your art, Samantha. Tell me what you would like to create, about the beauty you want to bring into the universe."

"Color," she said, her voice weak and broken. "I love to paint and...and just focus on the way the colors work with one another, the way they complement and contrast each other. The way they subtly change each other and create...*life*."

Something warmed within Arcanthus, and the sensation spread outward from his chest. It was far more than the constant state of desire and arousal she instilled in him, far more than sympathy or understanding. He wanted to take her in his arms, wanted to kiss her, wanted to caress her, wanted to pledge his eternal loyalty and devotion to her. Samantha was a priceless, one-of-a-kind treasure.

And she was his.

My mate.

"That sounds delightful." He brushed his thumbs across

her cheekbones. "I hope you have the opportunity to chase that dream soon."

He could set her firmly on that path now—could provide everything she'd ever need, could set her up so she could paint to her heart's content—but he sensed that wasn't what she wanted. More importantly, it wasn't what she needed.

She smiled sadly. "I think it'll only ever be that. A dream."

He vowed to himself then that he *would* give it to her. Whether she needed it or not, he would find a way to help her achieve that dream.

Samantha glanced over Arc's shoulder and frowned.

"What's wrong?" he asked, turning his head to follow her gaze. A groalthuun stood not far off, his arm raised with his holocom activated. Its screen flashed as though the groalthuun had taken a picture.

Normally, that wouldn't have concerned Arcanthus, but the holocom was directed at Samantha.

"I swear he's the same groalthuun I saw earlier. I think he took a picture of me then, too," Samantha said.

The groalthuun was well-dressed, his tailored clothing perfectly suited to a sector like this and bore no visible signs of criminal affiliation.

That provided Arcanthus with no comfort.

Arc shifted his body to shield Samantha from the groalthuun, lifting his arm to activate his own holocom. It was only then that he noticed the messages from Kiloq. They all amounted to the same thing—the cren, who Arcanthus had seen a handful of times at the mall today, had noticed a groalthuun taking an interest in Samantha.

Every time I silence my communications, something *happens.*

Arcanthus brought up his contacts, and within a moment

had sent their location to Drakkal with a simple message—*Time to go.*

"The day grows late, little terran." Arc slipped an arm around her waist, drew her close to his side, and guided her toward the nearest exit. "I think it's best we get you home."

Samantha offered no argument, and, to his relief, made no attempt to look back at the groalthuun.

There was no way to be certain whether the groalthuun was a slaver or a trafficker, no way to know without delving into the vastness of the plexus and hacking into the private, secured systems often employed by the city's criminal population, but the chances of it were uncomfortably high. Terrans were too new to Arthos to avoid being targeted by such scum. Usually, slavers avoided kidnapping anyone already registered in the Consortium system, but there were always individuals who could be tempted beyond good sense by money.

And terrans were worth a lot of money.

Drakkal met them with the car just outside the mall, and Arcanthus ushered Samantha into the vehicle. He paused before he climbed in and checked for pursuit, but he saw no sign of the groalthuun.

Just a curious person taking a picture of a new species.

But that reasoning didn't ring true, and the sinking dread in his gut remained intact.

Nothing would happen to his mate. Arcanthus would be sure of that.

Once he was inside the cab with the door closed, he exchanged a glance with Drakkal. The azhera's expression turned grim, but he made no comment as he piloted the hovercar into the air and started back toward Samantha's apartment.

"Take the scenic route," Arcanthus said.

Drakkal nodded; he didn't have to ask why or what Arc meant.

Arcanthus shifted close to Samantha. To his surprise, she didn't shy away when he settled his arm around her shoulders and pulled her against him. He wrapped his tail around her leg and absently stroked her upper arm with his hand. Though she said nothing about the potential danger she'd faced in the mall, the tension in her body conveyed a touch of unease.

They traveled in silence. Despite everything, Arcanthus found himself content merely to hold her. He only wished it was under different circumstances.

While it had taken no more than fifteen minutes to travel to the Ventrillian Mall, Drakkal's circuitous route extended the return journey to more than an hour. Throughout the drive, Drakkal monitored the camera feeds displaying the traffic around and behind their vehicle; he knew well enough how to spot a tail, so Arc didn't question him about whether they'd been followed when they finally landed around the block from Samantha's apartment.

As the hovercar's engines eased to an idling state, Arcanthus tipped his head to rest his chin upon Samantha's hair, inhaling her scent once again. It was soft, sweet, and floral, imbued by something uniquely her. A rush of desire swept through him, and he was damned thankful he'd secured the under wrapping of his loincloth before picking her up that morning, as it was the only thing that had prevented him from walking around with an extruded cock all day and was the only thing keeping him from extruding now.

He craved this female with every cell in his body.

Arc groaned. Standing up meant breaking this contact, and he found himself once again reluctant to release her.

Samantha turned her head, which forced him to lift his.

Their eyes briefly met before she looked toward her apartment building. Arcanthus glanced down to see her fiddling with her sleeves again.

"I know you've already spent so much of your time with me today," she said, "but would you...would you..."

Arcanthus couldn't hold back a smile. "I could invite myself in, if it's easier for you."

She smiled shyly and briefly returned her eyes to him. "It would be."

With any other female he'd been interested in, he would've interpreted this as an invitation for sex—though he'd never have gone to anyone else's home for it. His own place was far more secure, far safer. That he could simply have them escorted out afterward was a bonus. He would never have spent the day with any other female, would never have taken any of them to the Ventrillian Mall to take in the sights and enjoy hours of conversation.

He'd never even allowed a female into his bedchamber. He'd always kept his flings to the workshop, where he was guarded by four high-powered autocannons.

Arcanthus couldn't be sure of Samantha's intentions. She often looked at him with yearning, but she also made clear efforts to distance herself from him. When she'd said she wasn't a bold person, Arc disagreed; he believed she simply hadn't reached the point of acting on her desires. All she needed was some gentle guidance to claim what she wanted.

Whatever was about to happen, he couldn't give up this opportunity. He'd greedily take advantage of every moment he could spend with her.

"Samantha, may I have the pleasure of entering your apartment?"

"Yes." Her eyes widened, and she hurried to add, "But just for a little while! I just want... Well..."

He brushed his fingers down the back of her arm and coiled his tail toward her knee. "Whatever it is you want, Samantha, I'm sure I'll find a way to accommodate you."

She shivered, and her cheeks turned that adorable shade of pink.

He reached out with one arm and opened the door, allowing the ambient sounds of the Undercity—distant shouting, the echo of far-off machinery, and, somewhere high overhead, the airy whirs of speeding hovercars—to break the silence that had fallen over the cab.

"I'll be out whenever I'm out, Drakkal," Arcanthus said.

"I'm not doing this for you again," the azhera replied.

"Such a cheerful fellow, isn't he?" With great reluctance, Arcanthus released his hold on Samantha and climbed out of the car, offering her a hand once he was upright.

She slid toward the open door, placed her hand in Arc's, and looked at the azhera. "Thank you, Drakkal. From both of us, since he didn't say it."

Drakkal twisted in his seat to look at Samantha as Arcanthus helped her out of the car. "You seem like a good person, terran, so I will tell you this: he is a—"

Arcanthus slammed the door before Drakkal finished his statement. "Poor fellow. I must have him out well after his bedtime. Perhaps he'll have a nap while we're inside."

Samantha raised a hand—clutching the end of her sleeve in her fingers—to hide her grin. "I'm sure all he was going to say was that you are astounding."

Arc grinned at her. On the surface, her comment seemed a small thing, but it was another sign of Samantha opening up to him. A sign of her beginning to feel comfortable while he was near.

"I'm just happy that I've finally discovered someone who understands me." Keeping hold of her hand, Arcanthus gestured toward the building. "Shall we proceed toward whatever it is we're heading to?"

He caught a hint of something in her eyes before she walked away, something promising. Before they reached the front entrance, Arcanthus scanned their surroundings. He wouldn't doubt if the Blue Threshers were prowling the neighborhood, hungry for revenge, and he was in no mood to deal with them tonight.

Instead, he spotted a familiar face—the green-eyed cren, Koroq—leaning against the exterior wall of the complex across the street. Koroq's leisurely but solid posture suggested he was exactly where he belonged. His gaze met Arc's for an instant; the cren offered the sedhi no acknowledgement.

Arcanthus kept close to Samantha as they entered the building. The interior was run-down and bland but surprisingly clean, with doors on either side of the hall every few meters. Each of these buildings contained hundreds of apartments, many of which were tailored to the physical traits of specific alien species.

It wasn't glamorous, wasn't pretty, but it was nicer than some of the places Arcanthus had lived in his lifetime.

Still, being cooped up with so many people—even if they were behind closed doors—in an unfamiliar, relatively tight space made Arc uncomfortable.

I spent hours walking around the Ventrillian Mall today. I'm not going to have any ground to stand on when Drakkal chews me out later, am I?

This was foolish, made even more so by the fact that Arc recognized his own foolishness and would not allow that recognition to stop him. He was going to follow Samantha into her apartment and see what happened from there.

I should just bring her back to my place. It would be more comfortable. And safer for both of us.

But he knew she wasn't at that point yet. She needed a little more time.

They traveled up the elevator and stepped off when they reached her floor. As soon as they exited the elevator bank and entered the hallway proper, Samantha halted. Arc glanced up to see the cause for her sudden stop.

Of course.

The borian from earlier—Rakkob—stood around the midpoint of the corridor, leaning against the wall as he spoke to someone on his holocom. Rakkob turned his head and caught sight of Arcanthus. His eyes rounded, and he shoved away from the wall, scurrying into his apartment.

Samantha released a slow, relieved breath.

"Is this why you wanted me to come up to your apartment?" Arcanthus asked.

She looked contrite, chewing on her bottom lip. "Yes. Though...I would like it if you came in."

Even if she'd had an ulterior motive, Arcanthus viewed this as a victory—she *wanted* him to come inside. And he didn't mind her looking to him for protection. He felt a certain pride in it, a deep-seated satisfaction that could only be explained by his instinctual recognition of her as his mate. Samantha was a timid female, but she was learning to trust him.

How will that trust hold when she finds out you've been dishonest with her, Alkorin?

He batted aside the pang of guilt caused by that thought. Now wasn't the time to consider such matters; he wanted to experience this with his full attention.

"Good," he said. "I've already invited myself, regardless, so it doesn't matter if you want me to come in or not."

Samantha laughed and hurried down the hallway to her door and lifted her arm to the chip scanner. The door slid open, and she stepped through.

Arcanthus followed her into the apartment and swept his gaze over the small space. The room was about seven meters long and five across, containing everything she'd need—a bed in one corner, a kitchen in the opposite corner, and a living space in between with a small couch, a table and two chairs, and a desk against one wall. There were two doors on the right wall—he assumed one led to a bathroom and the other to a storage space.

The furnishings were simple, and, like the building's hall-ways, the room was devoid of décor. Apart from the coat draped over one of the chairs, a small pile of clothes on the floor, and the utensils in the sink, there was no evidence of anyone living here.

Samantha closed the door and hurried ahead of him. "Um, make yourself at home," she said as she bent to retrieve a shirt from the floor. When she rose, she pushed a nearby scrap of white fabric under the couch with the toe of her shoe. "I... wasn't expecting you to come, and I haven't had a chance to bring my laundry down, but..."

She shrugged and swept her hands to the side, smiling nervously. "Ta-da?"

Arcanthus's eyes lingered on the spot beneath the sofa where she'd hidden the white fabric; he'd only had a brief glimpse of it, but he had an idea of what it was. His blood heated further.

Oh, my delicate flower...what am I going to do with you?

What am I going to do to you?

"No judgment from me, Samantha," he said. "This ranks rather high compared to some of the places I've lived." He walked to the couch, stopped directly in front of her, and sat down with his tail angled to the side and draped over the armrest.

"I don't have much to offer, but would you like some *tea?*" she asked.

"Yes, if only to find out what it is."

"Oh! It's something I brought with me from Earth. My grandmother used to drink it and shared it with me when I was a kid, so I guess I just kind of grew up on it. It's made with dried herbs steeped in hot water."

"It sounds interesting, at the very least. I would love to try some."

She turned, stepped into the kitchen area, and reached up to open a cabinet and retrieve something from within. Her movement lifted the hem of her shirt, revealing the luscious curve of her ass through her pants—the ass he'd been gifted the briefest glimpse of during their call the night before. He stared hungrily at what he could not yet have As wonderful as this day had been, it seemed he was intent on torturing himself throughout it.

Well, what's a little more torture going to hurt?

While her back was turned, he shifted his tail, guiding it under the couch. It slithered beneath a piece of cloth, and he curled its tip to hook the fabric. He kept his central eye on Samantha and dipped the other two to his lap as he withdrew his prize, depositing it in his waiting hands.

A white pair of panties.

Her panties.

Arcanthus grinned, and for a moment, had to restrain himself; he had the overwhelming urge to raise the panties to his face and inhale her scent—her *intimate* scent—but that was too risky. He forced his lower eyes back to her as he folded the cloth, slipped it into his robe, and tucked it beneath the leather strap securing his loincloth in place.

She turned her face to look at him.

He stretched one arm along the back of the couch and lifted a leg, settling his ankle atop his knee. "Everything going all right over there, little terran?"

"Yes." She picked up two cups and approached Arc, offering him one along with a smile. "It's a little hot."

"I've never been bothered by a little heat," he replied as he accepted the drink.

She averted her gaze, took her cup in both hands, and brought it up to her face, holding it just beneath her nose. Her nostrils flared with a soft inhalation.

Arcanthus settled his cup atop his palm. "Are you going to sit? It's no problem if you're not. I really don't mind looking up at you."

It was almost comical how quickly she moved, perching herself on the edge of the cushion at the opposite end of the couch.

Eventually, she'd learn to relax in his presence. Part of him was disappointed in that knowledge. He found her reactions to him endearing. The world in which he'd lived before had necessitated bravado for survival; everyone had exuded confidence whether they felt it or not. And the females he'd joined with here in Arthos... Well, they'd been of a rather different sort than his little terran.

But a stronger part of him longed for her to be that comfortable with him because it would mean she trusted him completely. He found he craved her trust as much as he craved her attention, as much as he craved her body—if not more so.

He lifted the cup to his lips and took a sip. Though the liquid was hot, its heat was not unpleasant. Still, his brow furrowed at the taste, and the corners of his mouth tugged back as he fought a reflexive shudder. The drink had a hint of sweetness, but it was not enough to mask its bitter, herbal punch.

He forced himself to swallow. The sound of it was loud

enough to catch Samantha's attention. She studied him silently, searching his face before looking at his tail, the tip of which was flicking restlessly on the floor. He struggled to keep a neutral expression; that was the best he could've managed at that moment.

"You don't like it, do you?" she asked.

What's one more lie?

He studied her face, unable to deny the vulnerability in her eyes. Another lie, even a small one, was another crack in the trust he'd so desperately come to desire. He'd spent years of his life obsessed with trust, expecting betrayal at every turn—all while building a fortress of lies around himself.

Arcanthus smiled and glanced down at the brownish liquid in the cup. "I'm afraid it's not quite to my tastes. The tretin side of my people leaves us a bit fonder of...savory and salty flavors."

"Oh. I-I should have asked you what you'd like. I'm—" She set her cup down on the nearby table and leapt to her feet, moving toward the kitchen. "I'll get you something else."

Placing his cup beside Sam's, Arc stood up and followed her. As she was reaching into one of the cabinets, he caught her arm and spun her to face him.

"There is one thing I'd like to taste, little terran." He settled a hand on the side of her face, sliding his fingers into her long, brown hair, and leaned down to kiss her.

Samantha's eyes widened in surprise, and she pressed her hands against his chest as though to stop him—her palms were warm and soft, and he longed to feel them elsewhere on his body—but she offered little resistance as he claimed her mouth with his.

Tingles spread over across his face, burrowing deep to set his nerves aflame. He tasted a hint of the tea on her soft lips, but it was made sweeter by the flavor beneath it—by *her* flavor.

She curled her fingers, raking her nails over his skin. Her

eyelids fluttered shut in surrender as she parted her lips in a breathy moan.

Arcanthus closed his eyes, shifted his hand to cradle the back of her head, and deepened the kiss. Slipping his tongue into the warm depths of her mouth, he growled at her divine taste.

He needed *more*.

Arcanthus pressed Sam against the counter, trapping her, and wrapped his arm around her to place his hand on the small of her back. He clutched her closer. His cock strained against his loincloth's under wrapping with enough pressure that it threatened to tear through.

He'd never felt a need so powerful, had never felt the beast lurking at his core so active and aroused. He'd never had to battle the instinct to take, to conquer, like he was now.

He dropped his hand to cup her ass and grind her pelvis against his.

Samantha flinched and jerked her head back, breaking the kiss. She shoved against his chest. "No! No, stop!"

Awash in a lustful haze, Arcanthus opened his eyes; the haze dissipated the instant he met her gaze.

Samantha's eyes were rounded and glimmering, filled with desire and *fear*.

This sudden turn, combined with her vague answers to his questions and her overall timidity, sparked a realization in Arcanthus.

She was deeply hurt by someone she trusted.

His jaw clenched and his brows fell as anger rushed through him. He thrust the emotion aside as quickly as it had come; he couldn't risk Samantha mistakenly thinking he was angry at *her*.

Arcanthus eased his hold on his mate and leaned back, removing his hand from her backside as he gently ran the backs of his fingers over her cheek. "It's all right, Samantha. I mean you no harm."

Her eyes welled with tears. "I'm sorry. I just c-can't—"

"No, no. Shh. You don't need to be sorry." He wiped away the first of her tears. "This has been one of the most pleasant days I've ever had. I simply wanted to thank you in the best way I knew how."

She released a shuddering breath. Arc's gaze moved over her face; her lips were red from his assault on them, and her cheeks were stained pink. Despite the situation, he was tempted to kiss her again.

He moved his face closer to hers. "I *want* you, Samantha. I'll not hide that. And even if you don't see it, I know a simple truth about you—you're worth waiting for. Take all the time you need to understand that you want me, too." He stroked her bottom lip with his thumb. "I won't be going anywhere."

Samantha searched his eyes, and her fingers twitched against his chest. Indecision strained her features as she dropped her gaze.

"I don't want you to go anywhere," she said softly. "It's just... I can't. Not...not yet."

"I know, little terran, I know. Just remember that *this*"—he took hold of her wrist and smoothed her palm over his chest—"is yours, whenever you are ready."

Her cheeks reddened further, but she moved infinitesimally closer, tracing part of his *qal* with her fingertip before nodding.

Arcanthus smiled, and he couldn't keep his tongue from slipping out to lick her lingering taste from his lips. He knew what he had to do, but it was hard; he'd never imagined it could be so difficult to walk away.

He released his hold on her and stepped back. "Thank you for the tea, Samantha."

She leaned forward as though she meant to follow him, stopping herself by grasping the edge of the counter. "But you didn't like it."

"I very much enjoyed it from your lips."

She brought her fingers to her mouth.

"Dream of me, my flower. I'll dream of you again tonight."

Arcanthus left the apartment, ignoring the painful ache in his groin, ignoring the instincts demanding he go back to her, demanding he give her the pleasure she deserved. Demanding he erase the bad memories weighing so heavily upon her.

When her door closed behind him, he paused to glare at her neighbor's apartment. The borian was scared for now. How long before Rakkob's fear turned to anger and resentment and pushed him to make another move on Samantha?

Growling, Arcanthus forced himself to walk along the hall. As he rode the elevator down, he activated his holocom and sent a message to Kiloq and Koroq.

Borian living across the hall from the terran is a problem. Rakkob. Needs to be removed by the authorities.

Just as the elevator reached the ground floor, their reply arrived.

On it, boss.

Someone had harmed Arcanthus's mate. Someone had done lasting damage to her. He doubted it had been Rakkob, but the borian had only added to her emotional burden. Whether he had learned his lesson or not, Rakkob had not paid enough of a price, he'd not suffered enough for his mistreatment of Samantha.

As Arcanthus moved down the corridor leading to the exit, Koroq walked past, heading toward the elevators. He and Arc exchanged a nod; nothing more was necessary.

Arc's anger simmered while he walked to the car, and a fine layer of frustration gradually settled atop it. The best he could hope for was that Samantha would grow comfortable enough to tell him what had happened to her. Learning who had scarred her heart wouldn't necessarily enable Arcanthus to avenge her pain, but it would be a start toward helping her heal.

It only annoyed him more that, despite the complicated logistics, part of him was seriously considering a trip halfway across the universe—to Earth—to find the one who'd wronged her...

"I don't know anything about her situation," he muttered.

He'd only become more irritated if he followed that path of thought any further.

Arcanthus would do anything to ease her suffering and take away her pain. She was his *mate*. He didn't enjoy his sense of helplessness, but he couldn't do anything about it currently. She'd tell him when she was ready to, or she wouldn't tell him at all; either way, the choice was hers. She wouldn't share anything until he'd built trust with her.

Besides, it wasn't like he'd rushed to tell her all about his past, or how he'd lost his limbs, or even the truth about his name and profession.

He tugged open the front passenger door of the hovercar and climbed in beside Drakkal, slamming the door shut once his legs were inside.

Arcanthus sighed. "I already know what you're going to say. I'm—"

"I'm never going to sit in the car while you try to get a female to fuck you again," Drakkal said. "And if you disrespect me in front of her one more time, I'm going to break off one of your arms and shove it up your ass to show you what it's *really* like to be fucked."

Arcanthus stared at Drakkal with wide eyes and parted lips. "I suppose I *didn't* know what you were going to say, after all."

Drakkal's brows fell, and he grimaced as he turned his attention forward. "You're the predictable one here, Arc."

Chuckling, Arcanthus leaned back in his seat, settling a foot on the console. "You may well be correct there. Know that everything I said was out of the deepest respect and admiration for you."

"Funny way to show it. But you *have* taken many blows to the head over the years. Must be catching up to you." Drakkal guided the hovercar up, merging into the flow of traffic along the Undercity's ceiling. "You've never gone to a female's house before. That why you finished so quickly?"

"Do you truly think so poorly of me?" Arcanthus asked with a scoff. "We didn't do anything inappropriate."

No, nothing at all inappropriate. That kiss had been *right*, had made more sense than anything in Arcanthus's life.

"You're not nearly as funny as you think."

"Not a joke, Drakkal. Samantha is a...delicate creature, at least outwardly. I want her to be comfortable at every step along the way."

"Who are you, and what did you do with Arcanthus?" Drakkal glanced at Arc from the corner of his eye.

"This is different. It's...serious."

"Oh, *now* you want to be serious? You haven't taken any of my warnings seriously, but I'm supposed to suddenly give you the benefit of the doubt?"

"So, I've taken a few risks," Arc replied with a flick of his wrist. "I'm fine. I'm more concerned about her. Terrans are still considered exotic, and she's been accosted several times in the few days she's been in the city. There was a groalthuun taking pictures of her today."

Drakkal grunted and tightened his grip on the controls, his claws extending slightly. "Trafficker, probably."

"Hence my concern."

"You're the one who exposed her to it. Exposed yourself, too."

"Oh, I've not yet begun to expose myself, Drakkal. You'll know when I do so—even you won't be able to look away."

"*Kraasz ka'val*, Arcanthus. You're lucky I like you."

"Yes, I am."

EIGHT

Vaund didn't look up when a knock sounded at the door. He maintained his slouched posture in his kraug-hide chair, his long, claw-like fingers curled over the ends of the armrests. Reports flitted through his optical feed. Columns and columns of data detailed expenditures and earnings, all of it nonexistent as far as the Consortium was concerned—the records would be sent to the Inner Reach Syndicate's headquarters before local copies were destroyed.

The only sound in the knock's wake was that of his respiratory pumps maintaining a constant airflow into and out of his lungs. The years had, unfortunately, only increased his awareness of the noise.

He perused the currently displayed report to its end, tallying everything on a small side screen at the lower edge of his vision. Once he'd confirmed the totals were accurate, he allowed his attention to stray from his work; a minute had passed since the knock, and there'd been no follow up.

Vaund considered it a sign that his subordinates understood

him well. They knew to wait until he acknowledged them rather than cause a second interruption.

"Enter," he said, a low buzz running beneath his artificially replicated voice.

The door opened. Vaund didn't have to turn to see the groalthuun, Straek, enter the room; the cybernetic helmet encasing the ruined flesh of his head provided full view all around.

Straek stopped two meters away from Vaund's chair and blinked his large, black eyes. "Found a few prospects today, boss."

Vaund eased his hold on the armrests and lifted a hand, index finger extended. "Show me."

Straek activated his holocom, bringing up several still images on its projected screen. He swept them together with his fingers and flicked them toward Vaund.

The images appeared in Vaund's optical feed—three males and two females.

Vaund examined the stills one by one, assessing the candidates by species, build, and appearance. Two of the males were promising—a pair of daevah, twins with mirrored patterns on their violet-red skin. They looked to have athletic frames, which was a good start. Male daevah, who were always born as twins, were popular both with wealthy buyers looking for sex slaves and with the organizers of underground fights seeking entertaining combatants.

These daevah could pull in a decent payout on the Caldorian market.

But the last image was the most intriguing of all. It was a terran female with expressive brown eyes and long brown hair. She had a certain innocence to her features that would undoubtedly enhance her market appeal. The image only displayed her head and part of one shoulder.

"Give me everything you have on the last one," Vaund said. "The terran."

A moment later, fresh images appeared in his feed, all containing the terran, taken in what appeared to be one of the upper city malls. The crowd blocked her from full view in most of the images, and her baggy clothing made it difficult to determine the shape of the body beneath, but she seemed a slight, attractive thing.

Perfect.

"Who is with her?" Vaund asked. A tall sedhi stood near her in each image, often holding her hand; only the back of his head visible in most of the stills.

"Don't know, boss," said Straek. "Some sedhi she was walking with. They spotted me before the last one."

Something sparked in Vaund's gut as he neared the final image in the chain. The sensation was heavy and hot, and he somehow knew what he was going to see. He somehow knew *who* he was going to see.

In the final image, the sedhi had turned to face Straek directly. Vaund knew those yellow eyes, knew the *qal* on the sedhi's face and neck, knew the curve of those horns. He even knew the distinctive shape of those smug lips.

He's dead. I fucking killed him.

Vaund grasped the arms of the chair; the frame within creaked, groaned, and snapped. Arcanthus was *dead*.

"How long did you follow them?" he asked.

"Couple hours, maybe," said Straek. "They held hands while they walked around. Stopped in a few shops. Took in the sights."

Though Vaund could only speculate, it was likely that the terran was in a relationship with Arcanthus. It was likely that she was important to him.

Which meant there was a chance she could be used to locate the sedhi...or to lure him out of hiding.

"Find her. I want a name; I want a location."

"We'll get on it right away, boss. She's probably chipped, though. Might complicate things."

"We're not taking her yet. I just want her found. The sedhi she was with needs to die. Once he's dead, we'll capture the terran."

Straek's eyes widened. He opened his mouth, and Vaund could almost sense the questions that nearly tumbled out before the groalthuun snapped his jaw shut again.

Vaund twisted in his chair, turning his face—or rather the vague suggestion of a face his helmet presented—toward Straek. "This one isn't on the books. Do you understand?"

"Yes, boss."

"Leave me. I don't want to be bothered again until you know where she is."

The groalthuun nodded and hurried out of the room, closing the door softly behind him.

Vaund resumed his prior position, but restless, agitated fire pulsed outward from his gut to course through his limbs. He absently flexed and relaxed his fingers as the volume of his respirator increased.

The terran would fetch a high price, and that would benefit the Syndicate—Vaund had climbed the ranks by maximizing the profits he generated for the organization—but Arcanthus needed to die for Vaund's benefit. His subordinates had no idea who Arcanthus was; none of them had been on Caldorius those years ago, none of them were aware of what had transpired there.

But there were several people in the Syndicate leadership who did know.

And Vaund reported directly to some of them.

Ambition, ruthlessness, and a cold, calculating demeanor had brought Vaund this far, but it would mean little if his superiors discovered that he'd botched the job that had earned him a place within the organization a decade ago. It would make them question everything he'd said and done over the intervening years.

It would all mean *nothing* if they found out Vaund had failed to kill Arcanthus.

He grasped the armrests and wrenched them up, snapping them off the frame and tearing their hide covering.

This time, Arcanthus, I'm taking your head.

NINE

Samantha kept her chin down and held her purchases—clothing and food, all wrapped in different colored packages—against her chest as she strode along the street toward her apartment building. Her legs felt leaden, and her feet were sore. She was exhausted for a good reason. Sarai had given her a few hours of work today and had seemed tempted to allow Sam to keep working even after the borian woman's unreliable brother finally showed up. The labor had been satisfying, and it had kept Samantha's mind occupied.

Now, with little to focus on but the people milling around her on the street, she found herself reminiscing.

Two days had passed since she'd had last seen Alkorin. Despite her urges to call him, they hadn't spoken in that time. She felt miserable; confused and scared, too, but above all miserable.

She missed him.

By day, the sedhi had lurked in the forefront of her mind, and by night, he haunted her dreams, leaving her to awake a hot, sweaty mess with her sheets tangled around her. She kept thinking about the feel of his tall, strong body against hers, of his hands in her hair and on her backside, of his kiss.

Oh God, his *kiss*.

She'd never known that a kiss could steal her breath, that it could claim her mind, body, and soul all at once. He'd made her forget everything—her past, her pain, her loss, her doubt, and her trepidation. His lips had left room inside her for only desire and need. Alkorin had wound her up so tight that a single stroke would snap her.

Her time with him had been wonderful, like floating through a waking dream. He was playful, charming, protective, and kind. Though he treated her with thoughtfulness, he didn't act like she'd break at his slightest touch. He knew when to push and when to retreat. Though each time he pulled away, Samantha yearned to reach for him and bring him closer. He made her long for things she'd never experienced, made her long for things she never thought she could have.

She *wanted* him. More than anything in this universe, she wanted the sedhi who set her blood on fire.

She just didn't know how to overcome her uncertainty, her past experiences...

Didn't know how to overcome herself.

Worthless. Weak.

Samantha gritted her teeth.

Her father had died when she was eighteen years old. The loss had left her utterly alone and directionless. She'd drifted aimlessly for a few months, bombarded by an endless stream of bills and calls from collection agencies seeking payment on her father's debt, which had amassed because of her grandmother's illness and eventual death a couple years earlier.

And just as she'd realized she was at rock bottom—she'd been too naïve then to understand what *rock bottom* actually meant—her savior had swooped in.

But instead of the arms of a hero, she'd fallen into the clutches of a monster who'd taken almost *everything* from her— her trust, her worth, her freedom, her very self—before she escaped.

Samantha wasn't sure who she was anymore. She felt like a phantom, a fading echo of who she'd been, the ghost of a girl who'd once laughed and loved despite how little she'd had. And even though she was half a universe away from James, she still felt the tatters of her soul slipping through her fingers like sand; she was losing a little more of herself every day.

If it continued, there'd be nothing left of her at all before long.

Worthless. Weak.

James had hurled those words at her so many times over the years she'd spent with him that she'd come to believe them.

He'd shown her kindness at first. He'd been charming, he'd been dedicated. But once they'd begun building a life together —once she'd moved in with him and he knew she had nowhere else to go—he showed his true face. The mask had come off to reveal the monster who'd lurked beneath.

The hope he'd instilled in her had been a lie.

And now there was Alkorin—Alkorin, who many people on Earth would've considered monstrous in appearance. Alkorin, who'd been kind and devoted in the short time they'd spent together. She wanted so badly to trust him. Wanted so badly to believe he was the opposite of James. Alkorin gave her hope that everything would turn out fine. That she'd find a place here.

That she'd find *herself.*

But how could she know? How could she know the hope Alkorin provided was real, that he was real? How could she know that she wasn't following the same path from which she'd fled? She'd only known him a few days; that wasn't nearly long enough to see what truly dwelled in a person's heart.

Someone bumped into her shoulder, startling her out of her thoughts as one of her packages slipped out of her arms. She stopped, but something caught her eye before she could apologize to the person she'd walked into. There were two large hovercars—though *tanks* might've been a more accurate term—parked in front of her apartment complex, their gold and teal bodies matching the armor of the Eternal Guard peacekeepers standing nearby.

The building's entry doors swung open. Two peacekeepers walked out, dragging Rakkob between them.

"Fuck you!" The borian thrashed in their hold, his eyes wild. "It wasn't me, I didn't do it! It wasn't mine! You're fucking framing me!"

One of the peacekeepers beside the vehicles hurried forward and jabbed Rakkob in the chest with a staff-like weapon.

Rakkob convulsed, his body seizing for a couple seconds before he went limp. The peacekeepers didn't miss a step; they hauled him to the back of one of the vehicles and tossed him inside.

A light tap on her shoulder nearly wrenched a scream from Samantha's throat. She leapt forward and spun to face the alien who'd touched her, squeezing her purchases against her chest.

A male cren stared down at her, his yellow irises bright against his black sclerae. He had to be at least two meters tall—possibly a few centimeters taller than Alkorin, if she didn't count the sedhi's horns. The cren's nose was sharp and hawk-like, complementing equally sharp features that led down to a strong but narrow chin. A curving tusk jutted from either side of his wide mouth, and his thick eyebrows were angled down over the bridge of his nose, lending extra menace to his already intimidating appearance. His ears were long and pointed, adorned with numerous piercings. The sides of his head were shaved, and the long hair on its top—its navy-blue hue several shades darker than his blue-gray skin—was pulled back in a tight ponytail.

Samantha's brows lowered. For a moment, she could have sworn that she'd seen him before.

I did! He was one of the customers at Sarai's booth today.

But Sarai's booth was a twenty-minute walk from Samantha's apartment. What was this cren doing here now? Why had he approached her?

She swallowed and prayed the sound hadn't been loud enough for him to hear. "Yes?"

He lifted his hand; Samantha flinched back reflexively until she realized what he was holding—a blue wrapped package containing one of the shirts she'd purchased earlier.

"You dropped this," he said.

"Oh!" Adjusting the bundles in her arms, she reached out for it and met his eyes. "Thank you."

The cren nodded and smiled—or at least she thought it was a smile; his tusks made it difficult to tell. Either way, she chose to interpret it as a friendly expression.

"Be safe," the cren said before strolling away.

Sam watched him until he disappeared around a corner before turning back to her apartment building. The last of the peacekeepers climbed into his vehicle; within a few seconds, both hovertanks lifted off and sped away. The small crowd that had gathered outside, some of whom she recognized as other tenants of her building, dispersed slowly.

Samantha entered the complex and made her way to her apartment. She had no idea what Rakkob had done, but she couldn't deny her relief; he was gone. It felt good to traverse the corridors without fear of confrontation.

Carefully balancing her packages, she lifted her arm to the scanner beside the door and slipped through once it was open. She had made it several steps beyond the threshold before she realized she wasn't alone.

There was someone seated at her table.

The door closed behind her.

Samantha dropped her packages and whirled around to find another stranger beside the door—a goat-like groalthuun. Her eyes widened with sudden recognition; he was the same groalthuun who'd been taking pictures of her at the Ventrillian Mall. Her heart pounded, its beats echoing like thunder in her chest.

"W-What do you want? Why are you here?" she asked.

How did they get in?

"Have a seat," said the groalthuun, his dark eyes locked on her.

Samantha stared at him a second longer before she turned to look at the stranger seated at the table. "I...I would rather—"

"He wasn't asking," said the other alien. He was huge, with dull orange skin, long white hair, and four thickly muscled arms. It seemed impossible that the comparatively tiny chair was holding his weight.

Samantha was unfamiliar with his species, but she didn't need to know what he was to understand how dangerous he was. He looked like he could tear her apart with his pinky fingers.

The orange alien lifted a hand, gesturing to the chair across from him. "Sit."

Trembling, she walked to the table and stiffly lowered herself onto the chair. "Who are you?"

Goat sat on the couch, leaned forward, and rested his elbows on his thighs. "*You* are going to answer *our* questions, terran. Not the other way around."

"Who is the sedhi you were with two days ago?" Orange asked.

Samantha's blood chilled.

Were they after Alkorin? Her mind raced; she couldn't lie and say she didn't know who they were talking about because Goat had seen her with Alk, had been taking pictures of them.

"He's a friend," she said.

Orange shifted a hand to his face, pinching the bridge of his nose in a very *frustrated-parent* fashion. "Do you just not understand the situation? Your kind are new here, but I assume your people wouldn't have been invited to Arthos if you were dumb. Give me a name. Give me an address. We're here for tangible information, not for you to mull over the nature of your relationship."

Samantha placed her hands in her lap and clutched them together. "I-I don't know much about him. I only just met him. His...his name is Kolthar. That's all I know."

"Contact information," said Goat.

"I don't have any."

Orange pressed two of his hands atop the table and pushed himself up, leaning toward her; the table groaned beneath his weight. He bared his teeth and growled.

Samantha flinched back and threw her hands up, palms out. "I swear! We only just met! I don't know anything about him other than his name."

"You two seemed pretty damned close for having just met," Goat said.

The orange alien's fingers wrapped around the edges of the table, and the metal buckled in his grasp. "You'd better start giving us information, terran."

Tears welled in Samantha's eyes as terror clawed at her insides. She couldn't give them anything. Wouldn't give them anything. No matter what Alkorin might have done to these people, she refused to betray him. Not when he'd done so much for her.

"I don't know anything," she said shakily. "We only just met. H-He was fascinated with me being a human and flirted with me. We spent the day together and I haven't seen him since. That's all!"

Orange leaned closer to her. "How do you keep in touch with him?"

"I don't! I don't know how. He didn't give me anything. He came to me."

"When are you meeting him again?" Goat asked.

"I-I don't know. I *told* you. He just came to me."

The aliens exchanged a glance with one another.

"For your sake"—Orange reached across the table with surprising speed and grabbed her hair, dragging her out of the seat until her face was centimeters from his—"you'd better be telling us the truth. Our boss wouldn't appreciate you lying about this."

Sam cried out, her hands flying up to clutch at his fist as pain shot through her scalp.

Worthless. Weak.

The tears spilled from her eyes. "Please! Please, don't!"

"We'll be around." Orange shoved her away.

She stumbled backward, tripped over the leg of her chair, and fell to the floor. She remained there, shaking, and watched through the curtain of her hair as they left her apartment. The door closing behind them was like the gunshot signaling the start of a race, startling her into motion. Shoving herself to her feet, she darted across the room, hit the lock button on the door's control panel, and engaged the heavy deadbolt that slid into the floor.

She didn't know who they were, how they got in—how

easily they could get in again—but she would do what she could to prevent their reentry.

Pressing her back against the wall, Samantha slid to the floor. She sucked in one sharp breath after another. Panic threatened to overcome her; her heart raced, her throat felt tight, and chills shook her body. Black spots filled her vision.

No! I can't pass out. I need to tell him.

Samantha forced herself to take deep, even breaths. The darkness slowly receded.

Crawling away from the door, she sat up against the side of her bed and lifted her wrist. With trembling fingers, she activated her holocom and swiped through the menu to bring up her contacts.

She paused.

Why hadn't they made her show them her contact list?

Whatever their reasons, it didn't matter now. She needed to tell Alkorin.

She started a visual call.

Within seconds, Alkorin's hologram appeared on her display. He flashed his fangs in a grin. "*Samantha,*" he purred. "I was starting to worry that you wouldn't—"

"I need you," she said quickly.

His eyes narrowed and his brows fell low as he leaned closer, searching her face. "What's wrong? What happened?"

"There were people here looking for you. Th-they were asking me questions about you."

"What people, Samantha? Who were they?"

"They didn't tell me, but one of them was the groalthuun from the Ventrillian Mall. The one who was taking pictures." She wiped the moisture from her cheek with the back of her hand. "I didn't tell them anything. I swear. I even gave them a fake name for you. You have to believe—"

"Did they hurt you?" he asked, his third eye lingering on

her while the other two focused on something below the hologram.

Sam shook her head. "No."

"Stay in your apartment. I'll be there as fast as possible."

"They said they'll be around, Alk. They probably want you to come."

"They're probably listening to this conversation right now."

Her heart leapt and her eyes widened. Why hadn't she thought of that? Why had she been so stupid? Of course they would bug her apartment! It was probably why they hadn't demanded to look at her holocom contacts.

And she was giving them all the information they needed right now.

"It's okay, my little terran," he said, all his eyes now on her. "I'll be there soon. Don't open the door for anyone but me."

"Okay," she said, searching his face. "Please be careful."

TEN

The call ended, and the hologram of Samantha's face—so beautiful, yet so filled with terror—vanished. Arcanthus slammed his fists atop his desk, denting the metal, and shoved himself to his feet. His pounding heart pumped fire through his veins. He clenched his teeth hard enough to risk shattering them.

A wordless, furious cry rose from his chest, beginning as a growl and ending as a roar. Even if there were words to encompass what he felt at that moment, his rage was too great to find them. He'd known what she was to him—his *mate*—and had suppressed most of the instincts she'd awoken in him so far.

There'd be no stopping them now.

He wanted to destroy anything and everything in his path. Wanted to tear Arthos apart and make the city bleed until he had Samantha safe in his arms.

Bloodlust had always lurked in his subconscious; it was the part of him that had thrilled in the combat he'd seen in his brief days as a soldier, the part of him that had loved the bloody arena fights he'd been forced into as a slave, the part he'd always thought of as his *inner tretin*. As years had passed, he'd done his best to silence it.

But he would embrace it to save Samantha. He would unleash it upon the universe to protect her.

He stalked out of his workshop and down the corridors to the armory, sparing the walls and light fixtures along the way from his wrath only because they wouldn't bleed. As he moved, he sent a message to Kiloq and Koroq, informing them of the new situation.

Arcanthus threw open the doors to the storage locker and tugged out his combat armor breastplate. He pulled it on over his head and quickly hit the fasteners to activate the maglock seals along the seams; the armor covered his torso and pelvis, front and back.

"What the fuck are you doing, Arcanthus?"

Arc glanced over his shoulder to see Drakkal filling the doorway, his powerful arms crossed over his chest.

He's not my enemy. Not my enemy.

Arcanthus moved to the next locker and drew an auto-blaster from the rack. "Going to help her."

"Who? The damned terran?"

"Shouldn't that be obvious by now?" Grasping the weapon in both hands, Arc turned it to the side and checked the power charge; full. He slung the auto-blaster over his shoulder and pulled down a second.

"What happened?"

"Groalthuun from the mall showed up at her apartment. Was asking about me."

Drakkal growled. "I said you were being stupid, Arc. You think I was just messing with you? If you have people after you—"

"It could be anyone." Arcanthus took the second auto-blaster's grip in his left hand and settled his right hand on its foregrip. "*Anyone.* And it doesn't matter, because *she* is in trouble. You can suit up and come, or I'll go on my own."

Drakkal strode forward, throwing his arms out to the sides. He bared his fangs, and his claws protruded from his fingers. "All for that terran *ji'tas*? For a meek girl who'll be eaten alive by this city the moment you lose interest in her? Maybe try making decisions with your head instead of your cock, you selfish bastard. She's a piece of meat! You'll fuck her and move on just like you have all the rest. You're putting yourself at risk, this operation at risk, *all of us* at risk for a taste of terran slit."

The torrent of emotions whirling deep within Arcanthus—emotions he was trying to ignore so he could do what was necessary—surged to the surface. He lunged at Drakkal and clamped a hand over the azhera's throat, slamming him against the wall. Drakkal grunted, but before he could recover, Arc shifted forward, pressing his chest to the azhera's and tipping his horns against the azhera's forehead.

"She's my mate, you fucking *zhe'gaash!*" Arcanthus snarled through clenched teeth. "She's my mate, and she's in trouble, so I am going to go help her. You can come along or stay, but either way you're going to shut your fucking mouth about her."

"*Kraasz ka'val,* you really are stupid," Drakkal growled, grabbing hold of Arc's wrist with one hand and his horn with the other. The azhera's muscles strained against Arcanthus's hold.

Arcanthus released a growl of his own, tightening his hold on the azhera's throat as he poured strength into counteracting Drakkal's resistance.

"You should've told me sooner," Drakkal said, "and I would've called you stupid one or two times less. You're supposed to *trust* me with this stuff, Arc."

There was hurt in Drakkal's voice, nestled beneath his anger; it was just strong enough to make Arcanthus realize what was happening, what he was doing. He released his hold on Drakkal's throat and stepped back.

Drakkal shoved away from Arcanthus and moved to the storage locker, quickly donning his combat armor. He lifted his arm and activated his holocom, creating an open communication channel with the entire security team. "Need everyone who isn't posted geared up and in the garage five minutes ago. Move it!"

"I was ready to hit you, you furry bastard," Arcanthus said.

"Good thing you didn't. I would have had to carry you to the car to save your terran after I showed you your place." Drakkal pulled an auto-blaster from the weapon rack and turned to face Arcanthus.

"So choking you is totally acceptable?"

"Did it sound like I was choking, sedhi?"

Arcanthus shook his head, willing away the faint tremors coursing through his body. He rarely lost control like he just had. "Grab an extra set of armor for her. One of the smaller ones."

Drakkal nodded, tugged another suit of armor out of the storage locker, and fell into place beside Arc. They hurried out of the armory and through the halls. Four members of the security team were in the garage when Arcanthus and Drakkal arrived, all clad in armor and carrying auto-blasters—the large, blue-eyed cren, Razi, the two vorgals who usually guarded the entry to the workshop, Thargen and Urgand, and Sekk'thi, a female ilthurii with emerald scales.

"Should we wait for more?" Drakkal asked.

"No time," Arc replied. "I've already informed Kiloq and Koroq. They're on site but haven't seen anything."

He plucked the commlink earpiece from the shoulder of his armor and slipped it into his ear; the others followed his example. "I have no idea who we're up against, no idea how many there are, no idea what position they'll be in. Our only goal is to get a terran named Samantha to safety. She is a *very* dear friend of mine."

"So we're going blind," said Thargen.

"Basically, yes."

"Into a potentially deadly situation."

"Mhmm."

Thargen whooped. "About time we get a little action."

Arcanthus pointed to Thargen and grinned. "That's the kind of attitude we need here. Let's move."

His grin faded when he climbed into the hovercar's front passenger seat. The vehicle shook as the others piled inside. Settling the auto-blaster over his lap, Arcanthus lifted his arm and grasped the handle at the top of the door frame, squeezing. In moments like this, he missed his own flesh more than ever—he missed the feel of his muscles tightening, the pressure in his joints, the ache of exertion. He missed the slight pain that came with landing a solid blow on an enemy.

Please be okay, little terran.

Once Drakkal had situated himself in the driver's seat, he guided the hovercar out of the garage and through the express tunnels at immense speed, reducing the surrounding lights and vehicles to blurs. Arcanthus's racing heart seemed eager to match the vehicle's velocity.

He couldn't deny that Drakkal was right; Arc had been stupid. Incredibly stupid. He'd let his arrogance and desire cloud his judgment, had let his feelings tear down his guard and instill him with an uncharacteristic carelessness.

I should have brought her to the compound days ago. We would've avoided all this...

But would she have come? Even now, would she trust him enough to leave with him, or would she be frightened away by the dangerous people looking for him?

Getting into your own head again, Arc, you fool. What was the first thing she said when she called?

I need you.

Perhaps that was only because she'd had no one else to turn to, perhaps—

No.

He wouldn't allow himself to pursue those thoughts. Not now.

They emerged from the express tunnel leading into Samantha's sector. Hundreds of apartment complexes lay before them, but Arc picked hers out with ease, even from this height.

"What's the plan?" Drakkal asked.

"Funny thing about that," Arcanthus replied, "I don't actually have one."

"You really *did* expect to charge in blindly and deal with it as it comes?"

"Fuck yeah," Thargen barked. "My life philosophy."

"Don't encourage him, damn it," Drakkal grumbled.

Arcanthus snickered. "Look, I'm a fighter-turned-lover, not a strategist."

Drakkal snorted and shook his head. "We need a tactician for this, not a strategist."

"See? Yet another reason I'm not qualified. You just *had* to correct me on a technicality." Arc swept his gaze over Samantha's building as they neared it. The windows lining each floor were dark, tinted for the privacy of the residents, allowing not even a glimpse into any of the rooms. Arcanthus's lips curled upward in a smile.

He leaned forward and activated the display on the center of the car's console, fingers flying as he accessed the plexus and quickly located the Consortium-approved plans for the building. Within a few moments, he had the blueprints on the windshield display, overlaid atop the complex ahead in perfect scale. He entered her room number.

The windshield display highlighted one of the windows, showing the floorplan for the room beyond it.

"That one is hers," Arcanthus said.

"Okay. Where do you want me to park?" Drakkal asked.

"Keep up, Drak. Next to the window."

Drakkal turned his head toward Arcanthus, brows low. "You're serious?"

Arcanthus nodded. "Trying to use my head for once in all this, just like you want me to. That's the quickest way in and out."

"All right." Facing forward, Drakkal swung the hovercar around so it was alongside the building, guiding it up to the marked window.

Arcanthus brought up his holocom screen and sent a message to Samantha.

Stay away from the window.

Her reply came a few seconds later.

What? Why?

The hovercar came to a stop beside the window. Arcanthus swung his second auto-blaster over his other shoulder, pushed the door open, grasped the edges of the doorframe, and pulled himself partially out of it. A two-meter gap separated him from the window.

"Get me closer."

"Don't want to ruin the door," Drakkal said.

"Drak, I will—"

The hovercar lurched toward the building. Arcanthus growled a curse and wrapped his tail around the seat behind him, anchoring himself in place as he swayed forward. The car door scraped against the side of the building, producing a shower of sparks and the groan of metal-on-metal.

They were only twenty stories up; nothing to worry about, right?

"We're having a long conversation when we get home, azhera," he said as he straightened. The wind whipped his long hair around his face. He bent his leg and thrust it forward, kicking the window.

A circular, fist-sized crack formed in the glass. He kicked it again, and the damage spread; even against his enhanced strength and metal feet, the material they used for windows on these buildings was incredibly durable.

There were several hissing sounds from behind and beneath Arcanthus in rapid succession.

"Shit," Urgand growled from inside the cab. "We're taking fire from the street."

As Arcanthus bent his leg for another kick, a bolt of plasma zipped through the space between him and the building, passing close enough for him to feel its heat on his face.

"Kiloq, Koroq, see if you can get an angle on them," Drakkal growled as the hovercar drifted away from the building.

"Swing me back over," Arcanthus shouted.

"It's too dangerous, Arc."

More plasma bolts darted through the air. Arcanthus risked a glance down to see three people on the street below, firing their auto-blasters upward. The hovercar was armored, but that armor wouldn't hold out indefinitely.

He shifted his third eye toward the window, which had two circular points of damage with cracks radiating outward from them. It probably needed two or three more hits to break; he didn't have time for that. "Just get me some momentum, damn it!"

Drakkal uttered a curse. The hovercar moved farther away from the building before swinging back like a pendulum.

Arcanthus adjusted his grip on the doorframe and bent his legs, releasing his tail's hold on the seat.

What if it doesn't break?

It has *to break. I'm not giving it a choice.*

Arcanthus launched himself forward, lifting his arms, elbows in front, to shield his face as his body crossed the gap.

The window didn't shatter—it buckled and cracked, breaking out of its frame to fall into the apartment with Arcanthus atop it. Arc landed hard, his elbows smacking the floor while his abdomen caught on the window frame. He felt the impact even through his armor.

Gritting his teeth, he dragged himself fully inside and stood, swinging one of the auto-blasters into his hands. He scanned the room, heart lodging in his throat when he didn't catch sight of his mate.

"Samantha?"

"Alkorin?" Her head popped up from between the bed and the wall.

Relief washed over Arcanthus like a wave of cool water. For an instant, his knees felt impossibly weak, and he feared he'd collapse onto them.

When her frightened eyes met his, Sam leapt to her feet and raced toward him. She didn't hesitate; she slammed into him, wrapping her arms around his waist. "You're here! You're here," she said against his chest. "What's happening?"

He released the blaster's foregrip to wrap an arm around her, holding her trembling body close. "We're going to get you out of here, little terran."

"*Here's the spare armor,*" Sekk'thi said over the commlink.

Arcanthus glanced back to see the ilthurii in the open door of the hovercar. Plasma bolts from below struck the underside of the vehicle and filled the air between it and the building. She tossed the spare set of combat armor in through the broken window.

Drakkal's voice came over the comms. *"We have to break off. We'll land and try to clear an exit for you."*

Sekk'thi pulled the door closed, and the hovercar banked away and darted out of sight.

"All right." Arcanthus allowed himself a moment to press his lips to Sam's hair and take in her tantalizing scent. "Are you hurt, Samantha?"

"No." She pulled back and looked up at him. "I'm so sorry. I didn't know calling you would—"

He pressed a finger to her lips, silencing her. She'd said she gave her visitors a false name and hadn't told them anything about him. He believed her. She'd protected him despite her terror, despite knowing she was in terrible danger, despite barely knowing Arcanthus. She'd kept quiet. She'd refused to betray him.

That meant more to Arcanthus than he could ever express.

"You did the right thing." Though it pained him, he released her and stepped back, crouching to lift the spare armor. "We need to get this on and leave, all right?"

She looked at the armor with a concerned crease between her brows and nodded. "Okay."

"I will answer what I can once you're safe, Samantha," he said as he helped her into the armor; it was a bit large for her, but it would do. Once the armor was in place, Arc held up one of the auto-blasters. "Do you know how to use this?"

Her frightened yet met his. "No."

"Do you favor your left hand or your right?"

"My right."

Arcanthus stepped behind her, positioning the auto-blaster in front of her. He slipped the shoulder strap over her arm, guided her right hand to the grip and her left to the foregrip.

"Nestle this against your shoulder. Good. Don't point at anything you're not prepared to shoot and keep your finger off the trigger until you're going to fire. Point the barrel at what you want to hit and squeeze the trigger. It'll put out enough plasma to do the rest."

Despite her trembling, she nodded firmly and said, "Okay."

"I want you to walk behind me, little terran. Right on my heels."

When she stepped behind him, he slipped his tail around her waist, coiling it tight. "This is going to be frightening, but I'm here. You'll be safe."

Shouting from the hallway called his attention to the door. He positioned himself directly between Samantha and the entryway and moved forward, crouching behind the couch. Samantha followed, easing down behind him. Arcanthus aimed his blaster at the door.

An explosion consumed the doorway, its flash temporarily blinding Arcanthus. Something slammed onto the floor with a heavy *clang*. Samantha flinched and cried out.

Arcanthus squeezed the trigger of his blaster. The weapon made a series of high, thumping whines as it sprayed plasma bolts into the opening. Someone released a choked cry, the sound followed by the thump of a collapsing body.

Arc's vision cleared to reveal a warped, open doorframe where the door had stood a moment before. The smoke from the explosion slowly dissipated, leaving a haze in the room that wasn't quite thick enough to obscure the body lying across the threshold. The mangled door lay a meter inside the apartment.

"You're not getting out of here alive, sedhi," someone shouted from the hallway.

Narrowing his eyes, Arc shifted his blaster to the right, aiming at the wall beside the doorway. He fired another burst.

The frantic curse from the hallway told him his shots had

been close, but not close enough. Keeping his weapon raised, he hurried forward. Samantha lagged for a moment; a tug from his tail got her moving.

"Surrender and we won't hurt your terran," the male in the hall said.

Arcanthus replied with another volley of plasma bolts, these aimed slightly more to the right. He rushed into the hallway an instant later—keeping Samantha inside the apartment behind him—to see a volturian ducking away from the orange-glowing holes in the wall. The volturian had time enough to meet Arcanthus's gaze before the sedhi fired a prolonged burst into him. The alien's body shuddered and jerked before dropping.

Arcanthus swung his blaster to the left, checking the opposite direction along the wall. No one else was present. He guided Samantha into the corridor. "So, where do I need to go, Drak?"

"*Down,*" Drakkal replied through the commlink.

"Remind me, which direction is that?"

"*We're working on it, Arc. Got at least four here at the front entrance.*"

"*Three more out back,*" Kiloq added.

Blaster fire sounded briefly in the open feeds.

Frowning, Arcanthus kicked the volturian just to make sure he was dead. The still-smoking corpse bore no gang insignia, no discernable uniform, no distinct affiliated colors. Who were these attackers? *Why* were they after Arcanthus?

No time to speculate now.

He led Samantha toward the elevators.

A soft tone sounded from somewhere ahead of them. Arcanthus stilled.

Three aliens touting auto-blasters emerged from the

elevator bank; they were already facing Arcanthus and Samantha.

Releasing his blaster's foregrip, Arcanthus raised his right arm and activated his hardlight shield projector. He splayed his fingers and snapped them shut, bending his wrist inward. The circular shield expanded and changed into a rectangle nearly as tall as Arcanthus just before the first bolts from the elevator crew struck.

The shield flashed with each impact. Plasma bolts burst against the barrier, their normally blue-white light turned to a pale green through the translucent hardlight. Arcanthus bent his arm to angle the shield vertically, covering as much of the hallway as possible while the elevator crew advanced.

"Stairs?" he asked, glancing at Samantha over his shoulder.

Her face was paler than normal, her eyes as big as twin moons, and she clutched her weapon in two white-knuckled hands.

"Back this way." She gestured toward the hall behind them with the barrel of her auto-blaster.

"Good. Lead the way."

Samantha held his gaze for an instant before nodding. She moved in a brisk, shuffling sort of sidestep that allowed Arc to keep the shield protecting them without removing his tail from around her waist.

Unfortunately, the ever-friendly elevator crew sped their advance, continuing their steady stream of fire.

"*Vrek'osh!*" Drakkal spat through the commlink. "*I don't know who you pissed off, but more just showed up out here.*"

"*They are covering each other,*" said Sekk'thi. "*Attempting to get more of them into the building.*"

"Well tell them there's no room!" Arcanthus turned his body perpendicular to his attackers as he and Samantha reached the door to the stairs. Plasma bolts zipped around the edge of the shield, burning holes in the wall.

An excited, guttural voice crackled over the comms—Thargen, hurling insults at his enemies in an amalgamation of Universal Speech and Vorgalese.

Samantha opened the door. Arc wedged the shield against the wall at an angle to keep her protected and leaned through the doorway with his blaster at the ready. Once he'd confirmed the stairwell was clear, he swung his tail, forcing his terran inside. Stepping backward, he swept his arm down. The shield's lower edge embedded itself in the floor just in front of the doorway, effectively blocking off all but the uppermost half-meter of the entryway. He opened his fist, releasing the invisible field that kept the shield tethered to his forearm.

He returned his right hand to his auto-blaster's foregrip and led Samantha to the steps. The shield would hold out either until it had expended too much energy to sustain its form, or it was beyond the control unit's range.

At the very least, it would grant them some time to make their escape.

"At this rate, the Eternal Guard will get here before you're out," Drakkal said.

"As I recall, *someone* is meant to be clearing a path." Arcanthus hurried down the stairs with Samantha close behind. Her breaths were quick and ragged.

"Who...who are you talking to?" she asked.

"Drakkal and the others. They're outside."

When they reached the next landing, he glanced back at her.

Frantic pink splotches stood out on her cheeks, contrasting the heightened paleness of her skin. He had little notion of terran endurance and limitations; all he could do was hope she could push onward.

"Almost out, Samantha. This will be over soon," he said as gently as he could.

She nodded. "If we stop...I'm afraid I won't be able to keep going."

Arcanthus continued down, tightening his tail around her middle a little more. She wouldn't feel it through her armor, and he wanted to ensure he could keep her upright if she tripped or stumbled.

After what felt like both an eternity and a fleeting handful of moments, they finally reached the ground floor.

Arcanthus guided Samantha under the stairs; it was the only spot that provided cover from above and a little protection from the door leading into the main corridor. He looked down at the indicator on the inside of his right wrist. The shield wouldn't last longer than a few more seconds.

"Tell me one of the exits is clear," he said. "I don't have time to pull up city plans and puzzle out an alternate route."

"*Still hot out here,*" Drakkal replied.

"*They were reinforced,*" growled Koroq. "*Back is no good.*"

"I suppose they *really* want me dead," Arcanthus said.

Drakkal snorted. "*Don't they know there's a waiting list?*"

The shield's power indicator flickered off. Shouts sounded from high above. Arcanthus's heart raced almost as quickly as his mind; they needed a way out, and they needed one *fast*. His own skin being on the line should've been enough to push him to a solution, but his concern was solely for Samantha. For his mate. If he couldn't get her out of here, if he failed, the best she could hope for was a quick death.

Unacceptable.

Arcanthus turned his head toward her, and she met his gaze. He moved his right hand to her face and cupped her cheek. "We need to fight our way out, Samantha. Same as before—stay right behind me."

She closed her eyes, pressed her cheek into his palm, and nodded. The determination and resolve that hardened her features at that moment pierced Arcanthus to his core; he was nearly overcome with pride, and the fires of arousal sparked deep inside him. He *craved* her. He'd been patient, but this little terran was testing his restraint, and his bestial side was rampaging in the back of his mind with want for her.

He desired Samantha more than ever before.

Thrusting those thoughts aside, he forced himself back to the situation at hand. Heavy footsteps sounded from partway up the stairwell; at least two of the three members of the elevator crew were descending. According to Drakkal, more enemies were attempting to enter the building. Were they still outside, or had they succeeded? He had to assume his foes were in communication with each other, that they knew where he was.

Overthinking this again.

Arcanthus clenched his jaw, returned his hand to the foregrip of his auto-blaster, and strode toward the door. He turned the blaster upward as they passed into the open space, but the elevator crew chose not to peek down. He used his tail to guide Sam against the wall beside the door before pressing the button to open it.

The door slid open silently. Arc leaned through the opening slightly, checking the corridor to the left of the doorway before swinging to check the other direction.

A huge, orange fist sped toward his face.

Arcanthus instinctively tipped his chin down. The fist struck his horns with a dull, meaty *thwap*. The immense force behind the blow blasted through his neck and along his spine, clacking his teeth together, but he planted his feet and stood firm; tretin blood granted Arc's people naturally tough bones, but he'd reinforced his skeletal and muscular systems with cybernetics years ago to account for the strain caused by the enhanced strength of his prosthetic limbs.

He looked up to see a hulking, orange-skinned onigox standing before him.

Arcanthus swung his auto-blaster around. The onigox caught the weapon with the hands of his lower arms before Arc could take aim. Growling, Arcanthus poured more strength into the struggle. Despite his size and prowess, the onigox couldn't overpower the sedhi; the barrel of the blaster, trembling with the combatants' exertion, crept toward the orange brute.

At least until the onigox swung his upper arms simultaneously, catching Arc's head between his massive fists.

The sound of the blows was thunderous in Arcanthus's ears, and white flashed across his vision. He staggered backward. The onigox capitalized upon Arcanthus's brief disorientation by tearing the auto-blaster away and tossing it to the floor.

"Alk!"

Samantha's voice broke through the ringing in Arcanthus's ears. He shook his head sharply and glanced at her; plasma bolts rained from the stairs above, hitting the floor around her feet. She screamed.

Growling, Arcanthus spun, pulling Samantha out of the stairwell with his tail and sidestepping to draw her fully into the hallway. She stumbled from the sudden movement. Before Arc could right her, the onigox attacked again. Arcanthus released Samantha and raised his arms to defend himself from the onigox's rapid, powerful blows, deflecting and dodging as many as he could. Those that connected did so on his arms, which could absorb such punishment indefinitely.

"My boss told me to take you apart one piece at a time," the onigox said as he advanced. "Then I'll let Straek take your terran *ji'tas*. Maybe we'll sample her before we sell her."

A crimson haze fell over Arcanthus's vision, fueled by a furious, intensifying heat within him. He leaned backward sharply and braced himself on his tail to dodge one of the onigox's punches. The onigox overextended his arm; for an instant, his middle was exposed.

Arcanthus kicked the onigox in the gut, pushing forward with both his tail and his other leg. The onigox grunted and doubled over, forced back by Arcanthus's momentum.

Planting his leading foot on the floor, Arcanthus swung his right fist in a quick cross before the onigox could recover. His metal knuckles crunched bone and knocked the onigox's head to the side when they connected with the orange alien's cheek. Arc followed through with the punch, twisting his torso and hips. His tail whipped forward and coiled around his opponent's ankle.

Movement flickered in the edge of his vision—movement inside the stairwell.

"Alk, watch out!" Samantha called.

He dove aside as two members of the illustrious elevator crew opened fire on him from the stairwell; his tail tugged the onigox's leg forward, destroying the orange alien's balance and sending the brute to the floor. The sound of the elevator crew's blasters was amplified by the stairwell's acoustics, making the high, piercing shots almost deafening.

Arcanthus rolled onto his side, flicking his gaze toward Samantha. She'd fallen, but now sat with her back against the hallway wall across from the stairwell entry.

Pushing himself up on an elbow, Arcanthus reached back for his spare auto-blaster.

Samantha, still clutching her weapon with white knuckles, turned the barrel toward the stairwell. The fear never left her wide eyes as she pulled the trigger and screamed. Her voice was broken, pained, angry, *fierce*, conveying all her fears and frustrations without a single word.

Blue-white plasma bolts sprayed from her blaster in a wide cone, their spread increased by the trembling in her arms. There was no counting how many shots she fired; she just held down the trigger.

Arcanthus spun on his back, planted his feet on the wall, and shoved himself over to her. The two members of the elevator crew who'd descended were smoking corpses on the floor of the stairwell. Sam didn't seem to notice.

Sitting up beside Samantha, Arc placed his hands over hers to steady the weapon and ease her finger off the trigger. Her wide-eyed stare remained on the open door for a time before she turned her head toward him. Countless emotions swirled in her warm brown eyes, punctuated but made no more identifiable by her sharp, panting breaths.

A few meters down the hall, the onigox climbed to his feet and growled. "Stand up and face me, sedhi. I'm going to pummel you into a paste."

Perhaps in his younger, more rash days, Arcanthus would've welcomed the challenge of facing such an opponent in hand-to-hand combat, would've thrilled at the opportunity to prove his martial prowess. He knew he'd made some foolish decisions as of late, knew that he'd taken irresponsible risks, but if there was one thing Arcanthus had learned over the years, it was that he had nothing to prove.

He pivoted Samantha's auto-blaster, slipping his finger through the open trigger guard, and fired.

A burst of plasma bolts darted through the onigox and sizzled into the wall behind him. The orange alien glanced down at the holes in his chest, from which small tendrils of smoke curled, and grunted before crashing to the floor.

Arcanthus guided Samantha's hand away from the auto-blaster's grip and met her gaze. "Are you all right?"

Her lips parted, but no sound came out. She looked at the dead onigox, then swung her gaze to the dead aliens in the stairwell, before finally returning her eyes to Arcanthus. "I'm... I just... I'm..."

"Numb?"

She nodded.

"Let's get you up." Arcanthus took hold of her forearms as he rose, helping her to her feet. Her auto-blaster fell to hang from her shoulder by its strap. He slipped his tail around her waist again and kept hold of her arms; she seemed unsteady, and he feared she would fall if he let go. "Can you walk?"

Her tongue slipped out and wet her lips before she pressed them into a tight line. A little crease formed between her brows as they lowered. She nodded again, this time with more confidence.

Tentatively, Arcanthus released her arms. She wobbled for a moment before taking hold of her auto-blaster in both hands. The weapon seemed to help her reclaim her balance. Satisfied that she wouldn't topple over, Arcanthus swung his remaining auto-blaster to his front and glanced up and down the hallway; there was no one else in sight.

He led Samantha toward the rear exit, which was the closer of the two. "We're going to the rear doors. Kiloq, Koroq, how are you two holding up?"

"*Stalemate,*" Kiloq replied over the comms. "*We're outnumbered, and we'll be exposed if we move.*"

"Drakkal, what's your situation?"

"*We can make an opening to get into the car if we need to. That's as good as it's going to get,*" said Drakkal.

Arcanthus nodded to himself. He'd hoped for a smoother rescue, but having come into this without a plan, he'd not expected an easy operation. All he wanted was for Samantha to be safe. Was that really too much to ask? Was the universe really that intent upon screwing with him?

You give me my mate and at the same time throw in a bonus mystery organization that wants to kill me. If I had known, I would've declined the two-for-one and just taken the female.

"Be ready to make that opening, Drak. I'm going to free up Kil and Kor, and you can swing around back and pick us up." He glanced back at Samantha. "Almost there. Almost done."

From down the hallway, there came a soft, high, *familiar* tone.

"Kraasz ka'val," Arcanthus muttered, borrowing Drakkal's favorite Azheran oath as he looked past Sam.

The third member of the elevator crew stepped into the corridor near its far end. Arcanthus whipped around to face the lone alien, swinging Samantha behind him again. He raised his blaster and fired.

Plasma bolts darted down the hallway, hitting the walls, ceiling, and floor. Before any of the shots struck their intended target, the elevator crew's sole survivor shouldered a large weapon. The weapon flashed and roared, and a rocket—trailing smoke and fire—leapt out of its end.

Several of the bolts struck the alien a moment after his weapon fired; the falling body was obscured by the oncoming rocket's trail.

Arcanthus flicked his gaze to either side; there were doors nearby, but they would all be locked, coded to the ID chips of their residents, and he couldn't outrun a rocket. He did all he could; he wrapped his left arm around Samantha, tucking her against his body, let the auto-blaster fall away, and activated his already depleted hardlight shield.

He crouched over his terran and turned his face away.

The impact of the rocket against the shield blasted up his

arm and into his entire body, rattling his bones. A deafening explosion filled the corridor. Arcanthus clutched Samantha, and she clung to him as a wave of heat swept over them, followed by a dust cloud and raining debris.

Chunks of concrete, metal, and other substances clattered onto Arc, much of it striking with as much force as the onigox's punches. He gritted his teeth and held on. Samantha grunted and stiffened for an instant before her arms fell away, and she went limp.

In the ensuing silence, Arcanthus's heartbeat rose in a rapid, panicked rhythm. He blinked away the dust and shifted Samantha in his arm. Her head lolled back. The dust made her face look even paler than before and lightened the color of her hair, heightening its contrast to the dark trail of blood dripping down from her hairline.

"Samantha," he rasped, shaking her gently.

She groaned and almost lifted her head. Her fingers grasped his tail weakly, but she didn't open her eyes.

A blow to the head. How fragile are terrans when it comes to this sort of injury?

Shouts came from down the hallway, their origin shrouded by the slowly dissipating haze. He knew only that they weren't any of his people.

The hardlight projector on Arcanthus's right forearm sparked and powered down. Fortunately, his arm's functions were undamaged. He slipped the arm beneath Samantha's legs and lifted her off the floor, holding her against his chest as he stood.

A few moments before, there'd been a wall and an apartment door on the left side of the hall. Now there was only a gaping, jagged hole. The shouting in the corridor drew nearer.

"Almost there," he whispered, stepping through the breach. "Almost safe."

The apartment was small, set up just like Samantha's, with sparse furnishings spread around a single room—a room blanketed in dust and debris. The window looked out onto the alleyway between this complex and the next one over.

"Drak, new plan. Bring the car around to the alley. I'll meet you there. We'll get the cren brothers after."

The commlink crackled to life, and Drakkal said, *"On the way, Arc."*

Arcanthus stopped a few meters away from the window and lowered Samantha's legs to take hold of the auto-blaster dangling from his shoulder. He fired several bolts through the window. Rather than cracking the glass, they left glowing, oozing holes. But all he wanted was the glass weakened.

Releasing the weapon, he scooped Samantha up and strode forward.

The window gave after two kicks.

Once the buckled glass panel fell away, Arcanthus leapt up onto the windowsill, thrusting his tail out behind him for extra stability. The voices in the hallway were closer than ever.

"Bastard is around here somewhere with that *ji'tas*," someone said from just beyond the gaping hole in the wall.

Arcanthus leapt out the window.

It was a three-meter drop to the ground; his cybernetic legs absorbed the impact, allowing him to remain upright and reducing the jolt to Samantha. He turned his head to see the black hovercar speeding toward him.

The vehicle's rear swung slightly sideways as it came to a sudden halt in front of Arc. The back door swung open, and Sekk'thi waved Arcanthus inside. He passed Samantha in; the two vorgals took her and laid her carefully on the back seat.

"There!" came the shout from behind. Plasma bolts struck the back of Arc's armor and the vehicle around him.

Arcanthus dove into the hovercar. Sekk'thi slammed the door shut behind him as the vehicle accelerated.

Urgand was already kneeling beside Samantha, his medical kit open. Despite the size of his hand, his fingers were gentle as he parted her hair to check the wound on her head. In this crowded cab, around these aliens, she looked so small and frail.

Arcanthus fell to his knees next to the vorgal. His chest was tight, his body numb, and a dull ringing still undercut the thumping of his own heart in his ears. He took Samantha's hand in his own and squeezed it. She didn't respond to his touch.

"Swing around back so we can pick up the cren." Arcanthus's voice sounded distant and echoey, like a fading memory. "How bad is it, Urgand?"

The vorgal frowned. "Hard to say. Never treated a terran before. But the medpod back home should have her species' specs loaded. It'll tell us more."

Arcanthus settled his gaze on her face and curled his free hand into a fist.

"Any idea who those cowardly fuckers were?" Thargen asked.

"No, but we're going to find out who the fuck they are," Arcanthus said through clenched teeth, "and make sure they regret this decision for the brief remainder of their lives."

ELEVEN

Something feathered across Samantha's cheek. The faint sensation persisted, pulling her out of an abyss-like, dreamless sleep and easing her into consciousness. Her brows furrowed; the delicate touch shifted to them, soothing away their tension. Something else stroked her leg, moving from ankle to knee and back again.

"Samantha?" The familiar voice caressed her name and drew her the rest of the way to wakefulness.

Her eyelids fluttered open. She was looking up at a ceiling lit with a red ambience. Blue lines raced across it in intricate, angled patterns, never curving as they faded and retraced themselves ceaselessly. It was an oddly calming display but did not counteract her immense confusion.

Where am I?

The gentle touch shifted back to her cheek, following it down to trace the line of her jaw. Now that she was awake, it startled her; she flinched away and turned her head.

Samantha's breath caught in her throat, and her eyes widened.

She lay on a huge bed with dark red bedding, and Alkorin was reclining beside her. He was atop the blanket—just like her—on his side, his torso propped up on one elbow. Fortunately, she was fully clothed, but Alkorin wore only a black loincloth.

This was the first time she'd seen him in person without a robe. His holographic image had ended just below his chest during their visual call. For a few moments, she was unable to look away from the lean muscles of his abdomen, chest, and shoulders—or rather, *shoulder*. His right shoulder was covered by the uppermost portion of his armored prosthesis, which somehow made him more alluring. Her eyes followed the lines of his *qal* until they settled on his lips.

He smiled; it wasn't the sexy, seductive smile she'd come to crave—though she didn't think any of his smiles could be not sexy—but a relieved one.

"How do you feel?" he asked.

"Where am I?"

Alkorin turned his head to sweep his gaze over the ceiling and walls before meeting her eyes again. "My bedroom."

"Your—"

His bedroom.

Samantha looked around. The walls were black, sporting the same ever-changing patterns as the ceiling, though they were restricted to smaller panels between cones of soft, white light. Dark, satiny cloths hung on the walls at regular intervals, shimmering faintly in the subtly changing glow. If she went by human standards, this bed would've been considered...well, a triple-king, or maybe an *emperor*. It was massive.

And comfortable.

Why was she here? *How* did she get—

The attack. She remembered the aliens who had questioned her, remembered Alkorin coming to save her, remembered gunfire. She remembered the ceiling falling...

Samantha raised a hand and touched the top of her head. There was no lump despite the crust of dried blood in her hair, and only one spot was a little tender. She felt perfectly fine, which was surprising considering she knew she'd suffered a head wound severe enough to have knocked her out—it had been more than enough to have caused a concussion.

Alkorin brushed his fingertips across the back of her hand. "We healed you in the medpod. Fortunately, your injury wasn't serious, so it didn't take long."

"What happened?" she asked, lowering her arm. "Who were they? Why were they looking for you?"

His tail—which had been stroking her leg—curled around her calf. His smile tilted, becoming a gentle smirk. "Some people decided to use you as bait to lure me out, I don't know, and I don't know. But we're working on figuring it all out."

"But...*why*? You're a...a...a document verifier, aren't you? What could you have done to have people shooting at you?"

Arcanthus's smile shifted into something rakish. "Well, you know how you've been somewhat vague in answering some of my questions? I might've been somewhat vague in explaining what I do. And...who I am."

Unease bloomed in Samantha, rapidly thickening as it spread. She backed away from him.

No. Not again. Please no, not him.

He flattened his hand on the bed, pushed himself up, and curled his other arm around her waist. Her attempt to resist was futile; he dragged Sam closer and positioned himself over her, caging her between his arms. His dark hair fell in a silken curtain around his face, its tips tickling her cheeks.

Intending to push him away, Samantha flattened her palms against his chest—his warm, hard, enticing chest. Something small and hard pressed against her hand; his nipple piercing.

Her will to resist suddenly faded.

Still wearing his mischievous expression, Alkorin stared down into her eyes. "Just listen, Samantha. Allow me at least that much. I promise it's not as bad as it may seem. Or at least I think it's not as bad."

Samantha swallowed thickly. Despite her unease, despite the way he'd trapped her with his body, she...trusted him. She wasn't sure what to make of that. Was she doomed to repeat the same mistakes over and over? Was she doomed to suffer simply because she was a poor judge of character?

But he hasn't done anything to hurt me.

Alkorin had been her lifeline since she'd met him, her protector, her...friend.

"Tell me the truth," she said, forcing herself to hold his gaze.

His lips parted, and his tongue slipped out briefly. There was hunger in his eyes, and his body seemed to heat. The markings on his skin glowed a little brighter.

"Alkorin is one of several aliases I utilize to mask my identity," he said. "My name—my *true* name—is Arcanthus."

Samantha's brows lowered, and she frowned. He'd lied about his name? It felt, suddenly, like the very foundations of their relationship were in danger of shattering. She recalled when she'd first entered his hovercar—Drakkal had called him *Arc* before Alkorin interrupted him. She hadn't thought anything of it at the time.

"Why?" she asked.

Holding himself up on one arm, he moved a hand to her face and slowly combed his fingers into her hair. "Because I'm a criminal, Samantha, and it's safest if other criminals—and the authorities—do not know who I really am. Information is power in my world. I prefer to control the information that's available concerning myself. Very few know my real name, only those I trust...and I trust you. I should have told you sooner."

There was so much she should've been concerned with in that moment—that he'd lied to her, that he could very easily harm her, that he'd just admitted to being a criminal—but she *understood*. What he said made sense; he'd just been protecting himself.

"You had no reason to trust me," she said.

"When they came and asked you about me, what did you tell them?"

Samantha's heart skipped a beat. "I-I didn't tell them anything. I swear. I couldn't—"

Arcanthus pressed his thumb over her lips, silencing her. He held it there for a moment before he brushed it back and forth across her lower lip, following its path with his eyes.

A shiver coursed through Sam's body.

"I believe you, Samantha. You risked harm to yourself to protect me. That is more deserving of my trust than anything I can think of." He lifted his gaze to hers. "Which you are *never* to do again, is that clear?"

She nodded, though she knew she'd put herself in danger to protect him if a similar situation occurred. She'd risk herself for him again and again, even having learned of his deception. "Do you...kill people? I mean, apart from what happened at the complex..."

Oh God, I killed people.

The thought struck her with a blast of shock and guilt.

"I...I shot them, Alkorin. I..."

"Shh," he soothed. "You did what was necessary to keep us safe. You were very brave, little terran."

Brave.

That word cut through her shock. Had she been brave? She remembered being terrified, being nearly paralyzed with fear—both for her own life and Alk's.

Arcanthus, not Alkorin.

She hadn't thought they'd escape alive. And when those aliens had reached the bottom of the stairwell and fired their weapons at him... She'd simply reacted.

"I was?" she asked, her fingers curling against his chest.

Arcanthus nodded. "You were. Bravery is not a lack of fear but acting *despite* fear." He grinned, flashing his fangs. "I am proud of you."

The voice that always haunted her—calling her worthless and weak every moment of every day—fell silent for the first time in years.

"I have killed people. I told you I was a fighter before I came to Arthos, and that is true. I killed people then and I still do, from time to time, when they pose a threat to the safety of myself and my crew. And I do so without remorse." His smile faded, and a hard, intense light entered his eyes. "I'm not a good person, Samantha...but I would *never* harm you. Never."

Samantha stared into his eyes. She believed him without having to think about it. Everything he'd done for her, each of his actions on her behalf, had been to keep her safe. James would never have admitted anything like this to her. He would never have revealed his true self, not like Arcanthus was doing now. James had always blamed his emotions, or drugs, or *her* for his behavior. She didn't think he was even capable of acknowledging his responsibility for his actions.

Arc was being honest about things he'd done and would do again. About what he wouldn't do.

"I believe you," she said.

Relief softened his expression. "I wanted to tell you sooner, Samantha. I wanted nothing more than to hear my name from your lips, but I couldn't. I couldn't risk scaring you away. I couldn't bear the thought of putting you in danger...but it happened anyway."

Samantha still couldn't quite understand what he saw in her, why he considered her worth these risks.

"Besides...killing, what else do you do?" she asked.

"I'm a forger and a hacker. I craft false identities and install them in identification chips so people can fool Consortium systems." He grinned and tilted his chin up. "And I am the pinnacle of my craft."

Despite everything, Samantha laughed; somehow, he made arrogance charming.

His tail slithered a little higher up her leg, its tip brushing the back of her knee through her pants. "I think that has become my favorite sound," he said in a deep rumble.

He lowered his face, and Samantha stilled, eyes widening. His mouth stopped only centimeters from hers. His nearness, combined with his touch, his scent, and his heat, made it difficult for Sam to breathe, made it difficult for her to form a coherent thought. He overwhelmed her senses.

His eyes focused on her mouth. "I've decided to make it my goal to hear you laugh as often as possible, little terran. It drives me mad."

He settled the weight of his body on top of her, and Samantha's heart quickened when she felt the hard evidence of his desire through the fabric of his loincloth.

"Are there any other secrets you've kept?" she asked quickly, her cheeks flaming.

Arcanthus lifted his head slightly and cleared his throat. "I can't be expected to reveal *all* my secrets...but there is one pertaining to you that I should share. Our first meeting wasn't a chance occurrence."

Samantha's brow furrowed. "What do you mean?"

"I was following you the day we met."

"*What?*"

Arcanthus slid his thumb back to her lower lip and

resumed lazily stroking it. "I'd been keeping track of the terrans immigrating to Arthos when I found your file. The moment I saw your image, I wanted you—*needed* you. I had to find you, had to meet you. And when you stepped out of your apartment building and I had my first glimpse of you in the flesh, I knew you were the most beautiful thing I would ever see. So, I followed you."

Her lips parted, but no sound emerged. This big, beautiful, dangerous, wicked sedhi wanted *her*. Hearing him say it with such vehemence was startling.

Though she was shocked by his revelation, she was also thankful. If he hadn't been there that day, she could have died, could've been trampled under the feet of aliens who would never have given her a second thought. Sam didn't want to think about what could've happened when that gang had accosted her.

She offered him a small smile. "I...guess I should be glad you were, even though that *is* a little creepy."

Arcanthus grinned and brushed the backs of his metal fingers down the side of her face. "I'd prefer to think of it as devoted."

He dipped his head lower and slanted his mouth over hers.

Samantha's eyes flared briefly before she gave in to him and, eyelids drifting shut, returned the kiss in full. His tongue traced the seam of her lips, and she parted them to allow him entry. He groaned; the sound vibrated from his chest into her palms. Tentatively, she slid her hands up until they curled around his shoulders, one settled over flesh and the other over metal. His tongue coaxed hers into a sensual dance. She joined hesitantly, licking his fangs.

His kiss was scintillating, demanding, and seductive. Pulses of pleasure spread outward from her belly, leaving her breathless and wanting.

Wanting *him*.

She must have made a sound—a soft moan, or perhaps a whimper—because Arcanthus broke the kiss and pushed himself up on his hands.

Samantha looked up at him through half-lidded eyes.

He stared down at her. His slitted pupils were dilated, his yellow irises bright, and lust burned in his intense gaze. His glowing *qal* heavily contrasted his dark gray skin.

"I will never tire of your taste, my flower." His center eye remained locked with her gaze as the other two dipped, and he slowly licked his lower lip. "And I yearn to taste ever more."

Those words sparked a surge of arousal in Samantha. She pressed her thighs together, desperate to alleviate the ache blooming between them. James had never done *that* to her. He'd said it was disgusting, always in a tone that implied *she* was disgusting, and it had become just another degradation she'd begun to believe. But the way Arcanthus was looking at her now...

She didn't feel disgusting at all. She felt wanted.

Desired.

He leaned closer again, and anticipation fluttered in her belly. His lips stopped a hair's breadth away from hers.

"But I fear if I continue, I'll be unable to stop myself. You've had enough excitement already, I'm sure." Arcanthus unraveled his tail from her leg, pushed himself away, and slid off the bed, leaving the air above her suddenly cold and empty.

Wait...what?

He waved toward a door across from the foot of the bed. "There's a bathroom in there. Feel free to bathe. I've set clean clothes on the counter for you. They should fit." Arcanthus walked toward another door, this one to the left of the bed, with his tail swaying behind him. He slowed to glance at her over his shoulder, eyes gleaming ravenously. "Let me know if you require *anything.*"

Samantha watched in stunned silence as he exited the room and the door slid closed behind him.

The breath whooshed out of her in a bewildered laugh, and she covered her face with her hands.

"What just happened?" she asked.

Her cheeks were warm, her lips kiss-swollen, her skin overly sensitive. Her body felt bereft.

She was...horny.

Her pussy pulsed so badly that she was tempted to slip her hand between her thighs and touch herself. She hadn't experienced that impulse in years—not since she was a teenager exploring her body as she imagined her crush from school. Whatever sexual fantasies she'd once held had burned to ash while she was with James. He'd been her first, her only, and God had it *hurt.* He'd never been gentle with Sam, even before he started deliberately hurting her.

He'd never caressed her, had barely kissed her, and she couldn't recall a single time when he'd spoken in such a manner that his words alone were enough to arouse her. What she'd just experienced with Arcanthus...it was new, and it left her all kinds of confused.

Samantha lifted her hands from her face and paused when she saw her sleeves; they were coated in dust. She sat up. The sudden change in position blasted her with a wave of dizziness. Squeezing her eyes shut and pressing a hand to her forehead, she rode out the wave, forcing herself to breathe slowly until it passed. Once her head stopped spinning, she opened her eyes and looked down at herself.

She was a mess.

Understatement of the year.

Her clothes were filthy, covered in pale dust and sporting a few new tears and scorch marks. She couldn't help but wonder what her face looked like.

"Well, it's no wonder why he left," Samantha muttered, pinching the fabric of her shirt and stretching it out to stare at it in disgust.

Scooting to the edge of the bed, she swung her feet to the floor and rose slowly. There was no dizziness, no pain, not even any discomfort. The aches she'd collected over the last few days were just...*gone*.

She made her way to the door across from the foot of the bed and pressed the button. The door opened silently. Samantha's eyes widened, and her jaw fell as she beheld the chamber beyond.

The bathroom walls and ceiling were crafted of a black, marble-like material, through which ran glowing blue lines—but instead of tracing endless paths across the surfaces, these lines wavered and undulated to cast an ambient light on the walls not unlike sunlight reflecting off water.

A large rectangular pool lay in the center of the room, illuminated from within by soft blue light. The steps leading into it were positioned on the side closest to the bathroom entrance. Samantha guessed the rectangular panel suspended above the far end of the pool was the shower. The black, bowl-shaped thing in the corner was likely the toilet, and nearby it stood a wide counter with a deep, built-in sink. A tall mirror ran the length of the counter.

Sam's imagination produced an image of Arcanthus standing in front of that mirror, flexing and admiring himself, and she couldn't hold in her laughter.

She stepped through the open doorway, and sparkling lights came to life on the ceiling. Samantha turned her face toward them; they were like a field of white and blue stars, twinkling above an ocean. It was beautiful.

A pile of folded clothing rested atop the counter with a pair of slip-on shoes atop it and a hairbrush, toothbrush, and toothpaste beside it. Seeing those things, things she'd so often taken for granted, produced a grateful pang in her chest. She had nothing at the moment, and this little gesture meant the world to her.

Her sedhi was arrogant, but he was also kind and considerate.

My sedhi.

Samantha clenched her fists at her sides and bit her lip. She could still taste him on it.

Was he hers?

How long would his desire for her last? Was he only interested because she was part of a species considered rare and exotic here in Arthos? Would his fascination with her wither and fade?

Worthless. Weak.

She gritted her teeth and shook her head sharply.

"No!"

She wasn't weak. Arcanthus had called her *brave*. She hadn't cowered, whimpered, or cried when he'd come to save her; she'd followed his orders, had taken the blaster, and...

I killed them.

That knowledge made her sick to her stomach, but she'd done what was necessary. She'd persevered in the face of danger. She'd overcome her fear. And, when it mattered most, she'd defended someone she cared about.

I am strong.

She'd come to Arthos for a fresh start, for a new life, but what had she done to initiate that apart from changing her surroundings? When she'd stepped off that ship, she was still a scared young woman who was too afraid to speak up, who was frightened of everyone and everything around her. The same young woman who hid herself beneath baggy clothing. If she wanted a new life, she needed to make the effort. She needed to change.

She...needed to let go of the past.

James was countless light years away; he couldn't harm her anymore. Why was she still letting him suffocate her mentally? Why was she still letting him chip away at her soul?

Drawing in a shuddering breath, Samantha crossed to the toilet and relieved herself. It took a few moments to figure out the controls, but once she was clean, she tugged her pants up and walked to the sink. A stranger greeted her in the mirror.

Samantha rarely looked at her reflection. She'd always been afraid to stare into her own increasingly lifeless eyes, afraid to witness her sadness head-on, afraid to see the bruises and cuts James left on her body.

The woman staring at her now had the same large, dark eyes she'd known all her life, but there was something new within them, something in defiance of the sadness that still dominated her gaze—sparks of hope glimmered in the darkness.

And through those sparks of hope, she could see deeper— Samantha was still in there. She hadn't been defeated yet.

She picked up the toothbrush and toothpaste, squeezing some of the latter onto the former, and activated the brush. Its gentle vibration tickled her gums; she found it oddly relaxing. As she was finishing, she noticed a button atop the counter, nearly nestled against the mirror. She pressed it.

A small section of the mirror slid up to reveal a square storage space. Smiling, she placed her toothbrush inside, standing it next to another toothbrush that *had* to be Arcanthus's.

After closing the panel, she turned toward the pool and approached it. Her apartment only had a stand-up shower. This was impossibly luxurious in comparison.

She stripped, wincing at the small puff of dust that rose from her clothes when she dropped them on the floor. Her hair couldn't have been much better. She removed her socks last, and she was surprised to find the marble-like floor warm under the soles of her feet.

Moving to the edge of the pool, Samantha dipped her toes into the water. It was comfortably hot with wisps of steam rising from its surface, and its scent suggested it was already filled with some sort of cleaning agent. She descended the steps. The waterline was at her belly button when her feet touched the bottom of the pool. Smiling, she skimmed her hands over the water's surface before ducking down to submerge her shoulders.

She moved slowly toward the overhead panel, relishing the water's warmth. There were buttons along the nearby edge of the pool; she pressed one. Soft blue lights came on overhead. A moment later, hot water rained from the panel. Sam stood up, closed her eyes, and tilted her head back, content to let the water wash over her.

After a few minutes, she returned to the controls, and a bit of fiddling revealed another secret compartment. Its contents— a small collection of soaps and shampoos—rose from the floor beside the pool. She opened one of the bottles, and a little thrill coursed through her; its contents smelled like Arcanthus. Returning to the shower, she used the soaps to wash herself, paying particular attention to her hair. Sam loved that the scent on her skin would serve as a constant reminder of Arc.

She remained beneath the shower long after she'd rinsed, enjoying the hot water cascading around her body. For the first time in a long while, she was relaxed, and it made her reluctant to leave. In the end, it was only the knowledge that Arcanthus was waiting for her that lured her out.

When she exited the pool, the ceiling and floor suddenly

changed; each lit up with gentle while light, and the air around Sam warmed. It only lasted for a few seconds, but she was surprised to discover that the moisture had evaporated from her skin and hair when it was done.

Samantha walked to the counter and picked up the clothing Arc had laid out for her. She swallowed thickly at the sight of it. "Oh…"

For years, she'd dressed in baggy, shapeless clothes that hid her body. The dress in her hands was *nothing* like that. It was refined, form-fitting, *revealing*.

Her throat constricted as she glanced back at the pile of soiled clothes on the floor. She was tempted to put them back on, but they'd only get her dirty again.

"I am strong."

She returned her attention to the dress, closed her eyes, and released a long, slow breath.

"I can do this. It's just a dress."

Before she had a chance to change her mind, Sam slipped on the dainty, matching panties that had been bundled with the dress and stepped into the long garment. She slid the dress up her body and slipped her arms into the sleeves. Once it was in place, she glanced at herself in the mirror.

Samantha froze.

The dress was a deep red, making her skin look porcelain in comparison. The fabric was at once sheer and silky, flaunting the body beneath while concealing the details. The neckline— or lack thereof—plunged to her midriff, displaying a strip of flesh from her neck to just above her belly button. The slit running up the side of the long, flowing skirt ran nearly to her hip, baring her right leg to her upper thigh.

It was beautiful.

She *felt* beautiful.

But she also felt exposed.

She'd never worn anything like this—not even close—and she was scared as hell.

Her dark hair hung around her shoulders and down her back in long, loose waves, and her lips were still reddened from Arcanthus's kiss. A shiver coursed through her at the memory of his mouth coming down upon hers.

Picking up the shoes from the counter, Samantha slipped them onto her feet. Just like everything else, they fit perfectly.

Exactly how much did Arcanthus know about her?

Leaving the bathroom, Sam made her way to the door through which Arc had exited the bedroom. She hesitated as her hand was on its way to the control button. Would he be upset if she left the room and wandered around?

No; he hadn't told her to stay put, and she wasn't his prisoner. He would've said something if he didn't want her leaving the room.

Besides, she was curious. She wanted to know what was on the other side of this door, wanted to explore the place Arcanthus called home.

She pressed the button, and the door slid open.

Samantha stepped into the hallway beyond only to come to an abrupt halt when someone—a rather *large* someone—positioned himself in front of her. She released a startled gasp and retreated a couple steps, lifting her gaze.

The male's face was familiar, and that familiarity curbed her instinct to flee back into the bedroom.

He was the yellow-eyed cren who'd returned the package she dropped on her way home yesterday. The cren who'd purchased food from Sarai's booth.

"I-I know you," she said, brows falling low.

"I know you, too," the cren replied. "Samantha, yeah?"

Samantha nodded.

"Name's Kiloq. Boss told me to bring you to him when you got out."

"Boss? Ar... Er, Alkorin?"

Kiloq snickered. "It's okay, terran. Anyone he trusts enough to work in this part of the compound knows his name is Arcanthus."

Relief eased her tension. For a moment, she'd feared she had already violated Arc's trust by revealing his name. "Oh, okay. Good. You've...you've been following me, haven't you?"

"Yeah. He told us to keep you safe."

"Us?"

"Me and my brother, Koroq."

She waited for the flare of anger that should've risen in her gut. Arcanthus had selected Sam from her identification file, stalked her, lied to her, and sent some of his men to keep an eye on her. None of that was okay. None of that was *right*. And yet...she wasn't upset, wasn't angry, wasn't scared.

Because Arcanthus still felt right to her.

Being with him felt right.

She was glad for what he'd done; this city might well have swallowed her whole were it not for his intervention. Maybe she would've eventually found her way, her place, but there was a good chance she might've ended up kidnapped or dead first.

"It's nice to meet you, Kiloq," she said, offering the cren a smile.

He returned the smile. Despite the three-centimeter-long tusks protruding from his lower jaw, the expression had unexpected warmth to it. When she'd first encountered Kiloq, she'd been terrified of him. She realized now that he'd had a friendly, gentle air about him even then. She didn't doubt he was capable of ferocity, but that was true of Arcanthus as well, wasn't it?

"My brother, Koroq, is around somewhere," Kiloq said. "He looks like me, only uglier."

Samantha laughed.

He chuckled. "Boss is expecting you, terran. Come on."

The cren turned and walked along the hallway.

She followed him. The soft flow of air over the bare skin of her chest and right leg as she moved reminded her of what she was wearing, and her cheeks burned.

Kiloq led her through several long, high-ceilinged hallways, all of which exhibited a strange blend of the sleek luxury and wealth on display in Arcanthus's room and a gritty, industrial aesthetic. The bare, unpolished metal and dark concrete somehow paired well with the patterned crimson carpeting and elegant but practical light fixtures. Most of the doors they passed were large and looked durable, but they were made less imposing by the intricate isometric designs etched upon their faces.

The place was like a military bunker that had been purchased by a very rich individual with a taste for extravagant simplicity in his décor.

They turned down another corridor, which ended at a lone door. Kiloq tapped the control panel beside the doorframe.

"Yes?" asked Arcanthus through the speaker.

"Samantha is here to see you, boss," Kiloq replied.

The door slid open. The cren stood aside and gestured her onward.

Samantha remained in place for a moment, glancing at the cren before turning her full attention to the doorway. She'd been excited at the prospect of seeing Arcanthus again, but now that she was here, anxiety sank its claws into her heart.

I am strong. Even if I don't feel it.

Taking in a deep breath, Samantha stepped past Kiloq and crossed the threshold.

The doorway led her into a large, long, rectangular chamber. Several huge fish tanks, filled with creatures both vaguely familiar and utterly alien, were built into the wall across from Sam, separated from each other by sections of wall with soft red and purple lights that gave the room a moody luminescence. The strength of those lights was enhanced by the dark floors and furnishings. At the far end of the chamber to the left stood a huge blast door. A carpet, decorated with isometric patterns that were the same colors as the lights, ran down the center of the room. It was flanked by long, low couches on either side.

"You've finally come. I was getting ready to join you in the bath," Arcanthus said, calling her attention to the right.

At that end of the room, a set of wide, low steps led up to a raised platform. The desk set at the platform's front edge was about half the width of the platform, and it was covered with at least a dozen monitors and holo screens. More screens lined the nearby walls, interrupted only by larger equipment she couldn't identify.

Arcanthus stood just to the side of the desk. He wore a silky, royal purple robe; the garment hung open to reveal the muscles of his lean torso and his dark loincloth. His lopsided grin made her knees weak.

What was it that made fangs so damn sexy?

It's not the fangs, it's him.

The door closed softly behind her. She glanced over her shoulder to see an unbroken section of wall between two more fish tanks, displaying not even the slightest hint of an opening.

She faced Arcanthus again. There would be no escaping him.

And I don't want to.

He descended the steps at a leisurely pace, his tail swaying behind him, his glowing eyes locked on her.

"How was it? The bath?" He raked his gaze down her body, all the way to her toes, and ran it slowly back up.

"It was...wonderful," she replied breathlessly. "I've never seen anything like it."

"You look exquisite, little terran." His eyes, gleaming with desire, finally met hers again. "And Kiloq got to see you in that dress first. It should've been *me*." His lips pulled back with that last word, baring his fangs.

The hints of jealousy and possessiveness in his tone sent a thrill through her. She blushed and shifted on her feet, squeezing her thighs together. Her earlier arousal hadn't quite subsided.

He lifted an arm and gestured to the nearby couches. "Please. Sit. I want you to be comfortable."

Samantha slowly walked toward him, self-consciously clasping her hands in front of her stomach. When she neared the end of the closest couch, she turned and sat down upon it, keeping her eyes on him throughout. Her skirt parted, revealing her pale thigh; she tugged the material back over it and pinned it in place with a hand.

She was caught by surprise when Arcanthus strolled over and eased down on the cushion beside her. Sam wasn't sure why the move caught her off guard. Arcanthus wasn't the sort of person who would've seated himself on the couch across from hers, and she *knew* that.

He stretched an arm along the backrest behind her shoulders. His tail slipped between her body and the backrest, curled around her hips, and draped across her thighs, forcing her to lift her hands. Not sure of what to do, she settled her palms atop it. The skin of his tail was as firm, warm, and smooth as that of his chest.

"What is this place?" she asked. That was a safe subject, right?

Arcanthus slid a little closer, pressing his thigh against hers. "This is my workshop. I spend most of my time in here."

"Where you...forge identities?"

"Where I put my considerable *talents* to use."

Those words deflated her. She knew he was talking about what he could do for her, about what he wanted to do to her, but she couldn't ignore the darker implication of what he'd said. Of course he'd had other women here. A man like Arcanthus could've had almost anyone he wanted, and he'd likely slept with many females. She wasn't naïve enough to believe he hadn't.

Her chest constricted with disappointment and jealousy. Would she be just another name on his list of trophies? An exotic lay to brag about after he was done?

She stared down at his tail. "Did...did you choose the others the way you chose me?"

Arcanthus stiffened, and his tail twitched. "No, Samantha."

He curled his finger beneath her chin and turned her face toward him, forcing her eyes to meet his. There was a new intensity in his gaze. "*Nothing* about you—or how you've come to be here—is like anything I've ever done. You are the first I sought out personally. The first I've taken anywhere. The first I've fought for. You're also the first to know my true name and the first to have slept in my bed. And you will be the *only*."

Her stomach fluttered, but she furrowed her brow. "Why? Why me?"

Arcanthus stroked her jaw with his thumb and leaned his face closer, his lips nearly touching her ear. "Because one look at you was all it took to know that you're mine."

Samantha stilled. Her breath quickened, her heart raced, and ice crept through her veins. Her vision dimmed.

You are mine, James growled in her head. *You exist only for my pleasure.*

She could feel James's breath, hot against her face, could feel his rough hands around her throat as he pounded his cock into her again and again, could feel the burning, tearing pain of his assault.

"Samantha!"

Sam's eyes snapped open; she hadn't realized she'd closed them. Arcanthus was kneeling in front of her, his hands cupping her cheeks, his torso between her legs. She searched his face for something to focus on as despair threatened to overwhelm her.

Not James. He's not James. He's not James.

"Someone hurt you," Arcanthus said, his voice lower and deeper than it had been a few moments before. His center eye was narrowed to a slit. "Someone is *still* hurting you."

Faint tremors coursed through his hands. She wouldn't have thought it possible, considering his arms were cybernetic, but she couldn't deny it was happening. His dark brows were angled down harshly, his nostrils flared, and his lips peeled back to reveal his fangs.

For an instant, cold fear crystallized in her chest; she'd made him angry, just like she'd so often made James angry. But Arcanthus was much larger and infinitely stronger than James. She had no hope of defending herself against him.

It was the gleam in Arc's eyes that gave her pause and brought her to her senses. It was tinged with a helplessness that she knew all too well. She realized suddenly that he was not angry at her, but for her, angry for what had been done to her.

"Tell me, Samantha."

There was a pleading note in his voice, a hint of desperation. She guessed that few people, if any, had ever heard it.

"He was my fiancé," she said quietly.

Arc smoothed his hands down her arms to caress her elbows. "What did he do, little terran?"

Samantha held his gaze and took in a deep, shuddering breath. "My father died three days after my eighteenth birthday. It was a construction site accident. I was at work when I got the call. He was just...gone, without any chance to say goodbye. He was the only family I had left after my grandmother passed away two years prior. It was...too much. Too soon. I mean, there's *never* a good time to lose someone you love, but..."

Arc raised a hand and wiped a tear from her cheek. She hadn't realized she was crying.

"Go on, little one," he said.

"I fell into a deep depression. And no matter how much I worked—and I worked hours and hours just to keep my mind busy, just so I didn't have to *think*—I couldn't keep up with the debts his death passed on to me. I was losing the only home I'd ever known. I was losing...everything.

"And then he came. James. He was...good. So good. He treated me nicely, said all the right things. So when the house was finally taken away, I...I wasn't too upset because I had him. He gave me a place to stay, a place to call home—with him. He even asked me to marry him, and I said yes. I never cared that he had money. He was kind to me, and he made me feel safe. And I thought that I..."

The words lodged in her throat. She couldn't say them, didn't want to. She thought she'd loved James, but she hadn't. She'd loved the mask he had worn in those early days. And she'd just been a lonely, grieving, innocent woman.

The perfect prey for a man like him.

She felt something brush her leg and glanced down to find Arc's tail curling around her ankle. The gesture seemed...possessive.

"After that, things changed. *He* changed. It wasn't subtle either. But I...I had no experience, no knowledge of how things were supposed to be. My mom died when I was just a baby, and my grandmother was elderly. My father was too embarrassed to talk to me about things like that, and I was so insecure throughout my adolescence that I didn't have any friends to confide in. How was I to know?"

She sniffled, and more tears spilled down her cheeks. "It started that first night I moved in. We were getting ready for bed, and he was touching me. I was...excited. I was going to-to lose my vir-virginity to—" The words caught in her throat, blocked by the burning tightness brought on by her crying.

Arcanthus's thumbs, so gentle despite being made of metal, could not staunch the flow of her tears, which blurred her vision. He was reduced to a gray and purple blotch as he moved to sit beside her. When one of his arms slipped around her waist and the other beneath her legs, she didn't fight him. She couldn't.

He pulled Samantha onto his lap, guided her head to rest against his shoulder—his strong, solid, flesh-and-blood shoulder—and held her, one arm wrapped around her while his other hand smoothed down her hair.

Once her shuddering breaths eased, she continued. "It hurt. I knew it would hurt a little the first time, I knew that much, but oh God, it hurt *so* much. I told him to stop, but he didn't listen. I felt torn up inside, and he just kept...kept... He only stopped because I vomited, and then he was angry, disgusted. He hit me. He called me weak, worthless, and so many other names.

"He said I was his, th-that I existed only for his pleasure. He used me like that for three years. We never got married, but he knew he didn't have to marry me to keep me trapped. I had nowhere else to go, no one to turn to. And the more he wore me down, the more confident he became that I *couldn't* leave. His family had money, a lot more than I ever realized, and connections all over the place. I couldn't even go to the police, because his father was friends with the commissioner, and I didn't have any money to my name. He made sure of that.

"He'd apologize sometimes, tell me that he only acted that way because he loved me so much, because he was obsessed with me. *I* drove him mad. *I* made him act that way. But the only times he really eased up on me were when he brought another woman home, but...sometimes he'd force me to join, too."

Samantha fell silent. In that silence, she noticed three things—Arcanthus was no longer petting her hair, his body was trembling, and there was a loud, vibrating growl emanating from his chest. She lifted her head to find his markings aglow as though they were on fire. His eyes were focused elsewhere, and his pupils had contracted to such thin slits that they were almost swallowed by his blazing irises.

"Arc?" she asked in a small voice.

His third eye was the first to look at her, followed a second later by the other two. His features were strained; his lips were pressed into a tight line, his brow creased, his jaw muscles bunched. Then he brushed his fingers over her cheek, and his expression softened. "Would that I could've spared you all that suffering, my precious little flower."

His touch, combined with his words, was like a soothing balm to her wounded soul. "He's gone now. I'm here."

"But he's not gone. You've carried him with you across the universe, Samantha. Even if he were dead, which he *deserves* to be, you haven't yet left him behind."

Samantha looked away from him in shame. Arc was right. She had carried James with her.

"You don't have to hold on to him anymore, little terran. Cast him into the void."

"I'm trying, but—"

Arcanthus turned her face toward his again. "Let me help you, Samantha."

"How?"

"You deserve pleasure. You deserve ecstasy." A husky tone had entered his voice. He flicked the tip of his tail across the back of her knee. "And I would be delighted to provide it to you. Let me erase his stain from your memory."

Heat spread across her face. "I-I don't know if I can. I never felt…"

"You're sitting with the finest male specimen in Arthos, little terran. You have no idea of the pleasure I can make you feel." He tipped his head toward her, brushing his nose across her hair. His breath was warm against her ear.

He inhaled deeply.

She shivered, and her heart quickened.

"I'll offer you a deal, Samantha. Set aside your doubt, your hesitance, this one time. Let me *show* you. Let me make you *feel*. If you don't enjoy it…I won't push any further."

Could she agree? Could she let go of her fear and experience what Arc was offering?

In that moment, she wanted him more than *anything*. He was the embodiment of temptation, the epitome of seduction, and a simple glance from him was all it took to ignite a fire in her core.

Arcanthus flicked his tongue against the sensitive spot just beneath her ear, and Samantha gasped as tingles of arousal spread through her.

"What is your answer, my flower?"

"What do you get if you win?" she whispered.

"*You*."

TWELVE

Samantha pulled back and turned her head to look at Arcanthus. The desirous light in his eyes, paired with his wicked smile, promised unimaginable pleasure. Not for the first time, she couldn't help likening his looks to a demon—a demon of lascivious delight.

I'm about to make a deal with the devil...and I've never wanted anything more.

She kept her eyes locked with his. "Yes."

"Oh, my beautiful little terran," he purred, "I will open the universe to you."

He trailed his hand down from her face, his fingertips trekking over her cheek and jaw to the sensitive skin of her neck. It moved lower still, a feather-light touch that sent tingles across her flesh, brushing over her shoulder and arm, and finally stopped on her hip, opposite his other hand. The thin fabric of her dress was the only barrier between his palms and her skin; his heat radiated through the material, but the separation was too much.

She'd never felt so restricted by clothing.

Arcanthus lifted her off his lap and shifted beneath her, turning himself so he was leaning back against the armrest of the sofa. She was facing away from him when he lowered her onto his lap again.

"Lie back, Samantha."

Samantha looked at him over her shoulder. "But don't you need to...face me?"

"This is about you." Arcanthus snaked his arm around her middle and drew her backward until she lay against his chest with her head on his shoulder. He turned his face toward her, running the tip of his nose over her ear. "Don't focus on me. Focus on my touch, on what it makes you feel. Do not be afraid of your own body."

How could she not focus on him? His sensual voice filled her ears, his hard body and arms had her wrapped in their warmth, and his delicious scent enveloped her.

He flattened his palms on her lower abdomen and slowly slid them up. His fingers crossed the low neckline of her dress, sweeping warm metal over her skin and making it quiver. His hands moved higher and higher until they cradled the undersides of her breasts.

An involuntary sound rose from the back of her throat, and Sam grasped her skirt in her fists. She stared down at his hands; their black metal was stark against the red fabric and her pale skin, creating a startlingly erotic contrast.

He curled his fingers under her dress and slowly peeled it to the sides; the silky, sheer material brushed over her nipples as her breasts were exposed.

She shivered. Her breath grew ragged, and her nipples hardened, aching for more.

"Do you crave more of my touch, my flower?" Arcanthus whispered into her ear as his tail trailed along the outside of her right thigh, which was bared by the skirt's slit.

Samantha's cheeks warmed, and she bit the inside of her lip. She couldn't *say* the words, couldn't ask him. She nodded.

With the fabric of the dress fully parted, he returned his hands to her breasts, cupping their undersides once more. One of his fingers teased the edge of her nipple, causing another shiver to run through her. Sam arched into his touch.

"Tell me, Samantha. Let me hear your voice."

"Y-Yes," she rasped.

He pinched her nipples.

Samantha sucked in a sharp breath. Her body jerked against him, and she squeezed her eyes shut as she tipped her head back against his shoulder. The jolt from her nipples pierced straight to her core like a bolt of lightning. Her lips parted with her panting breaths, and she clenched her skirt tighter.

"Demand it of me, Samantha. Demand pleasure. Demand what you are due, what you deserve."

She whimpered before she could finally force the words out. "Touch me, Arc. I-I want you to touch me."

He increased the pressure on her nipples infinitesimally, rolling them between his fingers. "*Why* do you want me to touch you, Samantha? What do you want to feel?"

"Because I want you," she rasped. Liquid heat pooled between her legs as her sex pulsed and an empty pressure expanded within her core. "I want to feel you."

Arcanthus chuckled huskily, brushing his lips against her neck. "Then I am yours, my lovely little terran."

He released one of her breasts to grasp her chin and turn her face toward his. He captured her mouth in a searing, claiming kiss. Samantha moaned as his hand returned to her breast; he kneaded her tender flesh, pinched and stroked her nipples until she couldn't keep her body still. Her skin thrummed beneath his touch. Arc nipped her lower lip with a fang only to soothe the sting away with his tongue a few heart-beats later.

"You are so beautiful, Samantha," he said against her mouth. "So delectable. Give me your hands."

Intoxicated by his kiss and drifting in a haze of desire, it took Samantha a moment to process his words. When under-standing finally pierced the lust fogging her mind, she released her skirt, stretched her stiff fingers, and held her hands up.

Arcanthus caught her wrists and placed her hands over her breasts before covering them with his own. The action caught her so off guard that she opened her eyes to meet his burning gaze. The thought of touching herself in front of him was shocking, but it was also...thrilling. He guided her hands to caress and squeeze her flesh as though they were his.

The corners of Arc's mouth curved up in a smile. "Do you feel how soft you are?"

"Yes," Samantha said.

"Close your eyes. Good. Now imagine my lips upon them, my tongue circling those hard little peaks. Imagine me taking them into my mouth, sucking hard, surrounding them in heat" —he used her fingers to pinch her nipples, eliciting a gasp from her—"before taking them between my teeth."

"Arc," Samantha begged, rubbing her thighs together. She was so wet she could feel her slick dripping down her ass. Her body trembled in need.

"Yours is a body worthy of worship," he said, lifting his hands off hers. "Keep going."

He smoothed his hands down Samantha's abdomen as she breathlessly caressed herself. Though her touch wasn't the same as his, it fanned the flames he'd already ignited within her. His palms left a blazing trail in their wake along her thighs, and his fingers massaged her flesh on their slow journey to her knees.

She whispered his name; it emerged from her lips in a desperate plea. Arcanthus hooked his fingers under her knees and spread her legs wide. She wouldn't have resisted even if it had been possible.

One at a time, he draped her legs over his powerful thighs, forcing them even wider apart as he spread his own legs. With his left hand, he gathered her skirt and dragged it upward. The fabric glided over her skin until her pelvis was bare. Arcanthus swept the skirt aside and settled both his hands on the insides of her thighs, brushing his thumbs across the thin edges of her underwear.

Samantha trembled. She felt vulnerable and exposed, and yet, because it was Arcanthus, she felt *safe*.

"Ah, Samantha, do you know what you do to me?" He tilted his hips and forced her pelvis down; her backside brushed against the hardened answer to his question. "You have hidden yourself from everyone, but I will discover the wonders of your body. I will worship it." He teased the shell of her ear with his teeth. "I will *taste* it."

Samantha's breath hitched.

Arc curled his fingers beneath the waistband of her panties. "And I will conquer it."

He tugged outward with both hands. The waistband tore like paper, leaving only a scrap of fabric draped over her mound. The tip of his tail trailed up the inside of her thigh and slipped around the cloth, brushing over the hairless flesh of her pelvis, to pluck the red fabric away.

Arcanthus slid one hand back to her inner thigh and flattened the other over her abdomen as his tail crept toward her sex again. "Keep those hands moving, little terran."

Samantha had been so focused on his tail that she hadn't realized she'd stopped caressing herself. She set her fingers into motion again, but her attention remained transfixed on his hands and tail. She never would've dreamed he could use his tail for...for *this*. It was wicked.

The tip of his tail grazed her pussy, and her hips jolted in response. His breath was warm against her ear when he asked, "Do you want me to touch you there?"

She bit her lip and nodded.

"Command me," he rasped. "*Take* from me."

Squeezing her breasts in frustration, she released her lip and tried to roll her hips into his touch, but he pinned her in place with his hands. She'd never felt as much desire, as much need, as was coursing through her in that moment. Her limbs trembled, and her core clenched.

"Touch me, Arcanthus," she pleaded. "Now. I need you, now."

His tail brushed along her sex lazily, spreading her essence, while his hand slid down her abdomen. He cupped her pussy, spread her folds, and slipped his finger down her center. His fingertip traced a circle around her clit.

Samantha cried out, squeezing her breasts, as pleasure pulsed through her. He continued those maddening circles, slow and teasing, steadily building the staggering sensations. Heat coursed through her veins. Her lips parted as she panted, her brows dropping low. When she attempted to undulate her hips again, he tightened his hold on her, halting her efforts.

She stretched an arm up and wrapped it around the back of his neck. Her fingers delved into his long hair, clutching the dark strands in her fist. Her other hand grasped his metal arm. Her thighs and belly quivered with the overpowering sensations, which were still intensifying, winding tighter and tighter. The feeling was so strong it was frightening.

"Arc," she moaned, tilting her head back. She turned her face toward him.

He met her gaze, but his central eye—the most devilish of

them—remained focused on her body. His finger maintained its steady pace, circling her clit over and over.

"Please, Arc. It's too much. I can't..."

"Oh, but Samantha, you *can*." He spread her legs wider, and something nudged the entrance of her pussy. A second later, his tail filled her, sliding easily into her depths.

Samantha inhaled sharply. She tightened her grip on his hair as her sex clamped around his tail. She'd expected pain, had expected the burn of her tender flesh tearing, had expected the unforgiving bite of his fingertips in her skin as he drove into her relentlessly, but there was only *bliss*.

Arcanthus moaned and rocked his hips against her.

"So hot, so soft...so tight," he rasped.

His tail withdrew from her sex. The hollowness it left behind was agony, but Samantha couldn't look away as he raised his tail to his mouth and slipped it between his lips.

It was the most arousing thing she'd ever seen.

Arc sucked on the tip of his tail, tilted his head back, and groaned before sliding it out. "So *delicious*."

He touched the tip to her neck and slowly ran it down her body, trailing between her breasts and over her stomach before returning to her sex. His finger increased its pressure on her clit as his tail reentered her. He pumped in and out, enhancing her ever-growing pleasure.

Sam writhed upon him, her hips undulating in time with the thrusts of his tail and the strokes of his finger. Electric currents arced through her body. Her timid, throaty moans built in a crescendo, becoming overwhelmed cries. She was lost, drowning in sensation, in torment, in pleasure.

"*Yes*," Arc said. "Scream for me, Samantha. Let the whole city know you are in the throes of ecstasy." He pressed on her clit more firmly.

She gave in and let the sensations overtake her.

White-hot pleasure burst inside her. She came with a guttural cry that quickly turned into a scream as his fingers and tail quickened. Heat flooded Samantha, and her body spasmed, locking up tight. She squeezed her eyes shut, arched her back and reared her head, gritting her teeth as rapture tore her apart and pieced her together again. It was ruthless; it was blistering; it was *sublime.*

When the sensations finally diminished, Samantha's eyes fluttered open.

Arcanthus was watching her with half-lidded eyes that— along with his *qal*—glowed brighter than she'd ever seen. Hunger burned in his gaze. Slowly, he slipped out his tongue and slid it over his lips. His finger lazily circled Sam's clit, easing her down from the heights of euphoria, and his tail remained inside her, keeping her satisfyingly full.

Samantha lay atop him, breathing raggedly, as her body shuddered in the aftermath of her climax.

Arc lowered his head and captured her mouth. His kiss was ravenous and bruising, brimming with desire. Samantha moaned against his lips.

When he pulled back, he smiled lopsidedly, bringing his free hand up to stroke her cheek. "I win, little terran."

Though her cheeks were already flushed, another rush of warmth swept across them. She returned his smile with a big one of her own.

She felt...*free,* like a great weight had been lifted off her. She'd never thought sex could feel so wonderful. Hell, she'd never thought sex could even feel *good.* What Arcanthus had done for her... It was lifechanging.

He lifted his hand from her clit and placed it upon her thigh, giving it a gentle but possessive squeeze. "As per our arrangement...that was only the beginning. I'm ready for a *real* taste, now."

Arc's tail slowly slipped out of her. Her sex clenched, greedy to keep him there, and she tightened her legs around his thighs. But she wasn't strong enough to resist when he placed his hands on her hips, lifted her, and turned her to face him.

Her hair fell around her shoulders as he sat her on his abdomen and spread her legs to either side of his torso. Her skirt bunched around her waist and draped over his lap. His grin widened, flashing fangs as his central eye dipped to her pussy, which was slick with desire and bared to him.

Samantha shyly brought a hand to her chin as she stared down at him.

Cupping her ass, he pulled her closer, sliding her up his abdomen. "This flower is *mine*."

A high tone—reminiscent of the bells that had signaled the end of a period when Samantha was in school—sounded from Arcanthus's wrist, and he stilled. A moment later, the tone sounded again.

Arc gritted his teeth and growled, tightening his grip on her ass. "*Damn it.*"

THIRTEEN

Arcanthus was staring up at a fantasy made flesh, at the goddess of his desire, at everything he wanted and could ever need. Samantha's hair was in disarray, spilling over her shoulders in thick waves to brush the tops of her small, firm breasts, and her eyes were dark with lust. Her pale skin was flushed with excitement, her lips lush and swollen from his kisses. The smile she'd gifted him was more beautiful than anything he'd ever seen. Her joy was arousing and alluring beyond reason.

He inhaled deeply, taking in her mouthwatering scent, and returned his eyes to her bared sex. Its pink, glistening petals beckoned him. He was moments away from having his mouth *there*, moments away from drinking her nectar straight from the source.

The tone sounded again—someone was at one of the concealed doors.

A flash of irritation joined the fires of his passion. His cock ached, and there was only one thing—one touch—that could relieve his suffering.

But, of course, someone was at the *fucking* door.

Forcing his voice into as neutral a tone as possible, he said, "Just a moment, Samantha."

Arcanthus shifted his arms so his elbows rested lightly upon Sam's thighs and his hands were over his chest. He activated his holocom to access the door intercom. "Someone had better be dying, because I said *no interruptions*."

"Since when have I ever cared what you say?" Drakkal replied. "Especially since you locked me out, you bastard."

"I'm going to castrate you," Arcanthus muttered.

Samantha's eyes widened.

Arcanthus wanted to focus on Samantha's scent, her heat, her taste. He wanted to join with his mate, just like every fucking instinct inside him demanded. He clenched his jaw and said through his teeth, "I'm *busy*, Drakkal. What do you want?"

"We found him," Drakkal said.

"Found *who*?"

"The groalthuun from the mall. Now let me in so we can talk. I'm not talking to a door anymore."

Samantha turned her head, her gaze averted as she hurriedly righted her dress, covering her breasts and shielding her sex from view.

Arcanthus groaned and terminated the intercom connection. His head fell back; his body was suddenly too hot and too heavy. "Do you know your way back to the bedroom, Samantha?"

"I...can find my way."

He released a weighty sigh. "I'll have someone bring you some food in a little while. Just make yourself comfortable until then. I'll meet you as soon as I've spoken with Drakkal."

She nodded. "Okay."

After carefully climbing off his chest, she took a single step away, paused, and turned toward Arc to peck a kiss on his lips. She pulled back before he could catch her, smiling.

That simple little kiss struck him hard; he'd never been kissed like that before. It hadn't been an impassioned kiss, hadn't been a lustful kiss, but an affectionate kiss. Its warmth spread across his face, flowing directly into his heart.

Absently, he brought up the control on his holocom and opened the nearby door for Samantha—the same one through which she'd entered—keeping his eyes on her as she walked away. There was a sway to her hips now, extremely subtle but undeniable.

She'd not once walked that way in the time he'd known her.

Only after the door was closed did he sit up fully, swinging his feet onto the floor. He lowered a hand to his protruding cock and squeezed it through his loincloth, hoping in vain to alleviate its ache. He shuddered; there'd be no relief now.

The door alert sounded again.

Arcanthus's nostrils flared with an exasperated exhalation. He flicked the command to open the hidden entry on the platform before he dismissed the holocom screen, leaned back, and stretched his arms along the sofa's backrest. He laid his tail on the cushion beside him, unable to keep its tip from thumping up and down in irritation.

Drakkal entered the chamber on the platform, passing dozens of screens on his way to the steps. He descended and stopped in front of Arcanthus, staring down with his brows low. "Do I really need to see that?"

Arcanthus dipped his gaze to his groin, where his erect cock created a distinct, writhing bulge in his loincloth. "Yes. It's one of the consequences for interrupting me."

Drakkal shook his head and rolled his eyes. "I know she's your mate, but we do have other things to take care of."

"Taking care of *her* is my first priority, Drak."

"And did you?"

"Not to my satisfaction."

The azhera dipped his chin toward Arc's crotch. "Clearly. You ready to be serious now?"

Arcanthus tipped his head back onto the backrest and sighed. "I'm always serious, Drakkal." He couldn't stay angry at the azhera for wanting to address the problems they were facing, but it would be difficult to focus on anything when his body craved Samantha so badly it hurt. "What did you find?"

Drakkal eased himself down on the couch across from Arcanthus's. His tail lashed restlessly over the cushion. "We pulled surveillance holos from the Ventrillian Mall. Managed to get some good images of the groalthuun who was taking pictures of you. He pops up on yesterday's feed from outside Samantha's apartment building, too."

Lifting his head, Arc met Drakkal's gaze. "Show me."

A few motions of Drakkal's fingers in his holocom's controls brought up a wide, projected image in the air between them— the groalthuun, standing in the crowd at the mall. The image split to show the same groalthuun from a different angle, this time in front of the entry door to Samantha's building, with the large orange onigox beside him.

"That's the one."

"It took a lot of digging, but we found numerous aliases for him. Most common one is Straek."

Arcanthus tipped his chin toward the onigox's image. "The orange bastard said that name at one point. That he was going to have Straek take Samantha after I was dead."

Drakkal dismissed the image and lowered his arms, resting them over his thighs as he leaned forward. His expression was grim. "He's part of the Inner Reach Syndicate."

Something icy slithered into Arcanthus's gut, and his eyes flared. He pushed off the backrest and leaned forward himself, subconsciously mimicking his friend's position. "The Inner Reach? You're sure, Drakkal?"

The azhera nodded once. "Obviously, there's not much information beyond that, not without you looking into it yourself. They keep their activities under tight wraps."

"Understandably so." Arcanthus dropped his gaze to the floor. His cock finally retracted into his slit, its ache subsiding as numbness spread through him. If Drakkal interrupting hadn't been enough to dampen the mood, *this* was overkill.

"This can't be a coincidence, Arc."

"But why? Why after all this time? This...this was probably just because of Samantha. He was scouting her because she's a terran, and the Syndicate traffics in slaves. They just saw me as a potential threat—"

"You said they went to her apartment and asked her about *you*," Drakkal said firmly, calling Arc's eyes back to him. "You were recognized."

Arcanthus's heart pounded. Memories threatened to flood to the surface—memories of suffering, betrayal, terror—and he barely held them back. "But I've never seen this Straek before a few days ago. Have you? There's no way he could've known who I am."

"But someone who *does* know you must've seen those pictures."

"There's no way to say that with any certainty."

Drakkal's nostrils flared, and he lifted a hand to scratch his cheek. "Arcanthus, you asked me a long time ago to tell you when I thought you weren't thinking straight, and—"

"Caldorius is millions of light years away, and it was ten years ago. I'm dead as far as they're concerned. *Dead*. Now I'm supposed to believe they've found me here, in a city of billions? This doesn't—"

"*Arc*," Drakkal growled, his fur bristling, "shut the fuck up!

Kraasz ka'val, I don't want it to be true anymore than you do, but I can't sit here while you delude yourself. It doesn't matter who or why, we have to assume they know who you are, and that they're willing to finish what they started. I can excuse some of your stupidity—you needed to have your mate, whether you understood it or not—but it has to stop now. You're the smartest person I know. Start fucking acting like it."

Arcanthus snapped his mouth shut. A torrent of emotions roiled inside him, swelling from his gut to constrict his chest and throat. He struggled to hold his friend's gaze, but he couldn't.

"They know you're in the Infinite City, Arc. They devoted a lot of resources to take you out at Samantha's, and compared to us, their resources are essentially infinite—this is the damned Syndicate. The time for fooling around is over." Drakkal pushed himself to his feet and walked up to Arcanthus, crouching in front of him. He put his large hand on the back of Arc's head and forced the sedhi to look him in the eye. "I fought in those pits for years. I saw horrible things more times than I can count. But nothing was worse than the day I found you— the day I found what was *left* of you."

Arcanthus clenched his jaw. His breath was ragged, his throat on fire.

Drakkal's eyes were intent and unwavering. "If they come again, I will fight until the end. I will lay down my life for you. I would've died in those pits if you hadn't pulled me out. If you hadn't *trusted* me. But if they find you, Arc, they're not going to stop until there's nothing left for me to bring to a medic.

"From now on, you're not dealing with any customers face-to-face, and you're not leaving this compound. I'm not going to tolerate any arguments. You're going to listen to me for once."

Arcanthus shook his head and extended an arm, cupping the back of Drakkal's thick neck. Though he didn't feel humor inside—there was too much turmoil, too much worry—he forced a smile to his lips. "If I never listened to you, I'd have died a long time ago...and, consequently, your life would've been a lot less stressful."

Drakkal snorted, his mouth tilting in a smirk. "You can't even give a compliment without being an asshole."

"I'm always sure to utilize my strengths."

They lowered their arms, and Drakkal moved back onto the other couch.

Arcanthus raked his fingers through his hair, sweeping it back out of his face and behind his horns. "Is this Straek still alive?"

"As far as I know."

"I want to have a chat with him."

"You know what that means. They find out, and it's war."

"You were at the apartment complex, Drak. It already is."

The azhera frowned, and his mane stood up, but he offered no argument.

"Get some people on it," Arcanthus said. "We need to move as quickly—and discreetly—as possible."

"All right. I'll get it rolling." Drakkal rubbed the back of his neck, moved his hand to his face, and sniffed. "*Kraasz ka'val*, Arcanthus. You couldn't clean your hands before you let me in? It's enough that the air smells of her, but *I* don't need to smell like her, too."

Arcanthus lifted his hand and sniffed his fingers; they smelled of Samantha's nectar. He closed his eyes and extended his tongue, licking her faint, lingering taste from his fingertip.

"If you start touching yourself, I'm going to kick you," Drakkal said.

Arcanthus threw back his head and laughed. "If I start touching myself, you'll be in the blast zone." When his laughter faded, he glared at Drakkal. "Now go wash your mane. I'll kick *you* if you still bear her scent the next time I see you."

Drakkal shoved himself to his feet. "Don't try it unless you want to lose a leg, little sedhi."

As the azhera walked away, Arcanthus called, "Use soap! If you just lick your hand and wipe it off, that doesn't count as cleaning." He paused for a moment before leaping to his feet. "You'd better not lick that at *all*, do you hear me?"

Drakkal eyed him from atop the platform. "Open the door before I wring your neck."

Arcanthus didn't look away from the azhera as he brought up the door controls and opened the concealed door near Drakkal, who walked through without another word. Once Drakkal's tail was clear of the opening, Arcanthus shut it again.

He'd barely taken a step toward his desk when the door alert tone sounded. Arcanthus's tail flicked in irritation.

Switching on the intercom, Arcanthus growled, "If I have to come out there, Drakkal, you're going to regret it."

Drakkal triggered the tone again and snorted.

Arcanthus mounted the platform and sat in his chair, leaning back to peruse the many displays he'd already had active before Samantha arrived. There was work to be done—there was always work to be done—but how could he focus on any of it now? Though his arousal had faded, his body still ached, and what he'd hoped would prove a passing threat was far more dangerous than he could've imagined.

The fucking Syndicate.

The Inner Reach Syndicate was a conglomeration of numerous powerful crime organizations; though it existed in Arthos as a singular entity, one of many such groups, it was in contention for being the wealthiest and most influential of them all. Arcanthus's work as a forger had often necessitated accepting jobs from such organizations, but he'd never once met with any of their representatives directly, had never once let any of them see his face—because many of those organizations also had a presence on Caldorius.

The Inner Reach Syndicate kept its *headquarters* on Caldorius. It had been the Syndicate that moved against a pesky young sedhi fighter who'd had the audacity to cut into the profits they made from the gladiatorial arenas of that world. It had been the Inner Reach Syndicate that took Arcanthus's ambitions personally, and they'd demonstrated through yesterday's events at Samantha's apartment building that they were willing to do whatever it took to finish the job they'd started so long ago.

They'd used Samantha to lure him out.

Arthos had already been cruel to her, had already attempted to crush her on its own. She certainly didn't deserve to have the Syndicate after her, too.

The fear Drakkal's revelation had sparked in Arcanthus burned to ash in a blaze of fury. Samantha was Arc's terran, his female, his *mate*.

There'd only been a brief time when he'd entertained the possibility of finding a mate. Those dreams, indistinct as they were, had faded when he'd left home to become part of the Crimson Raiders, a wing of the Sedhi Defense Coalition. A life of combat and bloodshed had been the only future he'd truly been able to envision for himself.

A lonely life.

And even during that brief window during which he'd dreamed, he'd never once considered his mate could be from another species. There were stories of sedhi finding their mates amongst volturians, even a few—often relayed with some horror —whispering of tretin mates, but he'd never imagined any other possibility.

Certainly not a terran. He'd not even known of their existence until recently. Samantha's people had only entered his awareness when they began migrating to the city two short years ago, about a year after Syntrell Vantricar Caltraxion, a volturian ambassador from the Entris Dominion, had sponsored the terrans' formal request for admittance to Arthos. The Consortium had issued the invitation with surprising speed—they'd taken over a decade to approve the requests of some other species.

Then I'll let Straek take your terran ji'tas. Maybe we'll sample her before we sell her.

This went beyond them utilizing Samantha as bait to draw him out. The Syndicate didn't use someone and then let them move on with their lives; once a person's usefulness to the Syndicate had expired, they were silenced forever. *Silencing* just as often meant a trip to the slave markets of Caldorius as it did a plasma bolt to the brain. She was involved now, and that meant the bastards would come for her, too.

Arcanthus leaned forward and set his hands to work, issuing commands on the console to begin locating the sorts of near-invisible plexus access points organizations like the Inner Reach Syndicate often used for communication.

"I don't care how many resources you sewer skrudges have," he muttered, "you threaten *my* mate, and it's a fucking war."

FOURTEEN

Samantha was wary as she retraced the route back to Arcanthus's room, silently praying that she wouldn't run into anyone along the way, especially Kiloq. While she wasn't afraid of the cren—or anyone else who might've been in the building—she was afraid that he'd take one look at her and know what she and Arcanthus had just done.

She wasn't sure if she could die of embarrassment, but an encounter like that would probably get her close.

Fortunately, the corridors were empty, and she reached the bedroom without any issues.

Once she was inside, she leaned back against the closed door and drew in a shaky breath. Tremors still coursed down her legs, her inner thighs were wet with her slick, and her sex felt somehow heavy and hollow after her mind-shattering orgasm.

Arc dominated her thoughts. She'd already known his sensual voice alone could make her weak in the knees and flood her with heat, but his *touch*?

Sam's face warmed, and she pressed her hands over her cheeks. She was grinning like a fool, but she couldn't help it; she was just so damn happy.

It would've been stupid to think a man could fix her, and that wasn't what Arcanthus was doing; he was pushing her to fix herself. Through encouragement, praise, and compliments, he was helping Sam rebuild her self-esteem while earning her trust.

She never would've dreamed of wearing a dress like the one she had on now, even before James. Despite her misgivings and self-consciousness, she'd left Arc's workshop feeling beautiful, desired, and pleasured.

An hour ago, Sam had been fearful of sex. Now she couldn't wait until she saw the sedhi again. She wanted Arc to touch her more, and she yearned to touch him in return.

Samantha drew in another breath. Arcanthus's scent permeated the air, making it difficult to turn her thoughts away from him.

Am I going to just stand here trembling until he comes for me?

With little else to do, she forced herself forward and slowly explored his room, running her fingers along the walls to trace the ever-changing blue lines. She leapt back when her fingertips brushed over some sort of hidden console and a holo menu materialized in front of her.

Once her heart had stopped racing, she looked from the menu to the bedroom door. Arcanthus could walk in at any moment...

I really shouldn't.

You know you're curious, Sam.

But it's not my room! It's his!

All the more reason to look. Just a peek.

Biting her lip, she cast one more glance toward the door. Curiosity returned her attention to the menu. She raised a hand and flicked through the options. As she did, rectangular shapes lit up along the wall—eight of them were lined up in two neat rows around waist height, with two much larger, door-sized shapes to either side.

She manipulated the controls. The smaller glowing shapes slid out of the wall to reveal drawers, while the other two shifted up, opening on large, walk-in closets. Samantha stepped toward the nearest closet. An array of colorful, silky robes hung inside.

A giggle escaped her. "The man likes his robes."

She reached inside and lifted the sleeve of one of the garments, rubbing the satiny material between her fingers. As though driven by instinct, she leaned forward and brought the sleeve to her nose. It smelled exactly like him.

Letting the sleeve drop, Sam moved to the other closet and halted abruptly at the entrance. It was emptier than the first, but her brain couldn't process the clothing on display.

A few dresses, similar to the one she was wearing, hung amidst skimpier, naughty-looking garments, one of which appeared to be nothing more than a series of straps that would, quite strategically, cover very *little*. She went through the clothes one hanger at a time, studying them all. There were some shirts, coats, and pants in addition to the rest, even a couple robes in the same style as Arcanthus's—though they were smaller than his.

Sam might've thought they belonged to another woman if the shirts and pants weren't so similar to the sort she normally wore. She took down one of the shirts and held it up to her body; it seemed exactly the right size.

You're also the first to know my true name and the first to have slept in my bed. And you will be the only.

Had he purchased all these for *her*? Had he meant to bring her here all along?

The thought sent a rush of warmth through her chest.

She replaced the shirt and retreated from the closet, side-stepping to turn her attention to the drawers.

One contained what appeared to be Arc's loincloths, another was full of jewelry—including more earrings than she'd seen in her life—and the entire bottom row was full of methodically placed sets of sleek metal plates. It took her a moment to realize the plates were alternate coverings for his cybernetic limbs, each set with a unique color and finish.

A doorbell-like chime startled Samantha. Eyes wide and heart suddenly pounding, she hurriedly ran her fingers through the controls. The drawers slid in and out repeatedly while the closet doors opened and closed.

"Come on! Come on!" she begged when the chime sounded again. "Oh, you stupid thing, work!"

After several attempts, she finally got them all closed. She flicked the menu away, flattened her palm against the wall, and took in a few calming breaths. It couldn't be Arcanthus at the door; he would've walked in without warning, even if—*especially* if—he thought there was a chance she'd be undressed.

When the chime sounded a third time, Samantha hurried to the door and opened it.

A cren stood in the hallway, one hand raised to the button beside the door. The tray in his other hand had steaming food and a purple-tinted bottle atop it. The cren's green eyes met hers, and he grinned around his tusks. His hair, the same dark blue as Kiloq's, was short and spiked.

Sam crossed her arms over her chest as she recalled what she was wearing. "Are you Kiloq's brother?"

The cren nodded. "Koroq."

"You're not ugly at all." Samantha gasped and slapped a

hand over her mouth. She couldn't believe she'd just blurted that out. "I'm so sorry!"

The corners of his mouth lifted into a grin that put his tusks on full display. "Why would you be sorry?"

"I just— He said... Oh, never mind." Sam lowered her hand and gave him a shy smile. "I hope you don't beat him for saying you're...you know."

Koroq waved his free hand. "I let him believe it. Got to let him have something he thinks he's better at."

Samantha laughed.

"Anyway, got some food for you. Boss said you were probably starving after being knocked out since last night." He held the tray forward.

She took the tray with both hands. "Thank you. I am pretty hungry."

"Welcome. If you need anything else, there's a lounge that way." He pointed down the hall to the right. "Take the first left, follow the corridor all the way down, and then take a right. It's the last door before the next intersection. Bit of a walk, but there's usually one or two of us in there. Food and booze, too."

"I'll keep that in mind. Thank you."

Once he was gone and the door was closed, Sam sat on the bed with the tray settled on her lap. She studied the food, none of which she could quite identify. There were steamed greens and purple tubers, a hunk of grainy bread, and meat that almost looked like the kind Sarai cooked at her booth, smothered in a dark sauce. She picked up the bottle and opened it, bringing it to her nose to give it a tentative sniff. It smelled fruity.

Sam hadn't really thought about food since waking up—she'd been a little...*occupied*—but now that the savory and sweet aromas filled her nose, her stomach clenched. This was beyond hunger; she was *starved*.

She moaned as soon as the first bite of meat touched her tongue.

Samantha wolfed the food down. Before she realized it, she'd licked the tray clean, having consumed every morsel. It had been a long time since she'd eaten anything so delicious. All her meals over the last several months had been from instant-trays, nutritious and easy to prepare but terribly bland in comparison to this.

She set the tray aside—reminding herself to take care of it later—and returned to the console on the wall. Working the controls carefully, she opened her closet, stepped inside, and selected some clothes. Though part of her enjoyed the stickiness on her thighs, she carried the clothes to the bathroom and took a quick shower.

Once she was clean, dried, and dressed in a shirt and pants, she returned to the bedroom.

Her mouth opened wide with a yawn. Despite having just slept, she was suffused with weariness.

"Well, I did just have the strongest orgasm of my life..."

She chuckled and glanced at the door. Arcanthus was either working or still speaking with Drakkal. Either way, she had no idea how long he'd be. There was nothing wrong with taking a quick nap while she waited.

And it would make the time pass that much faster.

Sam drew the covers back, crawled onto the bed, and pulled the blanket over her as she lay down. She closed her eyes and took in a deep breath. Sandalwood filled her senses. Releasing the breath slowly, Samantha smiled. Only a single thought crossed her mind while she sank into sleep.

I am content.

SAMANTHA WAS ALONE when she woke. She had no idea how much time had passed while she slept; nothing in the room was different, but she felt rested. She sat up, propping herself on her arms.

Her hand bumped into something.

Turning her head, she looked down to see the food tray where it must've slid closer while she slept. She wasn't quite sure what to do with it. This wasn't a hotel or a restaurant, so she didn't feel right just setting it down somewhere for someone else to collect. She was a guest in Arc's home, and she would respect his home just like she respected him.

The lounge.

Koroq had said if she needed anything, she could go to the lounge.

Slipping off the bed, Samantha walked into the bathroom, where she brushed her teeth and used the toilet. She picked up the tray on her way to the bedroom door. After taking a moment to ground herself—she was heading into the unknown again—she pressed the button and stepped into the hall.

She followed Koroq's directions, to the best of her recollection, until she came to the door she hoped was the lounge. Sam shifted her weight back and forth between her feet, battling a swell of anxiety. She had no idea what awaited on the other side, *who* awaited, but there was one thing she did know— Arcanthus would never have brought her here if it was dangerous for her. Anyone she might encounter in this place was someone he trusted.

Samantha raised a hand to knock but paused, glancing at the control panel on the doorframe.

She pressed the button.

The door slid open. Samantha's brain didn't immediately understand what she saw; the room on the other side of the doorway could've been the breakroom of any large warehouse back on Earth. There were bare ducts cutting across the ceiling, a couple well-used couches facing three screens on the right wall—each of which was displaying some sort of full-contact sport Samantha wasn't familiar with—and three tables surrounded by chairs. The long counter directly ahead of the entry had a sink built into it and several appliances similar to those in the kitchen of her apartment. In one corner sat what had to be the largest free-standing refrigerator she'd ever seen.

One of the tables was occupied by three cren, including Kiloq and Koroq, and a female ilthurii with scales in a lovely, vibrant green. Bottles and snacks she couldn't identify—many of which were partially eaten—littered the tabletop.

Each person at the table had a small stack of credit chips piled in front of them, except for the unfamiliar cren—his pile was significantly larger than the others'. He was also the only one who didn't have any bottles nearby.

Some sort of projector was positioned at the center of the table, creating a translucent, holographic gameboard in the air above it. The three cren and the ilthurii each had sets of holographic cards hovering over their credits.

Kiloq turned his head to look at Sam and smiled. "Terran! Come in, sit with us. We need someone with fresh luck to break Razi's streak."

Samantha's brows lifted; she hadn't expected such a warm greeting. "Oh, um, okay?" She stepped inside, glancing around again before awkwardly lifting the tray. "I...wasn't sure where to put this."

"Over there is fine," Koroq said, gesturing vaguely toward the counter without looking up from his cards.

Sam walked across the room and set the tray beside the sink.

"You can sit here," the ilthurii said, scooting her chair aside and dragging an empty one over from the next table.

"Thank you." Samantha seated herself and settled her hands in her lap, struggling not to clasp them together nervously.

The ilthurii grinned, her lips peeling back to reveal sharp teeth. "My name is Sekk'thi. I would have introduced myself sooner, but you were unconscious the last time I saw you."

"Were...were you there?"

Sekk'thi nodded. "All four of us were there. And the vorgals, Thargen and Urgand."

The cren with the large pile of credit chips leaned forward, fixing his electric blue eyes on Samantha. He was larger than Kiloq and Koroq, and his white hair was chaotic, with short, untamed strands in the front and a thick bundle of braids hanging down his back and over his broad shoulders. His slate-gray skin contrasted his hair and eyes.

"Razi," he said in a deep voice. "Glad you're okay, terran."

Samantha smiled. "Nice to meet you, Razi. I'm glad, too."

He grinned.

Kiloq, who sat to her left, manipulated the controls on the holo. Six blank cards appeared in the center, and he flicked his fingers, sending them toward Sam. Once they were in front of her, foreign symbols appeared on their faces.

"You're in, terran," Kiloq said.

"I don't know how to play. And"—she glanced at the other player's credit chips—"I don't have anything to play with."

Razi settled one of his large hands over his pile of credit chips and slid it across the table until it was in front of her. Samantha stared down as he pulled his hand away; the pile he'd left for her was larger than everyone's but his.

Samantha pushed them back toward him. "Oh no, I can't."

"You're in," Razi said, dropping his gaze back to his holographic cards.

"I was going to win those back from you, damn it," muttered Koroq.

"You weren't going to win shit from him, and you know it," said Kiloq. "At least now we have a chance to win them from Samantha."

Sekk'thi shook her head and snorted. "Why do you think he parted with them so easily? He will win them back himself." She looked at Samantha. "This game is called Conquerors, terran. Watch carefully. You'll learn."

The game—with its alien symbols and daunting gameboard—seemed impossible to learn at first, but Samantha quickly picked up on it. The central game board was like a map, and the goal was to claim as much of it as possible before all the space was taken up. Each card had its own values, but it wasn't merely a matter of increasingly high numbers trumping each other—it was closer to a rock-paper-scissors scenario, with each symbol having strengths and weaknesses against the rest. Each card also had different traits depending on which way it was facing; a card strong on one side was often vulnerable on another.

By the fourth round, she had a fairly good idea of what was going on, and she'd managed to stifle the outward flow of credit chips she'd suffered for the first few matches.

That was when Sekk'thi opened a fresh bottle and slid it to her. "Drink, terran."

Sam accepted the bottle and leaned forward, peering inside. "What is it?"

"It is called *gurosh*," Sekk'thi replied.

"It's good," Kiloq said.

Samantha glanced around the table; each of them, apart from Razi, had several empty bottles of *gurosh* lined up nearby, and she'd seen them drinking throughout the games she'd played with them.

Why not?

Picking up the bottle, she brought it to her lips and drank. It burned going down her throat and roiled like liquid fire in her belly. She gasped and coughed.

Koroq leaned back in his chair and laughed. "I knew you terrans were soft, but I didn't think you were *this* soft."

Kiloq lifted his foot, bent his knee, and kicked Koroq's leg. "Want me to tell her about the first time you tried it?"

Sekk'thi pounded a hand against Sam's back until her coughing subsided.

"It's okay," Sam wheezed. "It was just...unexpected. I'm fine, really." She cleared her throat. The burn was gone, but warmth lingered in her belly. The *gurosh's* aftertaste was surprisingly sweet.

"You will grow accustomed to it," Sekk'thi said. "Just drink in little sips."

When Samantha returned the bottle to her lips, she followed Sekk'thi's advice and took a single, small sip; the burn was far more tolerable.

"Never cared for the taste," Razi said. Hunched forward, he perused his cards, his gaze occasionally flicking to the board. Given his size and the breadth of his shoulders, his posture looked almost comical.

"It's not about the taste," Kiloq said, "it's about the experience."

Sekk'thi leaned closer to Samantha, grinning. "Razi has refused to drink since he awoke one morning in an unfamiliar bed with a tralix beside him."

"He still won't tell us what happened," said Koroq. "Claims he doesn't remember. I don't believe that."

"Doesn't matter," Razi muttered, sliding one of his cards into place on the board. "She was clingy. And she was bigger than me. Made me uncomfortable."

Sekk'thi laughed.

Samantha grinned. "Might be why Razi wins so much. He keeps a clear head."

Razi met her gaze and lifted a finger to tap his temple, smiling.

She chuckled. She'd never been so welcomed by a group of people before, and it was an amazing feeling.

Koroq glared down at the gameboard with a scowl. "He always wins whether or not he's out of his wits. Just takes him longer to decide his moves when he's drunk."

"Always win because I never had competition before." Razi dipped his chin toward the board.

Samantha glanced down; his portion of the map was still the largest, but—to her shock—her territory was a close second.

"Beginner's luck," Koroq muttered.

Sekk'thi snickered.

They continued the match, and Samantha—who could've counted on one hand the number of times she'd had alcohol before this—continued sipping from the bottle. As time passed, she grew steadily used to the drink's taste, though she didn't chance taking another mouthful like she had the first time.

And her territory grew. By the end, she was only a few spaces behind Razi, with the other three players nowhere close. She took a larger portion of the prize pool than she had up to that point, and Razi offered her a wink as he gathered his payout.

"Why do we bother trying?" asked Kiloq as the gameboard reset.

"Because I buy the drinks," Razi replied.

They all laughed—all but Razi.

He kept a surprisingly straight face as he said, "What's funny? It's expensive. And I'm not even drinking."

They played a few more rounds; Sekk'thi offered a full

bottle at some point, which Sam accepted happily. By the end of their final match, only Samantha and Razi had any significant amount of credits remaining.

Koroq threw his hands up, rose, and walked to one of the screens by the couches. He flicked through the control menu, muttering to himself, until he found what he wanted. A twist of his hand raised the volume.

Music flowed from unseen speakers, beginning as light, electronic tones before building to a pulsing melody with a thumping beat beneath it. Unexpectedly, Koroq began dancing to the music—the sort of dancing she might've seen in Earth nightclubs had she ever mustered the courage to provoke James's ire by visiting one.

Sekk'thi pushed back her chair and joined Koroq, turning to give him her back as she pumped her hips and chest to the beat. Her long, thick tail brushed his leg. He reached out, grabbed it, and tugged her closer, placing his hands on her hips.

Samantha smiled and swayed gently in her chair as she watched them, continuing to sip her drink. Her body was relaxed, and her skin was flushed; she felt warm and fuzzy. She felt *good*.

A blue-gray hand appeared in front of her.

Samantha tilted her head back and blinked up at Kiloq.

"Come dance, terran," he beckoned.

"I don't know how."

"Doesn't matter." He rolled his shoulders and twisted his hips. "Just feel the music and move to it."

Samantha didn't allow herself any more time to think; she set her bottle on the table and placed her hand in his. She laughed as he pulled her up out of her chair. Her laugher became a delighted shriek when he spun her, and the room whirled around her.

She really was feeling quite giddy.

Razi leaned back, folded his fingers across his abdomen, and said in an oddly warning tone, "Careful, Kiloq."

Kiloq caught her hands, and they swayed to the hypnotic music. His eyes were locked on hers, and his lips were curled in a playful smirk. Samantha's cheeks hurt from smiling so much.

"We're just having some fun, Razi," Kiloq replied. "Boss doesn't need to worry."

FIFTEEN

"So there's nothing?" Drakkal asked.

Arcanthus shook his head and turned his chair to face the azhera. "The Syndicate uses rather advanced encryption for their offworld communications, but I've been able to crack it. I can't find any chatter about this situation. Locally, they're fairly silent. I would guess they prefer face-to-face communications on Arthos to avoid leaving any more of a trail than they already do."

Drakkal folded his arms across his chest. "Any logs of them sending word about it earlier?"

"None that I can find. And that worries me more. They have some big players here on Arthos, but there should've been *something*. The sort of firepower they threw at us doesn't get used without someone up the chain approving it." Arcanthus sighed and tipped his head back against the headrest. "I have a bad feeling about all of this."

Drakkal snorted. "Of course you do. They tried to kill you, Arc. That'd give anyone a bad feeling."

Arc turned toward his desk and stared at the screens. He'd

spent hours hacking and scanning Syndicate communication channels. Though that was a small amount of time in the big picture, it was odd for him to search for so long without finding anything of significance. "There's something more here. Something I'm missing, something I can't see."

"Guess that third eye really is for nothing."

"This is serious, Drak."

"That's what *I've* been telling *you* this whole time."

"We can argue over who said what to who later. For now, we need to focus on the task at hand."

"Ancestors, grant me the strength to spare his life," Drakkal muttered. "The only thing I'm going to focus on right now is getting some food in my gut. You should do the same. You've been in here all day, and I know for a fact you haven't had anything to eat."

Arcanthus waved a hand. "I had a few of those Kalatharian nuts."

"You did. Yesterday."

"Oh. Well, I—"

Drakkal grabbed one of Arcanthus's horns and dragged him up out of the chair.

Arc snarled.

"No excuses," Drak said. "Being short a few limbs is no reason to treat your body like garbage."

As soon as he gained his balance, Arcanthus yanked his horn out of Drakkal's hold. Straightening, he faced the azhera and smoothed his hands down his robe, tugging the fabric into place before he swept his hair out of his face. "First you demand I get to work, then you demand I stop. Do you have any idea how frustrating it is trying to keep up with your ever-changing whims?"

"Do you have any idea how frustrating it is to be your friend, bodyguard, and mother all the damned time?"

"I am quite capable of—"

Drakkal lifted a hand; Arcanthus stopped talking, brows falling low.

"As much as I appreciate a good laugh, Arcanthus, I'm too hungry to listen to your jokes. And I didn't think I'd have to remind you of this after what you've put me through the last few days, but don't you have someone you should be checking on?"

Arcanthus's stomach sank as he verified the time again. It had been hours since he'd sent Samantha away—and even if she didn't know it, he couldn't help comparing his dismissal of her to the way he'd dismissed so many other females in the past, females who'd meant *nothing* to him compared to this one.

"I didn't realize how satisfying that would be," said Drakkal.

"How satisfying *what* would be?"

"Seeing shame on your face. Don't think I've ever seen that before, and I've known you a long time, sedhi."

Arcanthus scowled. "Let's go, you overgrown sewer skrudge."

They left the workshop and walked to Arcanthus's room, where Arc left Drakkal in the hallway. His heartbeat quickened as he slipped into his bedchamber. Seeing her—especially if she were on his bed, or perhaps taking advantage of the bath —was a thrilling prospect, but, now that he realized what he'd done, he couldn't shake the guilt of having essentially ignored her for most of the day.

Though she would've been well within her rights to be upset with Arc, he didn't think she would be. Samantha was a kindhearted female—sweet, soft spoken, and compassionate. She already seemed to have forgiven him for so much. He understood how her nature had left her vulnerable to abuse, but he would never take advantage of her demeanor.

She wasn't in bed. Arcanthus paused to lean over the rumpled bedding and draw in a breath, inhaling her lingering scent.

His anticipation heightened as he walked toward the bathroom. Her fragrance was enough to heat his blood and rekindle his arousal, and his cock already throbbed with the need for release. Now he could finish what he'd started earlier—and if anyone tried to interrupt, Arc would just mute the door alerts until he and Samantha had both been satisfied.

He was thus greatly disappointed when he found the bathroom empty.

The dress Samantha had been wearing lay on the floor beside the dusty, rumpled clothing she'd been wearing before she woke. The sight of it brought a small smile to his lips; it was reminiscent of the first time he'd entered her apartment. He still had her white panties tucked away in a drawer beneath his loincloths.

He bent forward and plucked the dress off the floor, holding it up by the shoulders for a moment before shifting his hold to its waist. He lifted the garment to his face and inhaled.

The scent of her desire clung to the fabric.

A shudder coursed down his spine, continuing all the way to the tip of his tail.

"Fucking Drakkal," he growled.

He forced himself to place the dress inside the clothing cleaner, which was hidden within one of the bathroom walls, and adjusted the under fabric of his loincloth to prevent his cock from pushing farther out of his slit. Its ache spread through his groin and into his lower belly. Her old clothing went right into the trash chute; not only was it tattered and filthy, but she had no more need of it. He'd not allow her to hide in oversized clothes any longer—though the thought of her in one of his robes was tantalizing, to say the least.

After returning to the bedroom, he checked the closets just in case she'd somehow closed herself inside one. He noticed that her clothing had been moved, and one of the outfits was missing; it was oddly satisfying to know she'd likely snooped through his things. He'd have done the same were their places reversed.

He swept his gaze across the open space in the closet. Soon enough, he'd fill it completely with whatever clothing Samantha desired—and with whatever clothing *he* desired to see on her delectable little body. He'd have filled the closet sooner if he'd known things would move so quickly.

He exited the bedroom.

Drakkal stood in the corridor, leaning back against the wall. He frowned. "Where's your terran?"

Arcanthus shrugged. "She probably went exploring."

"So, bring up the surveillance feeds and find her."

"But that would bypass the thrill of the hunt. I'd much rather prowl the halls in search."

"I'm too hungry for you to waste that much time."

Arcanthus arched a brow and gestured toward the end of the hallway. "You don't have to wait on me, azhera."

"I do. It's the only way I'll be sure you eat."

Shaking his head, Arcanthus started toward the lounge, with Drakkal falling into place beside him.

"Are you going to start chewing my food for me, Mother Drakkal?"

"You keep it up, and I'll have no choice. It'd be hard for you to chew anything without any teeth."

Arcanthus laughed. "I'll remind you that the one time we fought each other, I emerged the victor."

Drakkal huffed. "That was a nonlethal bout. Doesn't count."

"Why wouldn't it count? Because the big, bad beasty lost and had his pride wounded?"

"Because it was nonlethal. Had to hold back so I wouldn't kill you."

"Really? It's strange you say that, because *I* was holding back so I wouldn't kill *you*."

"That why you were breathing so hard when it was done?"

"That's why *you* were almost unconscious when it was done."

Drakkal shrugged and lifted a hand, palm up. "Felt bad for you. You were trying so hard, I didn't want to crush your spirit."

The azhera stepped in front of Arcanthus when they reached the lounge entrance and pressed the button to open the door. Thumping music spilled into the hallway from within. Drakkal paused in the doorway, brows lifting and lips curling into a smirk.

"What is it?" Arcanthus asked.

"You'll see," Drakkal replied, shifting aside.

Arcanthus moved forward and turned to look into the room.

The music was coming from one of the entertainment screens. Kiloq, Koroq, and Sekk'thi were dancing to the rhythm while Razi, seated at one of the tables, was counting out a large pile of credit chips—likely his winnings from a game of Conquerors. It wasn't until Kiloq's dancing shifted his position that Arcanthus understood why Drakkal looked so smug.

The cren was dancing with Samantha.

And she wasn't merely dancing, she was enjoying herself, with her eyes sparkling and a huge grin on her face. Her cheeks were flushed, and one of her sleeves was rolled up. Though the clothing covered her flesh, it didn't mask her figure like her preferred attire.

Arc took a moment to appreciate the way the dark leggings

clung to her shapely calves and thighs, the way her top hinted at the flare of her hips and the gentle slope of her small breasts.

At the same time, a pang of jealousy struck him. She was here to enjoy her time with *him*, not with *them*. He shouldn't have buried himself in work—he should've been spending time with her, should've been making her laugh and smile, should've been showing her that he was here for her, that he belonged to her as much as she belonged to him.

"What is she doing?" Drakkal asked.

"Dancing," Arcanthus grated.

"*That's* dancing?"

Arcanthus tilted his head and shifted his focus to Samantha's movements instead of her body. There seemed to be little correlation between the music and the way she danced to it; her seemingly random, slightly unsteady motions were out of sync with the beat. But Arcanthus didn't care. Her smile and her carefree laughter lit a fire in him that could not be extinguished.

He'd never finished his earlier business with her.

Arcanthus strode through the doorway. Drakkal said something behind him, but the azhera's voice was muted and distant. Kiloq turned his face toward Arcanthus, eyes widening, and threw up his hands before backing away from Samantha.

The little terran didn't seem to notice that her dance partner had retreated. She pumped her arms as she slowly turned in place, granting Arcanthus a view of her curved backside.

Without hesitation, Arc stepped up behind her and dropped his hands to her hips, drawing her ass against his pelvis.

Samantha yelped and slapped her hands down atop his. "No touching there! Only Arrrrr"—she squeezed his hands and turned her head to look over her shoulder, her lips lifting in a wide smile—"canthus! You're here!"

"I am," he replied, those simple words made infinitely difficult with her backside brushing the protruding tip of his cock.

"I'm dancing!"

"You are."

"I never dance."

He chuckled and slightly tightened his hold on her hips. "Can't say that anymore, can you?"

"Nope." She turned to face him, forcing Arc to release her hips for a moment, and settled her hands on his shoulders. She beamed up at him. "Are you here to dance with me?"

Her breath—like the room itself—bore the scent of *gurosh*. It was no wonder she was acting and speaking so freely, no wonder her inhibitions had fled.

Arcanthus glanced at Razi. "How much has she had?"

Razi shrugged. "One and a half, maybe."

"That's *all?*" Arcanthus looked back at Samantha, arching a brow. "Are all terrans so susceptible to the effects of such beverages, or are you a special case?"

"No, not really. I just never touch the stuff." She rested her chin on his chest and looked up at him with those big, brown eyes.

She was absolutely adorable.

"Did you mean it? Am I?" she asked.

He arched a brow. "Are you what?"

"Special?"

Arcanthus smoothed a hand down her hair to cradle the back of her head. The sudden vulnerability in her eyes surpassed any he'd seen in them before—and she'd been shy and self-conscious from the moment he'd met her. "Of course you are, my precious flower. You are my once-in-a-lifetime."

Samantha closed her eyes and smiled softly. "I like the sound of that."

"But I'm not here to dance with you."

She opened her eyes, and her lower lip puckered. Arc was struck by an urge to suck that lip into his mouth.

"You're not?" she asked.

"No. I'm here to steal you away. I've something different in store for you."

He couldn't resist any longer; Arcanthus dipped his head and caught her lip between both of his, taking it into his mouth and nipping it with his teeth. He kissed her after he released it, relishing her taste despite it being layered with that of the *gurosh*.

Samantha moaned and returned the kiss without hesitation. Her hands slid from his shoulders, up his neck, and through his hair to wrap tight around the bases of his horns. A jolt of lust swept through him as she tugged his head closer, deepening the kiss, and he dropped his hands to her ass to pull her against him.

Fuck, I need *her. Now.*

Without breaking the kiss, he lifted her off the floor and guided her legs around his waist. She clung to him. The warmth of her core pulsed into his skin through their clothing. Arcanthus turned and carried her toward the door, keeping his hands on her lush ass.

"Arc, you're supposed to be eating," Drakkal said as Arcanthus passed.

Oh, I will be.

Breath ragged, Arcanthus entered the hallway. He left only his central eye open to guide the way as he hastened Samantha through the long corridors to his bedroom—to *their* bedroom. Their tongues twirled in an intricate, instinctual dance, exploring each other's mouths, sending tingling waves of pleasure across Arcanthus's face and straight to his belly.

Samantha caught his bottom lip between her flat teeth, and Arc grunted, his cock twitching.

When he reached the entrance to his bedroom, he pressed Samantha's back against the door and ravaged her mouth as he blindly felt for the open button. Samantha chose that moment to grind her sex against his slit and the tip of his shaft. A shudder wracked him.

Someone moaned; Arc couldn't tell if it was Samantha, himself, or both of them in unison.

His groping hand slammed the button and the door opened. He stumbled inside, clutching Samantha against him, until his knees bumped the side of the bed. Sam giggled. She released his horns and dropped her legs from his waist, wiggling her hips when he didn't release her.

He groaned deep, his fingers flexing on her ass.

"Put me down," she said.

"Never," he growled.

She pecked a kiss on his lips. "Please?"

All he could manage was a frustrated grunt. His body had no intention of relinquishing its hold on her—it needed this contact between them, needed *her*—but, somehow, he forced himself to comply. After he released her, his muscles tensed and strained. He clenched his fists at his sides to keep from grabbing hold of her again.

Samantha stood on the bed, leaving her half a head taller than him, and slipped her hands beneath his robe. Starting at his shoulders, she smoothed her palms down his arms, shoving the garment down. It fluttered to the floor a moment later.

She settled one of her hands on his chest, directly over his heart, and met his gaze for a moment. With a smile, she climbed off the bed.

Arcanthus turned his body to face her. When he raised his hands to reach for her, she shook her head.

"No. Not yet," she said with surprising firmness. Following its path with her gaze, she slid her hand down his chest and over his abdomen, stopping at the belt of his loincloth.

His skin quivered beneath her soft touch, his lips parted, and he released a slow, shaky breath. This was a side to Samantha he'd not yet seen—a side that might've taken weeks to awaken without the aid of the *gurosh*.

"I am at your command, little terran," he rasped.

"Good. Because I want to put my mouth"—she hooked a finger under his belt—"on you."

Arcanthus's eyes flared. His cock strained against the cloth holding it in place. "Tell me where, Samantha."

She worried at her lower lip—which was already swollen from his kisses—and dropped her hand to cup his groin. "Here."

He groaned against the shockwave of pleasure that blasted outward from her touch. The tip of his tail curled in delight. He wanted to give her control, to let her take what *she* wanted, but it was so difficult to restrain himself, so difficult to hold back.

"Show me," he said.

Samantha removed her hand and returned it to his chest. She pushed him toward the bed. "Sit." She hesitated for a moment before adding, "Please."

Despite the discomfort born of his need, Arcanthus chuckled. She couldn't possibly know what she was doing to him, couldn't possibly know his desire was being rocketed into the cosmos. She couldn't possibly know how *sexy* she was right now. He loved her bashfulness, loved how easy it was to make her blush, but he hoped she retained some of this confidence when she sobered up.

He eased himself onto the edge of the bed, settling his palms on the blanket behind him, and spread his thighs.

Samantha stepped closer, placed her hands on his knees, and slowly knelt in front of him. Arc barely held in another groan. Seeing her between his legs, knowing what she was about to do, was nearly his undoing.

Perhaps I should've taken myself in hand earlier. At least then I wouldn't stand as much a chance of embarrassing myself before she even touches me again.

He met her gaze and held it. His tail brushed against her hip. "Do with me as you please, my flower."

There was a glint of determination in her eyes as she scooted closer and moved her hands to his belt. She unclasped the buckles and peeled away the long front cloth, dropping it onto the bed beside him. Then her small, delicate fingers unfastened his under wrapping—the only thing keeping his cock contained in his slit. Anticipation welled in his chest; the pressure and heat within him were so immense, so powerful, he could scarce draw breath.

Her eyes flicked up to his briefly before she pulled the under wrapping away.

His cock sprang free of his slit. Though it eased some of the pressure, his discomfort only increased.

Samantha shrieked and fell backward, catching herself on her hands. Her eyes were wide and fearful as she stared between his legs.

Arcanthus's brows fell. "It's not going to bite you, Samantha."

"It-It's *moving*! It's *split*!" She slapped a hand over her mouth, leaving her voice muffled when she asked, "Did I break it?"

"It's not broken!" Arcanthus grasped the loincloth on the bed beside him, meaning to cover himself, but stopped before he did. Though his pride was stung, he had to remember she was a terran who'd only recently come to Arthos; what experience would she have had with alien genitalia? He'd seen what male terrans had between their legs—their species was rather tame compared to some.

He softened his voice. "You haven't even touched it with your bare skin, Samantha. *How* could you have broken it?"

"I-I don't know." Her gaze flicked down to his cock before returning to his. "Why is it...open and...moving?"

"The same reason you get wet when you're aroused," he replied. He hissed softly as he closed a hand around the base of his shaft, alleviating a little more of the pressure. The four prehensile tendrils comprising the end half of his cock quivered before squeezing together. "I want you so much it *hurts*. That's why."

Samantha eased forward, slowly closing the distance she'd opened between them. Her attention had fallen to his groin the moment he'd grasped himself and hadn't moved away since. A spark of intrigue, curiosity, and desire lit within her eyes. She settled on her knees and pressed her lips together. The light in her eyes took on a trepidatious glint.

It was her hesitance that pierced the lustful fog within which Arcanthus was helplessly drifting.

"Look at me, Samantha."

She dragged her eyes away from his cock and looked up at him.

He wanted her to touch him so badly, wanted her fingers, her lips, her tongue upon his flesh, and that want made his next words difficult to speak. "You have no obligation to me. You don't need to do anything you don't want to do."

He drew his discarded loincloth over his thigh, but Samantha reached forward and caught his wrist.

A tremor coursed through her arm. "No! No. I *want* to do

this. I want *you*. I want... I was just...surprised. You don't look human at all, so I wasn't expecting..."

He cupped her chin in his palm and brushed his thumb across her lower lip. "So long as you don't recoil in horror again, little terran. My ego can only take so much of a beating."

Samantha's cheeks turned scarlet. "I'm sorry."

Arcanthus released her and grinned. The amount of willpower it took to keep himself from displaying his discomfort, from succumbing to his overwhelming desire, was immense. "I'm sure you'll make it up to me. I am *yours*."

Samantha's gaze dropped again. The determination he'd seen in her eyes before returned tenfold. She settled one of her hands on his knee and extended the other. Arcanthus's breath caught in his throat.

Her finger touched the tip of his cock and brushed along one of the closed sections.

Arc gritted his teeth and shuddered; he didn't know if he could withstand this torture. He released his cock and placed his hands on either side of him.

She moved her fingertip to the crease between two of his tendrils and traced it. The tendrils split and writhed, hungry for her touch. Sam's breath hitched, and her eyes widened, but she didn't pull away.

Thank the fucking stars.

One of his tendrils curled around the tip of her finger as he clutched the bedding.

"What do I do?" Samantha asked.

Just the little bit of contact he'd already had with her was enough to threaten his tenuous control. "Whatever you want."

Samantha stroked his open tendrils with her fingers before dropping her hand to the base of his shaft. She grasped it firmly. The tendrils snapped shut, and Arcanthus groaned. Whatever trepidation she'd displayed before vanished.

She stroked her fist up to the tip of his cock, maintaining her solid grip, then back down again, repeating the motions in a steady rhythm. Her palm rasped over the sensitive nodules lining his shaft, and her pale skin was stark against the blue-gray of his cock. Each stroke sent an electric thrill through him; he shuddered against the rapidly building sensation.

Sam moved her face closer, eyes intent. Her warm breath flowed over his skin.

Arcanthus clenched his jaw, breathing heavily through his nostrils as her lips neared his shaft.

Her eyes flicked up to meet his. Dropping her fist to his base, she tightened her hold and parted her lips, taking him into her mouth.

Arcanthus threw his head back and hissed through his fangs. He squeezed his eyes shut, struggling against the onslaught of pleasure and heat, against the delicious torment, turning all his willpower toward holding on. He refused to let this end so soon, refused to spill his seed without first taking as much pleasure as he could withstand.

"Ah, my precious flower," he rasped. "Don't stop."

She tentatively took him farther into her mouth before pulling back slightly. When she drew him in again, she sucked him deeper still. Arcanthus's chest rose and fell with rapid breaths, and his pounding heart echoed in his ears. His thigh muscles tensed and quivered with exertion in his battle to keep his hips down as she rolled her tongue, teasing the creases between his tendrils.

Samantha moaned, and the vibration amplified the sensations she was causing in him.

He forced his head up and opened his eyes, fixing his gaze upon her; he wanted to watch, to savor every movement, to relish in every tiny change of her expression. Her eyes were closed, and her lips were stretched around his cock, which glistened with her saliva.

She adjusted the pressure of her hold around his base and pumped her hand in time with her mouth. Arcanthus's hips rocked in sync with her steady, maddening rhythm; he couldn't keep them still any longer.

Samantha shifted her knees and pressed her thighs together. Though her position obscured some of his view, he saw her free hand dip low, nearing her pelvis; she lifted it at the last moment to grasp a fistful of her shirt's fabric.

She was going to touch herself.

She's as aroused as I am.

That knowledge was enough to shatter his tenuous control; Arcanthus convulsed and threw his head back as he burst. A guttural cry tore from his chest and clawed out of his throat. He shifted one of his hands to her head, twining his fingers in her hair, and forced his tendrils to remain closed, fighting their instinctual drive to separate even as he pumped his hips and pulled her closer, making her take him deeper.

Intense pleasure cleaved through him. He growled as his seed flowed through the tiny opening at the center of his tendrils in great spurts. Samantha froze and made a small sound of surprise, her mouth locked tight around him as she drank. She moved her hands to his upper thighs and dug her fingers into his flesh. Spasms rippled through him, locking his muscles tight, until finally, the pleasure ebbed, leaving him breathless.

Samantha slowly lifted her head and released his cock. That last brush of her lips made him twitch. Finally allowing his tendrils to separate, Arc opened his eyes to see her pink tongue dart out and lick her lips before she wiped her mouth with the back of her hand.

"Did I...do good?" she asked.

His lips stretched into a grin, and he said, "Oh, my beautiful flower, there are no adequate words." He swept his hair behind his horns as he sat forward. "Do you trust me, Samantha?"

She reached up and lightly touched his cheek. "I do."

Arcanthus settled his hand over hers and removed it from his face, drawing her up with him as he stood. He managed to prevent himself from wobbling; somehow, she made him weak in the knees, a feat that should've been impossible considering they were cybernetic. His cock throbbed with echoes of that ravenous ache and refused to sheath itself in his slit. Despite the indescribable pleasure she'd given him, he hungered. His tendrils craved the feel of her inner heat; his body would not long be satisfied with what he'd received. He would need more soon.

Releasing her hand, he skimmed his fingers over her cheek, trailed them up into her hairline, and tilted her head back. He roved his eyes over her face slowly, letting them linger on her pink, kiss-swollen lips.

"Good. Then it's my turn, little terran." He tilted his head to the side. "Onto the bed."

Her eyes flared, and her little tongue slipped out again. She turned around and sat on the bed. Staring at him with those big, dark eyes, she placed her hands on her lap, one over the other, and slouched forward as though to hide herself.

Perhaps even the alcohol couldn't fully eliminate her discomfort in her own skin. Either that, or the effects were wearing off. It didn't matter—Arcanthus wouldn't rest until she knew how beautiful she was.

He stepped in front of her. "Sit up straight."

Her brow knitted.

"Now, Samantha."

Flushed skin paling slightly, she straightened her spine and swept her shoulders back. Her nipples pressed against the inside of her shirt, outlining themselves clearly.

He caught his tongue between his teeth to keep from licking his lips in anticipation. He couldn't wait to taste her, *all* of her, but he would delay it as long as possible—at least while that delay enhanced her pleasure. "Raise your arms over your head."

Confusion lifted her eyebrows, and she hesitated for a moment before complying with his command, slowly raising her hands.

"Now, little terran, I want you to close your eyes."

"Arcanthus, what—"

Arc caught her chin between forefinger and thumb. "*Do* you trust me, Samantha?"

"Yes," she breathed.

"Then close. Your. Eyes."

She swallowed audibly and obeyed.

"Good. Now, *you* are *mine.*"

SIXTEEN

Samantha trembled.

She should've been afraid, should've been terrified. How many times had James hurt her when he told her to close her eyes? How many times had he abused her trust?

But this was *Arcanthus*. Though she'd only known him for a short time, she did trust him. She couldn't help a twinge of fear for the unknown, for letting herself be so vulnerable, but excitement overpowered that fear.

She yearned for his touch. Her nipples were hard and aching, her sex wet and throbbing, and only Arc could satiate the excruciating need consuming her. She wanted him inside her. It didn't matter that his cock split into four independently moving parts, it was still him.

More than anything, she wanted to share this intimacy with Arcanthus. She wanted to make new memories with him, memories so heated and passionate that they'd burn away all the horrible experiences she'd endured, that the ghosts of her past would blow away like ash on the wind.

Sam could still taste him on her tongue, and that only

aroused her more. He tasted like lavender, floral and sweet. She'd been shocked at first; it, like his cock, had been wholly unexpected—but it was also wholly welcome.

What had she expected though? He was an alien. It was foolish to have gone into this as though he'd have human parts.

She'd always despised using her mouth as she just had, but she'd found herself eager to do so for Arcanthus despite her past experiences. She wanted to pleasure him again and again; she'd found satisfaction for herself in it. The act had been immensely enjoyable—especially when she'd watched him come apart in the throes of ecstasy. He'd been exquisite with his head thrown back, his brows low, his lips curled in a snarl that revealed those enticing, sexy fangs, and his body moving helplessly.

All because of her mouth, her lips, her tongue.

It had made her feel *powerful*.

Now...it was her turn to surrender. Her turn to be pleasured.

Arcanthus's hands settled on her thighs. Samantha started at the contact. His palms slowly trekked upward, their warmth radiating through her leggings.

"I want you to feel *everything*," he said.

He slipped his fingers under her shirt and hooked its hem with his thumbs, drawing it up as his hands continued their journey. Within moments, his fingertips were running over the bare skin of her sides, moving from her waist to her ribs. Sam's breath caught in her throat when his thumbs brushed over her hardened nipples. A moment later, her breasts were bare, and his warm palms slid over them.

Those fleeting touches were all he gifted her sensitive flesh; he lifted the shirt farther up, bunching it as it moved. His hands trailed along her arms, higher and higher, and drew the garment over her head. Her hair fluttered back down around her shoulders a few strands at a time. Once the shirt was off completely, the air flowed over her naked skin, carrying a chill in the wake of his heated touch.

Taking hold of her wrists, he guided her hands to his shoulders, both of which were warm and solid—one velvety flesh, the other sleek metal. Then his fingers smoothed downward, sweeping around her hips to slip beneath her backside. He lifted her bottom off the bed, hooked the waistbands of her leggings and panties, and drew them down her legs.

As the clothing neared her knees, something thick brushed along her pussy—the end of his tail. Samantha gasped and attempted to close her legs, but his hands kept them spread.

"Already wet for me, little terran?" Arc purred. He peeled her clothing off the rest of the way. "Open your legs wider."

Heat suffused Sam's cheeks as she slowly parted her thighs.

"Wider," Arc coaxed. "Show me that glistening pink slit."

Oh God.

His command sent a rush of desire through her; Samantha clutched his shoulders and opened her legs wider.

Was it possible to climax from his words alone?

"Such an alluring, delicate little flower." He lowered his shoulders and settled his arms over her thighs. His silken hair brushed over Sam's stomach and leg.

Her belly quivered. As he slid back, his arms looped around her legs, forearms nestling beneath her knees. He pressed his lips against her mons a moment later, right above her clit.

Samantha gasped, and her pelvis jerked forward. Her breath quickened, coming out in shallow puffs. She opened her eyes.

Arc's head was between her thighs, his lips curled into a wicked grin. Though his lower eyes were focused on her sex, his center eye was staring up at her.

"Eyes *closed*, Samantha."

She snapped them shut.

He exhaled, his breath hot and heavy against her wet folds. His chest swelled against her inner thighs as he inhaled deeply. "Ah, my sweet flower, you smell *delectable*."

Samantha whimpered. Her body trembled, aching for his touch.

"Do you yearn for the feel of my mouth against your slit, Samantha?"

"Yes," she rasped.

He turned his head and brushed his lips along her inner thigh, trailing slow, sultry kisses away from her core. As his mouth moved, he took hold of her wrists again, guiding her hands to his curved horns. "Lie back."

Sam grasped his horns and eased her back onto the bed.

Wedging his shoulders between her legs, he placed his hands on her thighs and parted them farther. He slid his palms closer to her pelvis. His thumbs settled on the soft outer folds of her pussy and spread her open.

She panted, clinging to his horns, simultaneously eager and afraid as liquid heat flooded her. "Arc..."

"*Feel* me, Samantha." His mouth pressed against her sex an instant later, followed by a long, slow stroke of his tongue, licking her from bottom to top.

Samantha couldn't hold in her gasp of delight as she arched her back. She tugged on his horns, pulling him closer. It was the most shocking, thrilling, *exquisite* thing she'd ever felt.

Arc's hands tightened around her thighs, and he moaned, licking again before giving her another kiss—this time directly on her clit. Her hips jerked at the jolt of pleasure, but he held her firmly in place. Arcanthus growled; the sound vibrated into her, heightening her pleasure as he sucked her clit into his mouth.

Samantha gasped, and her toes curled in rapture before her cries rose to fill the room.

He released her clit with a husky chuckle. "Your cries are the most beautiful music I've ever heard, and your taste is ambrosial, little terran. I don't know how I denied myself earlier."

Giving her no time to recover, Arc lowered his head. He ravaged her with his mouth, licking, sucking, and kissing every inch of her pussy. His tongue was ruthless as it delved deep into her channel, thrusting with surprising strength.

When his mouth moved back to her clit and he took it between his lips, stars burst in the darkness behind her closed eyelids. Ragged breaths tore from her throat, and she writhed in wild abandon as she came. Arcanthus eased his grip on her thighs; she undulated her pelvis, grinding her sex against his hungry mouth. Her cries were mindless as she succumbed to his erotic kiss.

The tremors coursing through her dulled as Arcanthus continued to leisurely lick and caress her with his lips. Her thighs quivered, and her core clenched. Though she'd come hard, she craved *more*. She felt as though there were something missing.

Arc.

She needed him inside her.

Samantha opened her eyes and raised her head to peer down at him. It was such a salacious, arousing thing to see his head between her thighs, to see his yellow eyes and markings bathing her skin in their soft glow.

He lifted his head just enough for her to see his mouth— which glistened with her slick—and ran his tongue slowly over his lips. "*Vrek'osh*, my flower, I could drink from you forever." He dipped his chin and slid his tongue along her sex from bottom to top, releasing a deep groan. "Are you ready for something more?"

Samantha shivered at his deep, rumbling voice. "Yes."

Arcanthus slipped his hands under her backside, bracing his arms along her back, and shifted her farther onto the bed. He climbed up a moment later and crawled over her slowly. His long, dark hair fell around him, brushing over her sweat-dampened skin as he moved up her body, his hypnotic eyes never leaving hers.

His mouth came down hard on Sam's. She felt the scrape of his fangs and tasted herself upon his lips and tongue, sending new spirals of ecstasy through her. She clutched his sides, smoothing her hands over his flesh, and hooked her arms around his back to draw him closer.

Arcanthus dropped his hands to her hips and rolled suddenly onto his back, dragging Samantha along with him. She pressed her palms against his chest as she came down atop him, straddling his hips. He grinned up at her.

The tendrils of his shaft tickled her backside, teasing her wet sex, seeking entry. Her core clenched at the thought of having them inside her, so alien and yet so arousing. What would they do? What would they *feel* like?

Arc stroked the back of a finger over her belly. "I am going to fill you, and you will feel *everything*."

Heat rushed to her face. "How did you...know what I was thinking?"

He chuckled, captured a lock of her hair, and caressed it, twirling it around his finger. "It's written upon your face. It's burning in your eyes. You can't hide yourself from me, Samantha."

Arcanthus released her hair and moved his hands down to cup her ass, grinding her against the base of his cock. Samantha gasped, her fingers curling upon his chest like talons.

"Do you want me, Samantha?"

"Yes. I want you."

"Then claim me. Make me yours."

Anxiety constricted her throat. She'd never been the one in control. "I-I don't…"

Tightening his hold on her, Arc lifted Sam so she was raised on her knees. "Grasp my cock."

Cheeks still aflame, Samantha reached between their bodies and slid her hand down his shaft; his tendrils brushed over her fingers, and a shiver coursed through him. Emboldened, she wrapped her hand around his base. The tendrils sealed.

Arcanthus slid his hands down her thighs. "Now take me into your body, little terran."

Samantha lowered herself until the tip of his cock touched her entrance. Her legs trembled. She bore down, and he breached her, sliding into her sex.

Arc groaned and squeezed her thighs.

She bit her lip, pushed back up, and dropped down again, welcoming him into her body, taking him deeper. He filled her, stretched her, and the nodules lining his cock stimulated her with every shallow pump.

"Yes, just like that," Arc rumbled, bringing her eyes to his.

Panting softly through parted lips, Samantha released his shaft to flatten both hands on his chest. She lifted her hips again and slammed down on him, forcing her body to take him fully.

Her breath hitched, silencing her cry. Arcanthus filled her completely, stretching her nearly to the point of pain, but the discomfort quickly subsided.

Only incredible, exhilarating fullness remained.

Arcanthus hissed through his teeth, his eyes momentarily

closing as he tilted his head back. When his eyes reopened, intense and burning with hunger, they fixed upon Samantha.

"Use me, my flower," he said. "Take what you will. I am yours."

Keeping her gaze locked with his, Sam set a steady rhythm. She and Arc moaned in unison as she rocked back and forth. She felt every one of his nodules against her inner walls; each stroke of his cock pushed her pleasure higher and higher.

Arcanthus slid his hands up to cup her breasts. He squeezed them, kneaded her flesh, and pinched her nipples, sending shock waves straight to her core. Her pussy greedily clenched around him.

"Do you feel how well we fit together?" he asked. "Do you feel how perfect this is?"

"Yes," she panted, eyelids fluttering. She could feel it, could sense her peak, so close and yet just out of reach. It was becoming difficult to keep rhythm—her elbows and knees were weak and trembling, refusing to support her weight as tingles spread through her limbs.

"Yes, my little terran." Arc chuckled through a moan, dropping his hands to her hips. "Let go. Seek your pleasure. *Demand* it from my body. Demand it from me."

His strong arms supported Samantha, lifting and dropping her to meet the upward thrusts of his pelvis, each of which was a little stronger than the last.

Her desire overrode everything else; he was all that mattered. He was all she needed.

Samantha's nails scratched and bit into his skin as Arcanthus quickened the pace. A fresh wave of pleasure blasted through her, and her elbows buckled. She fell upon his chest, and Arcanthus lifted his head, claiming her mouth hungrily. His lips dominated her, and she submitted, returning his kiss with a fervent sort of intensity.

Her body tensed, racked with tremors sparked by sensations she could not describe, until she'd succumbed to reckless abandon. She cried out against his mouth. Her thoughts fragmented as she was hurtled beyond the point of no return. Euphoria flooded her, sending torrents of rapture through her body.

She came apart at the seams, but she knew, in the end, Arcanthus would be there to put her back together.

ARCANTHUS GROWLED against Samantha's mouth as her sex clenched around his cock and a gush of liquid heat flowed from her. Her body pulled him deeper, greedy for what he had to give her. He thrummed with intense pleasure from top to bottom—even in limbs that were no longer flesh and blood—but he held on. He wasn't ready to be done; he'd not yet had enough of her.

Samantha tore her mouth from his and pressed her face against his neck, muffling her cries. Her breath was hot against his skin. Her entire body tensed and quivered over and around him, resisting his rhythm.

Something new sparked inside him—something deep, something ancient, something he'd never fully glimpsed.

It was the result of his people's mixed ancestry, a beast left dormant in his blood. A beast woken by its recognition of its mate.

He hooked an arm around her shoulders and rolled, flipping Samantha onto her back while keeping himself buried within her. As she writhed atop the rumpled bedding, Arcanthus shifted onto his knees, threw her legs around his waist, and grasped her hips. He yanked her down onto his cock, seating himself deeply inside her and producing another gasp from her kiss-swollen lips.

She clutched the blanket and looked up at him, eyes glazed and half-lidded. "Arc..."

He met her gaze and drew back his hips. He had no more words for her. When her pink tongue ran across her lower lip, any semblance of control he might've maintained burned away. He unleashed himself; he thrust into her hard, simultaneously slamming her against his pelvis.

Her cries gave way to ragged, panting breaths as he set a frantic pace, driven by an animalistic urge to have her, to claim her, to fill her with his seed. Guttural sounds rose from his chest and forced their way through his bared fangs.

His cock easily delved in and out of her wet channel, which sucked him in hungrily. He inhaled, filling his senses with the smell of sex, the perfume of his mate. Possessiveness tensed his muscles.

She was his. *His.*

Samantha squeezed her eyes shut and arched her back, thrusting her breasts into the air, as she crested again. She tightened her legs around him and dug her heels into the backs of his thighs, pulling him deeper.

The sight of his mate awash on a sea of ecstasy might've been enough on its own to send Arcanthus over the edge, but combined with the tightness of her convulsing channel, it was more than he could bear.

A maelstrom of sensation rushed through him. He held on for as long as he could, but the pressure was too great. Throwing his head back with eyes closed tight, Arcanthus roared. His muscles seized as his tendrils split open, latching onto her inner walls to force open the path to her womb, and his seed pumped into her.

Unimaginable pleasure blasted through his shuddering body, obliterating everything inside—it swept away every other feeling, every conscious thought, every bit of sensory input not related to her. For a few blissful moments, he didn't even know who he was. Only Samantha remained. Samantha, his mate.

His...everything.

When his awareness returned, he found himself bent over Samantha with his arms to either side of her head. Her dark hair was strewn about her, her pink-tinged skin glistened with sweat, her eyes were closed, and her lips were parted.

She was the most beautiful thing he'd ever seen.

Spasms raced through his body as his cock continued to flood her with his seed; his cybernetic limbs, in contrast, were locked in place, and refused to comply with his mental commands.

When he was finally able to move again, he lifted one arm and delicately brushed a few strands of damp hair away from Sam's cheek.

Her eyelids fluttered open, and she turned her face to look up at him. A contented smile graced her lips. She placed her palm on his chest, over his pounding heart.

"I'm not sure what that was, little terran, but I intend to have it again and again until my body finally fails me," he said.

Her smiled widened. "I...won't mind."

He grinned, sweeping his gaze over her face; he wanted this image of her forever in his memory. "I don't know if I'd give you a choice either way."

She grasped a thick hunk of his hair with her free hand and tugged him down. Helpless to resist, Arc bent and lowered his head as she tilted her chin up and kissed him. It was a tender kiss, an affectionate caress of lips, seeming to convey everything she felt but could not voice.

With any other female, Arcanthus would've panicked in that moment. He'd never wanted anything more than a fleeting physical connection; he'd never committed to anything beyond a bit of mutual pleasure. He didn't fully understand the things

Samantha made him feel, but he recognized them in her kiss, felt their echoes from her soul, and he accepted it all. So what if he didn't understand? This female was unlike anyone else, and her magnetic pull on him only strengthened with his every step closer.

Her hand slid up into his hair, and she broke the kiss. "I really like your hair."

"How could you not?"

Samantha laughed; the gentle vibration from her body flowed straight to his cock. It was only then that he realized it hadn't relinquished its hold. Her laughter only made his tendrils tighten their grip.

Her laughter died and her breath hitched. "Are...are you...*stuck?*"

"Yes. Yes, I am. Much as I'd prefer to tell you it's normal, I've never had this happen before—not for this long, anyway. My body seems rather covetous of you."

"Oh."

"*I* am rather covetous of you."

Sam's eyes rounded. "*Oh.*"

Arc grinned as he grazed one of his hands down her arm and over her hip to palm her ass. He kissed her again. A few days ago, she would've shied away from his slightest touch, and now she actively sought it, lifting her head to meet his lips. Her trust in him filled Arcanthus with warmth.

When his cock finally deigned to release its hold, Arcanthus reluctantly drew back his hips, slipping free of her channel. His seed spilled from her. The sight filled him with an unexplainable, savage pride, and a resurgence of possessiveness; though he'd withdrawn from her, part of him lingered inside.

His shaft slowly receded into his slit until only the tip protruded.

He slipped off the bed, reached forward, and pulled her toward the edge. Samantha didn't resist as he scooped her up; she looped her arms around his neck and shivered. Her flesh was hot against his, and the air was chilly in comparison.

Arcanthus carried her into the bathroom and stepped into the pool, flicking the nearby controls with his tail to lower the pool's floor. He sat on a submerged ledge, letting the water deepen until it was up to his chest, and positioned Samantha on his lap.

"This place is amazing," she said.

"I've always believed a home is a reflection of its owner." He dropped one of his hands onto her thighs and gently massaged her flesh, wiping away the lingering stickiness of their joining.

She turned her face toward him and grinned. "Have you always been this arrogant?"

"I can't be considered arrogant if it's all true. Only confident and self-aware."

She chuckled. Looking down into the water, she placed her hand on his arm. "The water doesn't affect them?"

Arcanthus huffed. "No. I spent good credits on these limbs. They weren't pieced together on some backwater planet, they're top of the line. Only the finest for myself...and my female." His fingertips danced over the soft flesh of her pelvis, just centimeters away from her sex.

How could he have experienced so much pleasure only moments ago and *still* hunger for more? How was his want for her so relentless, so insatiable?

She pressed her thighs together, trapping his hand.

"Hmm...I suppose you've earned a respite, if you feel you require one," he said, dipping his face to brush his lips against her cheek and nip her ear.

Arcanthus cleaned his mate, taking pleasure in the simple

task, especially when contentment relaxed her features as he washed her hair and massaged her back. By the time he was done, she was limp and nearly drowsing, her eyelids drooping.

He gathered her close, rose, and carried her out of the pool. She rested her head on his shoulder. He paused only long enough on his way out of the bathroom to let the auto-dryer do its work; the floor and ceiling briefly glowed white, and tingling warmth flowed over his skin, easing away the moisture.

Once he was beside his bed, he shifted his tail around to his front, hooked its tip beneath the bedding, and peeled the covers back. He gently laid Samantha in the open space. She curled on her side, and he pulled the blanket over her body.

After brushing the backs of his fingers over her delicate cheek, he turned to leave.

She caught his wrist.

Brow furrowed, he glanced down at her. "What is it, Samantha?"

"Stay with me," she said sleepily. "Hold me."

Her request caught him off guard; habit dictated that he never slept with *anyone*, that he never allowed himself to be so vulnerable. But what weight did habit hold when it came to Samantha? He'd already violated so many of his normal behaviors for her, had already risked so much. He'd demanded trust from her...and she deserved trust from him in return.

He lifted the blanket again and eased himself onto his side next to her. His heart pounded, and his mouth was suddenly dry. The logical part of his mind said this was just sleeping. What was there to be nervous about?

I feel for her so deeply, so wholly, and I don't know what these emotions are. They're so powerful, so intense...

And this was another step toward the edge. A little farther, and he'd plunge into the darkness of the complete unknown, he'd tumble beyond the limits of his experience.

As he laid his head down and wrapped his arms around Samantha to draw her against his chest, he realized that he *wanted* to delve into the unknown with her. He wanted to discover what their relationship would become, what it was meant to be.

Samantha rested her head on his flesh-and-blood bicep, and her soft, warm breath wafted over his chest. Her arms, with her hands curled into fists, were bent between her body and his. Within moments, her breathing slowed; she was asleep.

Arcanthus tightened his hold on her and wrapped the tip of his tail around her leg, wanting as much contact as possible. He rested his chin atop her head.

Even if he couldn't decipher his complex emotions regarding Samantha, one thing was certain—lying with her in his arms felt right. It felt like this was what had always been missing in his life. Like she was the piece that had been left out of him all along, and he'd only just figured out how she fit.

He didn't realize he was succumbing to sleep until it was too late; Samantha's intoxicating scent, mingled with his own, was the last thing he was aware of before oblivion claimed him.

SEVENTEEN

Arcanthus drifted up out of the depths of slumber, awakening to the darkness behind his own eyelids. His body was warm, his muscles blissfully slack, and a sweet, feminine scent pervaded the air. Something had touched his face; he was certain of it, though the notion was hazy in his dream-fogged mind.

Taking in a deep breath, he drew Samantha a little closer—her body felt just as warm and limp as his—and willed sleep to reclaim him.

A light brush over his cheek stirred his awareness to the surface again. He lifted a hand to his face, swatting at the phantom sensation without opening his eyes. There was room enough in his mind only for Samantha, and he'd not yet lain beside her long enough, hadn't yet held her long enough, hadn't yet dreamed of her long enough. This was where he wanted to be—in bed with his mate, the whole world nothing but a distant, unimportant memory.

Just as he was drifting again, something poked his cheek, squishing his skin against his teeth.

He moved faster this time, swiping at whatever was

touching him. His hand encountered something thick and heavy.

Arcanthus turned his head and forced his eyes open. The room was dimly lit, and it took his eyes a few moments to adjust to the gloom and bring the dark figure beside the bed into focus.

Drakkal stared down at him, eyes glowing faintly with reflected light.

Furrowing his brow, Arc glanced back at Samantha, who lay against him, face-to-face, with one arm wrapped around his side. She was in the same state of dress as him—naked. One small shift of her arm would expose her delectable breasts.

The realization sparked excitement in Arcanthus, immediately heating his blood—at least until his sleep-addled mind puzzled out the full situation. The same slight movement that would allow him so enticing a view would also reveal her to Drakkal, who was less than half a meter away and facing her.

Excitement gave way to fury.

Glaring over his shoulder at Drakkal—who stared back with an amused smirk—Arcanthus groped for the blanket with one hand without shifting his torso enough to move her arm. He found it bunched around their waists and quickly swept it higher, draping it over Samantha until it was tucked under her chin. His thumping heart echoed dully in his ears.

Samantha stirred. Arcanthus's breath hitched, and he turned his attention back to her. She sighed heavily, nuzzled a little closer to him, and eased back into stillness.

Arcanthus waited before allowing himself to inhale. Looking back at Drakkal, he scowled and pointed firmly toward the door.

Drakkal shook his head. He gestured with one hand, pointing first to Arcanthus, then himself, before moving his fingers and thumb like an opening and closing mouth.

Clenching his teeth, Arc struggled to hold back a frustrated growl. He didn't want *anyone*—not even his oldest, most trusted friend—anywhere near Samantha while she was naked. She belonged to Arcanthus; her body was meant for his eyes alone. And he certainly wasn't going to have a conversation here and now, not while it risked disturbing her rest.

Arcanthus gestured toward the door again. Drakkal repeated his prior hand movements with increased emphasis, this time pointing to the door afterward.

Get the fuck out, Arcanthus mouthed, wishing he could shout the words.

Get the fuck up, Drakkal mouthed in response.

I'm going to kill him, Arcanthus thought as he carefully disentangled his limbs from Samantha's.

Her nostrils flared with a heavy exhalation, and a soft moan sounded in her throat. Arcanthus froze and watched, muscles tense, as she pulled the bedding around her body like a velvety cocoon, nestled her face into the pillow, and settled.

Drakkal backed away, and Arcanthus, disturbing the bedding as minimally as possible, slipped off the bed. Arc kept his eyes on his mate briefly before he crept away, following the azhera to the door. The bedroom air was chilly against his sleep-warm skin, and his arms felt oddly...*empty*. He'd never been as content and comfortable as he was with her body against his.

He couldn't remember the last time he'd slept in the same room as another person—it had likely been during the chaotic, jumbled days following the loss of his limbs, as he and Drakkal had fled Caldorius, and only then because the azhera refused to leave him alone. In all the years since, he'd been too uncomfortable to share a bed with anyone. He'd felt too vulnerable.

Arcanthus cast a final, longing glance at Samantha before he stepped into the hallway. The door slid shut behind him with a tap of the control panel.

Drakkal leaned against the wall with his arms crossed. "About time you—"

Snarling, Arcanthus took a single step toward Drakkal and punched him hard on the shoulder.

The azhera grunted and staggered backward, catching himself only when he flattened a palm against the wall. He rolled his shoulder. "The fuck is wrong with you?"

Arcanthus jabbed his index finger toward Drakkal, anger burning his throat as he resisted the urge to strike again. "You are no longer permitted to enter my bedchamber without my direct permission."

Drakkal settled his hand on his shoulder, rubbing the spot Arcanthus had punched. "You're overreacting, Arcanthus."

Arc took a step closer and said through his teeth, "I'm *not* overreacting."

Drakkal laughed and shook his head. "You should see yourself right now."

"I'm serious, Drakkal."

"So am I. If you were almost any other species, your finger isn't the only thing that'd be wagging at me right now."

The azhera's words reminded Arcanthus of the cool air caressing his skin—*all* his skin. But that reminder did nothing to dampen the fire inside him.

"I would lay down my life for you, Drak. And that means a lot, considering how fond I am of myself. But when it comes to her...she's *mine*. Only for *my* eyes." Arcanthus lowered his hand, balling it into a fist. "I will not tolerate anyone seeing her naked, not even you. And that's not just me being a jealous, possessive asshole."

Drakkal's smile faded. He lifted his chin toward the bedroom. "So this is real, then? Not just the end result of you obsessing over the terran you couldn't have?"

The question triggered fresh rage in Arcanthus; he forced it aside. Drakkal had been looking out for Arc for years. He knew Arcanthus's moods, knew his weaknesses, knew it *all*. As much as it wounded his pride, Arcanthus could admit that he'd been saved from himself more than a few times by Drakkal, even if he'd only admit it in the privacy of his own mind. That's all this was—not an insult, but attempted vigilance.

"She's my *mate*, Drakkal. I didn't mean that as a figure of speech. My *qal* feels like it's on fire just thinking about her.

"I'm not sure if I should be happy for you or try to slap some sense into you."

Arcanthus shook his head and lifted a hand to sweep rogue strands of hair out of his face. "I've never been more certain of anything, Drak. And it scares the shit out of me."

Drakkal dipped his shoulder, leaning it against the wall again. "How does it scare you? Sounds like you hit it lucky. Found your one in ten billion."

"Because doubt is natural. I've approached everything in my life with some degree of doubt, and it's served me well even if it hasn't always saved my skin." Arcanthus's tail flicked back and forth through the air in erratic, restless motions. "I feel like I don't know what to do with it. Like I don't know how to move forward. My mind says there must be *something* wrong, that it's too good to be true, but my heart insists that it's real. This is true, and she deserves all the trust I've put in her."

"Don't know what to do? It's simple," Drakkal said, his voice thick with pent-up emotion. "You embrace it. Embrace *her*. Take it for what it is. There's no telling when the universe might decide to take it away.

A pang of guilt struck Arcanthus square in the chest, cooling his anger. "I didn't mean to diminish what you had, Drakkal."

"You didn't." Drakkal shook his head. "I admired her, I respected her, and I've spent a long time missing her. But it was a long time ago, and it wasn't the same as what you have with Samantha now."

Arcanthus stared at Drakkal's face. If he'd learned anything about his friend over the years, it was that Drakkal had an immensely deep well of emotions, but he rarely let those emotions rise to the surface. For a long time, Arc had thought it was a matter of Drakkal considering feelings a weakness and refusing to display that weakness to anyone, but he knew better now. Drakkal simply didn't want to burden the people he cared about with his feelings.

"You'll find what you're missing before long, Drak."

Drakkal bared his fangs. "Who said I was looking?"

"You're the one who walked in on my naked mate. You don't have any right to get angry with me."

"You punched me, Arcanthus."

"Fuck, azhera, you were a pit fighter for seven years. Are you really whining about one little punch?"

"Your hand is made of *metal*."

Arcanthus arched a brow and folded his arms, mirroring the azhera's stance. "You poor, poor thing. Now, what was so damn important that you had to drag me out of bed naked?"

"Just figured I'd see if you wanted me to find a slave collar in your size. We can get one with a tether so Samantha can lead you around the compound like her little pet."

"I *will* hit you again, Drakkal."

Scowling, Drakkal turned his shoulder slightly away from Arcanthus. "So sensitive lately, sedhi. I'd ask what crawled up your ass, but I already know."

Arcanthus stared at his friend.

Drakkal stared back before saying, "We picked up Straek."

Arcanthus pushed away from the wall, throwing up his hands. "Why didn't you say that to begin with, Drak?"

The azhera's nostrils flared. "Maybe because someone decided to punch me before I had a chance."

"It wasn't nearly as hard as you deserved."

"Don't make me give you what you deserve, sedhi."

"Focus, Drakkal. Where's the groalthuun? Downstairs?" Arcanthus strode forward, ready to act; he'd not forgotten the threat the Syndicate posed to himself and Samantha, and he was eager to address it now that an opportunity had arisen.

Drakkal stepped into Arcanthus's path and halted the sedhi with a hand on his shoulder. "Not yet."

Arcanthus ran his tongue over his teeth, swallowing a flare of agitation. "There's no reason for further delay. He has information I need. I'm going to obtain said information presently."

"You're still naked, Arcanthus."

"And?"

The azhera drew in a slow, deep breath. "You're not going to interrogate the groalthuun without clothes on."

"Why? A confident, nude individual in an unusual situation can be extremely intimidating."

"Because I have a responsibility to our security team, and you beating Straek to a pulp while wearing nothing but your *qal* has too great a chance of destroying their trust in me."

Arcanthus settled his hand on Drakkal's shoulder and gave it a squeeze. "Consider it a bonus for their exemplary performance over the last few days. A special treat."

"Go put on a loincloth," Drakkal said with exaggerated gentleness, "or I'm going to give everyone a turn to kick you in your damned slit."

Despite the prisoner waiting for interrogation, despite Drakkal's impatience, despite *everything*, Arcanthus stopped and stared at Samantha after he crept back into the bedroom. He couldn't help himself; she was so beautiful with her features relaxed by sleep, so lovely with all her cares and inhibitions smoothed away, so enticing. Curled up in the blankets on his massive bed, she looked tiny, vulnerable, and alone, a thing to be cherished and protected.

He knew in that moment that he'd give up anything, everything, for her. To keep her safe, to keep her at his side. His instinctual draw to her was irresistible, but his want for her was so much more than instinct.

Somehow, he resisted the urge to crawl back into bed, enfold her in his arms, and make sure she knew she wasn't alone, knew he was here, knew she was his. He forced himself to open the drawer containing his loincloths—noting with no small degree of irritation that, according to the menu, only two hours had passed since he lay down with his mate—removed one from within, and secured it in place as quickly and quietly as possible. He slipped into the closet next to pull on a robe, paying no attention to the color or subtle patterns on the fabric.

He paused again when he turned back toward the bed and his eyes fell upon Samantha.

I could just touch her once more. A simple little touch, just the brush of a fingertip over her cheek...

Arcanthus shook off that impulse. There were other matters requiring his attention, and he didn't want to disturb Samantha's slumber. She'd been through so much over the last few days, had seen so many dramatic changes to her life. He understood how that might've felt—he'd gone through sudden, drastic changes in his lifestyle and situation many years ago, and to say adjustment had been difficult would've been an immense understatement. All things considered, she was taking everything very well.

But he expected nothing less of his intriguing little terran. She didn't realize just how strong she was, but he saw it.

His stomach felt heavy and knotted as he exited the room, undoubtedly the result of denying his craving for her. He reminded himself once again that this was all for her, all to keep her safe, but it did little to ease his discomfort.

I need to seize control of my thoughts.

It was true, but part of him didn't want to turn away from Samantha and all the things they'd done together, from all the things he still wanted to do with her. They'd only begun to explore the erotic delights they could share—and he found her company thrilling even when they weren't engaged in such activities.

"You'd better have that thing strapped down," Drakkal grumbled as Arcanthus approached him.

Arcanthus blinked and turned his attention to the azhera, giving himself a mental shake to return to the present. "What are you talking about?"

"I know that look on your face. I know what you're thinking about. Keep it in your slit for once, would you?"

The sedhi offered no argument; he fell into place beside Drakkal, and they walked through the corridors and downstairs to one of the rooms below street level. The heavy door slid open with a rumble that Arcanthus more felt than heard, revealing a chamber devoid of furnishings apart from a few simple chairs.

The groalthuun was seated in one of those chairs, positioned in the center of the room beneath a single beam of intense light that made the rest of the space dark in comparison. He was facing away from the door, and a splotch of blood had dried on the fine scales on the back of his head, just beneath the knobby growths atop his skull. His arms and legs were fastened to the chair by thick tristeel manacles.

Straek twisted his neck to look back at Arcanthus with one large, dark eye. He snorted and turned away.

Sekk'thi and Thargen were seated to either side of the door, the latter sharpening a metal-bladed knife with a whetstone; it was an archaic method, but the sound of metal scraping rock was a powerful, primal thing.

"What has our guest decided to share with us thus far?" Arcanthus asked as he entered the room. Drakkal followed immediately behind him.

"Very little. He has been uncooperative," Sekk'thi replied.

"Just give me a few minutes. I'll get him to talk," said Thargen. "I'll even let him out of the chair, just to make it sporting."

"You may yet have your chance, my friend." Arcanthus picked up an empty chair and carried it past the groalthuun, setting it immediately in front of the captive. He eased down atop it, crossing one leg over his opposite knee and winding the tip of his tail around one of the chair's legs.

Straek's mouth curved upward in a strained smile. "No point in me telling you you're dead, I guess."

Rage had reawakened in Arcanthus—rage for what this groalthuun represented, for the danger Arc and Samantha had been placed in, for everything the Syndicate had taken from him. But they would *not* take his mate.

Arcanthus shrugged, forcing himself to hold his casual visage. "Is there a point in me telling you the same?"

Straek leaned his head forward and spat on the floor.

Pressing his lips together, Arcanthus glanced down at the glob of saliva near his foot. "That was rude, Straek."

"Fuck you."

"Someone has to clean this room when we're done. Now, any mess made by myself or my associates is understandable— this is our place, after all. But *this*...this is just uncalled for. You're a guest here. A show of respect could go a long way in your situation."

"You think I'm scared of you?"

"Clearly not."

"The boss is going to take you apart piece by piece, sedhi, and make you wish you were never born."

Arcanthus tipped his head back and sighed heavily. He'd learned throughout his life to always maintain the act—to always project confidence and calm no matter what he felt inside. He'd been slipping up in that regard more and more lately, and his current fury made it difficult to follow that rule, but he refused to show anything other than arrogance and indifference to this scum.

"I was worried you were going to go this route," Arcanthus said. "It's so...typical. The Inner Reach is going to kill me, me and my whole family are dead, you're not going to give me anything so I should go fuck myself. It's just *tiresome*, isn't it?"

Arc leveled his gaze on Straek. "If you're going to go this route, at least come up with original material. Your onigox friend said the same thing right before I killed him."

The groalthuun's expression hardened, and he bared his large, flat teeth. "I'm going to—"

"You're not going to do anything," Arcanthus growled.

Straek snapped his mouth shut and glared at Arc, nostrils flaring with heavy breaths.

Sighing again, Arcanthus smoothed down his robe and settled both feet on the floor, resting his elbows on his thighs as he leaned forward. "It seems you may be experiencing some difficulty understanding your current situation. Here's how it's going to work, Straek—I'm going to ask you a question, and you're going to answer. If you don't, or if I'm unsatisfied with your response, I'm going to move just a little closer to letting my vorgal associate do with you as he pleases."

"You think anything you can do to me is worse than what the Syndicate would do?" Straek laughed bitterly. "You have no idea what you're dealing with, do you?"

"A better idea than most, my friend. Why were you sent after me?"

"Fuck. You."

Arcanthus frowned. He leaned back in the chair, propping one arm on the armrest with his fist raised. He extended his index finger. "Why were you sent after me?"

The groalthuun's eyes shifted to Arcanthus's fingers. "What does that mean? What are you doing?"

Arcanthus raised his middle finger along with the first and repeated his question again.

Straek's jaw muscles ticked, and he released a huff of air. "I...I don't know."

Quirking a brow, Arcanthus began straightening his next finger.

"I'm not lying!" Straek said hurried. "I really don't know. Boss saw your picture and said you needed to die. As soon as he figured out a way to get you in the open, he sent a bunch of us to kill you."

Arcanthus halted the motion of his finger. "Why does your boss want me dead?"

"Like I said, I *don't* know."

Arc's third finger straightened. "Only two left, my friend."

"He doesn't explain that stuff to us, damn it! We just do what he says. He'd kill us if we questioned him. All I know is he kept it in our gang and threw a lot of people at you. You must've done something to piss him off, because I've never seen him get like that over one person."

An icy drop of fear tumbled into the blazing fires in Arcanthus's gut, making his stomach churn. This wasn't confirmation that the Syndicate knew his true identity; it didn't mean they were after him because of the events on Caldorius a decade before. It was far more likely that he'd slept with this *boss's* female and the tryst had been discovered. That would've been more than enough to be sentenced to death by a Syndicate officer. Before Samantha, Arcanthus had been rather promiscuous, and he'd made mistakes...

But that didn't ring true to him, and in this situation, he had to assume the worst, because regardless of their motives, the Syndicate wanted him dead. The only piece of good news—if it was even true—was that the hit hadn't been passed along the Syndicate's chain of command.

That meant there was still a chance of surviving this. There was a chance of stopping it.

Arcanthus coiled his tail tighter around the chair leg. "Now you're getting the hang of it, Straek. Loosening up. That warms my heart. This is the part when we get to the juicy information. What is your boss's name, and where I can find him?"

The groalthuun swallowed. "He's going to find you first, and you'll be fucking dead."

Frowning, Arcanthus raised his pinky. It took all his willpower to keep from smashing Straek's face, to keep from unleashing his fury on this groalthuun—the one who, as far as Arcanthus knew, had started all this trouble.

"Just when I thought we'd turned it around," Arc said. "I'm going to ask you one more time, Straek. I want you to think long and hard about this before you give me an answer. Think about what it means if you don't tell me what I want to hear. Think about what my friend is going to do to you. He's been quite upset since your people attacked us at that apartment building, and he's bristling to have an outlet for his frustration."

"Fuck yeah, I am," Thargen growled.

"Who is your boss, and where can I find him?"

Breathing raggedly through his nostrils, Straek stared at Arcanthus. His large eyes were filled with warring terror and hatred.

Arc could guess at what was going through the groalthuun's

head—would the consequences of betraying the Syndicate be worse than those incurred when Arcanthus lifted his thumb?

Arcanthus might've felt some sympathy for an individual in such a predicament, but not for this individual. At best, Straek had been scoping out Samantha with the intention of kidnapping her and selling her into slavery. That was inexcusable. *Any* threat against Arcanthus's mate, no matter how minor, could not be tolerated—and enslavement certainly wasn't minor.

The chamber door opened. Arcanthus looked over Straek's shoulder.

Razi entered the room, holding something in his hand. "Got his holocom here, boss. Made sure it wasn't reporting location before we brought it back."

The groalthuun's scales paled.

Arcanthus shifted his attention back to Straek. "Well, this new development doesn't seem very conducive to your continued survival, does it?"

Straek jolted forward; he was halted abruptly by his bindings. "No! No, you *need* me."

Smirking, Arcanthus curled his splayed fingers into a fist and lowered his arm. "Oh? Do I?"

"You do, yes, yes!" Straek twisted his neck to look at Razi, who stood just inside the doorway with the holocom on his open palm. "It's secured and encrypted. You're not getting anything out of it without me."

"Straek, old friend, I'm not sure if you're severely overestimating your importance or severely underestimating my capabilities. I suppose it doesn't make much of a difference either way, does it?" Arcanthus leaned forward and settled a hand on the groalthuun's knee. "Name and location. It can be that simple."

Straek shook his head and said in a weak voice, "They'll kill me."

A new layer draped itself over Arcanthus's anger. The time for calm had passed, and Straek's holocom would undoubtedly prove more informative than its owner—the technology could be tampered with but could keep no secrets from a person of sufficient skill.

He couldn't let go of the fact that, even now, Straek was more afraid of the Syndicate than Arcanthus. He knew it was petty, but he didn't dismiss the notion. Perhaps Arc *had* grown soft over the years. He preferred to build his operation on trust and quality work, and he'd relied upon violence and intimidation only when the informants who spread his aliases to potential clients forgot their places.

Perhaps Straek was too dumb to understand his inevitable fate. Perhaps his skull was too thick to comprehend the most immediate threat to his life.

Or, perhaps, Straek's boss truly was that terrifying.

Regardless, Arcanthus's patience had been exhausted.

Arcanthus turned his head slightly to meet Thargen's gaze and lifted a hand. "May I borrow your knife?"

Thargen scowled, turned the knife in his hold, and rose from his chair. He extended his arm and settled the grip of his knife on Arcanthus's waiting palm. "I wanted a piece."

Arcanthus nodded as he closed his fingers around the grip. "I know. But Straek chose to stalk *my* terran, and I will not allow that to go unanswered."

He held up the blade in the space between himself and the groalthuun, letting the overhead light gleam on the freshly sharpened metal.

Straek leaned back as far as his chair allowed, straining against his bindings. The entire chair rattled as his struggles grew in desperation. "Let me go. I won't tell anyone anything."

"Even were it not for my expansive experience with untruths, Straek, I wouldn't believe you on that."

"Then at least let me out of this chair like the vorgal said! Let me die fighting."

Arcanthus released a short, bitter laugh as a fresh surge of rage blasted through him. He shoved himself out of his chair and kicked Straek in the chest. The groalthuun released a choked grunt that couldn't mask the sound of his cracking ribs as the chair slammed backward and slid two meters across the floor.

Stepping over the chair, Arcanthus lowered his foot on Straek's throat and knelt on his other leg, bending forward so his face was closer to the groalthuun's. Scales that had paled to white not long before were now darkening, and Straek's eyes bulged in their sockets.

"Death in combat is a fate reserved for the brave," Arcanthus said through bared fangs. "You and your ilk know *nothing* of courage. You know *nothing* of sacrifice. You don't deserve a chance to fight for your life, you blubbering skrudge."

Arcanthus swung the knife in a downward arc. The blade sank deep into Straek's right eye, scraping the bone of the eye socket and stopping only when it punched through the backside of the groalthuun's skull and hit the floor beneath. Straek convulsed, released a few choked grunts, and stilled.

Keeping his foot on Straek's neck, Arcanthus tugged the knife free. Blood spurted from the open wound and splattered his arm, chest, and robe. Frowning, he wiped the blade clean on the groalthuun's shirt, stood up, and returned the weapon to Thargen.

The vorgal raised the knife to examine it. "You blunted the tip, damn it."

Arcanthus gritted his teeth and released a steadying breath. Anger simmered in his gut, undiminished by his outburst;

Straek's death had been too swift to alleviate Arc's pent-up aggression. Part of him regretted using the knife instead of his fists. His only compensation was the tiny satisfaction of having one less threat to his mate.

He forced an unconcerned tone into his voice and said, "Yes, and my robe got blood on it. We all have our problems."

Drakkal grunted; he was sitting against the wall to Arc's right, his tail rippling beside him. "I think he was about to talk. Right before you skewered his eye."

"You know just as well as I that torture is highly likely to produce false information," Arcanthus said. "There was no point in prolonging the inevitable."

"*That* was torture?" Sekk'thi asked, tilting her head. "Did I miss something during that exchange?"

"Yes, it was torture," Drakkal said. "He had to sit and have a conversation with Arcanthus."

Arcanthus turned his head to glare at the azhera.

Drakkal lifted his brows, sighed, and pushed himself up to his feet. He swept his arms to the sides and swung them back in a slow stretch before dropping his gaze to the groalthuun. "All right. Let's get this cleaned up. Our guest isn't going to find his own way out."

"Razi, drop off that holocom in my workshop," Arcanthus said.

The cren nodded.

Arcanthus strode out of the room without looking back. He knew there would be answers on the holocom, he just didn't yet know the correlating questions. It probably wouldn't help him identify Straek's boss, probably wouldn't grant any insight into why the Inner Reach Syndicate was suddenly after him again, but *any* information was welcome at this point.

Besides, Straek wasn't likely to volunteer any more information.

He clenched his fists at his sides as he stalked toward his bedroom, battling the urge to punch and kick the walls in blind, indiscriminate fury.

What is wrong *with me?*

The answer came with surprising swiftness and made it clear that his query had been poorly worded.

Samantha.

She wasn't what was wrong with Arcanthus—in fact, she felt like the only thing currently *right* in his life—but she had an undeniable effect upon him. Being called away from her earlier had sparked his agitation, but it wasn't merely that fleeting separation that had stoked the fires of his fury. She was in *danger*, and the beast lurking within him could not rest so long as that was the case. His instincts roared for him to eliminate all threats to her.

And where would that path lead? The Syndicate presented the most immediate danger, but what about this city, this planet, the whole damned *universe*? Everything could be perceived as a threat to Samantha. At some point, he would have to find a means of restoring his self-control.

But he wouldn't stop fighting for her. He'd *never* stop. More than anyone he'd known, Samantha deserved safety. She deserved comfort, security, and stability. Deserved to have a good life.

Arcanthus was jarred from his thoughts when he turned a corner, entering the hallway in which his bedroom was located, and collided with Samantha.

He released a startled grunt; she gasped and stumbled back several steps before righting her balance.

"Are you all right, little terran?" he asked, closing the distance between them. His heart thumped, and his skin felt hot; even the thought of accidentally doing her harm was almost too much for him to bear.

But she wasn't looking at him. Her wide eyes were fixated on her hands, which were smeared with blood.

EIGHTEEN

As Samantha stared at her blood-stained hands, her confusion became shock.

Not mine. It's not mine.

Then whose?

Samantha looked up at Arcanthus. There was blood spattered on his chest, soaked into his robe, and glistening on his hand. Horror, somehow fiery and icy at once, spread outward from her chest. Her heart quickened.

"Arc? What happened? Are you hurt? Did they attack again?" The words tumbled out of her mouth in rapid succession, sped by her growing panic.

He lifted his hands, displaying his palms, and shook his head. "I'm fine, terran, and we weren't attacked. Let's head back to the room and clean you up."

"If we weren't, then what happened? Whose blood is this?"

Arcanthus sighed softly. "You remember the groalthuun who broke into your apartment?"

The same groalthuun who was stalking us at the Ventrillian Mall.

"Yes."

"Well...he won't be bothering us anymore."

"What...what happened?"

He extended an arm, gesturing toward the bedroom. "Let's head to the room and wash up, and I will tell you, all right?"

Samantha didn't move. This situation felt familiar; how many times had James avoided her questions to hide what he'd done? How many times had he brushed aside her concerns so casually that it made her feel like she was insignificant—or, sometimes, like she was going insane?

Had she been a fool to let her guard down again? Had she misplaced her trust in Arcanthus?

"What happened, Arc?" Samantha asked quietly.

"Samantha..." He moved closer to her.

Sam retreated several steps.

He halted, hands falling to his sides. The hurt on his face almost made her resolve crumble. *Almost.*

"I had my people pick him up," he finally said. "He was part of the Inner Reach Syndicate, a powerful crime organization. I needed to know why they came after me."

A shiver coursed down her spine. "And you...you what? Tortured him?"

Please say no. Please say no. Even if you did it...please say no.

His brows fell low, and his expression hardened. "I'm not a good person, Samantha, but I gave him a chance to talk. He refused. There was no torture involved. His death was quick."

Samantha clutched the fabric of her loose shirt.

It was so easy for her to forget that Arc was a criminal, so easy to forget that he fought and killed without batting an eye. He'd offered her only sweet, coaxing words, gentle touches, and honeyed promises. Were it not for the attack at her apartment building, she might never have seen the darker side of him. She might never have known what he was truly capable of.

When would his kindness stop? When would he get angry enough to hurt her? To strike her, to beat her?

To kill her?

Arcanthus closed the distance between them before she had a chance to escape. He pressed her back against the wall, looming over her, and she stiffened with another jolt of fear. She felt tiny, helpless, weak, *trapped*; there was nowhere to go, and she'd done it.

She'd triggered him.

He raised his hands. She expected his powerful fingers to dig into her skin, expected the crushing force of his grip to fracture her bones, but there was only warmth, gentleness, and care as he cradled her face and tilted it up toward his.

"*Never* you, Samantha," he growled vehemently. "Anyone else, but *never* you."

Samantha stared up at him, heart pounding. His eyes burned as intensely as his *qal* markings.

Arcanthus leaned closer to her. "I will eliminate *any* threat to you, Samantha. I will do so without hesitation or remorse. But I would sooner plunge a blade into my own heart than do you any harm."

She swallowed thickly. The little voice inside her head that whispered doubts—*he's lying; words are cheap; don't fall for the act; he's just like James*—fell silent beneath Arcanthus's passionate gaze. Whatever lies he'd told, whatever truths he'd masked, whatever concerns she might've had couldn't discount the honesty and desire ablaze in his eyes. He was as silver-tongued as his sinfully demonic appearance suggested, but even one as talented and charismatic as Arcanthus couldn't fake the genuine emotion he was projecting.

His bared soul gleamed in his eyes, and it would've shown her the truth even without the aid of his words.

Samantha's stomach knotted with shame. She lifted her hands to cup his face but stopped when she noticed the blood on her fingers; she grasped his metal arms instead.

"I'm sorry," she said, eyes stinging with tears. "I shouldn't have... I know you're not him. I saw the blood, and I just—"

"Just acted like a rational person would." Arcanthus leaned his head down, closed his center eye, and tipped his forehead against hers. "You are new to this world. To *my* world. It would be foolish for either of us to expect you to have adjusted so quickly."

"I don't know if I've adjusted at all. I've just felt so...lost."

Through it all, Arc had been her one constant—he'd been the rock jutting from churning waters, and she'd clung to him desperately. Without him...she would've been hopelessly adrift.

"Come, my flower. Let's clean up," he said gently.

Samantha nodded.

They returned to his room quietly, and for the fourth time in what felt like a day—though she was fairly certain at least two days had passed since she was brought here—she bathed. Arcanthus joined her in the water, scrubbing the blood from his body and brushing his hands over her skin. His touch was soothing, and he kept their contact chaste. He seemed to understand that she wasn't ready for intimacy just yet. She needed something more from him; she needed answers.

She needed to know everything.

He didn't allow her to dress once they had left the water and dried—he said he wanted to feel her as he held her, that he wanted no obstacles between them.

Slipping his arms around Samantha, Arc lifted her off her feet and carried her into the bedroom. He pulled back the covers with his tail, laid her on the bed, and climbed in after her. She was in his arms again within a second. He drew her body against his and covered them with the blanket. His tail curled around her waist securely as he trailed a hand over her hair and down her spine.

Nestling against his chest, Samantha inhaled, taking in his scent. The mellow, spicy notes of sandalwood comforted her. Though she hadn't known Arcanthus for long, it felt like right here, in his arms, with his scent surrounding her, was where she was meant to be. Like this was...*home.*

"Why me, Arcanthus?" she asked.

She'd asked the question already, but she still couldn't wrap her mind around it. Why would he choose *her* when he could have almost any woman he wanted? Why her, when she was damaged, when she was broken, when she was timid and weak? Anyone else would've been a better choice. *Anyone.*

"I already told you, little terran. One look was all I needed to know you are mine. You're my mate."

Something about the way he said those last words gave Samantha pause. She leaned back and lifted her head to look him in the eyes. "What do you mean?"

"It means that my body, my instincts, and my...my *soul* recognize you as something more than anyone else could ever be to me. As my match. As the one person who can complete me, who can fill in what I'm missing."

Samantha's lips parted, her heart leapt, and something fluttered in her belly, spreading warmth outward. Joy unlike she'd ever known flooded her.

But on the heels of that joy crept her old friend, doubt.

He was just reacting to an instinctual drive. If not for that, he would never have paid her any attention. She would've been beneath his notice, and wasn't that what she'd hoped to accomplish? To be beneath everyone's notice, to be invisible, to make sure she never burdened anyone with her inadequacy?

Arcanthus's eyes narrowed. He swept her hair back and settled his palm on her cheek. "I *see* you doing it to yourself, Samantha. You let yourself be happy for a moment, and now you've crushed it. Speak to me."

"You..." She closed her eyes briefly and struggled to keep her voice steady as she said, "*You* didn't choose me."

His brows rose, and the corners of his mouth curved in a ghost of a smile. "I didn't? No, I suppose I didn't choose you. I feel I had scant choice in the matter. My body reacted to you immediately, told me I had to have you. But it was when we first spoke, it was during those first minutes we spent together, that I knew it was more than a need to have you. I *wanted* to have you.

"The pull I feel toward you...it is powerful, yes. But I have considerable willpower at my disposal, if I choose to employ it, and such instincts can be ignored. Things very likely would've been far simpler for me if I'd ignored it. I would never have been targeted by the Syndicate. I wouldn't have had to fight my way out of an apartment building. I wouldn't have my thoughts consumed by you."

Arcanthus brushed his thumb over her cheekbone. "And I do not for one instant regret following those instincts, Samantha. I'd have gladly blasted my way through a thousand apartment complexes to have you at my side. I cannot imagine how empty I would feel without you here, now that I know what I was missing."

Samantha stared down at him, her vision blurry from the tears welling in her eyes. Those tears spilled when she blinked. Her lower lip trembled against the power of the emotions roiling inside her; they were too strong to bear, too strong to hold in, but she couldn't speak past the tightness in her throat. So, she did all she could—she threw herself against Arc, pressed her face against his neck, and clung to him.

Arcanthus might as well have said *I love you*; his words carried the same weight as such a declaration, the same passion. And Samantha loved him, too. As outrageous as it sounded, she couldn't imagine life without him.

Oh, I can imagine...desolate, cold, lonely.

Arcanthus had brought more laughter into her life than anyone or anything else, had given her safety, friendship, and—though she had a long way to go—her first taste of self-confidence.

Arc wrapped his arms around her. "*That* is closer to the reaction I'd hoped for when I said you were my mate."

Samantha laughed; she could hear his arrogant grin in his voice. Her tears dampened his skin, but he didn't seem to mind. "How though? We're...two different species."

"Doesn't matter, my flower. Especially considering the tretin side of my ancestry."

"What do you mean?"

Arcanthus shifted back and propped his head on his hand so he could look down at her. "That depends on how in-depth a lesson you desire on biology and history."

She lifted her hand and brushed her fingers over his face, tracing the *qal* markings around his left eye and cheek. He closed his eyes as though her touch was bliss.

"I want to know everything, Arcanthus," she said. "I want to know all about you, your past, your people. The good and the bad. Everything."

"I suppose we should take all that one step at a time, shouldn't we?" he said with a soft smile, opening his eyes. "The tretins are a race of...well, they call themselves *intergalactic conquerors*, but their real drive seems to be to interbreed with every intelligent species in the universe. They have extremely adaptive reproductive systems that allow them to impregnate more or less anything they choose to mate with. They're particularly fond of seeding hybrid races, and there are cases of them essentially outbreeding entire species by creating new strains."

Samantha's eyes rounded, and she slid her hand down to her belly.

Arc's smile widened, showing his devilish fangs, as his eyes dipped to follow her hand. "Though I find the thought of you carrying my offspring immensely satisfying, you don't need to worry. I have measures in place to prevent that situation." He lowered his hand to cover hers; the metal of his palm was warm and strong. "Wholly reversible measures."

She never would've considered the possibility of inter-species breeding had he not said anything; it had seemed a given that they couldn't reproduce with one another. But now that the subject was out in the open, she couldn't help thinking about it.

James hadn't wanted anything to do with children—something for which she was incredibly thankful—and had forced birth control injections upon her. As soon as she'd left him, she stopped the treatments. Why would she have bothered? She hadn't expected to be with anyone else—hadn't *wanted* to be with anyone else—*especially* in an intimate manner.

The thought of having children with Arcanthus... It was a sweet one, and it filled her with warmth and joy.

What would their babies look like? Would they have horns, tails, and markings on their skin just like their father's?

They'd be...*adorable.*

But what kind of mother would she be? Samantha's mother had died while she was a baby, and though her grandmother had done the best she could, her age and failing health had limited her severely. Sam's father had never remarried. She'd never really had a strong maternal role model to learn from.

Still, Sam would do her damnedest to be the best mom she could be... When the time was right.

I would be a good mom... I will be a good mom.

Arcanthus's husky chuckle pulled her out of her thoughts. "I see the idea appeals to you, my flower."

Samantha blushed and smiled shyly. "It does... But not yet."

"No, not yet. We'd be getting a bit ahead of ourselves, wouldn't we? It may be some time before I'm willing to share you."

She reached up and brushed his hair out of his face, tucking it behind his long, pointed ear. "I...don't want to share you, either."

His *qal* glowed bright as he tipped his head forward and kissed her with more tenderness and affection than she'd ever experienced. His kisses had always been scalding, hungry, arousing, but this one was different—this was a gesture telling her he was here for her, that he'd always be here for her.

"Tell me more," Samantha said when their lips separated. "Tell me about your childhood and your life. I want to know you, Arc."

He shifted his hand as he leaned back on his elbow again, trailing his fingertips across his mouth. "I find myself torn between my desire to know more about *you* and the open invitation to talk about myself. You're feeding into an already dangerously large ego, Samantha."

Laughter bubbled up from within her. "I didn't think you could pass up a chance to talk about yourself."

His grin rekindled the light in his eyes. "You already know me so well. But as interesting as I seem, there's not terribly much to tell. My people are a relatively new race in the eyes of the universe. Our holdings are small, like those of your people, and life on sedhi planets is...*stressful* might be a good word. By virtue of our history and lineage, we have strained relations with the volturians and outright hatred of the tretins. Both races are far greater in number and power than us.

"It is a strange dichotomy in which we exist. We are terrified of random attacks from the volturians and the tretins, while at the same time our nature instills within us a *desire* for combat. At any rate, I learned the arts of war from a young age, like most sedhi children. It was normal for us."

"Is that why you said you used to be a fighter?" she asked, though his skills in combat suggested *used to be* was incorrect.

"I was a fighter, but not because of my childhood training. We'll get to the point in my story shortly—and I'll remind you that *you* wanted to know everything." He moved his free hand to her shoulder and twined a strand of her hair around his fingers. "When I came of age, I joined the Sedhi Defense Coalition, as is required of all my people. I joined the Crimson Raiders, knowing it was a branch that actively sought engagement with our enemies. Skirmishes with the tretins were frequent. I saw a great deal of combat in that first year. Part of me reveled in it. It made no difference whether I was fighting for my people, so long as I was fighting.

"But I was captured. As brutal as the tretins can be—and they truly are—they enjoy taking prisoners, and it's said the slave markets on Caldorius are fueled by tretin slavers. That's where they brought me. I was sold as a slave, and my owner immediately tossed me into an arena to fight for my life. I suppose it was a test. Survival meant I was worth further investment."

Samantha's dawning horror was counteracted only by disbelief—it seemed insane that he could lie there and remain so nonchalant as he talked about these things, idly twirling her hair around his finger as though its color and texture were more important than his story.

She swallowed down those emotions and flicked her gaze to his right prosthetic. "Is that how...you...?"

Arcanthus glanced at his shoulder. "No. That's a different story, for another time. I don't think it will spoil anything if I tell you I survived that first bout. Over my years in those arenas, I became one of the most popular and skilled fighters. A champion. Though the planet isn't known for placing much value on the law, there is a rule on Caldorius that is always honored—any gladiatorial slave who survives a certain number of bouts earns his freedom. It's used as motivation, mainly, a means of giving fighters a goal to strive toward. Something to keep them motivated.

"And I did it. One hundred and fifty matches, one hundred and fifty victories. I *earned* my freedom—freedom that should've been mine from the start. But what they don't tell you is that when you hit that milestone, your owner tosses you out without a credit to your name. The massive amount of money an enslaved gladiator earns for owners and promoters doesn't go to that fighter—not one bit of it. So, most of them have no choice but to sign on with a promoter, all of whom are connected to one crime organization or another, and continue fighting. Just as much a slave as before, but if you're winning for them, they might treat you nice. I refused to do that. I refused to be beholden to anyone. So I started doing it on my own. My skills, my winnings."

"And what happened?" Samantha asked.

"I realized that the whole apparatus they had in place—the promoters, venues, trainers, all of it—was unnecessary and deceptive. It was designed to make free fighters think there was no choice but to take a contract with a crime organization, and even though each of those organizations operated its own arenas in its own territory, they were all working together as the

Inner Reach Syndicate. So I formed my own organization. There were a few other fighters I knew who'd earned their freedom and were in situations similar to my own—Drakkal was one of them. We'd encountered one another frequently on the arena circuit. Only fought each other once, though."

His face became suddenly serious, his smile fading and brows angling down. "And no matter what he tells you, the truth is that *I* won. Fairly."

Despite how horrible Arc's story was, Samantha couldn't help but laugh at that. It was unexpected, and yet so like Arcanthus to preemptively shield his own ego.

Arcanthus's center eye met her gaze while the others remained on his fingers. He hummed softly, lips quirking, as his tail stroked up and down the side of her leg.

She prompted him to continue by asking, "And then?"

"Some of them accepted my offer. Many didn't. But as we demonstrated how successful we could be, how much money we could bring in for ourselves, more and more wanted to join. Unfortunately, the Syndicate wasn't particularly fond of our enterprise. Things became bad enough that I had to go into hiding. When they tried to kill me outright, Drakkal and myself fled the planet. We came here and started all this."

"Are you...still hiding?"

The corners of his mouth drew back, and his brow furrowed, but his features relaxed after a few moments. "I have to tell you that my natural instinct is to...*diminish* the truth on this one. I want you to feel safe here, Samantha. We *are* safe. But yes, I am hiding. As far as the Syndicate knows, I died on Caldorius ten years ago. I want to keep it that way. But with what's happened lately...there's a chance they know who I am, that I survived. There's a chance that's why the Syndicate is after me now."

"That's why Drakkal was so irritable with you when you took me to the mall," she said with a frown. Her eyes widened, and she clutched his arm. "It's because of me, isn't it? You exposed yourself because of me."

He smiled his disarming, roguish, utterly confident smile. "No, Samantha. It was because of me. You have no blame in the decisions I make. You have no guilt in this situation. I knew better, and I ignored my good sense. But whatever happens, I won't regret those risks—they're the reason I have you here with me now."

"But if—"

Arcanthus's head swooped down, and his mouth captured hers, silencing her words and thoughts. The caress of his lips, the stroke of his tongue, and his delectable taste eased her into a malleable, dreamlike state.

When he broke the kiss and pulled back, he wore a small but satisfied smile.

"Enough questions for now. Let's get back to what we were doing before Drakkal so inconsiderately woke me." He shifted his arm from beneath his head and slipped it under hers as he lay down fully. His other arm settled over her hip, and his tail coiled around one of her legs.

Samantha settled her hands on his chest; his heart beat strong and steady beneath her palms. The room was dim but for the faint blue light from the walls and the soft yellow glow of his *qal*. The golden marks were beautiful against his dark gray skin.

With a sigh, Samantha snuggled closer, letting his heat and scent envelop her. Though she felt like she'd been sleeping for days, she could still feel the heaviness of exhaustion lurking at the edges of her mind.

"You'll tell me more soon?" she asked.

"Soon, yes." He nuzzled his face into her hair. "Have to keep some mystery about myself in the meantime, or you'll lose interest."

She smiled and kissed the base of his throat before laying her head down. "I don't think that's possible, Arcanthus."

NINETEEN

Arcanthus sat with his chair tilted back and his feet, crossed at their ankles, propped up on his desk. His tail swept back and forth over the floor behind him, keeping time with the dull metallic clanks produced by the fingers of one hand tapping the knuckles of the other.

His central eye dipped to the holocom atop the desk—Straek's holocom. The screens in front of Arc, which displayed readouts from the programs he was running to overcome the holocom's security, were unchanging save for the slow cycling of tiny numerals.

Most holocoms were exceptionally secure devices, but Arcanthus's workarounds had been passed down from Zakarae, who herself had learned from some of the most skilled hackers on Caldorius. She'd taught him all he knew about hacking, and had thus laid the foundations for the life he'd led for the last decade.

Unfortunately, hacking was often a long, boring process, even after so many years to perfect his art. Were Zakarae alive, she undoubtedly could've accomplished this task in half the time.

He let his gaze wander around the workshop, paying little attention to what he saw; his mind seized the opportunity to turn toward Samantha.

He'd woken beside her a few hours ago, content and at ease. Though his problems hadn't been solved while he slept, they'd seemed less formidable after some rest, and his frustrations had diminished. Much of that was disrupted when he reminded himself that he had work to do—and that he would need to isolate himself from Samantha in order to finish it.

Despite all that, the most pressing matter upon his awakening had been Samantha. She'd turned to face away from him during the night, and her rounded ass had been pressed against his slit. His cock had already extruded, its tendrils slowly caressing her skin. He'd been unable to resist his urges—he'd teased her awake with his hands, tail, and lips, and she'd been hot and ready when he slipped into her from behind.

He waited until after they'd cleaned up and shared a meal to tell her that he'd need to spend much of the day in his workshop.

Samantha had taken it well. She'd even been understanding when he told her that, though she was free to explore the compound, he'd instructed his security team to prevent her from leaving. Keeping her locked in here made his stomach sink, but she'd only kissed him, said it made sense, and laughed about not having anywhere else she needed to be.

Her easy acceptance of the situation only heightened his determination to find a solution. He refused to spend the rest of their years cowering behind these walls, refused to let the Syndicate dictate the way he and his mate lived, refused to hold her here like a prisoner. Even if she decided never to go outside, he needed to ensure it was *her* choice to make—not anyone else's.

A soft chiming sound called his attention to one of the screens.

"About time," he muttered, expanding the screen and drawing it closer. The security bypass had done its job; now it was up to Arcanthus to extract the information within.

Using a secondary screen, he confirmed his usual protections were in place before he proceeded—the last thing he needed was the holocom somehow pinging its location despite his safeguards. Once he was satisfied, he brought up the holocom's internal menus on his main holo display.

There was little overtly incriminating data on the device—not that Arcanthus had expected there to be. The Inner Reach Syndicate had flourished because it was adept at minimizing evidence and bribing the right officials. Even low-level skrudges like Straek needed to be smart enough to cover their tracks. Anyone who leaked information in such organizations—whether the leak was voluntary or accidental—was dealt with swiftly and mercilessly.

After a little digging and cracking two more passcodes, Arcanthus gained access to Straek's stored images. To anyone who didn't know any better, it would've simply been a collection of pictures with exotic aliens as their subjects. But Arcanthus *did* know better.

Every individual who was the focus of those images was a potential target for Syndicate kidnappers and traffickers.

Arcanthus's rage reignited when he reached the series of images containing Samantha and himself. Based on the progression, Samantha had indeed been the groalthuun's focus—it wasn't until the latter images that Arcanthus's face was visible.

"Didn't even cover up your *qal*, you damned fool," he said as he perused the stills.

Despite their source, he found himself going back through the images. Samantha looked so happy in many of them, so carefree. It was how he wanted to see her for the rest of his days. She deserved all the happiness the universe could offer.

And, because the universe didn't seem particularly intent upon *giving* her happiness, Arcanthus would gladly seize it to pass along to her.

He forced himself to back out of the images after a few minutes and continued searching the device. Its geo-positioning software had been disabled, meaning it was unable to report its physical location, and its records on that regard were clean. It would've been too much to hope that Straek had accumulated a cache of location data that would point to the places he'd frequented.

The groalthuun's contacts were cryptic, listed in what Arc could only assume were nicknames—none of them followed any naming conventions or patterns with which he was familiar —that had no discernable means of organization. Just to be certain, he checked several against the Consortium database; the searches yielded no results; not an easy feat in a city of billions.

The Eternal Guard's database might've produced different results—the peacekeepers kept detailed records on anyone they detained, including known aliases—but it would take hours more of searching, and he wasn't done exploring the holocom's contents just yet.

Arcanthus paused when his eyes picked out something different on the list, backtracking a few entries to find it. While everything else was in the Universal Alphabet, one entry was listed in different characters, their shape and flow unfamiliar to him.

He copied them and ran a search on the plexus. The result came up instantly, and Arc stared at it for several seconds; his brain refused to believe what his eyes were showing him.

The characters had formed the word *Boss* in the native language of the groalthuun people.

He opened the entry, which contained, unsurprisingly, scant information—just the name and a commlink ID. Arcanthus knew the comm ID was a routing shield; it would contact the *Boss*, but it would do so through a seemingly endless chain of interconnecting IDs that would be obscured through dozens of different systems, making it almost impossible to trace.

There was nothing to gain by attempting to contact Straek's mysterious boss.

Was there?

Arcanthus stared at the commlink ID, running his gaze slowly over each character.

Even if there were nothing to gain—and he wasn't *entirely* convinced that was the case—there was also nothing to lose. Arcanthus could match the Syndicate's ability to make his communications untraceable; they stood no more chance of locating him through the commlink than he did of locating them. And, even if he knew he wouldn't get an answer, he wanted to ask this *Boss* why.

You're being stupid again, Arc. Just keep your head down and keep digging—discreetly.

Clenching his jaw, he lifted his hand, intending to dismiss the entry and continue searching the holocom, but he stopped before making the appropriate gesture.

The comm ID probably didn't even lead to Straek's superior in the Syndicate—it would be too obvious, too foolish, especially after all the deliberate obfuscation in place on the groalthuun's holocom. It was more likely to be some sort of joke, perhaps at the expense of one of Straek's associates who thought a little too highly of themselves.

He brought up a secure commlink channel on his secondary holo screen, engaged an additional layer of reroutes—claiming Straek's comm ID as his uppermost mask—and entered the comm ID for *Boss*. Without allowing himself further internal debate, he made the call. His voice-disguising software appeared onscreen as the commlink sought a connection. He quickly adjusted the settings, adding random distortions that would be difficult to filter on the other end.

The connection-in-progress tone ceased abruptly. For several seconds, there was only silence. Arc waited, lips pressed together, heart thumping.

"So, is he dead, then?" asked the person on the other end. The voice was deep, raspy, almost robotic.

Arcanthus's heart stopped, and his breath caught in his throat. He *knew* that voice.

"The sedhi?" he forced himself to reply.

"We both know this conversation wouldn't be happening if the sedhi were dead. Straek. You killed him, right?"

Arcanthus drew air into his lungs as quickly and quietly as possible.

"Just say *yes*, Arcanthus. Save us both the time."

The events fell into place in Arcanthus's mind, and he suddenly understood—Straek *had* been eyeing Samantha as a potential trafficking victim that day in the Ventrillian Mall. The groalthuun had reported to his superior within the Inner Reach Syndicate's hierarchy with the images he'd captured. A few of those images contained clear views of Arcanthus's face.

And Straek's boss just happened to be the individual who'd betrayed Arcanthus on Caldorius a decade before.

Vaund.

"Not often you're caught speechless, sedhi," Vaund spat. "I

seem to recall you always running your mouth when you were younger."

A swell of anger paralyzed Arcanthus for another instant before he found his voice; he would *not* show weakness, not to Vaund.

"And you certainly have a talent for running yours, Vaund, especially considering I cut off half your jaw."

"But who wound up the lesser man in the end? Who wound up whimpering on the ground in an alleyway?"

The memories—still startlingly vivid after all this time —threatened to rise to the surface of Arcanthus's mind. He gritted his teeth and shoved them aside. "If you just wanted to reminisce, you could've invited me out for a few drinks. You didn't need to send a hit squad to get my attention."

"You're tough, sedhi. Resilient as a sewer skrudge. But this time, I'll make sure you don't have anything left to drag your rotting carcass away with. Not arms or legs. Not your tail. Not even your wagging tongue."

"My only regret after all these years is that taking off *your* tongue didn't shut you up." Flames roared in Arcanthus's chest —flames that had burned for a decade. "I picked you up. I saved your life, I paid to have you fixed."

"You're the one who fucking broke me to begin with! Do you think I'd be loyal to you after that?"

"Would you have preferred death? Is that why you did it? You betrayed us all, Vaund."

"I would have preferred *victory*." The metallic buzz under-lying Vaund's voice grew more pronounced. "And I claimed it from you eventually. I *beat* you. Only to find out now you're still kicking—albeit with cybernetic legs."

"Is that why you haven't sent word up the chain, Vaund? Because a loss like that, a stain on your reputation, would end your career? Because you didn't actually win, despite what you've been telling your superiors?"

"I don't need anything but my own bare hands to kill you, sedhi."

Arcanthus snickered. "I suppose that's why you sent a dozen men after me the other day. I know this phrasing is insensitive, given your condition, but you need to face it, Vaund—in a straight fight, I'm the winner. Every time. You're going to need better than *you* if you want to take me out."

Vaund released a frustrated growl. The comms fell quiet save for the low rasp of Vaund's breathing before, frustration replaced by smugness, he asked, "How's your terran, sedhi? *Samantha?*"

Fury silenced Arcanthus, its impossible heat creating immense pressure in his chest that made it difficult to breathe.

"Hope you haven't used her too hard," Vaund continued. "It would be a shame if you diminished her market value. I could make a lot of credits off a female that delicate and innocent looking."

Arcanthus's nostrils flared with a heavy exhalation. Bracing his hands on the edge of his desk, he leaned forward. His arms trembled; he was a split second away from heaving the desk over, a split second away from smashing everything around him in helpless, hopeless rage. His instinct demanded he respond to *any* threat to his mate with violence, and only a diminished whisper in his mind told him that tearing apart his workshop would accomplish nothing.

"I'll give you this one chance, Vaund. Leave Arthos. Take whatever credits you've made from the Inner Reach and leave."

"You don't seem to understand how this works, Arcanthus. Even after all these years, you're still so naïve."

"I'm going to find you. And I'm going to take your metal skull between my hands and crush it."

"Mentioning the terran struck a nerve, did it, sedhi?"

"I was content to leave you be, Vaund. To put that part of my life behind me. *You* started this, and I will end it. Keep talking, and I'll change my mind about making it quick."

"Time for you to listen, Arcanthus, for once in your life. You're the underdog, just like you were on Caldorius. You can struggle all you want, you can fight, and it will always amount to *nothing*. The Syndicate would've crushed you even if I hadn't turned on you. It was just a matter of time. All I did was make sure I placed my bets on the winning contender for a change.

"You're a speck of space dust careening toward a star. There's only one way it will end, and it's not with you as the victor—it's with you annihilated. I *am* the Syndicate, and I'm going to stomp you out of existence once and for all."

The desk groaned softly as Arcanthus pressed down upon it. "The minutes are ticking away, Vaund, and if you don't hurry, you're going to wake up to your final sight—my grinning face."

Arcanthus terminated the connection. He remained frozen in place; his hands were clamped on the edge of the desk, his teeth were clenched so tightly they felt on the verge of shattering, and every muscle in his body was painfully stiff with tension. The deluge of emotions within him was too much; for a long while, he couldn't process them, couldn't sort them, couldn't even form coherent thoughts.

When he finally regained some control, his anger had risen to overshadow everything else.

Caldorius was ten years behind Arcanthus—why couldn't that chapter of his life remain in the past? Why had it surfaced to reclaim him now, when he'd found his mate, when he'd finally found some genuine happiness? When he'd finally found deeper meaning to it all.

He raged at his helplessness—he couldn't escape his past, couldn't hope to stand against the Inner Reach Syndicate if Vaund chose to utilize its full strength and resources, couldn't protect his mate from the danger looming just beyond the horizon.

Talk had always been easy; on their own, words held little power. They required actions to gain potency. What action could he take against an intergalactic criminal organization? More specifically, what action could he take that wouldn't get everyone he knew and cared about killed?

I never intended for things to go this way, Samantha.

He'd been dealing with trouble of one sort or another for most of his life, and had always found a way to persevere, but this...this situation felt too similar to his last days on Caldorius. He didn't need any more reminders of how well that had ended for him—his arms and legs served as reminder enough.

Memories pressed in at the edges of his consciousness—darkness; a pervasive, rotting smell; the slight sting of Caldorian rain. A ring of leering thugs, their features obscured in shadow, and the single familiar figure among them. The sound of machine-assisted breathing, the crackling hum of an energy blade, the hiss of raindrops evaporating upon it. And pain—so much pain, blazing through is body like hungry flames.

That deep, robotic voice, padded by the rainfall.

It's just business.

Arcanthus pried his hands off the desk; it now sported a pair of deep dents, each vaguely in the shape of his fingers. He stood quickly, kicked away his chair, and strode to the opposite end of the desk, where he bent down and tugged open the small refrigeration unit.

He rarely drank—which was why at least ten bottles of *gurosh*—given to him by Razi—stood neatly inside the unit, all full and sealed. As he gathered the bottles in his arms, he heard Vaund's voice in his mind again.

How's your terran, sedhi? Samantha?

Growling, Arc kicked the refrigeration unit closed and stalked off the work platform, muscles straining to not crush the glass containers tucked against his chest.

He wouldn't let his mind go back there. He refused to relive those experiences.

"I just have to find him first," he muttered as he dropped all but one bottle onto the couch. He opened the remaining bottle as he sat. "Find him and fucking kill him."

TWENTY

Vaund curled his fingers into the armrests, their bone-like tips tearing the chair's hide covering. Part of him knew Arcanthus's confidence was largely bluster, knew Arcanthus's threats were empty. If the Eternal Guard had yet to find the Syndicate outpost from which Vaund oversaw his portion of the greater operation, a single sedhi had no chance of it.

But his mind kept returning to the past, to their frantic battle in a Caldorian arena long, long ago. Even now, it remained clear in his mind's eye. Even now, thinking of it caused his chest to constrict—because Arcanthus *had* won. Arcanthus had been the better fighter. And it had been Vaund's need to prove himself, paired with his greed, that pushed him to accept the challenge offered to him—face a champion gladiator in a death match and ensure that champion didn't survive.

You're going to wish you had killed me by the time I'm finished with you, Arcanthus.

His respirator wheezed and hissed, and the monitors for his heart rate and breathing flashed in warning inside his optical feed. He cursed his failing flesh—cursed the weakness it represented. Even if he'd survived that day, his body had been slowly dying ever since, rotting away one little piece at a time...

All because of Arcanthus.

Vaund had left Caldorius years ago, had advanced his position in the Syndicate, and now stood to gain only more thanks to the current demand for terrans—and the particular talents of his retrieval crew in obtaining them. Why had a ghost from his past appeared now? Wasn't his own reflection reminder enough of his failures?

He dragged his hands along the tops of the armrests, shredding more of the material, and shoved himself out of the chair. He paced toward the holo screen at his desk console, where he stopped and stared. One message to his superiors would bring the wrath of the entire Syndicate down on Arcanthus—and upon Vaund himself.

It wasn't the threat to his life—or the pile of dead street soldiers he'd soon have to explain—that kept Vaund from sending the message. No, it was something much deeper, something contrary to the cold, calculating demeanor that had earned him his reputation in the organization.

He'd lost to Arcanthus, and Arcanthus had pieced Vaund back together and acted like everything between them was suddenly settled. Like Vaund should've taken his disfigurement and near-death in stride, like he should have been grateful to the sedhi, like what Arcanthus had done in saving Vaund's life made up for being the one who almost took it to begin with.

Like becoming part of Arcanthus's ragtag gladiators' union was some immense privilege for which Vaund should've been honored, and losing his fucking face was an insignificant entry price.

He squeezed his fists so tightly that the heat vents on his

cybernetic forearm implants opened, bathing the surrounding area in a hellish orange glow.

Things have changed since those days, sedhi. I have changed.

Vaund brought up the console's controls and sent a message to his remaining lieutenants with a single image attached.

FIND THIS SEDHI. SCOUR EVERY DAMNED SURVEILLANCE FEED IN THE CITY, QUESTION EVERY INFORMANT, DO WHATEVER IS NECESSARY. I WANT HIS LOCATION.

He flexed his fingers and drew in another ragged breath; had he a jaw, he would've clenched it. He'd deal with the Syndicate leadership later. For now, all that mattered was finding Arcanthus and tearing him apart until even the molecules that comprised his body were in tatters.

"You don't get to fucking hide anymore, Arcanthus," he said. "The minutes are ticking away."

TWENTY-ONE

Samantha had spent much of her day exploring Arcanthus's compound, growing increasingly familiar with the labyrinthine corridors. There were several doors that would not open to her, and despite her curiosity, she never tried any of them more than once. When she felt like she'd seen enough, she headed for the lounge, where she played a few matches of Conquerors with Koroq and Kiloq.

The shift change saw the cren brothers out, and the vorgals, Urgand and Thargen, took their places. An exchange of introductions found her sitting on one of the couches, watching a bloody action movie with the pair. Sam found herself cringing and looking away more often than not, but Thargen whooped and laughed at much of the violence on screen.

There was no denying that he frightened her a little.

She took her leave before the movie had finished and decided to follow a circuitous route to return to the bedroom. Her path took her past the training room. Poking her head inside, she found Sekk'thi in the middle of intense exercise. She watched the ilthurii for a little while before turning to continue her journey.

"Samantha!" Sekk'thi called.

Sam looked back to see the ilthurii jogging toward her. Before she knew what was happening, Sekk'thi was leading her into the training room. Samantha couldn't help her nervousness —she'd never been in a gym even once, and though she was working on overcoming her self-consciousness with Arc, this was a totally different setting. Sam was out of her element and had no idea what to expect.

They stopped in the middle of a large, square floor mat, and Samantha was surprised when Sekk'thi began instructing her on self-defense techniques.

Samantha raised her fists in front of her, copying Sekk'thi's stance. "Why are you showing me this?"

Sekk'thi adjusted the positioning of Sam's arms and kicked her feet farther apart. "Because I spent many years feeling helpless and vulnerable, and I have seen it in your eyes. I do not wish for anyone to feel that way."

"I'm sorry. For whatever you've been through."

"It was long ago. I am stronger for it. You will also be stronger for your pain."

Samantha's initial uncertainty and trepidation vanished as time wore on, and she dedicated herself to learning, going toe-to-toe with Sekk'thi even though she had no hope of winning. The ilthurii was stronger, faster, and infinitely more skilled, but Sam felt empowered for even trying.

If only she'd had a friend on Earth to teach her such things, if only she'd had the confidence and strength to stand up to James and say *enough*. She focused that deep-seated frustration into every punch, kick, and hold as she sparred with Sekk'thi.

When Sam's back hit the mat for what might've been the hundredth time, she finally gave up.

"Uncle!"

"Uncle?" Sekk'thi stood over Samantha with her head cocked to the side and her scaled brow low. "What does an uncle have to do with this?"

Samantha chuckled breathlessly. Sweat trickled down her temples and into her already damp hair. "It's an expression from Earth. It means I surrender."

"Humph. Why not say *I surrender?*"

"Fewer syllables?"

Sekk'thi's lips drew back to reveal her sharp teeth as she laughed. "You terrans are strange. *Uncle.*" She shook her head and held her hand out to Samantha, helping her to her feet. "You did well. Tomorrow?"

"You want me to come back to do this again tomorrow?"

"I asked, did I not?"

Samantha grinned. "Yeah. Okay. Tomorrow."

Warmth bloomed within Samantha's chest as she left the training room. She had no doubt she'd be sore and bruised by morning, but she'd pushed herself, and that was surprisingly satisfying. Plus...she was making friends. None of the people here had turned up their noses because she was human. They'd treated her like she was already one of them. Like she was...family.

It was a feeling she'd missed. Though her grandmother had been old and infirm, and her father had always been working, both had found time to spend with Sam, and they'd loved her unconditionally. They'd given her a place where she belonged.

When she reached the bedroom, she bathed, rinsing the sweat from her skin. As she was pulling on her shirt, her stomach cramped with hunger. She hadn't realized just how much time had passed until she checked her holocom; she'd kept herself busy for almost the entire day.

And she hadn't seen or heard from Arcanthus once.

He's working.

But he still needs to eat.

She latched onto that notion—it was a good excuse to see him without feeling like she was interrupting or being clingy, even if she knew in her heart that he wouldn't mind her showing up unannounced no matter the reason.

Samantha couldn't get over how he'd woken her that morning; he'd roused her from sleep with his clever hands and wicked tail before sliding his cock into her from behind. His fingers had explored her body as he thrust in and out of her, finally settling on her breasts to stroke her nipples. All the while, his lips had skimmed over her shoulder, neck, ear, and cheek, their contact broken only by his husky whispers. She'd shattered into a million glowing stars in his embrace.

She bit her lip and squeezed her thighs together as a thrilling thought came to her.

Maybe I could surprise him.

Brimming with excitement, Samantha all but ran along the corridors toward his workshop and nearly rammed into Drakkal as she rounded a corner.

She gasped, eyes wide, and reeled back. "I'm sorry!"

Drakkal halted abruptly and stared down at her, his expression unreadable. "In a hurry, terran?"

Her cheeks burned, and she clutched the sides of her shirt, ducking her head slightly. Her hair fell forward, partially blocking her face. She wasn't sure why the azhera intimidated her so much. He'd been kind, even if he was gruff, and he was Arcanthus's closest friend.

"I was going to find Arc to see if he was hungry," she said.

The azhera grunted.

Samantha cringed. "Sorry." She stepped around him. "I'll... slow down."

Drakkal caught her arm in one of his large hands, stopping

her before she passed. His grip was surprisingly gentle. "We haven't really talked, terran, have we?"

Samantha glanced at his hand before lifting her eyes to his. "Um, no. What...would you like to talk about?"

He turned to face her, dropping his hand away from her arm, and his shoulders rose as he drew in a deep breath. "I figured it's only fair you know where I stand. I want to be angry at you, Samantha. Part of me even wants to hate you. Because he's careless since you came into his life, and that carelessness has put us all in danger. It's my job to keep him safe, and he's making it impossible because he's so absorbed with you."

Samantha shrank back, chest constricting. "I-I didn't ask him to do any of it. I didn't know. I never would have—"

"I'm not like him, terran. Not as good with words." He grunted again and bowed his head slightly, dropping his gaze to the floor. "I'm trying to say that I *can't* be angry at you. None of this is your fault. I told myself at first that I would never understand what he sees in you, but I do. You've been here a few days, and you already have all three cren wrapped around your finger. That's no accident."

Samantha blushed and slowly raised her head.

He lifted his head as well, meeting her gaze again. "I've known him for a long time, Samantha. I've bled for him, and he's bled for me. Before we came to Arthos... I don't know what he told you, but I found him in a *bad* state. I don't want to find him like that—or worse—again. He's my oldest friend, my brother, and I trust him with my life, even if he acts like an arrogant asshole most of the time."

Drakkal stepped closer to her. She reflexively backed away, but she bumped into the wall, halting her retreat.

Moving his arm with deliberate care, he settled a hand on her shoulder. "You don't need to fear me. Arc doesn't give his trust easily, but he's given it all to you. So...you have mine, too.

I'm here for you, Samantha. To keep you safe, just like I want to keep him safe."

"I won't hurt him," Samantha said, voice full of conviction.

"I'm not worried about you hurting him, terran. I worry about Arc hurting himself."

She frowned. "I won't let him do that, either."

Drakkal swept his gaze over her, and his eyes softened. He lowered his hand and stepped back. "He's been in his workshop all day. Won't answer anyone, won't let me in. Get in there and give him a kick in the ass for me."

Samantha's brows fell as she glanced past Drakkal, toward the workshop. Arcanthus had been fine that morning. "What happened?"

Drakkal shrugged. "He won't talk to me. Usually, I want nothing more than for him to shut up. When he actually does, though... Something's wrong. Something bad. He gets like this every now and then, and there's always something behind it, but it can take days to get him to tell me what's eating him up."

Her stomach clenched, but it had nothing to do with hunger. Whatever was tormenting Arcanthus, he had locked himself away, was suffering alone. Momentary doubt flashed through her mind; would he even see her? Would he let her in?

"I'll do what I can," she said.

"I know." Drakkal nodded and walked away, slowing briefly to add, "Find me if he doesn't let you in, and we'll just break down a door."

The corners of Sam's mouth rose in faint smile. "Drakkal? Thank you."

He grunted and offered a wave as he strode down the hallway.

Samantha turned away from the azhera to face toward Arc's workshop again, and her smile faded. She strode down the hallway, pushed onward by her need to see him, to hear him, to know he was okay. Something twisted inside her—a nagging fear that something was terribly wrong.

She reached the door at the end of the corridor and raised her hand, pressing the call button on the wall console. There was no answer. She waited a moment before pressing it again, then once more.

She was about to press it a fourth time when Arc's voice came through the intercom.

"*Leave!*"

Samantha flinched.

At least he's alive in there.

She pressed the button again.

"Drakkal, I am not in the—"

"It's Samantha, Arc."

The intercom went silent, but she knew it was still on.

"Please let me in," she said gently.

Silence stretched between them for long enough that she began to doubt whether he would open the door. The tightness in her chest intensified, approaching the point at which she feared she'd no longer be able to draw breath.

The door slid open without another word from him. Samantha released a shaky breath and immediately filled her lungs with fresh air, steeling herself for whatever awaited beyond the threshold.

She stepped inside, and the door closed behind her.

The workshop's lights were turned down, leaving only the faintest red glow on the walls—the sort of light that would've been cast by a fire that had burned down to embers. The creatures inside the large tanks were reduced to dark, unidentifiable shapes, and the whole room was cast in a layer of obscuring shadow that gave it a gloomy air.

Arcanthus was sprawled on the center of one of the couches, his robe open and loose, his *qal* dim. He held an open bottle of *gurosh* in one hand. The gloom made his expression difficult to discern, but she knew his eyes were upon her by their yellow glow.

"How is it you look so delectable even in the dark, little terran?" he asked, but there was something different about his voice, something missing from it—his usual playful energy seemed forced.

Oh, Arc...

Samantha frowned as she approached the couch. She stopped in front of it, dipped her chin, and scanned the empty bottles littering the floor. The tip of Arcanthus's tail flicked, bumping one of the bottles and sending it rolling toward her foot; she toed it aside.

Stepping closer to him, Sam reached down and plucked the drink out of his hand.

"I was saving that one for you, anyway," he said, offering her a flash of his white fangs. The light of that smile didn't reflect in his eyes.

After placing the *gurosh* on the floor—well beyond his reach—Sam turned back to him. She leaned forward and cupped his face, looking into his eyes. "Are you drunk?"

Arcanthus shook his head slowly. "I wish I was. Sedhi have a very high tolerance...another tretin thing."

Sam brushed her thumbs over his sharp cheekbones. This... wasn't Arc. This wasn't the male she'd come to know, and seeing him like this tore her up inside.

"Arcanthus, what's wrong?"

"Nothing. I was just thirsty." He shifted his leg, and his foot hit another empty bottle with a clink. "*Quite* thirsty."

She stared into his eyes a moment longer and pressed a light kiss to his lips. His eyelids drifted shut while their lips were together, remaining so until she broke the kiss.

"I don't believe you," she said.

A crease formed between his eyebrows as he looked up at her, and a troubled frown tugged down the corners of his mouth.

"My past has come back to kill me," he finally said.

Samantha sat on the sofa beside him. Reaching up, she caught one of his long braids and gave it a gentle tug. He didn't resist, following her lead and lying sideways on the cushion, twisting his torso to settle the back of his head atop her lap.

She brushed the stray strands of hair from his face and traced a finger along his brow, soothing the tension there. "No one is going to kill you."

"He's going to try. He's already tried. And he'll keep trying, on and on, until either he succeeds or I kill *him*."

"Who, Arc?"

"Vaund."

"Who is Vaund?"

His eyes shifted to focus on the dark ceiling high above. "Did I leave out the part of my story regarding why we left Caldorius?"

Sam settled one of her hands on his chest while she combed the other through his hair between his horns. "You were a bit vague, but you can tell me now."

He drew in a deep breath and slowly released it. "We were doing good on Caldorius. The fighters who'd signed on with me were skilled, and we were able to pick and choose the fights we wanted. That meant we didn't have to fight in death matches if we didn't want to. It just became a matter of risk versus reward; would the potential payout be worth the danger?

"Drakkal was with me, and a hacker, Zakarae. She's the one who taught me how do all this"—he gestured at the nearby platform and all its screens—"and we used her talents to keep ahead of the Syndicate. They were upset because we were cutting into their profits. They were used to controlling all of it, used to taking a big cut of *everything*. They didn't like that our fighters were collecting their own winnings. Didn't like that we were bypassing their system. I kept an eye out for talented gladiators who were already free or close to becoming free, and I discovered one called Vaund. He was good. Had a lot of potential. And he was already free, so it should've been easy.

"I made him an offer. He knew who I was, and had a bit of a chip on his shoulder. A lot of fighters were like that, especially the ones who'd survived long enough to be freed. He thought that me being a champion was some sort of fluke, that I hadn't earned it, and said he'd think about my offer. Next thing I know, I get contacted by a promoter. Vaund was challenging me to a match. To the death. There was a massive purse on the line, big enough to upgrade our facilities and keep us operating for a long time.

"I went and talked to him before I gave an answer, tried to talk him out of it. He was dead set on fighting. Didn't care that there was a chance of him losing, didn't care that he had a chance to earn just as much fighting on our crew without putting his life on the line. To him, it was a guaranteed thing. An easy victory."

Arc's tail thumped softly against the couch's back cushions as he settled his hand atop hers, holding it tighter against his chest. "It was a lot of credits, and I didn't care for his attitude... so I accepted. A death match just means lethal weaponry is used. It doesn't have to end in death, even though they often do. I planned to toy with him enough to break his spirit and get him to walk away. I wanted him on my crew. He could've done well.

"But he didn't give up. I had him beat, and he knew it, but he kept fighting. And he was *vicious*. He wasn't just trying to win, he was trying to kill me outright. I couldn't let it go on like that, and he didn't give me a choice. So, I stopped toying with him. And my final blow sliced off most of his face."

Samantha inhaled sharply, her hand stilling in his hair. She could almost imagine the brutality and horror of Caldorius, could almost see the gladiatorial fights in her mind's eye, could almost understand the struggles those people had gone through to win their freedom, but what he'd just said... Even without a vivid description, her stomach twisted in knots at the things he must've been forced to do in those arenas.

"The bout was called, but...he wasn't dead. He was tough. His sponsors didn't care—he'd failed them already, and there were countless healthy fighters they could hire, so they left him. I made a choice, then, and even after everything that's happened...I'm not sure if it was right or wrong. I paid for him to be fixed. They had to use cybernetics due to the extent of the damage, but he lived. And while he recovered, I made my offer again. I guess I should've seen the signs, but I didn't. I just saw his potential. I was too blind, too stupid to understand that he *hated* me, especially after that fight.

"But he joined me, all the same. He was part of our crew for two years. And when it all came crashing down, when the Inner Reach Syndicate had finally had enough of me and my enterprise, who do you think they made an offer to?"

"Vaund," Samantha replied.

"Vaund," he echoed with a humorless chuckle. "Our security was tight, even then. Between Drakkal and Zakarae, we'd kept pretty well out of reach. But I thought Vaund had come around. I thought I could trust him. He led them right to us, and they...they were eager to make an example.

"They caught us off guard and killed almost everyone. It was a fight that actually meant something, a fight that had *real* stakes, and I couldn't do anything to turn it around. I couldn't help any of them. There were so many of those bastards, like a damned army had been dropped on our doorstep, and I fought and fought, but I kept getting pushed back.

"I ended up in an alley behind our base of operations. It was raining. I'll always remember that, because the rain on Caldorius is sometimes a bit acidic, and there was a slight sting to it that night. They swarmed me, finally disarmed me, beat me down to my knees...and I looked up, and there he was. Vaund. I hadn't known he was there until that moment. I thought he'd died with the others, fighting alongside us. But he'd been paid off by the Syndicate.

"He was there to finish what had been started a couple years before. Told me it was the Syndicate who'd hired him to fight me in the first place, that they would've paid him enough credits for him to never have to fight again. And I ruined that chance for him." Arcanthus laughed again, even more bitterly. "He took my arms and legs one at a time, pausing between each cut to make sure I felt it. And while I writhed in pain, he said *it's just business.*"

Samantha's heart constricted, and her fingers curled against his chest. She couldn't comprehend her own horror over what he'd just described. It hadn't been an accident that took Arc's limbs—it had been torture. It had been revenge.

"Arc..." she breathed, tears welling in her eyes.

"They left me in the alley, in a puddle of stinging rainwater and blood. You never realize just how much blood you have until most of it is spilled on the ground. I don't know how much time passed—I was in too much pain—but at some point, a pair of strong hands lifted me off the ground, and I looked up, and..."

He paused, pressing his lips into a tight line, and seemed to steady himself. "And there was Drakkal. He'd been out scouting new talent, so he missed the whole thing. He's beaten himself up over that ever since it happened. He thinks he should have been there to fight alongside me, that he could've somehow turned it around. That's part of why he's so protective now. He thinks he failed somehow. In his heart, I think he knows the truth. His absence saved my life.

"The energy blade had cauterized the worst of my wounds, but they'd beaten me pretty severely before that. Once Drakkal stopped some of the bleeding, he took me to the same place we'd taken Vaund to get patched up. And they...well, they did what they could, but I've indulged myself with some significant upgrades over the years."

"And then you came here," Samantha said.

"And then we came here, to build all this. I used what Zakarae taught me to keep us hidden. The Syndicate thought I was dead, and I wanted to keep it that way. It worked until we went to the Ventrillian Mall and that groalthuun took those pictures, which he passed along to his boss. Vaund."

Sam closed her eyes as guilt flooded her. She'd asked Arc to take her to the upper city on a tour. It *was* her fault. If she hadn't given in to temptation and called him, none of this would have happened. He'd still be in hiding. He'd still be safe.

She felt him turn to face her fully, and one of his hands caught her chin, forcing it down.

"Open your eyes, Samantha."

She sniffled as tears flowed down her cheeks, but she obeyed.

His bright eyes were narrowed. "I know that look on your face. This is *not* your fault. I chose to take you there, and I don't regret it. I would've taken you to a thousand other places afterward, whether you asked to go or not. You are not to feel guilt for my choices."

It didn't matter what he thought. Even if she and Arc were destined for one another, Sam carried some of the blame for what was happening now. She had to carry some of the blame.

"Does Vaund know where you are?" Samantha asked raggedly as she resumed combing her fingers through his hair.

"No, or he would be trying to kill me right now. We...spoke, earlier. I contacted him through the groalthuun's holocom. I think he hates me even more now than before."

Sam frowned. "Is that why you were drinking?"

"I was drinking because...because I thought I'd left all that behind. That I was free of it." He lifted his arms and gestured to the black metal encasing them. "Haven't I paid enough of a price? And now...I stand to lose *you* because of it, too, and I cannot stand the thought of that. I cannot stand that you are in danger because of my past."

She placed her hand on his cheek, stroking it with her thumb. "You won't lose me, Arc."

He took gentle hold of her hand and lifted it from his cheek, flattening her palm against his. He traced her fingers with the digits of his free hand. "I wish I could touch you with my own fingers just once. Just to have the memory of your feel forever."

"What do you feel when you touch me with them now?"

"Their warmth and their firmness. A hint of their texture. The same things I would feel with flesh, only lesser. It's all...off."

"Your hands are not the only things you feel with." Sam smoothed her other palm down his chest. "What do you feel when I touch you here?"

"*You*," he rasped softly.

She tucked her hair behind her ear and leaned down to brush her lips across his. Warmth filled her cheeks as she said, "You don't need your hands to feel me, Arc."

He briefly lifted his head to chase her lips. "You are too precious for this world, my flower."

Samantha smiled; his words sent a gentle, tingling sensation through her chest.

Arc needed something to distract him, something to lighten his mood. He was wallowing in his past, in his pain, in his despair, and Sam refused to let this continue.

She carefully slipped out from beneath him and stood up. "Well, that's too bad, since I signed an agreement saying I'd stay here at least a year." She took a couple steps away, nudging aside the empty bottles scattered on the floor, and glanced over her shoulder. "Though...I might stay longer if someone could convince me..."

His eyes were intent upon her as he sat up; their light had altered subtly, shifting back toward the wicked, ravenous gleam she'd come to appreciate so much. "I don't care what other agreements you've made, little terran. You're not going anywhere."

Samantha faced forward, a shiver running down her spine at his words, and walked toward the stairs leading up to his work platform. "Who's going to stop me?"

Her only warning of his approach would've been a barely audible whisper of fabric—had his foot not hit one of the empty bottles as he pushed himself off the couch and stalked toward her. Samantha took off running, mounting the steps as fast as she could. She grinned, her heart pounding in excitement, her breath coming in quick, shallow bursts.

She spun around once she was behind his desk, and he stopped at the foot of the stairs with his stance low and his tail extended behind him. He looked like a dangerous predator about to pounce.

One corner of his mouth ticked up. "There's nowhere to run, Samantha."

"There are plenty of places to run."

He placed a foot on the lowest step. "Nowhere that will get you away from me."

Samantha pressed her fingertips to her lips. When it came to flirting with Arcanthus, she was still shy, still nervous, but she couldn't stop grinning. Anticipation fluttered in her belly, desire flooded her veins, and a touch of pride swelled her chest. *She* had brought that smile to his lips. *She* had sparked that fire in his eyes.

"What will you do if you catch me?" she asked.

"*When* I catch you, little terran." He grasped the sides of his robe as he ascended another step, pulling the fabric apart. "When I catch you, I'm going to tear the clothes from your body." He shrugged off the robe, letting it fall away.

Sam's eyes trekked over his lean, powerful body, watching the play of his muscles as he moved. He wore only his loincloth, the fabric of which revealed his powerful thighs. She forced herself to slide farther away from him along the desk; it wouldn't be much of a chase if she stood there gawking until he grabbed her.

Arcanthus reached the top of the platform and placed his hand on the edge of the desk, turning his head to stare at her. "Once your clothing is in tatters, I'm going to run my tongue over every centimeter of your body. I'm going to taste every bit of you, and when I thrust my tongue between your thighs, my flower, your body is going to gift me your sweet nectar. I'll drink my fill of you, and you will beg me to take ever more."

She raised her gaze and locked it with his. Her heart quickened as ripples of eagerness swept through her, heating her core.

He braced his other hand on the desk and leaned forward. The muscles of his arm and chest flexed, and the light of his *qal* intensified. "And only when your need is so great that the only thing you can do is cry out my name in a desperate plea will I bury myself deep inside your body and claim you as mine. But even then, I'll take my time, because you are *my* prize. Each deliberate stroke will drive you mad, and when I finally deign to grant you release, you will shatter against me."

Samantha clenched the fabric of her shirt in her hands, close to tearing it off herself. His words alone might've pushed her to the edge. Her nipples hardened, her breasts felt heavy and full, and her sex throbbed with arousal.

"Then why are you still talking?" she asked breathlessly.

"Why aren't you running?"

They stared at each other for another second, and then Arcanthus burst into motion, darting around the desk toward her. Sam's heart leapt. She turned and ran, nearly slipping as she rounded the corner of his desk. She chanced a sideways glance to see Arcanthus plant a hand on the desktop and vault over it. His tail trailed behind him as his body passed through the holographic screens.

He landed in front of her, and Sam's momentum carried her directly into his arms. She hit his body, but he didn't budge. Tilting her head back, she looked up at him.

His lips stretched into a wide, triumphant grin. "You're mine, Samantha."

Arcanthus leaned forward, cupping the back of her head to prevent her retreat, and slammed his mouth down on hers. His kiss demanded as much from her as it promised—*everything*.

Electric waves spread outward from her lips to course through her body, lighting every nerve, setting her on fire. Samantha moaned against his mouth, returning the kiss without restraint. She tasted the *gurosh* on his tongue and smelled it on his breath; mixed with his taste, it was intoxicating and irresistible. She delved her fingers into his hair to clasp the back of his neck and pulled him closer, deepening the kiss as she rubbed her body against his.

Arcanthus groaned and moved his hands to the collar of her shirt. He tugged the fabric to the sides, easily tearing it apart. The brief caress of cool air against her skin made her shiver, but it was quickly replaced by the heat of his advancing body as he guided the tattered shirt down her arms and let it drop away.

He finally broke the kiss and eased down onto one knee, lips searing a path along her neck. Cupping her breasts with both hands, he skimmed his mouth over their tender flesh before sucking one of her nipples into it, swirling and rolling his tongue around her hard peak.

Samantha bit her lip to muffle a cry and tilted her head back, clutching him closer. "Arc..."

She started when he nipped the bud with his fangs—it sent a bolt of pleasure-pain straight to her pussy that made it clench in need.

She lifted her head and looked down at him. His center eye met her gaze as he placed a kiss upon the abused nipple before moving to the other. She watched, eyelids heavy, as he laved attention on her breasts, pulling her nipples into his mouth and sucking until they were sensitive and red, and she was a squirming, whimpering, helpless creature, trapped in his hold. Part of her felt like she could come from this alone, but it wasn't enough.

She wanted *more*.

Needed more.

As though reading her mind, Arc's mouth trailed down between her breasts and across her stomach. He dropped his hands to her hips and hooked his fingers under the waistbands of her leggings and panties. He drew them down slowly at first, his hands leaving tingling heat in their wake as they bared the skin of her pelvis, and moved his mouth lower until his lips were just above the cleft of her sex. He kissed her there. It was a feather-light caress, and she instinctively lifted her hips toward him.

Then he pulled the leggings down to her ankles in one smooth, quick motion.

She lifted her feet one at a time so he could remove those last pieces of clothing, and once she was fully bare, he ran his hands back up, cupping her calves, brushing his fingertips over the backs of her knees, following the outsides of her thighs.

His breath was warm and soft against her flesh. Sam trembled in anticipation. His nose brushed along her slit, and he inhaled deeply, his hands tightening on the backs of her thighs.

"I am going to *devour* you, Samantha," he growled.

Arcanthus rose, shifting his hands up to her ass. He lifted Sam off her feet and set her down on the edge of the desk, shoving her thighs apart. Sam's eyes widened at the feral look on his face, and she barely had time to catch herself as he dropped onto his knees, wrapped his arms around the undersides of her thighs, and yanked her closer to his hungry mouth.

Her lips parted in a sharp gasp as his tongue delved into her sex. She leaned back on her arms, hands flat atop the desk, unable to tear her eyes away from him as he kissed and licked her center, avoiding her clit—the one place she needed him the most.

Pleasure washed over her. She tightened her legs around him, eager to draw him closer, but he was as unmoving as a mountain.

Samantha moaned when his tongue speared her. He growled; the vibrations from the sound rumbled through her, teasing her, amplifying every sensation, but it wasn't enough. She shook with need and shamelessly rocked against his mouth, but still he ignored her clit.

He was keeping her at the cusp, right on the edge, balanced on the fine line between torment and rapture.

His eyes met hers; they were shining with lust, gleaming with wicked promise of what was to come.

She knew what he was waiting for. Knew what he wanted her to do.

Sam reached out with one hand and grasped his horn. "Please, Arcanthus," she begged. "My clit. Make me come."

Arcanthus chuckled huskily. "Oh, my lusty little terran, I thought you'd never ask."

He spread her thighs wider, and slowly—*maddeningly*—circled her clit with his lips. He gradually sucked it into his mouth, thrilling her with little flicks of his tongue; each graze of that sensitive nub made her hips buck.

The tip of his tail brushed against her ankle and slid up the inside of her leg. As it moved higher, he increased the strength of his tongue. Samantha's brows fell, and her toes curled, the building sensation within her soaring to new heights. She forced her eyes to remain open, forced herself to watch him.

When he slipped the tip of his tail into her pussy and sucked hard on her clit, Samantha came undone; she threw her head back and cried out in sweet agony.

She squeezed her eyes shut as waves of ecstasy crashed through her. Her body tensed, and Arc thrust his tail deep, over and over, as her sex—quivering with a flood of heat—clamped down on it. Tugging on his horn, she pulled him close and ground herself against his mouth and tail. She paid no mind to the sounds escaping her.

All that mattered was the searing pleasure consuming her entire being.

"Arc...please—ah! Oh, God!"

Her arm gave out beneath her, and she fell back atop the desk. His hold on her legs prevented her escape as she writhed. She came again suddenly, and her eyes flew open; all she could see were star-like bursts of light in the dim room.

Arc finally released her clit and withdrew his tail. He lazily lapped at her and released a deep hum of appreciation. When he placed a kiss against her sensitive clit, she jumped at the quick burst of sensation. He stood up, forcing her to release his horn, and slid his hands up her thighs and past her pelvis to curl his fingers around her hips.

Looming over her, he flashed his fangs in a devilish smile.

"You are glorious when you succumb to pleasure, Samantha."

He dropped a hand to his cock, and she watched avidly as his writhing tendrils swept over the moisture coating her inner thighs. They shifted to her sex, caressing her folds and clit, eliciting another moan from her. Arc grasped the base of his shaft, and the tendrils drew together. He guided their tips to her opening. Flexing his hips, he pushed into her.

"Oh, my precious flower." Arc returned his hand to her hip. He tightened his grip on her and pulled her closer, feeding himself into her body. "You are perfect. So...*ah—.*"

Samantha wrapped her legs around his waist and bit her lip as he filled her. Shivers wracked her, and she moaned in unison with him as he drew back and pushed in, again and again, with slow, measured thrusts that made her aware of every individual nodule along his shaft, that made her feel his tendrils' every tiny movement.

She tried to dig her heels into his back to pull him against her harder, faster, but he only solidified his hold, maintaining his deliberate pace. She whimpered and thrashed as another orgasm built slowly within her. Each slide of his shaft pushed her infinitesimally closer to a new peak.

When she reached for him, he caught her arms and pinned her wrists on the desk over her head with one hand, leaning over her to block out the room's scant light. All that remained was the glow of his eyes and *qal.*

"You have no idea how difficult this is, Samantha," he rasped. "No idea how much I want to ravage your delectable little body. But you need to feel this. To feel *everything*." He thrust deep, making her gasp. "Feel *me*."

The tips of his tendrils shifted within Samantha, stroking her core, and her inner walls pulsed with the beginnings of her impending climax. She clenched her fists as her breath hitched and her eyelids fluttered, but she kept them locked with Arcanthus's.

He shuddered and sagged forward for a moment, settling more of his weight atop her. His lips parted with a ragged exhalation, and his previously steady pace faltered.

"Come with me," Samantha begged. "Let go, Arcanthus. With me."

Arc's lips peeled back to bare his teeth. "Ah, my precious flower... You are my undoing."

His grip on her wrists tightened slightly as he forced himself up again. He drew back and slammed his hips forward, burying himself deep inside her, only to draw back and repeat it again and again, increasing his speed and force with each thrust. Feral grunts and growls escaped him, mingling with her soft cries. He took her hard.

She reveled in it and begged for more.

The pressure that had built inside her throughout his slow, deliberate seduction was suddenly too much; Samantha shattered. In that same instant, Arc's tendrils spread wide and pressed against her inner walls. Their bodies tensed in unison, and they both released strained, desperate cries as they climaxed. His seed gushed into her with enough force to send her into another crest.

Arcanthus released Sam's wrists to gather her close, pressing his mouth to hers as their bodies spasmed in the throes of ecstasy. The pleasure coursing through Sam was pure and explosive. His deep kiss swallowed her cries, and she clung to him as though he were the only thing holding her together.

His lips moved from hers to trail along her jaw. She felt his warm breath against her ear as he released a low moan. Faint tremors flowed through their bodies as they drifted down from the heights of their passion, and, even when his tendrils reluctantly eased their pressure, Arcanthus did not withdraw from her body.

He affectionately nuzzled her neck and whispered, "Even when I was a slave, I never belonged so wholly to anyone as I do you."

Samantha's breath hitched. Her heart, hammering against her ribs, swelled. She could barely breathe with the emotion welling within her.

She turned her face toward him and looked into his eyes, but he kissed her again before she could speak. In that moment, Samantha realized she didn't *need* words—she poured everything he made her feel into that kiss.

I love you, Arc.

I love you.

TWENTY-TWO

Six days passed without incident—no attempted communications from Vaund, no run-ins with the Syndicate, no sign of them taking action through any of the channels Arcanthus was monitoring. As grateful as he was for the quiet, he refused to grow complacent.

Something was going to happen. Some move would be made. He often reminded himself that his home was safe, secure, and well-hidden, but he found no reassurance in those thoughts. He had too much on the line, now. Too much to lose.

It was only Samantha's steady presence that prevented him from being consumed by dread.

And you're not going to give in to it now, Arc.

Only one thing mattered in this moment—finding Samantha. His core crew had taken quite a liking to her, and she'd spent a lot of time with them while he worked. Arc hadn't fully shaken his jealousy. The possessive, instinctual side of him wanted her all to himself, even though that would've meant locking her away in his bedroom, alone, for hours-long stretches, but he'd come to terms with it because she was *happy*.

Samantha had flourished during her stay here, faster than he'd ever thought possible.

The night after he'd spoken with Vaund, as he and Samantha had lain together in the dark of his bedroom, he'd turned his mind toward doing something just for her. They couldn't leave—the Syndicate could access surveillance feeds from around the city as easily as Arcanthus could, and Vaund knew Sam's face—so he wanted to give her something special to make up for it.

Though he couldn't deny that part of him wanted to give her a gift to make *himself* feel better, to assuage some of his guilt for her being trapped here, he just wanted to see her smile that big smile—the one that made her eyes sparkle—more than anything.

With the boxed gift tucked beneath one arm, he strode through the corridors, heading to the place where she seemed to spend most of her time when she wasn't with him—the lounge. His heart quickened with each step closer to his destination.

He knew their mating bond had something to do with her endlessly strengthening pull on him, but he knew, also, that this was something far deeper. Each time they were apart—even knowing that she was in the same building, never more than a few minutes' walk away—he found himself longing to get back to her side. The more time he spent with her, the more time he *wanted* to spend with her.

Arcanthus was finding it increasingly difficult to focus on his work, and increasingly difficult to care. He knew it should've alarmed him, but...why? They'd find a new normal eventually, despite Vaund and the Syndicate, and Arc had credits enough to maintain his lifestyle indefinitely thanks to several passive income streams he'd established over the years.

He paused when he entered the lounge. The only person

inside was Razi, who was seated upon one of the couches. Despite his hurry to find Samantha, Arcanthus walked up behind Razi and watched the screen that held the cren's attention. It was a volturian show in which a handsome male and a beautiful female were lamenting the hostility between their bloodlines—one of seemingly several factors preventing them from outwardly professing their love for one another.

Arcanthus snorted. "And people call me overly dramatic."

Razi started and spun to face Arcanthus with wide eyes, tipping the bowl that had been perched atop his lap. Dozens of assorted nuts scattered across the floor.

The cren scowled and muttered, "Not polite to sneak up on people like that."

"I pay you to be vigilant, Razi. That comprises the majority of your duties."

"Not when I'm on break." The cren grumbled to himself as he turned away and gathered up the snacks that had landed on his thighs. "And it's not overly dramatic. It's *tragic*."

Arcanthus smirked. "There is certainly a tragedy unfolding before my eyes. Do you happen to know where Samantha is?"

"Tried to get her to watch with me. She said she was heading to the training room."

"Why? Don't I give her enough exercise?"

Razi twisted and threw a handful of nuts at Arcanthus.

Arc raised a hand to shield himself, tucking the gift behind his body to protect it. "That's just uncalled for, cren."

When Razi launched another volley, Arcanthus retreated, pausing only after reaching the door. "You're cleaning that up!"

Before Razi could throw anything with greater mass, Arcanthus ducked into the hallway. He walked as quickly as he could without running as he made his way toward the training room, slowing only when he reached the entry.

He pressed the button to open the door and stepped inside.

Arcanthus froze just beyond the threshold.

It took his mind several moments to process what he was witnessing—Sekk'thi lunged at Samantha, grabbed hold of the terran's extended arm, and dropped into a roll, throwing Sam down onto the mat hard. Before Samantha could recover, the ilthurii trapped her in a full body choke hold, pinning the terran on the floor.

If there were logical explanations for what he'd just seen, they were lost on him; his instincts poured fire into his veins and blasted him forward, leaving room for only one thought —*protect my mate.*

It was his growl as he charged across the room that alerted the females to his presence. Sekk'thi and Samantha both looked up at him, the latter's face red with exertion, and their eyes widened in unison. The ilthurii released her hold and shifted onto her knees, and Sam sat up, shoulders heaving with her panting breaths.

She threw her arms up, palms toward him. "Arc, stop!"

Samantha's voice cut through the crimson haze that had settled over Arcanthus's mind; he skidded to a halt less than a meter away from her and shook his head sharply. "I don't... What *is* this, Samantha?"

Sekk'thi had risen to her feet behind his mate, her scaled brows slightly arched. Ilthurii didn't have many flexible parts of their face, but it was amazing how subtle changes could so powerfully alter their expressions.

Samantha glanced back at Sekk'thi before returning her eyes to Arc's. "She's been training me."

Arcanthus furrowed his brow, arms falling limp—save for the hold he maintained on the packaged gift. "Training you for what?"

"Just...training me."

"She was choking you!"

Sekk'thi scratched her snout. "She did not say uncle."

Arcanthus lifted his arms again, palms up, and opened his mouth to speak. After a few moments of stammering, he managed to ask, "Why the hell would she say *uncle*, of all things?"

Samantha's smile was tinged with a bit of self-consciousness as she laughed.

Sekk'thi snickered. "That is what *I* asked. She said it was an Earth saying. It means *I surrender*."

Arcanthus turned his attention to Samantha. "Why wouldn't you just say *I surrender*?"

"Fewer syllables," both females replied simultaneously. They exchanged a glance with one another and burst into laughter.

Pinching the bridge of his nose, Arcanthus lowered his gaze. "So...you're teaching her how to fight by throwing her around?"

Sekk'thi snorted. "How did you learn? By holding hands and talking until someone died of boredom?"

Arcanthus shook his head and sighed. "By being thrown around. In the mud, in my case."

The ilthurii threw up her hands and tilted her head, silently claiming victory.

"That doesn't mean it's okay to throw *her* around, ilthurii. She's...small."

Samantha pushed herself to her feet, narrowing her eyes. "That doesn't stop *you* from being rough." She lifted her chin, claiming her own little victory. "You don't hear me complaining. As a matter of fact, I believe I beg—uh..." She glanced at Sekk'thi, as though suddenly aware she had an audience, and cleared her throat, her already red cheeks darkening. "Anyway, I'm fine."

"Firstly, little terran, what we do in the bedroom, in the

bath, in my workshop, and that one time in the lounge, is entirely between the two of us and is a *completely* different situation. Secondly—"

"The *lounge?*" Sekk'thi asked. "Do not tell me you mated on one of the couches."

Samantha clasped her hands behind her back. "Um..."

"It was one of the tables," Arcanthus said. "Well, it started on one of the tables, and moved to—no, I'm not going to let you send me on a tangent. Secondly"—he pointed a finger at Sekk'thi—"you did not have my permission, as your mentor and employer, to toss my mate around, in a training scenario or otherwise."

Sekk'thi rolled her eyes. "As though I would ask your permission."

Arcanthus chose to ignore the comment. "Thirdly, I have to know—is she any good?"

"Samantha shows promise, and she has taken well to the blaster."

"You're training her with blasters? I can't believe that you would—" Arcanthus snapped his mouth shut and closed his eyes.

Instincts. These pesky instincts. Sam needs *to learn because of the world I've dragged her into.*

"My apologies, ladies," he said in a softer tone. "I simply would have preferred to have been informed when this training began rather than stumbling in on it. Now, Sekk'thi, if you're done abusing my mate, I'm going to take her."

Sekk'thi waved her hand. "I release her into your care."

Arcanthus turned to face Samantha fully, offering her his free hand.

Sam stepped forward and laced her fingers with his. "I wasn't keeping it from you. It...just kind of happened, and I never thought to mention it."

He walked her toward the exit, leaning closer. "I'm not upset, Samantha. I'm glad. And proud of you. But stepping in on that scene without any context... It triggered the instincts you've awoken in me."

She grimaced. "Sorry."

He turned his head to glance at her. Her skin glistened with a light sheen of sweat, and her hair was pulled back in a tight ponytail, revealing her slender, elegant neck. She was dressed in a shirt and pants, both of which were form-fitting. He was certain that the Samantha of two weeks ago would never have worn such clothing if she knew anyone would see her in it.

"Don't be sorry, little terran," he said as they entered the corridor. "I'm actually rather turned on right now. Maybe we can find some unconventional uses for what you've been learning..."

That Samantha still blushed when he said such things, despite how many times they'd joined since she'd come here, only made him want her more—and, on a deeper level, it made him *adore* her.

"Maybe," she said, peeking up at him with a grin.

His mouth curled into a grin of his own. "We both know there's no *maybe* involved."

She tucked a few stray strands of hair behind her ear and glanced at the package in his hand. "What's that?"

Arcanthus lifted it slightly. "A gift for you."

Her eyes rounded. "For me?"

"There are no other astoundingly beautiful terrans around, so it must be for you. But you'll have to wait until we're back in our room."

Sam's grin somehow widened, and Arc could almost feel the excitement radiating from her.

They headed to the bedroom at a brisk pace, matching each

other's strides perfectly despite their haste. Once they were inside with the door closed, Samantha released his hand, stepped forward, and turned to face him, bouncing on her toes with palpable anticipation.

Arcanthus shifted the gift behind his back, closed the distance between them, and slipped his free arm around Sam, drawing her into a deep, lingering kiss. She closed her eyes and moaned, her body going pliant against his as she slid her hands up to his neck.

The slightly salty flavor of her sweat reminded him of their past joinings, and arousal stirred low in his belly, causing his cock to partially extrude. When he broke the kiss, he ran his tongue over his lips to savor her taste. "Maybe the gift can wait..."

Samantha's eyes darkened, and she slid one of her hands down between their bodies to cup him between his legs. Arcanthus grunted. She smiled as she stroked a finger along his slit, teasing him through his loincloth.

"But can you?" she asked.

He caught his lower lip between his teeth to suppress a groan as faint currents of pleasure crackled outward from his groin. She'd learned, clearly, that his self-control was a delicate thing—that she could shatter it and take command with just a little boldness, with just a little touch.

It would've been so easy to toss the gift aside, tear off his loincloth, and give in. It would've been so easy to accept whatever pleasure she offered. There was no denying that he *wanted* it. The mere thought of her hand on his shaft was enough to send a thrill up his spine and almost make him spill like an untried whelp.

But he wanted to see her satisfaction more. He wanted to see if the gift made her face light up, wanted to see if it would coax that special smile out of her, the one she reserved only for him. The smile whose radiance was so great that it burned away all his worries and fears for a little while because it told him that, despite everything, Samantha was truly happy.

Arcanthus drew in a deep, steadying breath. He gently removed her hand from his groin, lifting it to his mouth to press a kiss atop it. "I can wait. For a few more minutes, at least."

He released her hand and raised the gift, holding the thin, rectangular package up on one palm. "For you, my flower."

She accepted the gift, glancing up at him for a moment before giving it her attention. Her fingers flexed around the box, and her smile softened. "I haven't been given a gift since the birthday right before my dad passed."

"Consider this the first of many," Arcanthus replied, battling the urge to take her in his arms.

She offered him another glance, flashing her white teeth in a widening smile, and tore away the paper wrapping from the gift. Her breath caught. "Is-Is this...?"

"A tablet, yes. I believe this is the preferred model for most artists in the city." He gestured to one side of it. "The stylus attaches itself there. It has touch controls, holographic projections, everything you might need. I figured it would be a good starting—"

Samantha threw herself against Arcanthus, clutching him in a tight embrace. Her tears flowed immediately onto his chest.

Arcanthus put his arms around her and held her close, cradling the base of her skull with one hand. "You're crying because you're so overwhelmed by my thoughtfulness, right?"

She laughed, the sound rich and genuine despite being made husky by her tears. "Yes. I...didn't know you actually listened."

He shifted his hands to her shoulders and leaned back to look down at her. "Samantha, I've been enraptured by your every word since the first one you spoke to me."

Though her eyes were watery, she smiled in exactly the way he'd hoped for. "I know that now."

Arcanthus moved a hand to her chin and brushed his thumb across her lower lip. "Good. Know it always. And I suppose it goes without saying that I am willing to offer my services, should you require a live model."

"I think"—she moved her hand to the clasps of his loincloth—"that I should take a closer look...just to make sure you're a subject I want to depict. I want to keep my artistic standards high."

She unfastened the clasp. His loincloth, under wrapping and all, slid down his legs to pool on the floor. Samantha pressed kisses down his throat and chest, stopping to take his right nipple into her mouth.

Arc hissed through his teeth as her tongue flicked around his piercing.

Samantha smiled and released it. She lowered herself to her knees, keeping one hand on his hip, and set her tablet down beside her.

Arcanthus groaned as his cock pushed out from his slit, tendrils writhing in eagerness for her touch. "Who taught you to be so wicked, little terran?"

She moved her other hand to his tendrils and stroked each in turn, allowing them to caress and curl around her fingers. Arc's muscles tensed, and he drew in a sharp breath, overwhelmed by the feel of her touch. His tail straightened for an instant before sweeping side to side, restless in his anticipation.

"A devilish fiend," she said, pulling her hand free of his tendrils to grasp his base.

The tendrils sealed, forming a solid shaft. Desire burned in the pit of his stomach. "Seems this *fiend* was an excellent teacher."

Samantha leaned closer and brushed her lips over the tip of

his cock. Her eyes were dark and hungry. "It helps when the student is so eager."

Her lips slid over him, and she sucked him deep into her hot, wet mouth. A hiss ripped from this throat. The gentle scrape of her teeth sent delightful jolts through his shaft.

He whispered something—it might have been her name, or it might have been a wordless utterance of pleasure—and reached forward. His fingers felt oddly clumsy as he removed the tie from her hair and spread her dark locks about her shoulders. He slipped his hands into her hair and grazed his fingertips along her scalp, transfixed by the way her lips stretched around his cock.

When she rolled her tongue—stroking the sensitive nodules along his shaft and pulling him deeper still—Arcanthus couldn't keep his eyes open any longer. His grip on her hair tightened, and his head tipped back. He feared any more would make his knees buckle, but he didn't want her to stop.

He never wanted her to stop.

"*Fuck*, you're good at that, my flower," he rasped.

She moaned, slid her hand from his hip to his ass, grasped the underside of his tail, and squeezed.

A strange, thrilling sensation arced up his spine, and his lower belly clenched, increasing the building pressure in his cock. He growled, and his hips bucked; he felt his tendrils stirring, felt them preparing to spread apart for his fast-approaching climax.

Samantha suddenly pulled her mouth away and stood, shoving her leggings down and kicking them aside. She pulled her shirt off over her head before crawling onto the bed, and—on hands and knees—presented her curvy ass and glistening sex to him.

Arcanthus shuddered, clamped a hand around the base of his shaft, and swiftly crossed the space separating them. He placed his free hand on her hip, positioned the tip of his cock against her center, and thrust into her.

"Arc..." Samantha gasped, pushing back against him, her sex clamping around his shaft.

Her heat nearly undid him. He bent forward, bracing himself with one hand on the bed, and drew in a deep breath. The air was perfumed with her intoxicating scent.

Keeping one hand on her hip, he straightened and ran the other up her spine, twining his fingers in her hair. He grasped the strands and pulled her head back as he gyrated his hips. He used his hold on Sam to tug her into his thrusts, slamming their flesh together, burying himself ever deeper. The tightness of her sex was amplified by the new position; before long, the pressure in him had risen to impossible heights, and his breath was ragged.

He pushed himself faster, harder, his eyes fixed on the sensuous flare of her hips, on the graceful curve of her spine, on the quivering flesh of her ass—on the erotic way his cock glided in and out of her, glistening with her slick.

Her body suddenly tensed. She gasped, her breathy moans rising in volume as she came; the tremors running through her sex were more than he could resist.

Arching his back, Arcanthus roared. His tendrils split apart and grabbed hold of her soft inner flesh, spreading her open inside, and his seed flowed into her in great spurts that coincided with the waves of pleasure blasting through him. He snarled, baring his teeth and grinding against his mate, unable to get close enough to her.

When the waves finally faded, leaving him shuddering, he eased his hold on her hair. Samantha sagged down and laid her cheek on the blanket. Arcanthus leaned over her, gently kissing her ear, her neck, her back and shoulders, sampling that enticing, salty taste, worshipping her with his lips. Unwilling to move away, he remained in that position even after his tendrils released her.

Panting, she reached up and brushed her fingers along his horn and into his hair. She hummed softly, lips curving into a smile as he rained kisses upon her.

"You, by far, surpass my standards," Samantha murmured.

Arcanthus grinned against her shoulder. "Was there ever any question?"

She wiggled her ass, sending another pulse of ecstasy through him. "I had my doubts."

"You shouldn't tell lies, little terran."

"The truth is...you're the most wonderful thing to have ever happened to me. And I..." Something had changed in her tone, and her body stiffened; her playful air had vanished in an instant.

Arcanthus gently withdrew from Samantha and rolled onto the bed, lying on his side next to her to look her in the eyes. There was a tightness in his chest, a heat that had nothing to do with their joining, a cloying sense of uncertainty and anticipation. "You what, Samantha?"

She glanced away briefly before turning onto her side to face him fully. She looked worried, looked vulnerable, like she was bracing herself for coming pain.

"I love you," she said quickly.

He wasn't sure what he'd expected her to say—anything else, perhaps. Anything but those words.

And yet he knew they were the right words. They somehow encompassed all of it—everything he felt from her, everything he felt *for* her—despite their simplicity. Those words sank deep into his core, into his heart, and radiated warmth throughout his body, even into the flesh of limbs he no longer possessed. He'd been foolish to think having his mate was the pinnacle of satisfaction, the peak of happiness.

Because having his mate's *love* lifted him to heights that shouldn't have been possible.

Arcanthus smoothed the hair back from her face, staring into the unfathomable depths of her eyes. "I love you too, Samantha."

She smiled, and it was so bright, so joyous, so beautiful that he almost couldn't believe it was real. She leaned toward him and pressed her mouth to his, cupping his face between her hands.

Arcanthus looped his arm around her waist and tugged her flush against him.

It didn't matter that they'd just joined; he needed her again. He rolled onto his back, pulling her atop him without breaking the kiss, and ran his hands up and down her back, over her ass and thighs, and along her arms before taking hold of his shaft.

Samantha lifted her hips, and he positioned himself at her entrance.

"I love you," he whispered against her mouth as he slid into her, raising his hips to push deep.

She exhaled softly and repeated the words back to him breathlessly.

He kept her within his embrace, sharing her breath through their kisses. Together they found a tempo that allowed the flames of their passion to flow freely until they were both consumed from within by a raging inferno.

Well after their desire had been spent—as Samantha lay against him, sleeping—Arcanthus looked upon his beautiful mate, and his heart swelled.

He had everything he could ever want, everything he could ever need, right here in his arms. And he would destroy *anyone* who tried to take it from him.

TWENTY-THREE

Days passed; Arcanthus spent as much of that time with Samantha as he could without neglecting his work. With her tablet in hand, she was often a silent presence in his workshop, her stylus never seeming to still as he alternated between the few identification chips he was under agreement to complete and the far more daunting task of locating Vaund.

He'd been mistaken to think she'd be too much of a distraction. Granted, his eyes strayed to her frequently, and he found himself stopping at least twice a day to have his way with her on one of the couches—or on the desk, the floor, and even once in the enveloping white glow of the body scanner platform—but he found her presence more grounding than anything.

She was often the only thing keeping him from sinking into despair as his repeated searches turned up nothing.

Samantha continued to spend time with the members of the security team, as well—watching shows, playing games, and training. Arcanthus accepted it; she always came back to him. Besides, he couldn't expect her to remain in the workshop for as long as he did. Its walls could eventually drive anyone mad.

Once he completed the ID chips, he turned all his focus to the search. Samantha didn't question his long hours of work. She talked to him about anything, about everything, when he needed a distraction from his mounting frustration, and was always drawing. She never complained when he crawled into bed hours after she'd retired—especially not when he woke her with his fingers or tongue.

Though she didn't share all her drawings with him, she shared many, and her confidence and skill grew by the hour. Her loose sketches—many of them depicting Arcanthus—gradually increased in detail and improved in form, and he adored the look of concentration that often fell across her face while she drew, especially when her tongue slipped out to press against her upper lip. It was clear to him that she loved art, and equally clear that she'd not created much of it over the last few years.

When she showed him a colored drawing of a creature she called Mister Wiggles—which had apparently been a tiny *cat* her grandmother had kept as a pet—Arcanthus grinned. He'd never seen such an animal before, but its resemblance to Drakkal was immediately apparent; its fur had the same coloration and nearly identical patterns, and its facial features were even reminiscent of an azhera's.

She was trepidatious at first, but Arcanthus convinced her to share the image with Drakkal.

Samantha held her tablet up to the azhera and said, "This was my grandmother's cat, Mister Wiggles. You reminded me of him the first time we met."

Drakkal's brows fell low, and he looked slowly from the image to Samantha.

"Um...cats are little animals from Earth that are often kept as pets," Sam said, "and...well..."

Arcanthus pressed his lips together and covered his mouth with a hand, holding back his laughter.

"I remind you of a tiny, domesticated animal?" Drakkal asked in a low voice.

"Yes." Her eyes rounded, and she hurried to add, "I mean... your fur and your coloration do. Obviously, you're not tiny, and you're not an animal." Samantha licked her lips. "He was really fond of cuddling, and he was really affectionate...and I think you probably are too, even if you don't show it."

Now Drakkal's brows rose.

Sam dropped her gaze to the floor. "Anyway, Arc wanted me to show you. You remind me of Mister Wiggles, and, well, that makes me think of my grandmother, and home...and its always kind of comforting to see you. It helps me...helps me feel at home."

A slight frown tugging down the corners of his mouth, Drakkal looked down at the image again. He was silent for several seconds before he said gruffly, "This is good, terran. You're good. Would you...send this to me? I would like a copy."

When she lifted her head, Samantha's eyes were huge and bright. She nodded enthusiastically. All the way back to the bedroom, she wore a big grin, and couldn't stop talking about how happy she was that Drakkal had liked it.

Arcanthus encouraged her to keep pushing, to keep practicing, to bring her imagination to life; she had such potential, and Arcanthus couldn't stand knowing that it might've been snuffed out completely.

It was on the seventh morning after he'd gifted her the tablet that Arc learned the true depth of her talent and passion.

He woke to find Samantha sitting up, naked, with her knees raised and her tablet settled over them. She glanced up from her work briefly to smile at him. It took him a few minutes of gentle coaxing to get her to share what she was working on.

"It's not completely done yet," she said, cheeks flushing, "but you can have a peek."

Drawing her legs closer to her chest, she turned the tablet toward him.

He wasn't sure what to say as he looked over the image; her statement about it being incomplete didn't at all match what he saw. There was no question of the subject—he was looking at himself, sprawled out on the bed with his hair splayed across the sheet, naked save for the crimson swathe of blanket draped over his groin.

He might've mistaken it for a photo were it not for the slightly more saturated colors. The work represented a masterful understanding of color and lighting and contained surprising subtleties—the soft blue glow from walls outside the frame reflecting on his arms, legs, and horns; the realistic folds in the fabric of the blanket; the barely perceptible texture on his skin.

There was no telling how long he stared at it before she pulled the tablet back into her lap.

She said in a small, soft voice, "I know it's not very good, and it needs a lot of—"

Arcanthus hushed her by pressing a finger to her lips. "Your drawings have been good, Samantha, but *this*...this is something else entirely. It's amazing. If this is your starting point, I can't even imagine how stunning your art will be in a year's time."

As only seemed natural, she set the tablet aside, and they made love again, the crimson blanket depicted in her painting tangling between their intertwined bodies. Afterward, they showered, dressed, and left the bedroom to eat. They went to the workshop once they were done, where Samantha settled atop one of the couches and Arcanthus resumed his tedious search.

Hours must've passed by the time Samantha stood up, yawned and stretched, and told him she was going to see if Sekk'thi was up for some more training. She kissed him and departed; it took a significant amount of willpower to remain in his chair and continue working.

Arcanthus's frustrations intensified as the day wore on. Simply knowing Samantha was elsewhere in the compound, out of sight but relatively close, eased his darkening mood, but could not curtail it. He reminded himself frequently that succumbing to his irritation would only make everything more difficult. When Drakkal entered the workshop that evening, Arcanthus found himself grateful for the interruption.

"Any luck?" Drakkal asked as he sat against the edge of the desk and folded his arms across his chest.

With a heavy sigh, Arcanthus angled his chair more toward the azhera, kicked his feet up on the desk, and clasped his hands over his sternum. "Nothing."

"Nothing from our usual informants, either—not that it's easy to get anyone to give up information on the Syndicate. Trying to expand our network, but it's slow going."

"As it should be. The wrong question to the wrong person could bring some very unwanted attention our way."

Drakkal grunted. "Definitely don't need any more of that, do we?"

Arcanthus looked toward the displays on the desk, staring at the nothingness between them. "He's like a damned ghost, Drak. There's nothing on him less than ten years old, and all that does come up is just promotional material from gladiatorial bouts he was in back on Caldorius. You'd think *he* died in that attack."

"Guess he learned more from you than we thought, Arc."

"Why couldn't he learn the right lessons?"

"Because right and wrong isn't universal, and what we

thought was right was also dangerous. We were doomed from the start. I don't regret any of it, but I can understand why so many good fighters turned us down."

Squeezing his fingers together, Arcanthus shook his head. "He's not perfect. He's ambitious, cold-blooded, cunning, and calculating, but he's *not* perfect. He's made a mistake somewhere, overlooked something... I just have to find it."

"Remember, Arc—you're not perfect either. None of us are."

Arcanthus turned his head to find Drakkal frowning at him, green eyes dark and troubled. "Speak for yourself, azhera."

Drakkal shook his head, though one corner of his mouth lifted in a begrudging smile. "How long have you been at this today, sedhi?"

Arcanthus shrugged. "A few hours."

"Samantha came out of here at least five or six hours ago, and I know you were in here for a while before she left."

"What's your point? If I don't keep looking, I'm not going to find *anything*. I can't just remain idle knowing he's out there." Arcanthus lowered his feet and sat forward, throwing his hands out to the sides. "If he finds us first, he's going to bring the fight to our home, and everyone—not just Samantha, but *everyone*—is in danger. It's not like he's going to knock on the door and wait patiently outside until I go fight him one-on-one."

"Yeah, you're right," Drakkal growled, angling his chin down and lowering his brows. "But what good will you be if you run yourself ragged? That'll hamper your search *and* make you worth shit in a fight."

"I'm a dangerous fighter whether or not I'm tired."

"So is Vaund. And we don't know how much better he's become after all this time."

"All the more reason to keep looking! If we find him first,

we can make sure the fight is on *our* terms, that every available advantage is ours."

Drakkal grunted and glanced up at the ceiling, scratching his cheek. "*Kraasz ka'val*, Arc, I'm not telling you to give up, just to take a damned break."

Arcanthus clenched his jaw and looked away. "I'm sorry."

"What was that? Don't think I heard you right."

"I'm sorry, Drakkal! Did you hear me that time, or are your ears too clogged with fur?"

"Oh, I heard. Not much surprises me these days, but you've sure made a habit of it since you found Sam."

Though he knew he'd changed because of Samantha, Arcanthus had no way of identifying those changes. Perhaps the word *change* was, itself, the wrong term. He didn't necessarily feel changed, but rather *more*—more himself now than at any other time in his life. As he'd been helping Sam bring her true self to the surface, she'd been doing the same for him. She'd been drawing out what was inside him all along.

For the first time in a long, long while, he was happy. Not just stimulated, not just entertained, but *happy*. She'd battered down the barriers around his heart and calmed the darkness at its core.

"She inspires me to be my best," Arcanthus said, looking at Drakkal again. "Samantha is the only person I've met who shakes my confidence in the best ways, because she shows me I can always do better, can always strive for more."

Drakkal held Arc's gaze, seemingly in search of something. "Well, Samantha is in the lounge right now, probably going head-to-head with Razi in Conquerors. The two of them have been going back and forth beating each other all week. You should head over there with me. We can throw together some food, have a drink, and lose some credits."

Arcanthus had known and trusted his core security team

for years, and, even if he wasn't as close to any of them as he was to Drakkal, he'd always enjoyed their company. It reminded him of his days on Caldorius, when, even during one of the darkest periods of his life, he'd found unexpected camaraderie with many other gladiators—even some of those he'd fought, like Drakkal. A little time with Samantha and the others could help alleviate some of the stress he'd accumulated lately.

"All right, Drakkal. Let me get a few autosearch and decryption programs up and going so the system keeps searching on its own. I'll catch up with you."

Drakkal nodded, dropped his hands, and pushed away from the desk. "Good. Don't take too long. If I have to come in here again, I'm going to drag you out by your braids."

Arcanthus leaned back in his chair. "Hmm... I *do* enjoy having my hair pulled, but I imagine you're a bit rough even for my tastes."

"You have ten minutes, sedhi. Get your ass down there or I'll give you to the Syndicate myself."

"Don't tease me with a good time, azhera."

Drakkal exited the chamber; had the door been of the old-fashioned, hinged variety, Arcanthus was sure the azhera would've slammed it behind him just for the sake of being irritating.

Raking his fingers through his hair to sweep it back between his horns, Arcanthus returned his attention to the screens on his desk. Even now, he was tempted to delve back into work, to bury himself in it, to keep trying either until he found Vaund, or he began bleeding from his eyes. For the first time, he regretted being so hasty in killing Straek; though the chances of it had been slim, the groalthuun might've eventually led Arcanthus to Vaund.

All this not knowing is driving me mad. Where is he? How much does he know?

No, forget Vaund for now... I need to see Samantha.

That easily, his thoughts turned to his mate, and he was grateful for it. He needed to see her smile and hear her laugh to remind him what was important. Needed to hold her to replenish his stores of hope.

His fingers moved almost of their own accord, pulling up the automated programs he already had running, along with a few others he'd not yet activated. He altered existing parameters and defined new ones, tweaking everything slightly, and set the programs to work one by one. He expected nothing to come of it—Vaund didn't exist in the Consortium registry as far as Arcanthus could tell, and the nature of his cybernetic prosthesis meant he would be exceedingly difficult to trace via facial recognition even if Arcanthus knew what it looked like.

Vaund's face was an interchangeable cybernetic helmet that could've been altered a thousand times over the years.

Arcanthus paused.

He didn't know what Vaund currently looked like, but he had detailed images of Straek. There had to be *somewhere* Straek had gone regularly to meet with his boss—and he would've been recorded frequently on his way.

Drakkal's ten-minute deadline had likely expired, and Arc was eager to see Sam, but this was an angle he couldn't ignore. How had he overlooked it up until now?

It could take days for the system to pour over the countless surveillance feeds blanketing the city in search of Straek; the sooner begun, the better. Bringing up the proper program, Arcanthus fed in as much data as was readily available—including every image of Straek he and his people had obtained—and initiated the search.

"Can't hide for much longer," he said, smirking.

He pushed up from his chair and left the workshop with a new lightness in his stride. It was premature for celebration, but he'd finally recognized a lead with a strong possibility of producing results. That was more success than he'd had during the entirety of this search.

When he reached the first intersecting corridor, he paused. One way would lead eventually to the lounge, the other more directly to his bedchamber. He glanced down at his robe and frowned; he'd been sitting in it all day and felt dirty. What would another ten minutes matter when he was already late? He'd rather face Drakkal's inevitable admonishment while freshly cleaned and clothed.

He'd rather face Samantha while freshly cleaned and clothed; only the best for his mate.

He hurried to his bedchamber, stripped, and bathed. He selected a crimson loincloth when he was done—one that matched the color of the fabric draped over his pelvis in Sam's painting—and had just opened his closet when the bedroom's lights switched to pulsing orange and yellow, accompanied by a high, whining alarm.

The excitement that had been fluttering in his stomach petrified and sank, coalescing into a lump of dread.

He pulled up his holocom control screen and tapped the flashing alert. It split into several surveillance feeds from around the compound. Armed individuals were at several of the outside entrances, overwhelming the door guards with speed and firepower.

Arcanthus watched as several members of his security crew were gunned down in the alleyways they'd been posted in, their bodies collapsing in unidentifiable puddles and filth. He curled his left hand into a fist while the attackers rushed to the entry doors and placed explosive charges.

Not yet. Can't be this soon. Can't be here.

The ice in his blood turned to fire when he shifted his attention to the main-level entrance—the only entrance that didn't let out onto the street two floors below—and saw a tall, slender figure clad in black striding along the path opened by the attacking gunmen. Arcanthus knew who it was just by the way he moved.

Vaund.

Simultaneous explosions at several doors filled the corresponding feeds with static; he heard their roars echo distantly through the corridors outside his room.

Arcanthus's heart skipped a beat when he realized that Samantha, his sweet, precious little flower, was in the lounge—nearly on the opposite end of the compound from him, but only twenty meters away from the main entrance.

Only twenty meters away from Vaund and the Syndicate.

TWENTY-FOUR

Samantha flashed Koroq and Razi a triumphant grin as she pulled the credit chips toward her growing pile. "I win. Again."

Koroq groaned and threw his hands up in frustration. "Never should have taught her to play!"

Kiloq snickered, leaning back in his chair. "No chance of *ever* winning now. The terran's too good."

"Beginner's luck," Razi muttered. "It'll run out. Eventually."

Thargen barked laughter and took another swig of his drink. "You're just pissed because you got knocked off the top of the hill, cren."

Razi frowned, brows falling low over his piercing blue eyes. "No. I'm happy for the competition. Not like any of you ever gave me a challenge."

"That's cause you're a cheat," Koroq said.

"I don't cheat. You're just too dumb to understand the game," Razi growled.

Koroq pushed himself up, but Kiloq—grinning as though he

enjoyed the spectacle—stopped him with a hand on his shoulder. "He doesn't cheat, Kor. You just suck."

"You're not any better," Koroq said.

Kiloq shrugged. "Don't want you to feel bad, so I lose on purpose."

"No you don't, you lying—"

Someone cleared his throat; Sam looked toward the doorway to see Drakkal standing just inside the lounge with his powerful arms crossed over his broad chest—his signature stance.

"Everyone's getting along great, *right?*" the azhera asked.

"You always spoil the fun," grumbled Thargen. "I was just about to start taking bets on who'd win the fight."

Samantha chuckled. "We're playing Conquerors. Do you want to join us?"

Drakkal dropped his arms to his sides and strode to the table, glancing down at the stacks of credit chips in front of the players—not that anyone had much left, apart from Razi and Sam. "Might be tempted to when Arc gets here. It's more fun when I know he's losing, too."

Excitement thrummed inside Sam. "Arc is coming? Is he finally taking a break?"

"He'd better come. He agreed, and I gave him a deadline. He'll be late, because he always gets distracted, but I think he'll get here eventually."

"He'll come," she said.

Thargen laughed. "Oh, I'm sure he'll be *coming* all right, but it won't be here."

Samantha blushed, ducking her head, but a faint smile tugged at her lips—because Thargen was likely right.

Though her gaze was averted, she swore she felt Drakkal glare at the vorgal.

"I think you're the only reason he's left that room at all over the last week, Samantha," Drakkal said. "He'll come. Time just works a little different for him. I said ten minutes, so he'll be at least half an hour."

"It takes time to look this good," Razi said in a voice startlingly similar to Arcanthus's.

Samantha laughed. "That was pretty good, Razi."

The cren shrugged and reached forward to reset the holographic game board, a shy smile touching his lips.

Despite his complaints, Koroq anted up at the start of the next round. Within a few turns, Razi and Samantha had clearly pulled ahead, the former wearing a look of intense concentration throughout. Drakkal remained beside the table, watching with a smirk.

When her turn came again, Samantha considered the board, making subtle calculations even she couldn't fully understand. For her, a large part of the game was driven by instinct. She was reaching for one of her cards when the lights in the room changed abruptly.

Orange and yellow flashed overhead, and an alarm blared.

A chill ran down Samantha's spine. "What's going on?"

Everyone around the table leapt to their feet in unison, their features hardening. Drakkal quickly activated his holocom. Within a second, he'd pulled up what looked like surveillance feeds from outside. There was gunfire, and attackers advancing; the screens were too small for her to see what exactly was happening, but it clearly wasn't good.

An explosion sounded in the hallway, loud enough to shake the walls and floor, occurring in time with several other explosions that terminated some of the surveillance feeds on Drakkal's holocom.

"That was the main door," Drakkal growled.

He and the others drew their blasters.

Arcanthus's voice, tinged by a faint, electronic buzz, came

through everyone's holocoms simultaneously. "Everyone fall back to the workshop immediately! They've breached multiple entrances. Get to the damn workshop!"

Tremors of fear coursed through Samantha as she watched everyone but Drakkal rush out of the lounge. She looked at the azhera with wide eyes. "What's happening?"

Drakkal rounded the table and clasped her upper arm with his free hand. "We're under attack. We need to move, terran."

Samantha nodded and stood up.

He led her into the hallway, where the others—Koroq, Kiloq, Razi, and Thargen—had spread out with weapons ready. There were shouts from around the nearby corner, and a haze of smoke in the air. Of everyone, only Thargen looked unconcerned; his lips were curled in an anticipatory grin, like he was eager for what would come.

Drakkal guided Samantha to flatten herself against the wall and positioned himself in front of her, blocking her view. Her heart thundered as, at his direction, she slowly retreated, backing away from the shouting.

Only a moment had passed before the whining thumps of firing blasters filled the hallway. Blue-white bolts of plasma darted past Samantha. Across the hall, Thargen returned fire, roaring with a gleeful light in his eyes as he squeezed the trigger of his blaster over and over.

"Fall back!" Drakkal roared.

Despite his half-crazed excitement, even Thargen slowly backed away.

Samantha looked in the direction they were heading; the next intersecting corridor was only a few meters away. She wasn't sure which way to go—to her knowledge, there were at least four doors into Arcanthus's workshop, but she'd only learned a few specific routes to traverse the compound despite her frequent wandering. Were any of those paths safe?

The blaster fire died down for a moment. In the lull, Drakkal sped their pace, practically shoving Samantha down the hall and around the corner.

To her relief, the others joined them, all seemingly unharmed.

"There's more coming in," Drakkal said. "Too many. We need to hurry."

"Quickest way is through the big door," Thargen said. Delighted fire burned in his eyes; this was his element, this was what he lived for.

Samantha was glad he was on their side.

They raced along the corridors, working their way ever deeper into the compound. Sam had never seen most of the hallways they ran through and didn't have time to orient herself; Drakkal kept her slightly ahead of him, ensuring his body shielded her back. She tried not to acknowledge the fact that none of them were wearing armor of any sort.

We'll be okay. We're going to make it, and we'll be safe, and then Razi and Koroq can get back to arguing about who won how many credits from who in that last game.

Someone yelled behind them. More blaster fire darted back and forth, and Drakkal growled out what must've been a curse. Samantha pressed her lips together and forced her legs to keep moving. Her nostrils flared with her heavy, burning breaths.

"Doing good, Sam. Keep going," Drakkal said.

The steadiness of his voice granted Samantha strength; she'd learned how terrifying these situations were when Arcanthus had rescued her from the apartment complex, but she'd also learned how grounding it was to be around someone who held his cool even when his life was in danger.

Someone like Arcanthus.

God, Arc, please be okay. Please.

She had no idea where he was, no idea what he was facing right now—no idea if she'd ever see him again.

No, I will see him again. *This isn't the end, damn it. We're both getting through this.*

Though she was grateful to have Drakkal there, she longed to have Arc beside her so she could cling to his warm, solid body, so she'd know he was safe.

Hell, she would've felt more comfortable—or at least less powerless—with a blaster in her hand. She wasn't a great shot, but it would've been *something*; even the illusion of being able to fight back might've been enough. Having no practical means of defending herself was frightening. It reminded her too much of how helpless and weak she'd always felt around James.

"Shit," someone yelled; it might've been one of the cren, but Sam wasn't sure.

Samantha ducked as plasma bolts struck the nearby wall, punching orange-ringed holes in concrete and metal. Drakkal shoved her into the shallow recess of a doorway and blocked the opening with his body. She pressed her face against the door and clenched her jaw, caged in the tight space as a cacophony sounded around her—shouts, gunfire, growls—all underscored by her rapidly beating heart.

We're going to be fine.

Drakkal hissed as a bolt zipped past his head; an instant later, the acrid odor of singed fur stung Sam's nose. Smoke curled from the spot on his bristling mane that had been burned away.

We're going to be fine.

Unfortunately, she found her own thoughts unconvincing.

TWENTY-FIVE

Arcanthus clenched his jaw as he retrieved the blaster from its hidden compartment beside his bed. Fear had coiled through his insides, touching everything with its cold, slimy fingers, but it could not extinguish the firestorm of his rage.

Once again, Vaund had violated Arc's sanctuary. He'd attacked Arc's *home*.

My home, my friends...now my mate. You don't get to take everything again.

He checked the surveillance feeds as he hurried to the door. Fighting had already spilled into the compound, but he couldn't tell how many Syndicate attackers had entered, couldn't tell how many of his people were up and fighting, couldn't guess which corridors would be safe to travel. Samantha, Drakkal, and a few others had escaped the lounge and were involved in a fighting retreat toward the workshop, and more of Arc's people were battling elsewhere in the compound, all outnumbered. Two of them—Sekk'thi and Urgand—were a relatively short distance from Arcanthus, caught in a firefight with several of the invaders. There was minimal cover available to them.

Arc's deepest instincts demanded he ignore everything, everyone, and charge across the compound to reach Samantha as quickly as possible, but he couldn't obey them this time. He had to help his people, his friends, as best he could along the way. He would not allow a repeat of the slaughter on Caldorius. He would not fail the people who followed him—not again. Arcanthus had no doubt that Drakkal would do everything in his power to protect Sam.

That had to be enough for now.

He dismissed the holocom screen, formed his hardlight shield, and entered the corridor, hurrying to Sekk'thi and Urgand. Each step forward intensified the furious heat in his chest.

My home. My friends.

My mate.

Arcanthus raised the shield as he turned into the hall where Sekk'thi and Urgand were fighting. Two of the gunmen at the far end were dead, but the rest—four or five, at least—shifted their focus to Arc and fired. Plasma burst and dissipated in flashes across his shield. He spread his fingers wide, pushing the shield to its maximum size, and advanced toward his friends.

He moved just beyond Sekk'thi and Urgand's positions, allowing them to duck behind his shield. Both the ilthurii and the vorgal were clad only in what appeared to be undergarments; they had likely been sleeping between shifts in their quarters when the alarm had sounded. They fired around the edges of the shield, taking down another attacker.

"At least we're all dressed for the occasion," Arcanthus said without humor as they retreated down the hallway backward.

"Where's everyone else?" Urgand asked.

"Scattered. They hit us from all sides, and we were spread too thin," Arcanthus replied.

The energy he was expending to maintain the shield was creating a build-up of heat in his right arm; it wouldn't be long before that heat reached a critical level and caused internal damage to the prosthesis. But cutting off the flow meant the shield would collapse within seconds—the enemy's fire was too concentrated and unrelenting.

There was undisguised concern in Sekk'thi's voice when she asked, "And Samantha?"

"With Drakkal. They're fighting their way to the workshop."

They turned at the next intersection. Arcanthus slammed the shield into the floor and released its tether, blocking the entrance of the corridor. He and his companions spun around and ran. Arc's right arm hissed as its heat vents opened to expel scorching steam and draw cooler air over its power cells.

They encountered another group of Syndicate attackers in the next hall, igniting a frantic exchange of fire that filled the passage with so much plasma the air wavered with heat. Despite the superior fire rates of the Syndicate's auto-blasters, Arcanthus and his companions managed to put their foes on the defensive; two more invaders fell before the rest took cover. Arcanthus followed Sekk'thi's lead through a staggered retreat —he, Urgand, and Sekk'thi moved from doorway to doorway, two maintaining suppressive fire as the third fell back to the next bit of shelter, constantly alternating roles.

Arcanthus quashed his urge to check the surveillance feeds again and find Samantha; he couldn't afford a distraction that would slow him down. He'd have trouble getting to Samantha if he was shot.

He and his companions continued toward the workshop, harassed at every step by aggressive and plentiful attackers,

who seemed to swarm the halls like fast-multiplying vermin—
sewer skrudges equipped with auto-blasters and low-grade
combat armor. For every enemy who fell to the trio's blaster fire,
two more seemed to appear.

When the gauge on his arm indicated the hardlight shield
had failed, Arcanthus growled; it meant even more invaders
would be rushing toward them. He summoned a new shield,
but because the overburdened power cells hadn't fully recovered, he couldn't expand the barrier beyond its default one-
meter diameter circle, and it wouldn't survive much
punishment.

His intensifying rage demanded he shift the battle to his
terms, that he charge his enemies and get close enough to put
his real skills to good use, close enough to feel their blood
splatter his skin as he sliced them to pieces with his sword and
crushed their bones with fists and feet. But his judgment was
not so clouded as to succumb to that wild, primal urge.

At least not yet.

They encountered a few more members of the security
team as they retreated, doubling the size of their party, but
there were distressingly few people about; many of the
personnel under his employment served as guards for the alley
accesses that led to the compound's numerous entrances, and
thus had likely been killed in the initial surprise attack. The
new additions to the group were better equipped, if nothing
else, wearing combat armor and carrying auto-blasters.

Still, the battle raged without cease throughout their journey. What should've taken a few minutes felt like days, and
Arcanthus's worry for Samantha only grew more pronounced.
He continued firing, continued killing, but the stream of
enemies was endless. He felt impotent, ineffective, *useless*, as
his security crew rallied around him and defended his body
with theirs.

When a plasma bolt pierced Sekk'thi's right arm, and her blaster fell, she growled in pain, crouched to retrieve her weapon with her left hand, and resumed firing. Flecks of molten metal sprayed from the wall as it was torn apart by plasma bolts, splashing on Urgand's face to sizzle tiny portions of his flesh, but the vorgal didn't even flinch.

Arcanthus's small group turned, finally, into a short corridor that ended at one of the workshop's concealed rear entries. Once everyone was in the passage, Arcanthus sealed the opening—from the other side it would look like a section of the hallway wall, indistinguishable from the rest. Their pursuers would've seen the open passage, meaning they'd eventually find a way through, but every extra second Arc could claim to help his people escape was worth it.

Arcanthus opened the workshop door, and his group rushed inside. They were greeted by a few more members of the security team, some of whom already looked bedraggled and battered.

But there was no Drakkal. No Samantha.

"Cover the other entrances," Arcanthus said as he hurried to his desk to pull up the surveillance feeds.

"*You there, Arc?*" asked Drakkal over the holocom.

"Where are you?" Arcanthus spread out the surveillance screens and expanded them.

"*Almost at the big door. Coming in hot. Have it ready.*"

"Is Samantha—"

"*She's okay.*"

The immense pressure that had strained Arc's breathing eased a bit. A moment later, he found them on one of the feeds; Samantha was running in front of Drakkal, who kept his body between her and the invaders giving chase. Dead Syndicate gunmen littered the hallway, but there were more advancing. A mere ten or fifteen meters separated Arc's people from the

Syndicate—and at the enemy's rear was a faceless specter, calm and controlled amidst the chaos.

Arcanthus opened the huge blast door at the far end of the chamber, halting it about a meter high; that was enough to allow the others to slide beneath without exposing everyone inside the workshop to hostile fire. Then he opened the hidden escape hatch on the platform behind him.

An explosion sounded in one of the corridors outside, and the corresponding camera feed went out. The Syndicate was blasting their way into the workshop.

Arc turned to look toward the door through which he'd just entered. How long before the invaders breached it? He had to assume they had adequate equipment to penetrate the defenses—this attack was meant to erase Arcanthus from existence, and Vaund was the sort who would've equipped his men with excessive firepower to ensure the job was done.

"*Vrek'osh,*" Arcanthus growled. "Once Drak and the others are inside, we're leaving."

He swung his attention back to the surveillance feeds to see Samantha and Drakkal nearing the wide landing in front of the big door. The azhera slowed, turning to shoot at the Syndicate and allowing Koroq, Kiloq, Razi, and Thargen to move past him.

Arcanthus's eyes widened when Vaund burst into motion, charging toward Drakkal like a vengeful shadow blasting out of the void.

"Everyone into the hatch," Arcanthus shouted as he leapt over the desk. He landed heavily at the base of the steps and sprang up, breaking into a sprint.

Faster, damn you! Faster!

SAMANTHA'S LUNGS and throat burned as she ran. Her feet felt like they each weighed a hundred pounds, and her back itched, anticipating the deadly sting of a plasma bolt at any moment.

"Go, go," Drakkal shouted behind her.

Thargen and the cren brothers entered her peripheral vision as she reached the staircase landing, running alongside her. The others dove in unison, sliding beneath the large blast door just ahead. Despite her terror, despite her heart pounding so fast and loud that she almost couldn't hear anything else, her mind registered Drakkal's absence.

Samantha risked a look over her shoulder to see Drakkal near the corridor entrance, only a meter or two from the steps, firing his blaster into the hallway. Her breath hitched when a black figure, moving faster than seemed physically possible, darted out of the corridor. The tall, slender figure ducked low, beneath the barrel of Drakkal's blaster, and swung a crackling blue energy sword up. The blade left an after-image of its trail through the azhera's arm; the limb detached from Drakkal's body a fraction of a second later.

Drakkal's roar—as filled with rage as it was with pain—was deafening, reverberating off the walls. He swung his free arm, catching his foe in the head with a heavy blow that produced a dull metallic *thunk.*

The figure spun aside with the force of the blow, but shifted the momentum into a kick, slamming his heel into the side of Drakkal's head.

The azhera staggered, one of his legs buckling beneath him, but lunged forward, swiping his big, dark claws across the figure's chest. Cloth shredded and viscous, dark blue blood glistened on the fabric of the figure's coat. Drakkal fought savagely despite his injury.

The figure reeled before replying to Drakkal's assault with

his own series of quick attacks. Drakkal narrowly avoided the arcing blade, but he couldn't defend himself from the figure's powerful kicks.

A blow to his gut doubled Drakkal over. The snarling azhera was unable to recover before his foe kneed him in the face. Drakkal staggered backward, and the dark figure kicked him twice more in the head.

Drakkal collapsed.

Everything had happened so quickly that Samantha had barely been able to register it. She didn't realize until that moment that she'd stopped before reaching the door; it hadn't been a conscious decision, just like it wasn't a conscious decision that had her charging toward the black figure, who now loomed over the fallen azhera.

Samantha was terrified; she knew she was outmatched. She couldn't stand against anyone who'd dropped Drakkal so quickly.

Drakkal's voice sounded in her mind, echoing the words she'd heard him say to Arcanthus so many times—*don't be stupid*.

This was, perhaps, the stupidest thing she'd ever done, but she couldn't run to safety while her friend was killed. Her greatest regret had always been her failure to fight for herself. She wouldn't add failure to fight for a friend to that regret, not if there was some chance, no matter how tiny, of making a difference.

The dark figure stood with his back to Samantha and his head angled toward Drakkal. Slowly—as though relishing the moment—he raised his sword and reversed his grip, directing the tip downward.

Clenching her teeth, Samantha launched herself at her foe.

The figure turned suddenly, facing Sam with his featureless metal mask. She knew in that moment this was Vaund, the devil risen from Arc's past.

Vaund's empty hand darted out with lightning speed, and he closed his long, skeletal fingers around her throat in a vise-like grip, halting her in midair.

The pain was immense, and her airway was immediately squeezed shut. She grasped Vaund's forearm with both hands, desperate to relieve the pressure, desperate to breathe. His arm had a strange feel through his shirt—like hard leather stretched over a dense metallic core.

"So, he let his little terran wander away from his side," Vaund said, his raspy voice pervaded by a buzzing electronic undertone.

Panic and helplessness pressed in on all sides of Sam's mind, chased by rapidly encroaching darkness. She clawed at Vaund's arm and kicked his torso, but his grip didn't falter.

Worthless. Weak. Stupid.

No! She wasn't going to listen to those doubts anymore. She wasn't going to be James's victim—*anyone's* victim—ever again.

Focusing past the pain in her throat, the fire in her lungs, the building pressure in her head, she recalled what Sekk'thi had taught her.

Every foe has a weakness, but you must survive long enough to discover it and take advantage.

Samantha had, at best, seconds to act. She raked her gaze over Vaund, searching for something, for anything, but he was covered from head to toe in black, and her vision was already darkening...

He tilted his head, and her eyes fell on the hoses connected to the side of his helmet, just behind where a human's ear would've been.

Throwing all her strength and willpower into the movement, she bent her abdomen, swung her legs up, and kicked the hoses. Her heel hit one of the connectors, and it loosened. Air hissed from the damaged valve, and Vaund let out a raspy grunt. Samantha hurriedly hammered her heel into the hose again, breaking it free.

Vaund released her and dropped his sword, clawing at the disconnected hose and open valve. His wheezing breath sounded painful; were she not otherwise occupied, Sam might've found something poetically just about that. She landed hard on her backside, immediately moving her hand to her neck as she sucked in several hungry breaths.

She glanced at Drakkal. He was unmoving save for the shallow rise and fall of his chest.

Focus, Sam. Don't have much time.

Her eyes landed on the fallen energy sword, which had embedded itself in the floor with its handle angled upward. It slowly sank deeper and deeper into the concrete as its blade melted the surrounding material.

Samantha scrambled forward and grasped the sword's handle. The blade's dull vibrations coursed up her arms as she pulled the weapon up; it slid free with unexpected ease. She forced herself to her feet, ignoring the weakness in her knees and the fire in her throat as she swung the sword at Vaund.

Vaund swayed back, his gangly frame twisting to avoid the pulsing blade. He kept one hand on the disconnected tube as Samantha recovered from her first swing and attacked again. He raised his other arm. The blade burned through his sleeve and bounced off some sort of dark metal beneath, leaving a narrow, glowing orange trail.

"A spirited creature," he said, his voice seemingly unaffected by his labored breathing. "I may have to break you in myself."

"Samantha!" Arcanthus yelled from somewhere behind her.

Growling, Samantha reversed the blade and lunged forward, taking another swing.

Vaund deflected the blade with his forearm again, but this time, he released the hose. His hand clamped over both of hers, locking her arms in place. His other hand joined the first immediately, and before Samantha could react, Vaund had pried the sword out of her grasp. He spun her like she weighed nothing and clamped an arm around her neck, tugging her against his rigid chest.

She found herself facing Arcanthus. He stood in front of the workshop door, staring past her with glowing, hate-filled eyes. The blaster in his left hand was aimed at Vaund, and his tail flicked restlessly behind him.

"Arcan—"

Vaund tightened his hold, silencing Samantha. She clutched his forearm with both hands, but he was too strong for her to break free.

He drew in a strained breath as heavy footfalls approached from the hallway behind him. "Don't shoot the sedhi. I'm going to take care of him myself."

Several of the gunmen who'd been chasing Sam and her companions entered her peripheral vision with their weapons aimed at Arcanthus.

Vaund raised his sword, stopping the thrumming blade a centimeter from Samantha's eye. She tried to lean back, but there was no way to move, nowhere to go. Half her field of vision was Arcanthus, his features more demonic than ever in his rage and worry, and the other half was dominated by her imminent death.

She wished that she could tell Arc again how much she

loved him. Wished she could tell him that, for once, she *wasn't* sorry. When it came to him, Samantha had no regrets.

TWENTY-SIX

Arcanthus's heart went several moments without beating, and his breath remained caught in his throat. The slightest twitch of Vaund's hand would cause immense pain and damage to Samantha. Consuming rage and chilling fear warred for supremacy inside him.

"Drop the weapon, sedhi," Vaund said.

There were only a few meters between Arc and Sam, between Arc and Vaund, but he couldn't take a shot. There was too much danger to her. Too great a chance that Vaund's helmet was armored against blaster fire.

Gritting his teeth, Arcanthus dipped his central eye to Drakkal; the azhera appeared to be breathing but was otherwise still. His left arm lay on the floor a meter away from his body, severed cleanly just above his elbow. That sparked fresh anger in Arc's gut. It was too close to what Vaund had done to him all those years ago.

Arcanthus slowly shifted his finger off the blaster's trigger, angled the barrel down, and tossed the weapon toward Vaund. It clattered to a stop near Vaund's feet.

"If you hurt her, Vaund, I'll—"

"You're in no position to make threats, sedhi." Vaund inclined his chin toward the door behind Arcanthus. "Tell your people to come out."

"They're not in there," Arcanthus replied. He could only hope they'd moved fast enough—and that they'd closed the hatch behind them.

Vaund was silent but for the strained sound of his breaths.

An explosion boomed inside the workshop—near Arc's desk, by the sound of it. It was followed by the sounds of raining debris and crackling electricity.

"All of you get in there to support the other team. Kill anyone you find," Vaund said.

The Syndicate goons hurried forward, keeping to the sides of the partially open blast door. Arcanthus held his gaze on Vaund as flash grenades went off in the workshop; the detonations left a ringing in Arc's ears that almost drowned out the sound of the Syndicate gunmen storming into the room.

Vaund maintained his hold on Samantha, whose eyes were wide and fearful. The energy blade was impossibly steady in his hold.

"Release her," Arcanthus said.

"I should kill her." Vaund tipped the blade infinitesimally closer to Samantha's pale skin.

She cringed and whimpered softly.

Arcanthus's insides knotted, and he clenched his fists.

Vaund's laugh was like electricity arcing out of a broken power casing. "But I'm not going to. I'll hurt her—you can be sure of that—but I'm going to keep her afterward."

"No one's in here, boss," someone shouted from inside the workshop.

"Where are they, sedhi?" Vaund demanded.

"It's just the two of us, Vaund," Arc said, struggling to keep his voice steady. He couldn't allow himself to forget one of the lessons he'd learned long ago—a battle could be won before the first blow was thrown if you could get into your opponent's head beforehand.

Arcanthus focused his rage into a tiny point, into a powerful, controllable shape, and let his instincts and fear make it cold; it would be a weapon to wield deliberately against his foe, a deadly tool. He could not allow it to control him, or he'd lose.

Vaund laughed again and shoved Samantha aside. She stumbled half a dozen steps before crashing heavily to the floor. To Arcanthus's relief, her head snapped up immediately, but there was a concerned look on her face. Her shoulders heaved with her quick, shallow breaths.

"The two of us and twenty of my men in the room behind you," Vaund said.

"I thought this was meant to be a fair fight," Arcanthus said. "Or is it that you still can't beat me without a gang to hold me down?"

Vaund reached up with his empty hand and tore off his shirt, tossing it aside. His bared torso was lean, with hard, irregular ridges of muscle, and armored plates jutted from beneath the ashen skin of his forearms. Tattered flesh, smeared with dark blue ichor, dangled from his chest. He looked more skeletal—and less alive—than ever before; his chest didn't even move with the wheezing breaths flowing through the damaged tube on his mask.

"I don't need any help killing you, sedhi."

"Good. I just wanted to ensure we had an understanding." Arcanthus lifted his arm, engaged his neural link to the autocanons mounted on the workshop's ceiling, and flicked his wrist to enable their automated threat elimination mode.

The heavy *whumps* of the canons' rapid firing was joined, for a few brief moments, by the shouts and screams of the uninvited guests in the workshop. Flashes of light pulsed from under the open blast door, casting strobing shadows around Arcanthus. It was over within seconds; the only sound remaining after the canons fell silent was Vaund's strained respiration.

"It doesn't matter how many more you have outside," Arcanthus said. "You'll be dead before they get here."

Vaund released a buzzing growl. "I'm going to cut off your limbs again, one by one, and your terran is going to watch. She's going to be haunted for the rest of her miserable life by what I'm about to do to you."

Arcanthus opened the compartment on his left forearm, dropping the hilt of his hardlight sword into his waiting hand. He activated the weapon, and the translucent yellow blade materialized, extending from the hilt.

Vaund circled slowly to his left; Arcanthus mirrored his foe's movement, maintaining the distance between them as Vaund neared the big door and Arcanthus approached Samantha, who had moved to Drakkal's side.

"You could've just accepted my offer all those years ago. We could have avoided all this. All this pain and strife," Arc said. But he didn't regret the way things had happened—didn't regret having been forced to flee Caldorius—because that chain of events, that long, torturous road, had brought him to Arthos and, ultimately, his mate.

"And you could've just *died*." Vaund pointed the tip of his energy blade toward Arcanthus. "You had no right to be on top. No right to act like any of us should've bowed down to you and fallen into what you thought were our *places*."

"*Our* place was on top." Arcanthus rolled his wrist and halted his legs as soon as his body was between Samantha and Vaund. "That was my point all along. My goal. We brought in all that money, and it should've been ours."

"My place is on top. Yours is face down in an alleyway puddle."

He was never this much of a talker before a fight. He's fueled purely by hatred.

"Samantha," Arcanthus said softly, "stay with Drakkal. We're going to leave as soon as this is done. It won't take long; I don't have the patience to toy with him this time."

"I love you," she said firmly, though her voice was hoarse. "Be careful."

"Love you, too, little terran." He raised his voice to say, "Now, Vaund—which side of your face do you want me to remove first?"

With another robotic growl, Vaund took his weapon in a two-handed grip and charged. Arcanthus rushed forward to meet him; he needed to keep the battle as far away from Samantha and Drakkal as possible.

Their blades met with a flash and an instant's resistance; that fleeting clash was enough to throw Arcanthus's mind back more than a decade. He could almost feel the roar of the crowd sweeping over him, could almost feel the floor vibrate with the stomping of their feet. Fighting in the arena had always been a thrill—even as a slave, he'd enjoyed it—but now he had so much more to fight for than glory or a victor's purse. Now he had so much more to lose.

He had Samantha.

Their blades separated, and the dance began in earnest.

Energy crackled through the air, tracing blue and yellow arcs as the combatants swung, thrust, parried, and dodged, their movements faster than conscious thought could enable. More than once, Vaund's energy blade passed close enough for Arcanthus to feel its heat on his skin.

Vaund's performance had to be attributed to more than

another decade of experience—he was immensely faster and stronger than he'd been the last time they'd battled.

Arcanthus's rage intensified, sharpening to a finer point; despite his cybernetic prostheses, he and Vaund were a near match as far as their physical capabilities.

But there was a key difference between them—despite his cunning, despite his coldness, Vaund still fought with the same savagery as before. His attacks were meant to be overwhelming in force and speed, were meant to overpower rather than outmatch his foe.

"You seem out of breath," Arc said, deflecting a powerful blow from Vaund's blade. "We can pause for a moment to rest, if you'd like."

Vaund snarled and launched into a succession of rapid, heavy-handed strikes, his movements too quick to leave Arcanthus time for an adequate counterattack but too sloppy to land a blow.

"Wouldn't want you at a disadvantage, Vaund." Arc swayed aside from a downward swing, narrowly avoiding the blade.

Vaund recovered, twisted his hand to reorient his blade toward Arcanthus, and swung backhanded. The sharp angle of the attack—aimed at Arc's face—left Vaund overextended, with his chest exposed for an instant.

Arcanthus swatted the energy blade aside with the flat of his sword and twisted his hips, throwing significant power behind a punch that connected with Vaund's ribs. The jolt of the impact ran up Arc's cybernetic arm and into his flesh; his hand struck with a dulled metallic clang, like he'd punched a padded metal plate.

Vaund stumbled aside from the force of the blow but kept on his feet. His immediate, frenzied counterattack had Arcanthus once again on the defensive, backpedaling toward the stairs.

When Vaund drew back for an overhead swing, Arcanthus retorted with a quick slash.

Vaund released a choked sound and abandoned his attack to leap backward. The hardlight blade grazed his chest, leaving a long, horizontal cut that split wide and oozed dark blood. Backing away farther, Vaund hissed through his open respirator valve and lifted a hand to the wound, digging his clawlike fingers beneath the damaged flesh to peel it back—revealing not muscle and bone beneath but dark metal.

"My dying flesh has forced me to make a few changes over the years," Vaund said. "A small price to pay for another chance to kill you."

Arcanthus kept his blade up and ready. He'd not had a fight like this in a long while—he'd never really met his match during his time as a gladiator, though a few had come close. He turned his head slightly, keeping Vaund in sight while shifting his center eye to look at Samantha.

She stared at him with those big, dark, frightened eyes, her skin pale but for the blotches of red on her cheeks and the dark bruises already forming on her throat. She'd positioned herself in front of Drakkal, as though to shield the big azhera with her little body.

The sight made Arc's chest tighten; he was so proud of her, so fiercely in love with her. She should have fled into the workshop with the others, but she'd gone back to help Drakkal. So foolish, but also so brave, so loyal, so selfless.

Arcanthus could learn so much from her.

For Samantha, for Drakkal, for all those who yet lived and all who'd been lost, Arcanthus needed to finish this.

"You talk too much," Arc said. He leapt into an attack of his own, pushing himself beyond the limits of his strength, speed, and agility. Blade, fists, feet, elbows, knees, and tail blended together in an unrelenting, blistering assault.

Vaund released more grunts and growls as Arcanthus's strikes broke through his defenses; the hardlight blade sliced off chunks of pale flesh and bit into the underlying metal, and Arc's unarmed blows hit with resounding force, steadily beating Vaund back toward the partially open blast door.

Arc caught Vaund in the chest with a side kick; Vaund flew backward a few meters, slamming into the blast door. With a bestial growl, he raised his empty hand, directing his palm at Arcanthus. The armor on his forearm slitted open, pouring out a wave of heat and an intense red-orange glow. An energy blast of the same color burst from the center of Vaund's palm.

Arcanthus dove aside. The blast struck his left forearm, and an electric jolt raced through the nerves connected to the prosthesis. He rolled onto a knee and glanced down with his center eye; the outer casing of his left arm glowed with residual heat, and wisps of smoke wafted off it. His hardlight blade was gone. When he bent his fingers into a fist, the digits moved slowly, stutteringly.

Vaund tossed his energy blade aside and straightened his other arm. Its heat vents opened.

Curling down into as tight a stance as he could, Arcanthus threw up his right arm and formed his shield. Vaund's blast struck the hardlight barrier dead center. The shield flickered, and heat flowed around its edges, but it held; after a moment, the energy blast subsided.

Arcanthus sprang forward, swinging his arm and releasing the shield's tether to throw it at Vaund. The hardlight disc hit Vaund as he was charging another shot, knocking his arm aside and sending the blast into the nearby wall. Arc struck an instant later, driving his knee—with all his weight and momentum behind it—into Vaund's chest.

Caught between Arcanthus and the blast door, the subdermal armor beneath Vaund's skin buckled, and he released another choked grunt. Vaund swung a fist at Arc's head, but Arcanthus raised his damaged left arm and blocked the blow. When Vaund angled his other palm —the circular opening at its center still glowing orange—at Arcanthus, the sedhi caught his wrists and forced them up.

Vaund shoved off the blast door, forcing Arcanthus back a few steps before the sedhi braced his feet and halted Vaund's advance.

Their bodies trembled as they struggled against one another, and Vaund's wheezing breaths intensified. Not for the first time, Arcanthus was grateful that he'd undergone the expensive and painful procedures to reinforce his bones and muscles; his flesh would not otherwise have withstood the immense strain placed upon it in these moments.

The heat vents on Vaund's arms flared, making the air around them waver. Arcanthus lost a centimeter of leeway on either side. He gritted his teeth and forced more out of his already overburdened muscles and prostheses.

Vaund snapped his head forward. Arcanthus dipped his chin, blocking the headbutt with his horns. The blow sent a jolt through his skull and down his spine.

"I was going to cut off your head," Vaund said, "but I think I'll rip it off with my bare hands, instead. Just for the satisfaction of watching your blood ooze from your tearing flesh."

TWENTY-SEVEN

Fear had spread through Samantha like frost across a windowpane, chilling her limbs and forming a sinking weight in her stomach. She'd known she never stood a chance against Vaund, even before seeing him and Arcanthus fight; it was a small miracle that she'd done any damage at all in her desperate attack.

But Arcanthus was struggling. She knew he was pushing himself to his limits, *beyond* his limits, and what if that wasn't enough? What if she lost him?

She clenched her jaw and curled her hands into trembling fists. There had to be something she could do. Some way she could help.

She refused to let fear prevent her from protecting her man, her mate, her everything. Even if she wasn't nearly as skilled or capable as Arcanthus, she would fight just as hard as him to protect the people she cared about.

Samantha forced her body forward, dropping onto hands and knees to pick up Arcanthus's discarded blaster. She pushed herself to her feet and adjusted her grip on the weapon, accounting for her clammy palms. She aimed the barrel toward Vaund—he and Arcanthus were locked up like two goats butting heads—and advanced.

There was no point in trying to shoot from anywhere but point-blank range; the chance of hitting Arcanthus was too great, and her shots wouldn't do any harm to Vaund. He'd taken at least three direct blasts from Drakkal without slowing, and she'd heard the dull, metal-on-metal clangs when Arcanthus's fists and feet connected with his body. He had armor *beneath* his skin.

To her knowledge, Vaund only had one exploitable weakness—but she had to get close to make sure it worked.

Damned close.

The first time she'd attacked Vaund from behind, he'd reacted as though he'd seen her coming; she had to assume he could and act accordingly.

She crossed the space that separated her from the males quickly but cautiously, giving Vaund a wide berth as she circled around to his back. Her eyes repeatedly flicked to his hands as she moved; though Arcanthus had managed to keep Vaund's palms pointed up, all it would take was a miniscule gain by Vaund to angle those arm-canons lower. She had no chance of evading such a blast.

Once she was facing Vaund's back, she pressed straight ahead. Her thundering heart and ragged breaths dominated her hearing. The paces between Samantha and her target diminished, and thoughts swirled in her head—deriding her foolishness, questioning her apparent death wish, telling her she would fail now just like she always had. James's voice bubbled up from her memory to say she was worthless and weak, that she needed him, but she shoved it aside and clenched her jaw.

I never needed you. I need Arcanthus—and he needs me, too.

I can do this.

Vaund wrenched his head back from Arcanthus's as Samantha neared. Her chest constricted and her stomach knotted for an instant; in that instant, Vaund growled and twisted his body, sending a kick backward—directly at her.

This time, she'd been expecting it—had been counting on it. She dodged to the side; Vaund's leg brushed over the fabric of her shirt as it cut through the air in front of her, narrowly missing her abdomen. The way he'd moved had angled the side of his helmet toward her. Before she could think, she slid her leading foot forward, closing the last bit of distance between her and her foe, and pressed the barrel of her blaster against the valve opening on his helmet.

Samantha pulled the trigger twice.

Fiery sparks flared from the other connections on Vaund's helmet. The sound he released was unlike anything Samantha had ever heard, unlike anything she could've imagined, even in her wildest nightmares. It was at once bestial and robotic, guttural and staticky, agonized and furious; she couldn't know if he was even making the sound himself or if it was a malfunction caused by the internal damage to his mask.

Arcanthus swung Vaund around by his wrists and heaved him toward the blast door. Before Samantha could move, he spun to face her again and leapt at her. His body collided with her heavily, knocking the blaster from her hand. He wrapped his arms around her as they fell; they landed hard, but his arms absorbed most of the impact and prevented his full weight from coming down atop her. Arc shielded her with his body.

She pressed her hands to his chest; it expanded and contracted with his quick, ragged breaths, and the rapid pounding of his heart matched the pace of hers.

The terrifying sound from Vaund continued, gradually diminishing into a static hiss that ultimately ended with a drawn out, gurgling release of air. Seconds passed; anticipation kept Sam's muscles tense, but whatever she was waiting for didn't come.

Sam and Arc lifted their heads and turned to look toward Vaund. He lay unmoving, pale gray smoke curling up from his helmet.

"Is he dead?" Samantha asked.

"I would hope so," Arcanthus replied. He turned his face toward hers. "Are you all right?"

Samantha reached up, grabbed his jaw, and pressed her mouth against his. She kissed him hard, kissed him with the despair she'd felt at the possibility of losing him, with the relief she felt for having him safe in her arms, with all the love brimming inside of her. She slid her hands up and wrapped her arms around his neck, pulling herself tighter against him. He returned the kiss with the same raw, unguarded emotions that flowed through her, holding her like he'd never let go again.

Arcanthus groaned when they finally broke the kiss, slipping his tongue out to lick his lips. "There's a little voice in the back of my mind that says it's an inappropriate time to want to make love to you, Samantha, but I am unreasonably aroused right now."

Laughter burst out of Samantha; it hurt her sore throat, but she didn't care. She could feel the evidence of his arousal against her thigh, and she'd have been lying if she said she wasn't feeling a spark of desire herself, but...

Sam's eyes widened. "Drakkal!"

Arcanthus's brows rose in alarm. He slipped his arms out from beneath her, pushed himself to his feet, and took her hand to help her stand. "Go to him. I'll be right there."

Samantha rushed back to Drakkal's side. He lay exactly where she'd left him, blood matting his mane. She pressed her hand to his neck, searching for a pulse through his thick fur, and gasped when he stirred. She settled her palm on his chest and leaned toward him. "Drakkal?"

Arcanthus grunted behind her. Samantha glanced over her shoulder to see him standing over Vaund with the blue energy sword in his right hand. He leaned down, grabbed something with his free hand—his body was blocking her view of it—and swung the blade. Straightening, he tossed the object aside—Vaund's armored head, now cleanly detached from his body.

Movement from Drakkal called Sam's attention back to him. He lifted his head off the floor slightly, eyelids fluttering open, before dropping it again. "*Vrek'osh,*" he grumbled, "my skull feels like a tralix stepped on it."

Relief flooded Samantha. "You got hit pretty hard. You might have a concussion."

Drakkal's expression hardened. "Can't feel my arm. How bad did he get me?"

"The good news is that your arm looks fine," Arcanthus said from behind Samantha. "It just happens to be separated from your body."

Samantha turned her head to look at Arcanthus with disbelieving eyes. "Arc!"

The azhera's nostrils flared with a heavy exhalation, and he opened his eyes again; they were clearer, this time, more alert and determined. "Still three limbs ahead of you, sedhi."

Arcanthus moved to Drakkal's side and crouched, slipping a hand beneath the azhera's uninjured arm. "Let's get you on your feet, old friend. We need to leave before any more *guests* show up."

Samantha stood up. "The others?"

"They made it into the escape tunnel," Arcanthus said as he helped Drakkal up, taking the azhera's weight on his shoulder. "Anyone who didn't is probably already dead."

Her heart seized at the thought of losing any of her new

friends—her new family. She'd only just found the place she belonged, and they'd taken her into their fold so readily, had treated her as one of their own from the start. She couldn't bear to lose any of them.

Arcanthus used the tip of his tail to activate his holocom and opened the workshop blast door fully, revealing the destruction within. The couches were charred, the floor scorched with blast marks, and bodies—or at least pieces of bodies—were scattered everywhere, blasted into ash. The air was thick with the stench of burned flesh.

Sam walked beside Arc as he and Drakkal entered the workshop. Neither of the males seemed affected by the carnage around them. She tried to emulate their indifference, telling herself that those *weren't* corpses, that the blackened piles of ash *hadn't* been people a few minutes ago. Her stomach churned and twisted, and she pressed her lips together, clutching Arcanthus. He slid his tail around her waist, offering wordless comfort.

They mounted the steps to the platform. His desk was in pieces, and much of the equipment against the surrounding walls was damaged or destroyed, though several of the screens were still operational. One of the entrances had been blasted open, and the door lay in several large, deformed chunks nearby.

Arc input a command on one of the surviving holo screens; a hatch slid open at the center of the platform, revealing to a set of steep, illuminated steps. The opening was too narrow for them to descend side-by-side. Arcanthus directed Samantha down first.

Her gaze lingered on Arcanthus and Drakkal before she took in a deep breath, turned, and descended into the narrow tunnel.

She was greeted by several blasters pointed at her. Her eyes widened and her heart stopped.

"Samantha," Sekk'thi gasped. Razi, Kiloq, Koroq, Thargen, and Urgand stood near her, blocking the tunnel with their bodies. Several other people Samantha didn't know were behind them; they must've been more members of the security team.

They all lowered their weapons, looks of relief softening their expressions.

Sekk'thi shoved her way forward and pulled Samantha into a tight, one-armed embrace. "You tough, stupid little terran. I am glad you are safe."

Samantha pulled away from Sekk'thi and glanced at the ilthurii's right arm, which was tucked tight against her side. "You're hurt!"

"I will be fine, Samantha. I have had worse."

"You were supposed to be with us, terran," Kiloq said, scowling.

"I had to help Drakkal," Sam replied.

"Is he..."

"I'm not dead," Drakkal growled from behind Samantha.

She looked back to see him moving down the stairs, supporting himself with his uninjured arm against the wall. Arc was just in front of him, keeping close. As soon as Drakkal was low enough, Arcanthus closed the hatch overhead.

"You lost an arm," Koroq said.

"*Kraasz ka'val,* do you think I didn't notice that?" Drakkal replied through his bared teeth.

"To be fair, you didn't," Arcanthus said. "But we can talk about all that later. We need to move. We'll get a clean-up crew in as soon as possible once we're out."

The tunnel shook with an explosion from overhead, the force of which resonated through the walls and floor.

"What's happening now?" Kiloq asked.

"Just destroying some evidence," Arcanthus replied. "Now, if you'd all be so kind as to *move*, it would be greatly appreciated."

"This was a bucketload of skrudge piss," Thargen grumbled. "Why'd you make me wait in a damned tunnel when I could've been out there fighting?"

"If you want a fight, I will gladly beat you into unconsciousness," Arcanthus replied, "*after* we get out of this place. I thought I was keeping the best of the best on my security team. What the hell am I paying you for if you can't follow a simple order? Go!"

The group moved forward, with Thargen muttering curses to himself as he turned to follow.

Samantha lagged to step closer to Arcanthus. "Where are we going to go?"

He brushed the backs of his fingers down her cheek. "I have a safehouse on standby. It might be a bit dusty, as I've never used it, but it's something. From there"—his mouth tilted up at one corner into a roguish grin—"we'll have to find a new home together."

She leaned her face into his touch and smiled.

Together.

EPILOGUE

"Close your eyes," Samantha said.

"I've been wagging around a stump for two months," Drakkal replied, raising his left arm, which had been cut off four or five centimeters above his elbow. The lower half of his bicep was covered in a sleek, surgically implanted metal sleeve. "I shouldn't have to wait any longer."

"It's only another minute or two. Now close your eyes, Drak. It's supposed to be a surprise!"

Drakkal growled, took a moment to glare at her, and squeezed his eyes shut. His long tail flicked in annoyance, but Samantha knew he was excited.

"No peeking." She took a step away from the table Drakkal was sitting beside and turned toward the open doorway. "He's ready now."

Arcanthus walked into the room with a long, cloth-wrapped bundle in his arms. "Wouldn't it be more fun if we told him they botched the order and he had to wait a few more weeks?"

"I'm sitting right here, sedhi," Drakkal grumbled. "My eyes are closed, not my ears."

"He's agitated today, isn't he?" Arc asked with a smirk.

Samantha poked Arc in his chest. "You'd think as someone who lost a few limbs of his own, you'd be a little more sympathetic."

Arcanthus snickered. "You should've heard him calling me a whiner while I was in recovery. This is payback on the smallest possible scale—far less than he deserves."

He knelt in front of the azhera and peeled back one end of the cloth, revealing the cybernetic prosthesis's connector. He inserted it into the slot on Drakkal's metal sleeve; it locked into place with a heavy click.

"You can open your eyes now," Arcanthus said.

Drakkal opened his eyes and glanced down, scowling. "Why did you make me close my eyes if you had it covered up all along?"

"It's not too late for me to return this, azhera. You're lucky Samantha worked so hard on the design, or I'd have given you the ugliest, most generic prosthesis I could find."

"You realize I have plenty of credits to my own name, don't you?"

"Don't you dare take away what little satisfaction I can find in this," Arcanthus snapped. "Besides, I paid for it from your account." Before Drakkal could reply, Arc loosened the cloth wrapping and tugged it off with a flourish.

Drakkal's eyes flared, transfixed on the prosthesis.

Samantha clasped her hands together and raised them to her chest, wringing her fingers. Despite Arcanthus's encouragement, she'd doubted herself ever since she had the idea to design the aesthetics of Drakkal's cybernetic arm. It seemed like such a big thing, such an *important* thing, and she wasn't sure of Drakkal's tastes. Would he appreciate the stylized limb she'd designed, or would he have preferred the sort of prosthetic that looked like a living body part down to the finest detail?

She'd gone for a look meant to emphasize Drak's prowess. Gladiatorial armor from ancient Earth had served as a core inspiration—she thought it was fitting, given his history—but she'd added a few special touches to make it unique. It sported some of the sleeker designs evident in many of Arcanthus's prostheses, but had a traditional flare in the subtle patterns she'd had etched into the dark metal, all of which were based on Azheran art.

Drakkal raised his new hand and turned it, examining it front and back. It was larger than his other hand, clad in segmented, gauntlet-like armor. His brow furrowed as though in concentration. Hardlight claws formed at the tips of his fingers, long and hooked like his natural claws.

"With a little practice, you'll learn to alter them," Arcanthus said.

Flexing his fingers, Drakkal dismissed the hardlight claws and turned his gaze to Samantha. "You designed this?"

"Do you like it?" she asked hopefully.

He stood up, pushing the chair away, and stepped to Samantha. For a moment, she stared up at him; he was about the same height as Arcanthus, but far broader. His expression was unreadable. When he leaned down and drew her into a tight embrace, she was caught completely off guard.

"Thank you, Samantha. For this...and for my life."

Samantha smiled and wrapped her arms around him, returning the hug. Elation flooded her, spreading warmth outward from her chest, and tears stung her eyes. "I'd do it again."

"But you *won't*," Arcanthus said firmly.

She chuckled, turning her head to look at him. All three of his eyes were narrowed on Drakkal in displeasure.

Arcanthus stepped closer. "All right, that's enough. Hand the female over."

Drakkal laughed and whispered, "Run away with me, terran. I'll treat you better than he does."

"Are you looking to lose a few more limbs, azhera?" Arcanthus said. "I already treat her better than I do even myself. It's impossible for you to do more."

Samantha laughed and patted Drakkal's cheek affectionally. "Maybe another time."

Arc slipped his arm around her waist, wrapped his tail around her leg, and pulled her away from Drakkal. "No, not *any* time. You're mine, Samantha."

She grinned up at him. "Prove it."

His answering smile was devilish and full of promise. He stooped down and swept Samantha over his shoulder, looping an arm around her thighs and settling his other hand on her ass.

She shrieked with laughter and pressed her hands against his back to claim some stability as he turned around. Shaking hair out of her face, she looked at Drakkal, smiled, and waved. "Enjoy the arm!"

Arcanthus carried her to the bedroom they'd been sharing while they stayed in this safehouse; everything was smaller here, but it didn't matter, because she had him. She didn't need a sprawling compound—though she knew he was preparing a new one for them to move into sometime soon.

Once the bedroom door was closed, Arcanthus tossed Sam onto the bed and lowered himself over her, caging her between his arms and wedging his hips between her thighs. His long, dark hair fell forward, and he stared down at her hungrily with glowing eyes. "So you need some proof, do you?"

Samantha settled her palms on his chest, curling her fingers in the fabric of his robe. Desire pooled low in her belly, sending a rush of heat to her core. "I mean, Drakkal *is* pretty hot with that new arm..."

Arcanthus pressed his lips together, closed his eyes, and made a sound partway between a hum and a groan. "All our worst habits have rubbed off on you, my flower. You tease me." He dipped his head and brushed his lips over her cheek. His warm breath tickled her ear. "And damn if I don't love it."

She giggled. "You love it when I call your friend hot?"

He lifted his head and met her gaze. A new, tender light had joined the hungry gleam in his eyes. "I love that you're comfortable enough to tease me. All I have to do is look at you to know you desire *only* me." Shifting one arm, he cupped her cheek, brushing his thumb across the same skin he'd just kissed. "You're still the same little flower I plucked off that Undercity street months ago, but you're so much more now. You've blossomed and found yourself. And I am so much better for it."

Her smile softened as she slid a hand up, lightly tracing his *qal* with her fingertips until she reached the dot on his bottom lip. "I did a little research about your *qal*."

"Oh? And what did you learn? Please tell me you figured out how to turn these marks into an erogenous zone."

She chuckled and shook her head. "I learned that the volturians take the markings of their mates upon themselves. Humans have a symbolic exchange, too, but it's nowhere near as permanent, when we get married. We exchange rings and vows."

His smile broadened into a grin. "Are you asking me to marry you, Samantha? Trying to tie me down?"

Her cheeks warmed, and she glanced up at him for a second before returning her eyes to his *qal*. "I...guess I am. That is...if you..." She grimaced. This wasn't turning out at all how she'd hoped. "I thought with us being mates—"

"Samantha Dawn Wilder," he said, calling her attention back to his face, "would you do me the indescribable honor of becoming my wife?"

Her brows rose in surprise that was rapidly swept aside by joy. "That's exactly how a human would ask…"

"You aren't the only one who's done some research, Samantha. And, according to *my* research, I would traditionally present you with the ring I purchased…but it was unfortunately destroyed along with the rest of the compound. I was planning to wait until we were settled into a more permanent residence to find a worthy replacement."

"A ring doesn't matter." Sam smiled up at him through tear-blurred vision, taking his jaw between her hands. She couldn't believe he'd already obtained a ring, that he'd already been planning to propose to her according to human tradition. "I would much rather take your *qal*."

"Hmm." His eyes swept over her face, and his thumb continued its lazy back and forth across her skin. "As flattered as I am by that, I don't want my marks on your skin."

His words struck her like a heavy blow to her chest. She turned her face and dropped her hands. "Oh."

"Ah, Samantha." Arcanthus grasped her chin and forced her to face him again. "I am not rejecting you. Sharing *qal* is a volturian tradition, one that my people abandoned long ago. And I am two decades removed from my culture, on top of that. I don't need you marked as my property. When I look upon you, I want to see *you*, not a reminder of myself. I have mirrors if I want to see my *qal*, but there is only one of you. I want to see your face, your skin, your beauty."

"I just thought…" She took in a shaky breath, and a tear fell from the corner of her eye to disappear within her hair. "I wanted to show you that I was yours. Always."

"Ah, my precious flower. You show me every day, in everything you do. Every time you look at me. Every word you speak to me. Every little touch, every smile, every moment. As jealous as I become when other males look at you, I *know* you are mine, just as I know I am yours"—he moved his hand down, settling it over her heart—"here. There is much in this universe that we may doubt, Samantha, but you and me? We're one of the few certainties."

With a small sob, Samantha threw her arms around his neck and pulled herself up, pressing her mouth to his. Arcanthus groaned as he returned the kiss, his lips and tongue moving with hers in a sensual dance. He slipped an arm around Sam, holding her against him as he ground his pelvis between her legs.

A breathy moan escaped Samantha's lips as delighted shivers stole through her.

"You never answered me, little terran," he said against her mouth. "Will you be my wife?"

Samantha smiled, meeting his eyes as she pulled back. "Yes. Your wife, your mate. Yours."

"*Mine*," Arcanthus growled as he reclaimed her lips in a searing kiss. When he pulled away, he raised his torso and hooked his fingers beneath the waistband of her pants. "As my wife-to-be, you are to enjoy certain benefits. Terran traditions are not the only things I've researched."

Panting softly, Samantha stared at him while he drew off her pants and underwear. Her nipples were hard and achy against her shirt, and her sex pulsed in need. "What benefits?"

Arcanthus grinned that devilish grin and lowered his mouth between her thighs to show her *exactly* what he meant.

AUTHOR'S NOTE

Thank you so much for reading Shielded Heart! We hope you all enjoyed it.

If you've been loving our Infinite City, check out *Untamed Hunger* featuring our big ole pussy cat Drakkal. This burly, furry guy needs someone to love.

As always, we give updates, share teasers, and more on our in our Facebook Reader Group. We hope you consider joining! Or if you'd prefer to join our newsletter, we also share monthly updates and new releases there.

And if you do feel so inclined, please leave a review! We would appreciate it dearly. <3

The Weaver

The Delver

The Hunter

<u>THE CURSED ONES</u>

<u>His Darkest Craving</u>

<u>His Darkest Desire</u>

<u>ALIENS AMONG US</u>

<u>Taken by the Alien Next Door</u>

<u>Stalked by the Alien Assassin</u>

<u>Claimed by the Alien Bodyguard</u>

<u>Saved by the Alien Crime Boss</u>

<u>STANDALONE TITLES</u>

<u>Claimed by an Alien Warrior</u>

<u>Dustwalker</u>

<u>Escaping Wonderland</u>

<u>Yearning For Her</u>

<u>The Warlock's Kiss</u>

<u>Ice Bound: Short Story</u>

<u>ISLE OF THE FORGOTTEN</u>

<u>Make Me Burn</u>

<u>Make Me Hunger</u>

<u>Make Me Whole</u>

<u>Make Me Yours</u>

<u>VALOS OF SONHADRA COLLABORATION</u>

<u>Tiffany Roberts - Undying</u>

<u>Tiffany Roberts - Unleashed</u>

<u>VENYS NEEDS MEN COLLABORATION</u>

<u>Tiffany Roberts - To Tame a Dragon</u>

<u>Tiffany Roberts – To Love a Dragon</u>

Tiffany Roberts is the pseudonym for Tiffany and Robert Freund, a husband and wife writing duo. The two have always shared a passion for reading and writing, and it was their dream to combine their mighty powers to create the sorts of books they want to read. They write character driven sci-fi and fantasy romance, creating happily-ever-afters for the alien and unknown.

Sign up for our Newsletter!
Check out our social media sites and more!
http://www.authortiffanyroberts.com